THE

"Dredd!" Trager's shout came a fraction too late.

A perp had jumped onto one of the boxes and pointed a sawn-off shotgun in the lawman's direction, letting off a deafening blast. Dredd threw himself sideways, feeling the high-calibre ammo shred the back of his uniform and pepper his skin with buckshot. He rolled, twisted and fired in one movement, pumping the trigger of his Lawgiver, but the pain igniting his back threw his aim off as he drilled a series of holes in the wall before catching the creep in the leg, shattering his kneecap. He squealed and dropped to the ground behind a stack of boxes, but Dredd sensed he wasn't out of the game just yet.

Trager scuttled alongside him, ducking low, and laid a hand on the senior Judge's shoulder. "Bad?" he asked.

"Had worse," Dredd answered, looking back and seeing a fine spray of his blood on the wall. "More pressing, spugwit ain't finished with us. I think I just winged him."

"OK, stay here. I'll deal with him."

"You're worse off than I am."

"Yeah, but I'm younger than you, old man. I carry it better."

"Shame your instincts weren't sharper. You might've spotted the punk earlier before he nearly plugged me."

Judge Dredd from Black Flame

#1: DREDD vs DEATH
Gordon Rennie

#2: BAD MOON RISING
David Bishop

#3: BLACK ATLANTIC
Simon Jowett & Peter J Evans

#4: ECLIPSE
James Swallow

#5: KINGDOM OF THE BLIND
David Bishop

More 2000 AD action

Durham Red
#1: THE UNQUIET GRAVE
Peter J Evans

Rogue Trooper
#1: CRUCIBLE
Gordon Rennie

Strontium Dog
#1: BAD TIMING
Rebecca Levene

#2: PROPHET MARGIN
Simon Spurrier

The ABC Warriors
#1: THE MEDUSA WAR
Pat Mills & Alan Mitchell

Nikolai Dante
#1: THE STRANGELOVE GAMBIT
David Bishop

Judge Dredd created by
John Wagner & Carlos Ezquerra.

Chief Judge Hershey created by
John Wagner & Brian Bolland.

JUDGE DREDD

THE FINAL CUT

MATTHEW SMITH

For Lucy.

A Black Flame Publication
www.blackflame.com

First published in 2005 by BL Publishing, Games Workshop Ltd., Willow Road, Nottingham NG7 2WS, UK.

Distributed in the US by Simon & Schuster, 1230 Avenue of the Americas, New York, NY 10020, USA.

10 9 8 7 6 5 4 3 2 1

Cover illustration by Dylan Teague.

ISBN 1 84416 135 8

A CIP record for this book is available from the British Library.

Printed in the UK by Bookmarque, Surrey, UK.

MEGA-CITY ONE, 2126

PROLOGUE: LIFE, AND AFTER

Of all the wounds on Emmylou Engels's body, it was the three-inch slash across her throat that had ended her life. As the blood fountained from her severed jugular, it had taken her last breath with it, her lungs emptying into open air with a soft rasping hiss like a punctured tyre. Her mouth had been bound with tape, so she died with barely a sound. Her nostrils flared, her eyes bulged, then rolled up into their sockets, but any cries died at source. Her feet kicked a brief rhythm on the cold plascrete floor, but she was firmly held and seconds later ceased all movement. Emmylou was two weeks shy of her twenty-fourth birthday when her arteries spewed their red spray in a five-foot parabola, a distance that everyone who'd seen it later agreed was impressive.

And yet that cut was the kindest she'd received in the five hours between groggily opening her eyes and the light dimming from them forever. It had been administered by a strong hand that wielded the knife with authority and skill. In truth, she'd prayed for a death blow long before she was granted one. Her torso and arms were a patchwork of abrasions caused by a plethora of instruments, from a pair of pliers to several lit cigarettes. They had used some kind of small chainsaw to cut off her left leg just above the knee – one of the goons held the limb aloft like a trophy, only to drop it because his hands were slippery with blood – and she had blacked out for several blissful minutes. Slapped back into consciousness, she wondered if she would go insane. The prospect of being able to crawl away into a dark hole in her brain and shut out the atrocities being wrought upon her person was welcoming. Her mind, however, remained typically, screamingly rational. Emmylou's mother had always said her daughter had no imagination.

So torture piled upon torture, in all its cruel ingenuity. Sometimes her captors improvised and sometimes they followed strict orders, but they never addressed her personally, never yelled abuse in her face, or indeed seemed to be aware that she was a living human being at all. Their faces bore the expressions of professionally bored people who had done this sort of thing many times before, and would continue to do so long after she was just a faded crimson stain on the seat of the chair they had strapped her to. She was just a body, upon which pain was to be conveniently writ in big, bold and deep red marks.

And once that sharp steel had parted the flesh from her throat, that's all she'd become: a body. Her lifeless form was of no use to them anymore, and so her bloodied husk was untied and dragged away to join the five others in the back of the small, black speedster van parked outside. Emmylou was the last to be loaded, and the evening's work needed disposing of.

It was like a mobile abattoir in there: limbs entwined, vermilion streaks painting the walls, the corpses tumbling together with the motion of the vehicle as it drove through the city, headlamps from passing cars occasionally shining against the darkened windows and highlighting a glazed eye impassively staring up from the tangle of corpses. The two-man team charged with dump duty knew the route and the course of action intimately, and they worked quietly and efficiently.

They arrived at their destination, the cloud-heavy night sky adequately concealing their task from passers-by. They backed the van up to the chem-pit, opened the doors and began to empty the contents. Although the furnace of the pit would have been enough to destroy the cadavers' clothes, the men knew enough about Justice Department procedures not to take the chance, and began to remove any personal effects that would identify them too easily. If they had had the time, they would have removed all the teeth and fingertips – those that still remained – but complete dismemberment was a luxury they couldn't afford. Anyone with any experience of disarticulation knew just how long and tiring it was to take apart a human body, so they would just have to rely on the dissolving qualities of the chemicals in the pit. Similar sites had proved useful for such purposes and there was no real reason for the Judges to come sniffing around here, provided they were careful.

Except...

Perhaps it was the heat. The night was sultry and the seething surface of the chem-pit ratcheted up the temperature by a good twenty degrees. Perhaps it was because one of the men was unknowingly incubating a viral infection. Perhaps he was worrying about his kid's eye operation in a couple of days' time. A lapse of concentration can usually be traced to a specific point of origin, from which the consequences ripple outwards and all tales take flight.

Whatever the cause, the man in question paused for a moment in his work to wipe his brow, and dirt, blood and sweat smeared across his forehead. The fumes stung his eyes and made his saliva taste bitter on his tongue. His partner looked up from rolling a corpse down the bank and into the chemical soup and admonished him for his slowness. He whispered at him to pick up the pace, reminding him what the boss would do to them if they fouled up. The first man didn't need telling twice, but still the heat made him dizzy and he stumbled as he finally pulled Emmylou's body from the van in his haste to be finished. He stripped her quickly, removing two rings from her fingers, and squinted through streaming eyes to check for any other belongings. His colleague slammed the van's back doors and hissed at him again to hurry.

Head pounding and a sickness rising in his chest, the man angrily released Emmylou without a second thought and she rolled down the bank, following where the others had gone into the greenish-yellow cocktail of substances. The bubbling surface closed over her form, accepting her into its fiery embrace, and by the time the van had disappeared into the darkness, all trace of her had vanished from sight.

Already the mix of chemicals was at work on the bodies, disassembling atoms. Marrow cooked and meat sloughed off bone. It would take several weeks for the cadavers to be reduced to little more than a liquid film on the boiling surface, but the soft parts were quick to be eaten away: the skin, lips, eyes, cartilage. Emmylou's right ear was gradually separating itself from the side of her skull, now not much more than a discoloured globule. But within it, where it had been hidden by the top of the lobe, was a titanium stud. The man who'd stripped and dumped her had missed it with his cursory glance, his mind on other things. And there it remained, a hard, black rock amidst her transient flesh. While the woman she had been collapsed around it, her earring resisted any corrupting touch.

The earring had been given to her by her boyfriend, Callum, shortly before she left the Pan-African States for the Big Meg. He'd said he wanted her to have something that she would carry around forever – necklaces could be broken, rings mislaid. But the stud would always be there, a permanent reminder. At the time, she'd found the sentiment touching, if a little overbearing. She'd never been one for overt displays of romantic sentiment and discouraged Callum from acting too much like a simp over her, but secretly she loved the attention. He could well have been the one she would end up throwing her lot in with, she'd decided, and never intended her move to Mega-City One to last more than a couple of years. The plan was that she'd make some creds, get her face known around the studios, prove herself as an actress, then decamp back to her home country with the weight of experience behind her and watch the offers come flooding in. As a rule, the money was in MC-1, but their pictures were loud and dumb. Emmylou fancied herself maturing into a dignified elder thespian of the holographic image – a Guinevere Cathcart, for instance, or a Dame Marjorie Pickering. Sedate, respectable films, where she didn't have to scream at some big rubber monster for days on end, or shed her clothes at opportune moments.

Emmylou's parents had supported her career choice from the beginning, though in truth they felt she was a rotten actress (a view held by the majority who'd seen her performances in the handful of movies she'd actually had speaking parts in). Dudley and Janice Engels knew enough about their daughter's ambition not to even try to stand in her way, despite their reservations about the limitations of her talent and the unreliability of show business. Fourteen years ago, in Brit-Cit, Emmylou's fifteen year-old sister Roxanne had, for reasons unknown – though the Judges attributed it to Lemming Syndrome – leapt from the bedroom window of apartment 2234/B Nicholas Blake Block where the Engelses had lived all their lives. She fell to her death on the pedway thirty stories below. Ten year-old Emmylou was watching cartoons at the time. Dudley and Janice – driven by grief and a strange, shapeless guilt – had initiated a move from the country of their births to make a new life as far away as possible in Pan-Africa, and ploughed all their energies into always making sure their surviving daughter's wishes were granted.

Emmylou never wanted anything else but to appear on the Tri-D: she wanted to attend the premieres, wanted the glamour, the illicit affairs with her dashing leading men, the column inches written about her. She wanted all this to stoke the fires of her own vanity, sure, but she also wanted to give the trappings back to her parents, in a kind of reciprocal show of love. Once she had the wealth, she would get them out of their shabby, cramped apartment and fix them up somewhere as befitting the mother and father of a superstar.

Needless to say, none of it turned out like it does in the movies. After a long period of inactivity, firing off her expensive publicity pics to every studio in New Nairobi, all she got was a succession of bit-parts in dubious, low-rent quickies that wouldn't be appearing on her CV anytime soon. She eventually had to sack two successive agents for repeatedly putting her name down for unsuitable material.

She wanted to be taken seriously as an artist, but for some reason she couldn't break out of the Z-grade ghetto. It wasn't as if she was the archetypal blonde, with an arresting cleavage and a breathy voice, the sort that seemed to drift towards trash as if driven by a hardwired homing device. But apparently she had a homeliness about her – or so she was told by embarrassingly transparent directors – that would endear her to a large proportion of their audience. She was "the girl next door" or "the childhood sweetheart", and by the way how did she feel about taking her top off for the beach party scene?

This wasn't how she had envisioned an actor's life. It was just cheap and tawdry. The films she reluctantly took roles in – *Hard Justice VIII: Caught Handling Swollen Goods*, *The Day They Took My Son Away*, *Frat Party Massacre II*, *Confessions of a Resyk Assistant*, *Blood Worms of the Meteor* – were funded by shady Euro-Cit producers and made in the full knowledge that they were rubbish by the very people putting them together. They believed that filling the shelves with crap product was better than no product at all.

It was dispiriting, but she found her fellow thespians shared the same laissez faire attitude, reasoning that they were lucky to have jobs at all. It was one step up from vidverts, and if the producers had any more money they would be using digitally generated models, and so could do away with the inconvenient human livestock altogether. When her third agent rang her to say that he'd got her a part in *Death Block: The Block That Eats*, she realised something had to be done.

To the desperate, Mega-City One can seem like a place of golden opportunity. As it was becoming apparent Emmylou wasn't going to break into the upper stream of quality Tri-D movies on her own terms, she considered maybe a change of scene was required. Film lore often spoke of unknowns being plucked from obscurity to become the toast of the Big Meg; all it took was one breakout part and some clever PR, making sure she was seen with all the right people.

She'd discussed the possibility with her new beau Callum, whom she'd met on the set of a washing powder vidvert – she was the ecstatically pleased young housewife, he the smarmy salesman – which, despite the romantic outcome, she thought represented her lowest ebb and demonstrated just how far she had fallen from her original lofty ambitions. Ironically, her parents were quietly proudest of this piece of work, beaming at the Tri-D screen every time she appeared in an ad break.

Callum had been ploughing a similar furrow to hers for the past couple of years, trading on his good looks, boyish charm and, most importantly, his willingness to take virtually any role that was offered to him.

Her boyfriend thought the idea of moving to MC-1 made sense, if that was what she really wanted. He couldn't go with her because he had a sick father to care for, but he could see that fame was something she yearned for. Where it left their relationship was left unspoken – she imagined herself returning to him full of star-struck tales, and he sensed that as soon as her first invite arrived for a glitzy premiere, he would be the next, new citizen of Dumpsville.

Three months later, Emmylou said farewell to her parents and Callum at the spaceport. She would get a flight to Brit-Cit, then change onto the zoom train that would take her through the Atlantic Tunnel and on to the North American metropolis. She'd found herself a room lodging with a landlady in one of the southern sectors, and early in-roads into finding work over there had yielded promising results. Callum gave her the earring, and she felt her eyes filling up. They told each other that they would speak every day, though neither of them truly believed it at the time. In fact, it all felt weirdly like something was coming to a close, but they couldn't have possibly guessed where Emmylou's final destination lay. Callum kissed her on the lips for the last time ever and she passed through the departure gate. She turned and waved once, and was gone.

Throughout the journey, she fretted that she had made the right decision; Mega-City One was as famous for its levels of crime and violence as it was for its size and population. Horror stories filtered across through the Pan-African media: tales of supernatural ghouls murdering citizens in their thousands, of wars and disasters, of attempted coups and the harsh brutality of living under the Mega-City Judicial system. Halfway beneath the ocean bed, she began to feel homesick and wondered if she had sacrificed everything meaningful in her life for a shot at something so transitory and insubstantial.

An old woman sitting across from her noticed her discomfort and tried to soothe her fears. The woman – travelling back from a vacation – told Emmylou that MC-1 was unlike any city on Earth, and that if it ever fell, mankind would never see its like again. It was noisy, overcrowded and dizzyingly vast. The rattle of gunfire was never far away, and if you looked out over the skyline of an evening, you could often see the distant flicker of block wars burning into the night. The people were by turns selfish, greedy and breathtakingly gullible. And the Judges, they were like your guilty conscience made flesh. Those faceless lawmen patrolled the city weeding out troublemakers like grud's own avenging angels, coming down hard on anyone that stepped out of line.

"But," the old woman said, raising one eyebrow, "no other city makes you feel so *alive*."

Once the zoom pulled into the Mega-City terminus, the disembarking passengers had to pass through customs. Emmylou nervously presented her luggage and papers to the Judges on duty.

"Business or pleasure?" asked one, flicking through her documents. His badge said his name was Holden. His colleague was running a scanner over her suitcases.

"Business, I guess. I've come looking for work."

"You and about four hundred million others," he replied dismissively. "Says here you came in from Pan-Africa. Sounds like a Brit accent to me."

"I'm British by birth, yes."

"Well, either way," he reached behind the counter and retrieved a clipboard, handing it to her, "read through that and tell me if you've had any of those diseases. Bear in mind, failure to do so constitutes a crime. We'll have to give you a quick medical, anyway."

Emmylou glanced at the list and blanched. To her left, a respectable-looking businessman was being frogmarched into an adjoining room. "I lived in New Nairobi," she said indignantly, "not in the middle of the Radback. Where am I supposed to have caught *this*?" She pointed to one of the names on the list.

"You'd be surprised," Holden said. "Kid came through yesterday claiming to be from Emerald Isle, and had buboes comin' out his ears." He stamped her papers and passed them back to her. "You've been granted a six-month stay. You want to stick around any longer, you'll have to apply for an extension in writing."

"That was the plan."

"Don't build up your hopes. This city ain't exactly the land of milk and honey." He motioned towards a female officer. "Judge Campbell here will conduct your physical examination."

Two humiliating hours later, Emmylou was given the all-clear and allowed to enter the city. She recalled the old woman's words and thought that "alive" wasn't exactly how she would describe how she was feeling at the moment; more like utterly degraded. However, nothing could have prepared her for the adrenalin rush that hit her the moment she stepped onto the street. New Nairobi was bustling, but nothing compared to this; the Big Meg in full flight was disorientating to the point of nausea. Pedways criss-crossed above her like gossamer strands between looming buildings, sky vehicles honked at surfers and bat-gliders as they soared and wheeled, and behind it all the ceaseless roar of the meg-ways as sixteen lanes of traffic thundered constantly through the city. Bodies seemed to be everywhere, every way she turned, and she gave up apologising as she was bundled through the crowd and eventually barged into the mêlée like a natural.

The robot cab drivers she found surly and unhelpful. Once she managed to master the art of flagging one down – which seemed to involve a lot of shoving and shouting – she then had to deal with their peculiar temperament. Evidently, whoever had programmed them had decided to channel into their circuitry every obstinate and teeth-grindingly frustrating trait known to mankind. After the driver had insisted on lecturing her on the full safety guidelines, she had had to repeat her destination several times while it checked the route with its internal map software, making an odd tutting noise at the back of its voicebox. Then, once they were in the air, the droid attempted conversation, though it sounded like it was building up to a monologue.

"You on holiday?"

"No. No, I'm here to find work."

"Work?" The robot emitted a barking noise, which she presumed was the equivalent of a laugh. "Not a lot of work around here, luv. They give it all to us poor sods. Now, me, I'd be happy if a few more humes had a little more responsibility, you know what I mean? Might get them directing their energies into something a bit more worthwhile, 'stead of killing one another all the time. And if foreigners such as yerself want to come over and help us out, then all power to yer. Not as if we're short of jobs to do. What skills have you got? You looking for factory work, construction, what?"

"Um, no, not really. I'm an actress."

The driver looked at her in his rear-view mirror. "Actress, huh?" It paused. "Well, that's got its... merits, I suppose. Has its place in the social hierarchy. Must give people pleasure, I guess..." It trailed off, as if it couldn't think of anything to add.

Emmylou took advantage of the silence to look out the window and take in her surroundings. They were flying at mid-height, the blocks stretching below her to City Bottom and reaching up as far as she could see to scratch the sky. Their enormity was terrifying. Off in the distance, she caught sight of the Statue of Judgement, something that she'd only read about, and again the size of the Big Meg was brought home to her. She had only caught a glimpse, but even from a couple of miles away it seemed to tower over everything.

She suddenly realised the droid was talking again.

"Of course, the city would fall apart if it weren't for us. We build your homes, make your food, sew your clothes, and recycle your dead. Thousands of years of human evolution have come to a complete standstill, to the point where you're prepared to sit back and let technology take charge." It sounded like the openings of a pet theory that the robot had been rehearsing for some time. "What's going to happen to you, eh? You rely more and more on meks to do your dirty work, and what are you doing with all this extra leisure time? Sitting at home and scratching your arses? You're becoming *redundant*, you know that? Humes gave away all their responsibilities because they felt it was beneath them, only to discover that they'd just lost their reason for living. And they couldn't get it back 'cause they knew we could do a damn sight better job than they ever could. So what's left open to them? *To destroy*. Man kills so he can feel alive."

"And art," Emmylou said, believing she should speak up for the human race. "We can create art: music, literature, paintings, films. Something no mechanical can do–"

"Art?" The droid sounded genuinely disgusted. "Since when has *that* ever changed the world?"

Feeling more depressed than ever, Emmylou alighted at the slightly rundown George Bush Snr Block and found her lodgings. Her landlady, Mrs Petri, proved welcoming and not the least bit surprised by her aspirations to become an actress. She said she'd had plenty of prospective thespians come and go under her roof, though she had to admit that she'd never heard from or seen any of them again. Emmylou once more felt a twinge of panic pluck at her heart.

Her search for work proved no more rewarding than it did at home. The parts she was offered were the same level of garbage that she'd attempted to escape, just done on a bigger scale. So many creds had been poured into these films that they had to secure a wider distribution to recoup their costs. While Emmylou tried to keep a straight face as she spoke her lines in movies such as *Kazan's Legions* and *I Loved a Traitor General*, she reconciled in her mind that her profile was wider than ever before and somewhere out there, an executive was watching a test shoot and seeing her as his next leading lady. Somewhere in the back of her mind, though, she knew this was a long shot.

She never did receive an invite to a premiere – the nearest she got were the lacklustre wrap parties, which were spectacularly ramshackle affairs – but grew to find it mattered less and less to her. She spoke to her parents and Callum at least every week via vid-phone, and their absence occupied her thoughts more than she'd anticipated. Once again, she considered what she'd traded, and resolved to put a finite length on her Mega-City adventure.

On the evening of Tuesday, 6 April 2126, she was alone in the apartment, Mrs Petri having gone to visit a niece in the North-West Hab Zone. Emmylou was using a particularly lean period workwise to spruce up her CV, but found her attention was wandering from the computer screen. She gazed out of the window at the cityscape, watching a passing H-wagon swivel its arc-lights over the rooftops and walkways. Despite the press of people on every side, she felt alone.

There was knock at the door. She glanced at the clock to see that it was 9:36 pm. Emmylou wasn't expecting anyone, but she knew her landlady was friendly with several of her neighbours and they often dropped by. When she padded across to the door and peeked through the peep-hole however, she was surprised to see a familiar face. The visitor was for her.

She opened the door to the man standing there with two companions. They chatted briefly before she invited them inside. The three men crossed the threshold and quietly shut the door behind them.

Now, as recent past events disperse like vapours, Emmylou dissolves too, matter changing form into liquid and gas. The earring shifts as molecules break down, and it catches in her skull. It will snag in a fracture in her cheekbone and there it will be found.

At that moment, Dudley and Janice were sitting in their small apartment talking about their daughter and wondering what to get her for her birthday. They were hoping that she'd make the trip back to see them. Callum was acting in another vid-vert, this time for kneepads, and he was thinking that he wanted to get the hell out of the business.

And Mega-City One, as ever, lives on.

PART ONE:
DISAPPEAR HERE

ONE

"The advice from Justice Department is to keep all windows shut for the next couple of weeks until the swarm moves on to another nesting ground. If possible, seal doors and vents. Remember, their sting is highly toxic – symptoms include vomiting, organ malfunction and internal bleeding. Any citizens who spots one within the city walls are asked to alert their local Sector House immediately."

"Ugh! I wouldn't want to wake up with one of those in my slipper, Jerry."

"Heh, me neither, Belinda. The Judges have issued a warning saying the little critters are extremely aggressive when provoked, so viewers would do well to let trained Verminator squads deal with the situation. We don't want Grandpa Joe going after one with a rolled-up newspaper and collapsing with a subdural haemorrhage."

"Ha ha! But seriously, folks, let's be careful out there. Onto local news now, and the beautiful people have been out in force tonight for the opening of the brand-new Fred Quimby Block in Sector Thirteen. This upmarket apartment block has been under construction for the past year as part of Councillor Matheson Peat's programme to rejuvenate destitute and irradiated areas. His high-profile campaign to repopulate sections of the city with a more moneyed class of clientele has brought criticism from civil rights groups claiming that this kind of selective housing is driving a further wedge between the 'haves' and the 'have-nots', but Councillor Peat has stated that he feels he is merely rebuilding what has been shattered by conflict. Mike Johansson is on the scene now. Mike, how's the party mood?"

"Hi, Belinda. Yes, as you can see I'm in the main reception hall of Fred Quimby and behind me the party is in full swing. There's been a strong turnout of famous faces, all adding their celebrity endorsements to this new project. Harry Hartley is here, fresh from filming the second *Body Count* movie, with his lovely wife Alissa. Gameshow host Barney Cannon is holding court over there, and I can see Tony Tubbs has just squeezed through the doors. The one guest that the crowds outside are all waiting for though, is reclusive model, singer and actress Vanessa Indigo."

"I should imagine the security must be pretty tight..."

"Yes, the Judges are certainly making their presence felt tonight and keeping the onlookers under control. There have been a few arrests for minor disturbances, but nothing serious. The atmosphere is mostly good-natured and relaxed."

"Mike, what can you tell us about the background to Councillor Peat's rejuvenation scheme and the significance of this block's star-studded opening?"

"Well, Jerry, I'm hoping to grab a few words with the man himself in a moment, so you'll be able to hear it from the horse's mouth. But Councillor Matheson Peat has been in the public eye for many years now, most notably with his Phoenix Campaign, in which he has pledged to clean up areas of Mega-City One left ruined by disasters such as the Apocalypse War and build upon them anew. By no means camera-shy, the media-savvy Councillor Peat's track record so far has been very impressive, with a number of blocks dotted around the sector standing testament to his vision. His vocal patriotism and what seems an unabashed love for this city has lent him a great deal of support amongst a select cadre of very powerful friends, and it is well known that he has a cordial relationship with Chief Judge Hershey. As he's not reluctant to point out, they both share a common goal in, and I quote, 'pulling the city up by its bootstraps to face the demands of the twenty-second century and beyond.'

"For Councillor Peat, high-profile coverage of openings such as this are vital to keep his campaign on the front pages and in the minds of his electorate. He's smart enough to know the attraction of celebrity, and has no doubt hired a quality PR agency to make sure all the right people have received invites. You only have to look around to see that this is a very tasteful cross-section of high society, and that sums up Councillor Peat's perfectly judged project – everything in its place at exactly the right moment.

"And talking of perfect moments, here comes the instigator of tonight's celebrations... Councillor Peat? Mike Johansson, *MCC News*. Could you spare a few minutes?"

"Certainly, Mike. I'd be glad to. I trust you're enjoying the festivities?"

"Ha, yes, it's quite a party. You must be very pleased with so many guests arriving to witness the unveiling of another of your achievements."

"Oh, I'm over the moon that so many of the great and the good could make it. This is a very important night, not just for me, but for the whole area and indeed for Mega-City One. Fred Quimby is a symbol of how we can pull ourselves up from the brink and stand tall. The Phoenix Campaign is all about rising from the ashes, and this magnificent building sends out a message to the world that the Mega-City spirit can never be broken."

"It is indeed a truly spectacular piece of architecture. You used Barnfold and Robinson again, I believe?"

"That is correct, Mike. Architects with a unique and daring sense of design, famous for constructing buildings that are as bold as they are revolutionary."

"And quite prohibitively expensive, I would imagine. There is the criticism that whilst your clearance programmes are beneficial to the city in general, they are only creating residences for the wealthy."

"Mike, it would be very easy for me to throw up slum tenements in disused sections of the city. But does that ever solve anything? One only has to look at somewhere like Cuidad Barranquilla to see the problems that that kind of housing causes. It was always my belief when I first undertook this personal mission of mine that I wasn't just going to cement over the ruins of the past, but draw something new from them, something to be proud of. And, yes, that does cost. But quality always does. I felt if I was going to do something for this city, it was going to be done right and proper and true."

"So where now for Councillor Matheson Peat? Are you going to continue to build upon your successes?"

"Oh, of course. I feel it would almost be an insult to Mega-City One to turn my back on it with plenty of work still to do. This great metropolis is constantly evolving, growing and changing with the times, and I want to be at the forefront of its bright new future. Don't worry, Mike, your viewers haven't heard the last of me."

"I'm sure they haven't. Councillor Peat, thank you for your time."

"It's a pleasure."

"Jerry, Belinda, I'm off to get myself a glass of shampagne. This is Mike Johansson, live at the Fred Quimby Block opening, back to you in the studio."

"Thanks, Mike. Seems like it's going to be quite some night, eh, Belinda?"

"Certainly does, Jerry. Hopefully, Mike will be joining us tomorrow at six for our showbiz hour, filling us in on all the celebrity gossip that's fit to print."

"Look forward to it. Now, men, do you suffer from weak bladders? Always making those inconvenient dashes to the public facilities? Well, the boffins at Tek

Twenty-one have announced that they've been working on a very unusual device that could be the answer to your prayers..."

"That's her, Dredd."

Dredd turned his gaze from scanning the crowd to watch a sleek, white limo pick its way through the excitable throng. The windows of the vehicle were mirrored, but still the various members of the press were pushing up against the barriers as far as they could, lenses thrust towards the glass. Several Tri-D crews were positioned beside Fred Quimby's main entrance, their cameras all automatically sweeping towards the newcomer, eager to frame her the moment she made her appearance.

The car came to a halt and the chauffeur nimbly jumped out and opened the rear door. A six and a half foot minder clad in a tuxedo and wraparound shades unfolded himself from the back seat, then stood to one side as a petite woman in a tiny black dress elegantly emerged behind him. A short, fat man followed and took the woman's arm in his. A second bodyguard was the last to leave the vehicle to tower over them on their left.

The crowd went nuts. The air was suddenly thick with whistles, catcalls and cheers. Flashbulbs exploded like concussion grenades and the evening lit up in staccato bursts as pressmen all yelled at the woman at once to pose for them. She looked startled at first, as if it was a reaction she wasn't expecting. But that expression held for only a split second – imperceptibly, her professionalism kicked in and a calm, bland serenity came over her face. She tightened the shawl around her slim shoulders, smiled and waved, eyes only occasionally blinking at the barrage of cameras popping off from every direction. She made a seductive effort to play the journalists' game, adopting modelling stances with an ironic degree of detachment, but all the while she was gently guided up the red carpet by her chaperone who was intent on keeping her under public scrutiny for the shortest possible time. Interviewers pointed microphones at her, shouting questions which she gracefully declined to answer. Ordinary citizens held out their hands as if they were hoping to touch something angelic. Throughout the spectacle, her smile never wavered, but her mind was clearly elsewhere.

"She knows how to make an entrance, I'll give her that," Dredd grunted.

"If you think this is insane, you should see how they go crazy for her in Euro-Cit. Almost made her birthday a national holiday."

"Control not working you hard enough, Geest, that you've started taking an interest in pop music?"

Geest shrugged. "Pays to know what makes the citizens tick," he said. "First time Vanessa Indigo visits the city, and there aren't many people that *don't* know who she is."

"There are still a few of us with more important things to do," Dredd replied. "Just keep your mind on the job. Crowd's getting a little too restless for my liking."

Geest sighed inwardly and tightened his grip on his daystick. By grud, attempting small talk with Dredd was hard work. He wondered how the man could stay uptight twenty-four-seven and not feel the need to relax once in a while. That wasn't to say he didn't respect him – how could you not admire the living legend that had led the fight against War Marshal Kazan and Nero Narcos, who had returned from exile to defeat the Dark Judges, whose very teachings on enforcement of the Law were required reading at the Academy?

When Geest was a cadet, the name Joe Dredd had been the byword for greatness. He represented everything a Judge should aspire to be: morally beyond reproach, rigidly disciplined, supremely confident and have an unshakeable faith in the Judicial system. To the young boys and girls training to be the city's protectors and regulators, Geest supposed, Dredd was himself a kind of celebrity, a Justice Department pin-up, not that any of them would have admitted as much. That degree of hero worship implied you weren't fully devoted to your duties.

And, of course, no man could live up to such a reputation. As much as the stories of Dredd's deeds circulated amongst the cadet dorms, so too did rumours of a darker side: of his doubts in the very Law he espoused so fervently, of clashes with former Chief Judges and, most worryingly of all, of a possible defect in the Dredd DNA dating back to the Father of Justice himself, Fargo.

Dredd's clone-brother Rico and the ex-Judda Kraken – all from the same genestock – had exemplified a leaning towards evil and corruption that seemed to have bypassed the old man altogether. But who knew if there was something in the blood, some rogue element waiting to surface, unchecked by Tek Division? It was a scary thought, to imagine this man, whom Mega-City One had relied upon so much over the years and would no doubt continue to do so in the future, was essentially a mystery to them. He wasn't even human, in the conventional sense, just a blueprint from a past life. He had no parents, no memories from before the Academy and could simply be described as a tool created for a job, a weapon engineered to combat crime. Nobody knew him, not really. And now Justice Department scuttlebutt had it that there were other Dredd clones being developed, the programme accelerated to meet the demands of the citizenry, and all presumably equally humourless with the same rods shoved up their backsides.

Geest sneaked a glance at Dredd standing at his side. Close-up, you could see the signs of age etched on the senior Judge's face. There was no doubt he was probably fitter than rookies that had just graduated onto the street, and that set-in-stone jaw showed scars and crags wrought by experience. Eleven, twelve years ago, following his battle with the Sisters of Death, Dredd had undergone rejuve treatment to get him back up to strength, yet the man clearly couldn't go on forever. The presence of the clones suggested that the Council of Five knew it too, and were taking pre-emptive measures to groom his replacements. Even legends had a shelf life.

"Vanessa, I love you!" a gimp in the crowd suddenly shouted, clambering up onto the barricades and waving an obviously home-made banner depicting a crude picture of the actress, assembled from magazine cuttings. Dredd strode forward without hesitation and used his daystick to sweep the fan's legs from under him, knocking him back into the crush.

"Behind the barriers, all of you," he barked, "or else I'll start making some arrests."

"How much longer are we going to have to stay nursemaiding these creeps?" Geest asked.

"Probably go on all evening," Dredd replied, constantly watching the hordes of autograph-hunters and photographers. "Some of these cits have been camped out here since yesterday. A personal appearance by a supposed megastar always brings the crazies out of the woodwork."

"Seems to me this sort of thing should be kept under wraps, not paraded in front of a bunch of infatuated halfwits."

"Two words: Matheson Peat. You can bet he'll be wanting to get as much media mileage out of this as possible."

"You reckon he's cut a deal with the Chief Judge?"

"Councillor Peat makes some very generous contributions to Justice Department funds," Dredd answered carefully, finally looking at Geest. "He gets a little leeway now and again. But Hershey's smart, she can see right through him and knows what a fame-hungry, self-obsessed creep he is. It just happens that he's also a very well-connected and extremely rich creep. Plus he seems to have the city's best interests at heart."

Geest peered up at Fred Quimby Block, stretching above them into the night sky. "I guess it is something to be proud of, giving people a new start, a new home..."

"For the few," Dredd muttered tersely. "It's the *many* we have to worry about."

Despite appearances, Peat was nervous. Usually, this kind of social gathering was his bread and butter, a chance to shine amidst the upper strata of Mega-City's artistic community and allow his ego to expand that little bit further as it absorbed every insincere word of praise. He was under no illusions that his guests were particularly interested in his work, or indeed even liked him that much, but they needed the oxygen of publicity as much as he did. It was a relationship that served all of them well, allowing Peat to bask in the glow of assorted luminaries. But right now, even he was apprehensive at meeting Vanessa Indigo.

She had the bestselling album of the year, her latest movie *Baring Bloody Teeth* was wowing audiences all over the globe, and she was currently dating Evan Frick, the aeroball player who was presently on tour in Hondo City. Peat's PR agency had performed a minor miracle to get her across from Euro-Cit to open the building tonight – though he wouldn't be surprised to learn that she was in town for reasons of her own as well – and he was unsure on how to handle her. The scandal rags, which he trusted more than any studio spokesperson, said she could be difficult. He would just have to rely on the old Matheson Peat charm when he finally met her.

He glad-handed his way across the hospitality area, warmly welcoming those he plainly didn't recognise as if they were old friends. The turnout had been exceptional and if all went to plan this evening, it would be another benchmark in his remarkable career. He reached the exclusive VIP room and knocked gently on the door. A goon in a tux opened it a crack, looking him up and down, and for a moment Peat thought he would have to embarrassingly identify himself as the host of the party, but he was admitted without a word.

On first impressions, he wished he was back outside amidst the celebrations. The room was dour, with a stultifying atmosphere, the few celebrities present whispering amongst themselves and trying too hard to enjoy themselves. That old ham Harry Hartley was here with his bimbo wife, talking with a couple of ancient, besuited executives, and a vaguely infamous rock singer—whose name escaped Peat—was drinking himself towards unconsciousness. Vanessa sat on a chair against the wall, cradling a glass of water, while another of her meatheads hovered at her shoulder looking uncomfortable, his shirt collar straining to contain his six-inch neck. She seemed bored out of her mind.

It was a peculiarity of the celebrity animal, Peat knew from his many years throwing bashes like these, that the higher you moved up the ladder of fame, the more miserable you became. At any function, A-list stars would insist on having their own private corners, where they demanded to be left undisturbed, and consequently spent much of their time silently on their own, feeling too self-important to venture outside their bubble of sycophants and hangers-on. It never looked as if their fortune had bought them much happiness, but rather it had trapped them in a self-deluding circle of anxiety and vanity. Whilst Peat spent much of his life rubbing shoulders with household names, he regarded them only as a means for his own ends. Most of the time, they were no use to anyone.

The councillor cautiously walked towards Vanessa and coughed lightly, perhaps a little too theatrically. She gazed up at him and he wondered if she'd taken something; her eyes looked glassy and her movements appeared cumbersome, as if her senses were dulled. He got the immediate impression that she didn't know who on earth he was.

"Ah, Miss Indigo?" he said slowly. "I'm Matheson Peat, the organiser of tonight's event. I just wanted to let you know how much I appreciate you coming here this evening. No doubt you saw the crowd outside. The whole of Mega-City One is going crazy for you, and we're all very excited to have you here."

"Hmm?" she blankly looked up at him.

"I'm sure Miss Indigo thanks you for your kind welcome," said a voice behind him. Peat turned to see a squat, rotund man returning from the buffet balancing a plate of finger food in one hand and a flute of shampagne in the other. He had a thick moustache, complete with a sprinkling of crumbs, and his thinning hair had been pulled back into a ponytail. He performed a quick juggling act with the cutlery, and extended a free hand, which Peat shook. "Maurice Lubular. I'm Miss Indigo's manager." He, like the actress, had an accent that was difficult to place; there was a lilt to it that Peat found pleasantly musical, if unrecognisable.

"I was just saying what a great honour it is to have you here." The councillor lowered his voice. "Is she OK?"

Lubular glanced to each side, as if to check no one was in ear-shot and cleared his throat. "Can you be discreet?"

"Of course." Peat nodded.

"Miss Indigo has, um, a slight addiction to FX," he said quietly. "Nothing life-threatening, of course. Just a little escape route from reality."

"She needs an escape?"

"If you had her life, screaming fans throwing themselves at you day and night, you'd want to get away from it as much as possible too. As I said, it's not serious. She's probably just imagining gremlins are eating the sausage rolls. But she's developed quite a habit for the hallucinogen. I think it helps her come to terms with the real world when she's sober."

"Jovus, I had no idea..."

"Why should you? It's not something we're planning on releasing to the press. But Miss Indigo is the perfect professional. She will not let you down."

"She'll be OK to cut the ribbon?"

"Oh yes. I will be there to guide her, have no fear. What time do you want us?"

"In about fifteen minutes. I'll start rounding up the rest of the guests, then make the announcement to the baying hordes outside."

"No problem."

Peat cast a worried glance at the star, who was staring into her water enraptured, then headed back to what he hoped was normality.

Dredd threw the perp into the back of the catch wagon and slammed the doors. It was his tenth public order arrest of the evening and he had a feeling that there were going to be plenty more before the night was over. The crowd was becoming more boisterous by the hour, stoked by constant announcements from the block's PA system that Vanessa Indigo would shortly be making an appearance to officially declare the building open. Right now, the cits were chanting some inane countdown.

Like Geest, Dredd was impatient for the whole farrago to be over. In fact, he was beginning to think that maybe Hershey had played this one wrong and underestimated just how easily this gathering could spiral out of control. Peat had been given too much room to celebrate himself at the expense of the Judges' rule.

Dredd was ambivalent towards the councillor. The man was charismatic and fanatically pro-Justice Department, but there was something about him that you couldn't pin down. On the couple of occasions that Dredd had been introduced to Peat, he was left with the impression that the councillor saw everyone around him as suckers to be used at his whim. Every meeting was a photo opportunity, every publicity stunt stage-managed to attain maximum exposure.

Peat's past too, was a strange mixture of genuine bravery and revisionism. During the Apocalypse War, Peat had led his local Citi-Def unit against the invading

Sovs and had won some significant victories, with McGruder personally commending him for his actions once the conflict had ended. But in his early steps into politics, he made some extremely controversial, right-wing, anti-Sov speeches that upset many and he later had to apologise for offending anyone in the more enlightened, hands-across-the-ocean times. Of course, there was a section of the populace that thought he'd gone soft and felt no apology was necessary as they agreed with his statements that it was about time somebody destroyed East-Meg Two as well.

Dredd wondered what the real Matheson Peat truly believed. Did he change his opinions to fit with the political mood? Did Peat have so little faith in his policies that they were something to be picked up or dropped depending on which way the wind was blowing? The man seemed to be pure artifice.

And now there was this Phoenix Campaign of his. His intentions were laudable, but again it was a case of style over substance. Rather than genuinely solving the chronic housing problem, the campaign merely reinforced the divisions between the wealthy three or four per cent of the Big Meg's population and the struggling remainder of it. Because only those with serious cash could afford to live in these new blocks of his, it simply ghettoised the poor, driving them ever further into the margins of society. Peat never did anything that didn't benefit himself directly, and by creating these new homes for his rich peers he was ensured of their support come election day.

"Ladies and gentlemen," boomed the PA. The crowd roared in response. "Tonight is a special night for Mega-City One, for tonight we are playing host to one of the most famous women on the planet. You cried along with her in *Twilight of the Dead*, you made 'Twenty-Second Century Blues' number one for eleven consecutive weeks, you voted her the person you'd most like to be stranded in the Cursed Earth with, and now she's here in the flesh.

Put your hands together and give a huge Mega-City cheer for Vanessa Indigo!"

Dredd was sure that the technicians up in Weather Control heard the roar that erupted from the mob; it was thunderous. Flashbulbs started popping again as Peat emerged from the front doors, leading a confused-looking Indigo, the tubby guy and the two minders to a podium that had been set up with a microphone. Beside it were two small posts with a length of red ribbon tied between them. The other celebs filtered out behind the main attraction, standing in a semi-circle to the rear, trying hard not to look envious of the reaction Indigo provoked. Tri-D cameramen moved closer as Peat raised his hands pompously for quiet, which his audience roundly ignored.

"This..." He winced as he struggled to make himself heard against the chants of Indigo's name. "This is indeed a special night. This building behind me is a symbol of the indomitable Mega-City spirit, growing from the ruins of the past and refusing to be broken. I am very grateful and honoured to be involved in such a project that brings hope to the citizens of this illustrious metropolis, and it seems fitting that it should be officially declared open by someone who means so much to all of you. Ladies and gentlemen, it gives me great pleasure to hand you over to Vanessa Indigo."

Peat stood back and allowed Indigo and fatman to move towards the mic. Fatman was whispering in her ear, guiding her with his hand as if she was incapable of acting without his support. She bent forward, not looking at the crowd, and said, "Hi."

It was enough for the fans, who bellowed back their approval. Dredd watched as one of the Tri-D cameramen adjusted his position, circling around to Indigo's side, though strangely he wasn't paying much attention to what he was supposed to be recording. He kept looking behind him, as if he was checking the distance between himself and the nearest Judge. Something was up, and

Dredd was moving before his brain had even assimilated the information.

"T-thank you so much," Indigo was mumbling. "I love you all..."

The cameraman suddenly took his video camera with both hands and cracked it open, retrieving a small blaster from the hollow interior. He pointed it at the actress.

Dredd's Lawgiver was clenched in his fist within seconds as he ran forward. "You!" he shouted, his voice straining to rise above the background noise. "Drop the gun! Now!"

The man had heard him and was clearly panicked, swinging round to bear down on Dredd. Indigo's entourage immediately became aware that something was going on, and the actress's chaperone pulled her away from the podium, the woman emitting a sharp yelp of surprise. Her bodyguards both pulled hand cannons from shoulder holsters and levelled them at the perp. The crowd had gone deathly quiet.

"You two!" Dredd snapped at the bodyguards. "Lose the weapons or you'll be going down too!"

"Drokk you," one of them spat, with a thick burr of an accent. "We were gene-engineered to protect her."

The cameraman looked distressed, his eyes flickering nervously between Dredd and Indigo's minders. Other Judges were moving towards the confrontation so there was nowhere for him to go, though he probably knew that from the start. "V-Vanessa..." he whimpered. "I c-came for you."

"Last warning," Dredd growled.

"Vanessa, answer me!" the man cried, raising the gun. A fraction of a second later his head disappeared in a red drizzle as one of the bodyguards' pistols bellowed fire. Dredd reacted instantly, putting two bullets through the minder's chest. He staggered backwards, gazing down at his wound with an expression of utter disbelief. Dredd swapped targets and drilled a hole in the other bodyguard's forehead before he could aim. They both dropped heavily to the ground simultaneously, as if their nervous systems had been synchronised and somebody had just pulled the plug. The audience, who had just watched this brief firefight broadcast across giant vid-screens, took a collective breath and began to find their voice again, screaming for the superstar.

Giving the bodies only a cursory glance, Dredd headed over to Indigo, who was being helped to her feet by the fatman and Peat. She was sobbing uncontrollably.

"You want to tell me what that was about?" the senior Judge asked gruffly.

"It happens, unfortunately," fatman said and introduced himself as the singer's manager. "A person of Miss Indigo's stature tends to attract obsessive types. He was not the first."

"That doesn't explain the mini-arsenal those two meatheads were carrying," Dredd replied. "There's the small matter of smuggling illegal arms into the city."

"I cannot take this," Indigo was moaning. "I cannot... I cannot *face* them..."

"She all right?" Dredd asked.

"She's in shock, as you would expect," Peat piped up indignantly, attempting to regain his composure. "I have to say, Judge Dredd, I was disappointed with the way that situation was dealt with. Surely there was no need for further bloodshed–"

"You break the Law, you pay the price," Dredd snapped, his temper rising. "I will not stand by and see crimes committed, no matter how famous the person. My authority will *not* be undermined."

"Dredd, it's Geest," a voice crackled in his earpiece. "Crowd's losing it. Going to need some back-up."

Dredd turned and saw cits pulling at the barricades, their shouts now angry and frustrated. The celebs were fleeing into the building as bottles and debris began to be thrown at the screens and the entrance facade. Helmets were pushing the throng back, daysticks swinging to and fro, cracking heads. "OK, request riot foam," Dredd instructed. "Start making arrests. Let's stamp down on this *hard*."

He returned to Peat. "Looks like the party's over, councillor. I suggest you and your guests stay out of harm's way before anything else happens." He looked at Indigo and Lubular. "I don't want either of you to attempt to leave the city. There's still some questions I'd like answered."

Before they could reply, Dredd headed out into the heart of the disturbance, unsheathing his daystick. His radio mic sparked into life again. "Control to Dredd, Senior Judge required, Elizabeth Short Block construction site. Body dump discovered."

"Kinda got my hands full," Dredd said, bringing his knee up into a rioting cit's face. "Isn't there anyone else?"

"Negative. You're the nearest unit."

Never rains but pours, Dredd thought as he waded his way through the chaos towards his Lawmaster and the first of the H-wagons roared overhead.

TWO

So I'm sticking my gun in this geek's face and he's moaning and twitching like he's plugged straight into Power Tower. I twist the barrel between his lips and tell him to open wide. He resists at first and I'm tempted to slam the butt against his jaw, perversely interested in seeing those tiny yellow teeth shatter like crockery. Instead, I just increase the pressure slightly, my left hand gripping his shirt collar at the back of his neck, my right forcing his head back as I push harder with the gun. He relents and the barrel slides into his hot, stinking mouth like it's making a home for itself. His eyes water with fear and his breath comes in short, sharp bursts. Looking at his sweaty, grime-encrusted skin, cheap jewellery, thinning hair and stained white suit, the temptation to squeeze the trigger and empty the contents of his skull all over the warehouse wall has never been greater.

A voice calls behind me. "Yo, Pete. Take it easy, man." I look behind me and Brett Dansky, leaning against a crate of grenades, makes a casual calming motion with his hand. I stand back a pace, but don't remove my gun from the gimp's mouth, letting him suck on it like a baby pacifier. His wide, panic-stricken eyes turn beseechingly towards Brett, as if believing *he's* all that stands between me and the drokker's brain exploding in party-popper streamers.

If it were anyone else, I would consider him even more of a fool for appealing to a Dansky. You didn't have to spend long in their company to realise they had no redeeming qualities and zero sense of compassion or sympathy for their fellow man. Business is business to them, and if that involves dropping a competitor off a flyover or gunning down a rival gang boss in front of his family, then it goes with the turf, daddio. The Danskys don't consider anything off-limits if it stands in the way of them making a whole heap of moolah.

However, this guy sucking on my blaster, this Banana City contact, he's *known* to them. They've used him before, and to all intents and purposes they probably trust him. But it doesn't hurt to make sure an associate is on the level, so while they've asked me to go through the heavy routine, this greaseball's still got his uses to Brett and Jonny. The charade is just to make sure the drokkwit is fully aware of just who he is dealing with. The brothers have put together scams with this character before, previous to my entrance into the Dansky empire, but since he's never dealt with me, I can be the wild card that keeps him on his toes, scaring him into submission.

Brett saunters over and lays a friendly hand on the geek's shoulder. "You know we've always been happy with your work in the past, Martinez. There's no reason why we can't come to an amicable arrangement again, right, bro?" Brett glances at his younger, slightly dumber brother Jonny, who is sitting at a small card table, his feet up, cleaning the serial number off an ex-army assault rifle. Jonny grunts and nods. Brett turns back to Martinez, smiling. "You see? That shipment you brought in last time contained some high-quality merchandise, something our clients can't get enough of. Right now, we could do with more of that. As you can see, our stocks are running low and there are crazies out there with wars to fight, and Citi-Def units looking to procure untraceable weaponry. You're our *connection*, man." Brett puts his arm jovially around Martinez's shoulder, pulling him close. The gimp tries to smile around the gun barrel and only manages a nervous grimace. "But I swear if you screw with us, if you ever try to drokk us over," he continues, his mood darkening, "I'm gonna let Trager here put a bullet through your worthless, lowlife heart." Brett turns his attention to me. "You hate spics, ain't that right, Trager?"

I don't reply but simply pull back the hammer on my pistol.

"Old Petey's a real mad dog," Brett says. "Better get on his good side. So whaddya say, Martinez? Can we do business like grown-ups, or am I gonna have to dump your dago corpse in the Black Atlantic? Trager, let the man speak."

I slide the revolver out of his mouth. As soon as it's gone, he swallows several times and licks his lips, probably trying to get the taste of gun oil off his tongue. He fishes in his trouser pocket and pulls out a handkerchief, which he uses to wipe his eyes and forehead, then blow his nose.

"You have no reason to doubt me, Señor Dansky," Martinez says quickly. "I have always played straight with you. You say yourself, we have done good business together."

"As far as I'm concerned, our past means as much as a week-old hottie, and in my experience, relationships sour just as quickly. Only thing I trust is the deal before me. So, what have you got for us?"

"I receive your message, and pass it on to the relevant people. My suppliers are keen to provide you with more of the same material, for the right price, of course."

"Price remains the same," Jonny interjects, not even looking up from his task. "Otherwise we'll take our creds elsewhere."

"Well said, my brother," Brett says. "You're not dealing with a couple of hopheads looking to score cheap arms, Martinez, and I find it personally insulting that you even *think* you can start dictating terms to us."

Martinez is flustered. "I intended no disrespect, señors. I simply meant that my contacts in Cuidad Barranquilla are willing to sell for a mutually agreed price. I'm sure they are open to negotiation."

"So are we," Jonny remarks, working the rifle's bolt release with a sharp *krr-chak* that echoes around the warehouse.

"Indeed," Brett says, grinning. "So, Martinez, this material. What exactly are we looking at?"

"Three crates of zip guns. A dozen rocket launchers, with twenty-eight boxes of ammunition. Laser parts removed from an orbiting defence battery, enough to build a military-grade weapon, or so I am told. Five crates of stub guns and a dismantled sonic cannon. There is more, but I did not bring a list, in case I was stopped by the authorities. You will be able to see for yourself, once you agree to the meet."

I can see Brett's eyes gleaming. I imagine the thought of all that shining killware makes credit signs *ping!* in his head. The Danskys have been dealing in illegal arms for several years now and have found that it is easily the most profitable of the gang's sidelines. When they started out, they had their fingers in the usual pies – extortion, robbery, prostitution, perp-running, Umpty-bagging – but nothing was more in demand in Mega-City One than readily available and unlicensed weaponry.

For the most part, their clients are the various criminal factions wasting each other in drive-bys and contract hits, but they have built up a formidable reputation for providing heavy-duty ordnance for block wars and Cursed Earth hunting parties as well. Nothing was beyond them. Somewhere in this vast building were boxes filled with satellite components, deactivated Mechanismo parts and Land Raider tracks. Mark I Lawgivers stolen from dead Judges' hands now collected dust, experimental devices that never left the prototype stage had been sold on to the Danskys by disgruntled Tek Division employees out to make a quick sale.

Some of the Danskys' buyers were genuine collectors, obsessed with picking up assorted pieces of hardware from the Big Meg's bloody past – the gun that Chief Judge Volt used to commit suicide was a big seller on the black market – but more often than not it was the business of killing that kept the money rolling in.

"Quite a cache," Brett says, impressed. "And the source?"

"Ah, as you know, Señor Dansky," Martinez replies carefully, "my suppliers like to keep their own contacts, how you say, close to their chests. They have their own interests to protect, as much as you do."

"I just want to be sure we're not being sold ten year-old junk, or cheaply made knock-offs from Sino-Cit. We have something of a rep to maintain amongst our regulars."

"Let us just say somebody very close to Cuidad Justice Department's main armoury is benefiting very nicely from the arrangement and leave it at that."

Brett shares a look with his brother, then glances around the room. Besides myself, there are four other members of the Dansky gang whose principal roles are muscle, intimidation and donkey work. Strodem, Mauser and Cavell were all cut from similar cloth; their lack of intelligence ensured an unquestioning and unswerving loyalty. I wonder sometimes what path led them to their current employment as gun-runners. They look almost vat-grown for the job: all over six feet, built like tanks and with creepily blank expressions, as if breaking some poor sap's neck is no different to opening a can of Popp's Cola.

The fourth, Hogg, is different. Small, dark and quiet, you can see a brain working behind her desensitised eyes, but she's probably more insane than the rest put together. Rumour has it that she used to work as a slab-walker for the Danskys until she started cutting up her johns and the brothers realised her talents could be put to better uses. The way they reason it, they're doing the city a service by channelling her energies into something more pro-active. Left on her own, she'd probably run wild on a thrill-kill rampage.

I'm sure there are plenty of tawdry tales of their pasts that I'm not privy to and they're in no great hurry to divulge – I'm sure as hell not about to start telling them *my* life story – and so an air of general mistrust hangs over us all, like a background smell you eventually become accustomed to.

For people who live their life by the moment, you never know what's coming around the corner, and whether you might have to just drop your colleagues and walk away. Sometimes you might have to make the decision to whack them, if there are no other options available. Experiencing life on a day-to-day basis like that, friendships are fleeting, and therefore unnecessary.

"Whaddya think?" Brett asks us in general, though his decision's already made. He and his brother like to make us feel we're part of a collective, as if we've got some say in the business side of things. Truth is, the Danskys would put a bullet in the back of any of our heads if it turned out to be financially rewarding.

"I don't see why we should trust this little runt," I say, still acting my role.

"Trager, your sense of suspicion is both welcome and gratifying," Brett replies, smiling, "but while Martinez may look like something you'd wipe off your boot, he's still the man with the keys to the kingdom. The gangbangers, survival nuts and warmongers out there are queuing up for some Banana City boom-boom, and we're just the guys to sell it to 'em." He looks at Martinez. "Right?"

The greaseball smiles sickly. "Absolutely, señor. Just say the word and I'll set the wheels in motion."

Jonny straightens up, putting the rifle down on the table, and moves over to stand next to his brother. "Where are they gonna want to do this?" he asks.

"The docks, I think. I will get in touch with them and arrange a place, date and time, but they will be bringing the shipment in by boat, so the pay-off will have to be done there and then."

Brett nods in agreement. “OK, let us know the details, as and when. We’ll wait on your call.”

Martinez turns to go, then hesitates. “There is one other thing, Señor Dansky,” he says slowly. “My contacts said they have come into possession of more of the… specialised equipment.”

Brett and Jonny make eye contact for the briefest of seconds and something unspoken passes between them. It goes unnoticed by the rest of the goons – you could kick any of them up the ass and it would take their brains a full minute to assimilate a reaction – but the crackle of nervous energy visible in the glance they share piques my interest. It’s not something I’ve ever seen before. The Danskys looked, well, *frightened* for a moment. There’s no doubt that the brothers knew instantly what Martinez is talking about, and it’s something they’ve dealt with before. The immediate desire to gabble questions has to be suppressed. I’ll have to pick up as much as I can between the lines without arousing any suspicions.

Brett coughs, clears his throat. “Is that right?” He’s struggling to reassert his authority.

“Yes,” Martinez answers. From his expression, there’s no suggestion he’s aware of the subtle shift in power, but you’d have to be pretty dense not to spot it. I’m beginning to think the dirtbag is as good an actor as me. “They say they are willing to sell for a special price. You still have your buyer who collects such pieces?”

Brett looks again at his brother before replying. “I… I haven’t spoken to him for a while, but… yes, I can get in touch with him.”

“From what I understand, I believe he would be interested in this shipment. My suppliers tell me they are antiques, recently discovered. A good find. And a good profit for yourselves, I think.”

“We’ll contact our buyer, tell him we may have something for him,” Jonny says, a touch too quickly.

"See that you do. An opportunity like this does not often come up, eh?" Martinez heads towards the door, opens it and turns back to us. "You shall hear from me soon, señors. Adios, and here's to good business!" He grins and disappears into the city.

Silence descends on the warehouse. The inquisitive demon inside me won't be denied for any longer. "Specialised pieces?" I say as casually as I can, holstering my gun beneath my jacket. "What the hell was he talking about?"

Brett looks at me as if he is seeing me for the first time. He blinks, then attempts to wave the question away. "Just some stuff we've sold on in the past. There's a collector we've dealt with a couple of times that has a particular interest."

"What's that?"

"Weapons of torture," he replies. "Thumbscrews, blades, that kind of thing. Y'know, from South-Am death squads. Banana City has a good supply of it."

"Torture? What in grud's name does he want with those?"

Brett shrugs. "Drokked if I know, and quite frankly I don't *want* to know, but I'm sure you can guess. As long as he pays the massive mark-up we make on 'em, that's as far as my interest goes."

"So who *is* this guy?"

Brett and Jonny once more lock stares, but neither of them answer.

It's late as I make my way across sector along the still-crowded pedways. The city never sleeps. As dusk falls, when the respectable cits are tucked away in their cosy apartments, a different kind of citizen emerges, with a different kind of business to attend to. Pimps and dealers unglue themselves from the shadows, quietly hawking their wares: sugar, Uncle Umps, stookie, cigarettes, coffee beans, young bodies. Gangs of Uglies loiter menacingly on street corners, preening and showing off their boils, while in the depths of dimly lit alleyways, vagrants gather around spluttering fires. Gangbangers roll past in souped-up vehicles, hanging out the windows and passing comment on the pedestrians. The clubs are heaving, pounding music cutting through the night, the freaks and weirdos crawling out of whatever hole they spent the day in to queue up outside and impatiently wait to gain entrance.

Somewhere, perhaps a couple of miles away, a siren blares before it is cut short by a burst of gunfire and the dull thud of a small explosion. No one even looks round. To live and survive in Mega-City One is to grow immune to the turbulent surroundings, to internally adapt some kind of insanity filter that acts as a blinker. Those that fail, that buckle under the pressure, can lose their minds from sheer sensory overload. Better to ignore the craziness, to let it fade out into the background, otherwise you'll end up straitjacketed in a kook cube, drinking your meals through a straw.

I hop on a zoom for a brief ten-minute journey, avoiding a hostage situation on Clancy as some spugwit tries to negotiate his way out of the dump he's burrowed himself into. The Judges call this time of night the Graveyard Shift, when every nutjob and looney-toon seems to explode into violence simultaneously. You can feel it in the air: the anger, frustration and boredom looking for an outlet, spreading like a psychic virus, infecting others with its touch of madness.

I alight at Freddie Starr Interchange and from there it's just a short walk to my destination. The building looms large over its neighbours, and even at this time of the morning it's extraordinarily busy. As I pass the off-ramp leading to the underground bike pool, two Judges come roaring out, one giving me the evil eye before they both speed off into the distance. I decide to avoid the main entrance – too many helmets, too many unnecessary questions – and instead find one of the many side doors, punching in a six-digit code on the keypad beside it that will grant me access. Once the voice-identification software confirms that I am who I say I am, the door slides open and I'm inside the Sector House. I take the empty service el' to the twenty-third floor and then it's a brisk jaunt along a nondescript corridor to Hendry's office.

As usual, the anxiety hits me the moment I leave the street. Out there, it's my home, the buzz of the city is my lifeline, and amongst the cits, I pass unnoticed, a face in the crowd. Here, in this sterile environment, I'm the proverbial sore thumb. I feel strange and ungainly, like I've taken a misstep. I lock stares with whoever I pass, daring them to say something, to demand to know who I am, so I can turn this fear into something aggressive, but they seem to sense that I belong here. The shift happens before I'm aware of it; as soon as I enter this other world, my training takes hold and my posture grows more confident, my demeanour more purposeful. Something that was ground into me many, many years ago rises from the depths of my being and asserts itself. I lose the cowed, suspicious look of a Mega-City perp and transform myself back into a Judge.

I rap on Hendry's office door and enter before he can answer. He glances up irritably from the papers strewn across his desk, then does a double-take of surprised recognition. I slump into a chair opposite him, noticing that he looks considerably older since the last time I saw him. The frizzy hair at his temples is greying and his forehead seems more lined than I remember, but this is the first time I have seen him in person for over six months.

"Trager," he says evenly, trying to sound as nonchalant as possible. "To what do we owe this pleasure?"

"Oh, you know me, Hendry," I reply. "Never been one for predictability."

He smiles, a rarity for him, and offers his hand, which I shake firmly. Hendry's been my liaison since I first joined Wally Squad some twelve years ago, and in a job in which trust and deception are our stock-in-trade, there's no man whose hands I would more willingly place my life in. His knowledge and guidance has ensured that my cover has never been blown on any operation I've been involved in, and his three decades of experience on the streets before a recurrent leg injury forced him into taking a backroom role has enabled him to develop almost a sixth sense when it comes to pulling out an officer if the situation threatens to become compromised. Never a man to mince words, his seriousness is only matched by the respect he engenders in the rest of the department.

"You haven't reported in for..." he checks his computer screen, "eight weeks, at least. We were beginning to wonder if you'd gone native."

"The Danskys have spent the past month shifting a tonne of gear," I reply, amused at the thought of Hendry sweating over one of his officers disappearing. If he had truly been worried, I would've known about it, one way or another, probably with a couple of helmets pulling me in on a bogus charge. "That small block war over in Jim Carrey the other week? Half the ordnance was Sov-made. The Danskys shipped it in via a freight carrier bound for Luna-One. We offloaded the cargo when it was meant to be refuelling. So, as you see, they've kept me busy on one or two little errands like that."

"Even so, some names and dates would've been nice," Hendry says sternly. "They're flooding the sector with firepower and it's about time we nipped their enterprise in the bud."

"Hence the reason you see me before you this very night," I say, opening my arms wide and grinning. "The brothers are making a big buy off their Banana City contacts. They're bringing it in by boat, further details to follow."

Hendry raises his eyebrows. "Big?"

"It ain't chickenfeed, that's for gruddamn sure. These are guys they've worked with before and it seems they're getting it straight from Cuidad JD. Major players. We're talking one hell of a bust here."

My superior sits back in his chair. "And you don't know the location yet?"

I shake my head. "They're using some runt called Martinez to act as a go-between. He's getting back to them with the specifics of the meet. I should imagine the Danskys would want it fairly soon. Their stocks are running low and it's drokking hunting season out there."

Hendry nods. "That would be Enrique Martinez. We got a file on him long as your arm. Worked as an informant for the Banana Cit Judges as well as fix-it man for the Conquistadores."

"I got the impression the Danskys have a history with him. There was something else too," I add. "This piece of stomm Martinez mentioned something about antique torture devices he can get for them, alongside the regular weaponry. It seems the brothers have a specific buyer who collects the stuff."

"Torture?" Hendry frowns. "You get a name?"

"Drokkers wouldn't say. Fact is, soon as the greaseball piped up about it, the Danskys looked ready to just about drop a brick there and then. Whoever this guy is, the brothers – and let's not forget who we're talking about here – are *scared* of him."

"Antique torture pieces," Hendry muses, looking thoughtful. "Not exactly a wide appeal..."

"Exactly. And I want to follow it up. Go through with the deal. Find out what this sicko is doing with 'em."

"Keep the bust under wraps, you mean?"

"Yeah, total media blackout. Far as our nameless friend is concerned, let him think the buy went ahead as planned. I'll go ahead and meet him with the merchandise after the bust to find out what this character is up to."

"You've got your teeth into this one, haven't you?"

I smile. "You know me too well, Hendry. Yeah, I got a hunger to see it through. Curiosity is driving me crazy."

"Sounds dangerous too. What you're saying makes sense and it's a lead we've got to follow, but don't push too hard. If this creep makes the Danskys have sleepless nights, then let's keep a level head."

"Wilco, skip."

Hendry studies me for a long moment. "How are you finding it out there, Trager?"

I shrug. "Same-old, same-old. Perps are becoming more inventive and ruthless by the day, while the cits grow ever more complacent. It's a warzone at times, and I don't think it's a battle we will win. Trying to stem the tide of crime in this city is like trying to put out a raging inferno with a thimble of water. But there's nowhere else I'd rather be."

Hendry taps his keyboard, glancing at the screen. "Your message drops have become increasingly erratic over the past two or three years. You're not enjoying it *too* much, are you?"

"Gotta play the game," I murmur. "You of all people know that, boss."

"Not at the expense of forgetting who you represent. What side of the *Law* you stand."

"Is this some kind of warning?"

"No, just some advice," Hendry says with an audible sigh. "You're a natural for this kind of work, Trager, and you get results. But remember you are a Judge. You have a code of honour to uphold and a duty to protect the citizens. I've never lost an undercover officer yet and I don't want to start with you."

I hold up my hands and smile. "Hey, I'm the very dictionary definition of professional."

Hendry meets my gaze and shakes his head. "Just keep your reports up to date. And get me the Banana City meet details asap. I don't want to mobilise helmets at short notice and risk blowing the op."

"You'll know as soon as I do," I say, leaping to my feet and heading out the door.

"Keep it clean," Hendry calls after me.

"Don't I always?" I reply before returning to the street, where I belong.

THREE

When Dredd arrived at the Elizabeth Short construction site, it was teeming with life, like ants crawling over a carcass. Med and Tek Divisions had already established a base of operations, and there were a couple of helmets standing guard, regulating the inevitable rubberneckers who were craning to get a view of the crime scene. The Judges on duty saw him approaching and motioned him to pass with a curt nod.

Arc lights had been set up, casting the area in an eerie, hard white glow and throwing stark shadows on the ground and walls. Dredd dismounted his Lawmaster and made his way to the hub of activity which had been covered by a tent; as soon as he entered he was hit by the heat of the chem-pit which lay at its centre. Rubber sheeting had been placed on its banks upon which there was an odd collection of bones wrapped in plastic, as if somebody had attempted to piece together several human bodies and found that too many parts were missing. Dredd saw a skull with nothing attached beneath the jawline, while next to it was what looked like a ribcage and a pelvis with a couple of femurs below it.

A maintenance crew was at work draining the pit, the sludge steaming as it was sucked out by an industrial vacuum pump. They had nearly reached the bottom and it looked like the pit was giving up the last of its secrets, with a few more remains coming to light. At a rough estimate, Dredd reckoned it had held about fourteen bodies.

A female Tek-Judge was crouching by the bones and writing notes. Seeing Dredd surveying the scene, she stood and walked over to him, introducing herself as Garrison.

"What have we got?" Dredd asked.

"Construction droids were working on the foundations of the block when they realised the chem-pit they were building over was leaking into the rockcrete. They decided to clear the pit and discovered it was filled with human remains."

"Fourteen, at my count."

"Well, we haven't fully established just how many we're dealing with because we're having to match DNA samples of every piece of bone we come across. And of course, that doesn't account for those that could've been in there for years and have simply vaporised. But yes, from our preliminary calculations, we're looking at something approaching that figure."

"How long do you think they've been in there for?"

Garrison studied her notes, frowning. "The scorch marks on the bones, caused by the chemical reaction, vary from one to the next, which suggests some have been in there longer than others. It seems whoever has been using this as a dumping ground has returned on more than one occasion. They could date back over a few months."

"It'll solve some missing person cases, if nothing else," Dredd muttered. He strode over to the nearest of the remains. "Cause of death?"

Garrison joined him, bending over to pick up a skull. It rolled inside its bag and left a black, sooty stain. "That's another variable. See the contusion here, just above the eye socket? That suggests a blow caused by a blunt instrument. Ragged tearing is a sign of a limb being either broken or amputated, which a few of them seem to have suffered. In one, the chest cavity was snapped open, the likely reason being to remove internal organs. Hands and feet have been shattered, which could've been done by either a hammer or a bullet. Teeth have been forcibly removed, sometimes leaving the root. Whoever murdered these people slaughtered each in a different way with a number of different weapons. And it's likely the majority of the damage was done before the victim was dead."

"You don't think we're dealing with a serial killer then?"

Garrison shook her head, replacing the skull on the sheet. "It doesn't fit with the profile. Pattern killers tend to stick to one method, and there's usually a recognisable similarity between the victims, whether they're young women, children or people of a certain ethnicity. I can see no correlation between these carcasses; they're a mixture of men and women, young and old."

"Terrif. So we've got no through-leads and most of the evidence has gone up in smoke."

"Get ready for some more bad news," Garrison said, grimacing. "I don't think we're dealing with just one person. I think we're looking at an *organisation* here. The number of victims that have been dumped – and I'm fairly sure they've been disposed of in groups of threes and fours, if I've got my timings right – suggests at least a two-man team. There may be more involved, if not in the actual dumping then in the murders themselves. The varying causes of death calls to my mind an orgiastic killing."

"A cult?"

"Possibly, though even ritual sacrifice tends to be fairly straightforward – just a quick knifing on an altar. This seems more measured and sadistic. They took their time with the victims, and covered their tracks well, knowing exactly where to come to dispose of the bodies."

Dredd looked over the burnt and blackened remains of what had once been citizens of Mega-City One, thinking he couldn't possibly imagine the suffering they must have gone through before they ended up here. It certainly wasn't the first mass grave he'd been called to in his years as a Judge. Hell, it was a drop in the ocean compared to the landfill sites outside the West Wall containing the thousands of dead that had perished in Necropolis. But just when he thought he had the measure of this city's inhabitants, they would suddenly throw something up at him that was so despicable and callous it made him wonder if anything he did really made a difference. Justice Department did not hide the fact that it came down hard on lawbreakers, but it was debatable whether it worked as a deterrent. When perps could be so cold-bloodedly methodical as this in the act of murder, no laws could prevent it from happening. Dredd suddenly felt an overwhelming urge to bring in the guilty party more than ever.

"Have Psi-Div been through?" he asked. Telepaths could probe the final thoughts of the deceased for latent images that could sometimes show the face of the killer, or the location of the victim's death.

Garrison nodded. "He left just before you arrived. Couldn't get anything of any use as the bodies are all too far gone. Though he did say something about war..."

"War?"

"That's all he said. Just had a feeling of war. Nothing beyond that. He said he just had a 'psychic waft'."

Dredd snorted. "Psi Div as useful as ever. This whole case feels as if it could blow away like smoke in a second. We need some ID on those remains. Start chasing up the backgrounds of the victims, see if we can make some connections."

"We'll do our best," Garrison said. "We're following up dental and hospital records and cross-referencing them with missing persons. We could get lucky."

"Let me know as soon as you find out anything." The heat inside the tent was beginning to make Dredd feel uncomfortable. "The construction droids that called it in, are they still here?"

"Outside. They've been making statements."

He left Garrison to the task of placing names to the remains and walked out into the relatively cool night. Above him the skeletal framework of Elizabeth Short was silhouetted against the sky like it had been cut out of the darkness itself, the gentle wind whistling through its exposed beams. He headed off across the muddy expanse, passing a forensic team that was examining the soft earth.

"Anything?" he enquired.

"We've got tyre tracks, but unfortunately they could be any number of construction vehicles that may have come and gone over the past couple of days," a middle-aged, bearded man told him. He, like the rest of the team, was clad in gloves, boots and a white boiler suit, so as not to contaminate any potential evidence. "We'll run 'em through the computer, see if we can single out anything that looks unusual, or shouldn't be on the site."

"Garrison thinks they were dumping the bodies three or four at a time," Dredd told him. "So we're looking for something slightly bigger than a ground car. Probably a small van, something that wouldn't draw too much attention."

The man nodded. "OK, we'll keep an eye out for anything that matches that description. We've also got footprints around the banks of the pit, but again these have been obscured to a degree by other sources, most notably the droids who made the discovery." He motioned to the three robots that were being interviewed by a Judge in a quiet corner, away from the main investigation. "They weren't very careful, I'm afraid. You know how clumsy mechanicals can be."

Dredd strode towards the droids. He could see that one had been designed for wrecking, with a large iron ball hanging from its left arm, currently lying at rest between its feet. It was a good eight feet tall, with a wide, barrel-shaped torso, and it towered over its two colleagues, whose principal duties were not immediately obvious. One was squat and boxy and had a flatscreen face, with arms that had been fashioned into guns, probably to dispense nails or rivets; the third was the most humanoid, with a thin, spindly body. The latter was gesticulating wildly to the Judge that was standing before them.

"You gotta believe us, we never did nothin'!"

"Harrick," Dredd acknowledged, cutting the droid short. "What have our witnesses got to say?"

"Plenty, though not much of it useful. At 9:45 pm they were working on the foundations of the block, securing the supporting walls. Call-Me-Kevin there," Harrick nodded to the wrecking robot, "was clearing some nearby rockcrete when he noticed a substance seeping through cracks in the bricking. He pulled out some slabs and discovered that the chem-pit had eaten away at the 'crete and was spilling through into the basement. He pointed this out to his two workmates, Geraldo and Robert here, and they decided to cement the rim of the pit to stabilise it before 'creting over it again."

"You gotta understand, we had no idea what was in it," the humanoid robot was starting to protest again, his digitised voice a reedy whine.

"Shut up," Dredd said. "You can answer questions when they're put to you. Geraldo, is it?"

"Robert," the droid murmured.

"Anyway," Harrick continued, "in the process of shoring up the chem-pit, they realised the chemicals had become too unstable and the 'crete's just going to be eaten away again. So they decide to empty it entirely and Call-Me-Kevin starts to pull apart the banks to channel the sludge away, and that's when they first saw the bones."

"We called Judges straight away," Call-Me-Kevin said with a low rumble. Dredd couldn't help but recall the first Robot War and its revolutionary leader, Call-Me-Kenneth; the two robots closely resembled each other. Dredd didn't entirely trust mechs. With the problems they'd caused the city in the past, it was a sensible suspicion, and it wasn't easy to gauge what was in their heads. A Judge shouldn't have to use a lie-detector when interrogating a droid since theoretically, it was against one of the laws of robotics for a mechanical to tell a deliberate untruth. But robots were just too damn inscrutable.

The only droid Dredd knew of that wore its emotions on its sleeve was his old servant Walter, and even *he* had managed to surprise Dredd with his deviousness and ability to cause trouble. No, droids were a double-edged sword, a potential menace everyone had to live with. It was impossible for the city not to use them. They were more efficient, they never tired, they didn't require wages and could be used for situations which were far too dangerous for a human being, and yet mankind had grown used to relying on an artificial intelligence they couldn't always understand or even control.

"Why was the pit not cleared before construction began?" Dredd demanded. "Did you know it was there already?"

"We knew the history of the land," Robert said. "We had been briefed beforehand that it had been heavily irradiated. A Sov missile came down not far from here at the start of the Apocalypse War. But that was the point of Councillor Peat's restructuring programme–"

"Wait," Dredd interrupted. "You're saying this block is another of Peat's Phoenix Campaign buildings?"

"Yes. This was started just as Fred Quimby was in the closing stages."

"Can't seem to get away from the councillor tonight," Dredd muttered under his breath. He looked at Geraldo, who had remained quiet so far. "So you knew you were building over the chem-pit?"

"As far as we were aware," Geraldo replied in a high-pitched wheedle, "the pit had been covered over. We would not have started construction if we knew the chemicals were going to eat into the rockcrete. It would have eventually destabilised the entire building, putting the residents at risk."

"I don't understand why the pit just wasn't emptied first," Dredd said, more to himself than the others. "Surely that would've been the safest option?"

"Councillor Peat wants this built quickly," Robert said quietly, as if debating with himself about whether he should spill the beans on his boss. "Why do you think we're working at this time of night? He's put the whole thing on a fast-track, making us work overtime to get it up and ready."

"So much for Peat's 'quality first' statements," Harrick said. "Looks like he's cutting corners and neglecting safety issues simply so he can get another of his buildings up as quickly as possible and his face back on the Tri-D."

Dredd didn't reply. It didn't seem like Peat to so wilfully disregard the well-being of those he'd want to live in the block once it was completed. After all, they were going to be his wealthy friends and peers, whom he relied upon to stay in office. Why risk incurring their wrath for the sake of delaying the opening of the building? From what Dredd had seen of the councillor, the man was exacting and a stickler for detail; he did nothing without reason.

Of course, it was also perfectly possible that Peat knew nothing of the pit his workforce was building on; while he may be the instigator and figurehead of the Phoenix Campaign, he wasn't necessarily in charge of clearing the land or making the day-to-day budgetary decisions with regard to materials. Dredd would have to have a word with the councillor himself and see what he had to say. He would have to be informed in any case that his latest project was now the site of a multiple-murder investigation, which would no doubt cap his day off nicely.

"Y-you don't think we had anything to do with those bodies, do you?" Robert asked. "As I told the Judge here, we just found 'em. We never knew what we was building over. We called the authorities as soon as we knew what they were. You gotta believe it, it's the truth–"

"All right," Dredd snapped, holding a hand up. Grud-damn thing sounded as if its voicebox was stuck. "No, you're not suspects. But make sure you give Judge Harrick all your serial numbers and manufacturers' details because we may need to question you again. There'll be no more work done on Liz Short until this inquiry is over, so I suggest you find other employment. Harrick, get contact numbers."

The droids looked at each other, though none of them said anything. If it was possible for a robot to feel relief, Dredd guessed, that was what was passing through their circuitry. Once again, he felt a twinge of distaste for the machines; it was as if they were privy to information that he couldn't obtain. There was too much of a divide between human and mechanical for his liking, with the latter too easily capable of concealing matters from their masters.

"Dredd!"

The senior Judge looked around and saw Garrison beckoning him to return to the tented area. Dredd marched off towards it and he could see from the excited expression on the Tek-Judge's face that they had a breakthrough.

"We've found something," she said, leading him back to the remains. "It was something on one of the last to be pulled from the pit."

"What is it?" Dredd asked impatiently.

Garrison lifted another bagged skull before him. "Look closely, under the cheekbone. It's a complete fluke that it's caught there. It could've easily disappeared amongst all that effluent."

Dredd took the cranium in his hands and tilted it into the light. The skull appeared fairly fresh compared to some of the others that had been dragged out, and even he could tell it was female. Beneath the cheekbone was a silver pellet, half the size of a pea, which had become welded to the bone.

"Is that... *metal*?" Dredd wanted to know.

"Titanium," Garrison replied, barely able to contain the pride in her voice. "I'm pretty confident that it's an earring and as the flesh surrounding it disintegrated, it came loose and caught in the skull. As I say, absolute thousand-to-one shot. We've taken scrapings from it and are running tests now, but we think it originates from outside the Big Meg."

"The titanium survived the chemicals in the pit?"

"Just about. That's why we're sure it comes from overseas. It's probably been mixed with other polymers as it was fashioned into a piece of jewellery, and that's what enabled it to stay virtually intact despite the heat."

"Could they be imported?"

"It's very likely, which means that we should be able to run a trace on any purchases that were made in, say, the past ten years. Even though I don't think this woman was killed all that long ago – we could possibly be talking only months – she may have bought the earring a while back. However, just by looking at her skull, I can tell she was in her early to mid-twenties, so we wouldn't have to go back much more than a decade."

Dredd handed the skull back to her. "Even so, a trace running across the entire city over that period is going to take time."

"There is another possibility that would narrow it down some," Garrison said. "That she came from overseas *herself* and had the earring when she entered the city. If she was a tourist or an immigrant, then they should have records of her at customs. If we can pinpoint the source of the titanium, then we can match it with anyone visiting from that country within a certain timeframe."

Dredd nodded, feeling progress was made at last. "Good. Get on it, Garrison. Any leads, any names, pass on the info immediately."

The Tek-Judge lifted the skull up again and looked at the minute earring with something approaching wonderment.

"Amazing how one little detail can throw a case wide open, isn't it? And it's sheer luck that this victim happened to be wearing something that was near indestructible, as well as it sticking to the body. From tiny acorns, eh?"

"Ironically," Dredd replied, heading out of the tent, "I'm about to tell someone just how far his mighty empire could fall..."

Matheson Peat sat in the dark in his luxury apartment in Michael Douglas, with a glass of water and a couple of tablets for his nerves. His nineteen year-old girlfriend Sondra had long since gone to bed, and from his chair in the living room he could hear her rhythmic breathing. He found it soothing to listen to, but sleep for him seemed very far away. His brain was too wired, the events of the evening playing over and over again in his head like a movie stuck on a constant loop. How could something that had been arranged so meticulously, that had seemed to be going so well, fall apart so quickly? One minute he had the press hanging off his every word and any Z-list celebrity that was worth his or her salt was desperate to scrounge an invite to the biggest night of the year. The next minute, three men lay dead in a vicious gun battle, sending one of the world's most famous women – who was here at *his* invitation – round the bend.

Lubular had taken Vanessa back to their hotel, the Mega-City Excelsior, via a back route that avoided the riot going on at the front of the building. He said he would try to wean her off the narcotics until she calmed down so they could decide what their next move would be. His other guests had similarly dispersed as quickly as they could while the Judges contained the trouble, and though he made an effort to help clear up the remains of the party afterwards, his listlessness made him more of a hindrance. In the end, he too headed for home, a strange, unfamiliar feeling gnawing at him. A feeling of failure.

He'd been sitting here for over an hour, visibly trembling. Thoughts tumbled through his head: what the headlines were going to be on tomorrow's newspapers, what his friends would think of him after such a debacle, whether it was his fault for inviting a superstar like Vanessa Indigo to an inane, dumbed-down city such as this. He really should have known better.

But the image that occupied his mind most of all was of the mysterious man who had kick-started all the trouble, the would-be assassin who was gunned down by Indigo's bodyguards. Lubular had waved away the reasoning behind such an attack, saying such crazies are par for the course when you're in the public eye, and perhaps that was true. Trying to apply logic to something as random and maniacal as this was pointless. And yet, Peat couldn't help but be haunted by the man with the gun, prepared to murder someone he loved with all his heart, possibly because he couldn't have her for himself. If he had succeeded, then Peat's name would have been synonymous with a night everybody would remember for entirely the wrong reasons.

There was a knock at the door. At this time of night, he knew it could be nothing trivial, but even so he was disinclined to answer it. He just wanted to shut his eyes and forget that this evening had ever happened. The knock came again, louder, and he heard Sondra stirring in the bedroom. He struggled to his feet and padded across to the door, opening it a crack, keeping the chain in place. When he saw who it was, he sighed and opened the door fully, letting his visitor in.

"I trust I'm not disturbing you, councillor."

"No, I couldn't sleep anyway." Peat went and sat back in his armchair, reaching for his half-glass of water. "What can I do for you, Judge Dredd?"

Dredd stood, arms folded. "There have been developments of which you should be aware. Construction droids working on Elizabeth Short discovered a chem-pit beneath the foundations. This pit proved to contain the remains of at least fourteen bodies. We believe they have been murdered and dumped there."

"My grud..." Peat's jaw dropped. "D-do you know who they are?"

The Judge shook his head. "We're working on that at the moment. Just so you know, all work on Liz Short has been halted for the foreseeable future pending the outcome of this investigation."

Peat swallowed a gulp from his glass. "OK."

"I also have to ask you, councillor, did you know there was a chem-pit beneath the construction site?"

Peat leaned back in his chair, frowning. "No... not specifically. I mean, I knew the area once had a high rad-count, because that was the reason behind my campaign – to make such areas habitable again. So I suppose I must've assumed there was every chance there might be chem-pools on the land. But it was the collective responsibility of the architects and construction companies to clear the land before building was to begin."

"Did you authorise the block to be constructed over the chem-pit, without it being cleared first?"

"What? Who's said that I did?"

"Just answer the question."

"No, of course not. It would be a recipe for disaster."

Dredd paused for a moment, glanced at his lie-detector, then levelled his gaze at the man. "Our paths seem to keep crossing, Councillor Peat. I'd hope for your sake that it's just coincidence, if you believe in such a thing. Right now, you're involved – however remotely – in a multiple-murder case, so I'm instructing you not to think about leaving the city until we say otherwise. We may require you for further questioning."

"Matheson, what's going on?" Sondra emerged yawning from the bedroom in her dressing gown, her hair tousled.

"Nothing to worry about, dear," Peat replied. "Judge Dredd has just relayed some rather surprising news regarding business."

"We'll talk again later," Dredd said. "I'll bid you citizens goodnight." He headed towards the door.

Peat followed, and as he got out of earshot of his girlfriend, hissed: "I shall be contacting the Chief Judge in the morning about your heavy-handed tactics at the block opening this evening."

"That is your right, I suppose, Councillor Peat."

"Don't think you can bully us around like everybody else, Dredd. We're not *like* everybody else. I could have your drokking badge." Peat slammed the door on Dredd before making his way back to the living room.

"Matheson, you look terrible," Sondra said. "You always work so hard. I wish you'd let me help you."

Despite her protestations, Peat had refused to let her come to the opening; partly because he wasn't keen on everybody seeing his teenaged girlfriend for fear of what rumours would start circulating, but mostly because he knew she'd steal the limelight from him.

"Why don't you come to bed?"

Peat didn't argue. He let her lead him by the hand into the bedroom and beneath the sheets. But even wrapped in her arms, he found he was shaking more than ever, and he stayed awake until the first fingers of dawn pierced the sky.

FOUR

It is three nights later when I get the call telling me the buy is going ahead. Brett instructs me to pack as much killware as I can surreptitiously conceal about my person, and to meet them at warehouse four-two-three on the north-east docks at 2:00 am. I can glean nothing from his voice that tells me how he thinks the night's events are going to go down. He just barks brusque directions and suggests that I would be a fool to leave without adequate firepower.

The call comes through at 11:25 pm, which will give Hendry a couple of hours to mobilise the back-up units and stake the area out. I go down to a public phone and leave a coded message on an automated reply service that feeds directly into Wally Squad, and tell my superior the where and the when. Then I head back to my apartment in Nic Cage and try to think of something mindless to do to fill the hours and take my mind off the upcoming bust.

In my experience, too much thinking can be just as dangerous as a lack of preparation – with your brain wired over what to expect and how you'll deal with it, should the eventuality arise, it can blunt your instincts. I feel I work better fuelled by adrenalin, living off my intuition and natural reflexes. Certainly, in undercover work, the moment you start doing things by the book, you risk blowing your identity as your years of training start to filter through. In the end, I elect to channel-surf my Tri-D set, maybe catch a crappy movie that will require next to no concentration.

I've been living out of my apartment for virtually my entire career as a Judge. There are tens of thousands of habitats like this one, dotted around the city and owned by Justice Department for its covert operatives, and they're not so much homes as bases. I have no personal effects or photographs on the walls, my bed is a mattress, tucked into a corner of a bare room, the cupboards in the kitchen are all but empty save a few packets and some mouldering vegetables. I have no need for luxury, for it plays no part in my life. I receive no salary from Justice Department, but it supplies me with everything I require to be a Judge, and being a Judge is all that I require. When I entered the Academy of Law, I willingly relinquished the chance of marrying or having a family, of ever being wealthy or travelling, of making my own choices. I traded it all in.

Perhaps my one concession to normality is my Tri-D set, which can be vital in linking me to the rest of the city. Whilst your average street Judge operates best when he or she's aloof from the citizenry, to be a Wally Squad officer is to be in tune with the fashions, crazes and dialogue of your regular Joe on the slab. If anything, this side of the job is just as dangerous to your health as having a blaster rammed in your face; overexposure to the insanity that this city dreams up can send your brain sideways, with every goofball quiz show and vidiot pirate channel competing for your attention. It's well known that a proportion of undercover Judges have a slender hold on reality as it is, forced to plunge into the mind-sapping maelstrom of plastic pop music and twenty-four-hour soaps.

Living in Mega-City One is a stressful business, crammed into a melting pot of bizarrity, with four hundred million borderline psychopaths jammed either side of you that can snap at any time. To submerse yourself too far into the populace brings with it the risk that you too can succumb to the intense pressure experienced by your fellows, and jeopardise your ability to think coherently. For a Wally Squad officer, the trick is to never forget what you *are*; that while on the outside, you're indistinguishable from the next cit. As long as my moron act stays just that – *an act* – then I have some hope of survival.

But nobody ever said it was easy. Stupidity in the Big Meg is everywhere, like it's one of Otto Sump's lifestyle choices that's never stopped being all the rage. Right now, as I flip channels, the vapidity steals out of the Tri-D set and tries to lower my IQ. I can feel my eyes glazing over as the stations change, but the inanity remains the same: a cookery programme presented by a microwave telling viewers in clipped female tones how to reheat leftovers; an embarrassingly cheap drama about teenaged sky-surfers that was obviously filmed by a very unskilled cameraman on a powerboard; a right-wing chat show hosted by a guy claiming to be the reincarnation of Bob Booth; alien seduction techniques; celebrity bean-counting; and so on and so on, like a descent into cathode-ray hell...

Enough, I tell myself, resisting the urge to wheel through a further hundred channels, my forefinger hovering over the buttons on the remote. I stick, as expected, with a movie, a fairly old propaganda job retelling moments from the Apocalypse War, clearly made with Justice Department approval. The simplistic black-and-white moralities on display make even me wince; the Sovs are portrayed as warmongering animals, slaughtering women and children with dastardly quips while the Meg Judges ride out of a rising sun, bringing justice to the invading hordes. It typically plays fast and loose with the facts, inventing laughable romantic sub-plots between Sov lieutenants and cit fraternisers that sit uneasily with the carnage it unashamedly glorifies.

I was a cadet at the time the conflict kicked off, so my experience of the realities of the war were limited to a bunker beneath the Academy, but even so, you'd have to take a full hit with a Stupid Gun not to smell the bullshit this movie was peddling. Watching the shots of Sov tanks rumbling through the occupied streets makes me think of my eight year-old self lying on a makeshift campbed deep underground with the other greenies, listening to the shriek of missiles streaking overhead and realising at that moment just how much we had changed, how much our tutors had moulded us into proto-Judges.

Other children of our age would normally be terrified to be so close to the noise and heat of battle, but all we felt was a steely determination and a shared desire to be out there, defending our city. I suppose if we'd been asked to visualise our emotions, they would look not unlike this piece-of-crap flick, this child's-eye view of a nuclear exchange. Fiercely patriotic and breathtakingly naive, with caricatures mouthing clichés, the programme reduced the war to the level of something like the Tri-D talent show *You Stink!* – easy consumption for people who don't like to think too much.

In the end, the toe-curling acting and lines like "But War Marshal, haven't you ever truly loved someone?" are enough to make me want to kill someone, so I flip the set off before I lose my temper. I go into the bedroom and lift up a couple of floorboards, removing two Justice Department blasters with the serial numbers burnt off to make them look unlicensed. The small ammo store I have here contains probably the most valuable items in the entire apartment. It's not a significant arsenal by any means – several hand cannons, a little explosive, some bladed weapons – but enough to make me feel secure.

I slot a loaded Zirgman P28 into my shoulder holster, then work the slide on a compact Roundlock before slipping on the safety catch and jamming it beneath my belt at the small of my back. I tape a boot knife to the inside of my trouser leg, then I pull on my jacket and drop a snubnose Jameson .38 into the pocket with a few spare slugs. The weight feels reassuringly heavy, like I've got some solid protection. I look myself over in the mirror and don't see any awkward bulges that would give me away. Ideally, a bullet-proof vest would be useful for this kind of deal, but its bulkiness would be too obvious.

I replace the floorboards then take a final look in the mirror. Breathing deeply, I stare back at my reflection and silently tell myself that the Danskys are not going to know what's hit them, and they will *never* know, because everything is going to go nice and smooth. I have no reason to panic. I am smarter than them by several billion degrees.

I switch off the light and my reflection is lost in darkness as I head out into the night.

I'm due to meet Cavell at a hottie house on Johnson, so I grab myself a synthi-caf while I wait. It jangles with the zizz I scored on the way and snorted in the restaurant's toilets, but it helps flatline the paranoia that was starting to creep up on me. The drug is boosting my perception, and in the building's sickly, yellow flickering light, everything is in deep focus: the group of arguing eldsters at the next table, the droids working behind the counter, the steam rising from the frying hotties, the puddles of sauce on the tiled floor. I feel hyper-alert, but it should level off shortly into a sense of pleasantly heightened awareness.

Somebody's left today's *Mega-Times* on a chair beside me and I leaf through it, conscious of the Roundlock rubbing uncomfortably against my waist. A news item on page two about a body dump discovery catches my interest. Reading between Dredd's typically terse statements to the press, it looks like the victims were all tortured before being buried beneath a block development for some time. The story sets alarm bells ringing in my head that I know is more than just the zizz talking, and Dredd's vague comment at the end about following up "significant leads" makes me ponder. I tear the article out and stuff it in my pocket.

The scarred, hulking visage that is Cavell appears at the door and nods. I finish the synthi-caf with a gulp, then join him, the meathead already striding away before I'm out the door. Conversation has never been Cavell's strong point, and the welcome silence between us as we catch the zoom over the docks gives me more time to mentally prepare. We arrive at our destination and I follow the big lunk through the maze of warehouses, his long coat flapping ahead of me. The wind brings with it the smell of the Black Atlantic: a harsh, eye-watering stink of pollutants. In the distance I can hear the cries of dog-vultures, probably wheeling above the sluggish waves, searching for carrion, but otherwise it is unnaturally quiet. The roar of the city seems a very long way away.

I try to imagine the forces of Justice Department moving in the shadows, surrounding the area, getting into position. It gives me a small amount of comfort to envisage that our movements are being tracked by infra-red binox and rifle sights, that somewhere out in the darkness my back-up is waiting to pounce. My hand slides inside my jacket pocket and brushes against the snubnose. I hope that events don't spiral so out of control that I have to blow my cover too soon.

Cavell halts at an anonymous door and raps on it four times as I check my watch: 1:45 am. The door opens and we slip inside to be met by the sight of the rest of the gang thumbing shells into shotguns. On the other side of the warehouse stands an empty truck, waiting to be loaded with the merchandise.

"Guess we're all here," Brett says by way of greeting, snapping shut the breech on one of the weapons and throwing it to Cavell, who silently hides it within his coat.

"You expecting trouble?" I ask, nodding towards the ordnance. Hogg is strapping a wicked-looking blade to her thigh.

"They ain't gonna be welcoming us with candy and flowers," Brett remarks, adjusting the holsters under each arm. "Pays to have a little insurance."

With the amount of killware on display here, I realise that if it all goes down then I'm going to be in the middle of a small war. Even with several helmets standing over me like guardian angels, they're not going to be able to pull my fat out of the fire before both factions start swapping lead. I'm walking into a highly volatile situation, and if they get any whiff of the fact that I've set them up, then I'm going to have a dozen or so gangbangers looking to tear my lungs out and eat 'em. I've gotta hope these guys mean business and don't dick the Danskys around too much. With slimeballs from Banana City, you can never be too sure.

"OK, we set?" Brett asks the room, picking up a briefcase. Most of them are wearing long coats similar to Cavell's to hide the shotguns hanging at their sides. "From here on, let me do the talking. That includes you, Jonny. No threatening gestures, no throwdowns unless necessary. Don't underestimate these dirtwads, they'll slice your drokking throat as easily as shaking hands with you. Clear?"

Mauser, Strodem and Hogg nod, and Cavell remains impassive, like a mechanoid awaiting instructions.

Brett leads the way through the darkened alleys to the docks until we're overlooking the black expanse of the sea. The smell off the water is ripe with decades of decay and I struggle not to cough as it gets into my mouth. I keep my lips tightly sealed and breathe through my nose.

"Martinez..." Brett mutters testily, looking at his watch. I check mine and see it's just after two. I can sense the Danskys' anxiety; they obviously want this over as quickly as possible.

A light flares in the shadows to our right and we turn as one and see Martinez emerging from a doorway, casually smoking a cigarillo. He looks like he's out for nothing more than a midnight stroll, wearing the same white suit that I last saw him in. He saunters towards us as if he's deliberately toying with the brothers' nerves. I can detect again that subtle shift in power. Martinez performs as if he's holding all the ace cards.

"Señors," he says with an insincere smile, blowing smoke out the side of his mouth. "Glad you could make it."

"Martinez," Brett acknowledges, visibly trying to control his temper. "So, the deal still on?"

"Si, my people are here," he replies, tapping ash onto the ground. "But there has been a slight change of plan."

"What?" Jonny growls.

"Nothing serious, I assure you, señors, but my contacts, they have their own protection to think of. They would prefer that the deal went ahead on the boat."

"Wait, wait," Brett says. "You mean we make the exchange out at drokking *sea*?"

Martinez nods. "It is anchored just a couple of miles outside Mega-City docks." He gestures towards the water and the darkness beyond. "They have a small craft that will take you there, and they will help you offload the merchandise once the deal is complete. But they want to keep the negotiations on the ship."

"Why?" Brett demands.

"They are reluctant to enter Mega-City One, as you would expect. But they would also prefer it if the two parties met on ground where there is little opportunity for... unforeseen circumstances."

My mind is reeling. This is bad. My back-up is going to be snafued out in the middle of the drokking Black Atlantic, and I can only hope that Hendry is picking this up and making some fast changes, otherwise I'm on my own and up to my neck in it. My zizz-induced confidence gets the better of me and before I know it I'm saying: "This is bullshit. Why the drokk should we trust these greasers?"

"Trager," Brett shoots me a look. "Keep your damn mouth shut."

"But we'll be right where they want us," I protest, playing for time.

"Trager, make another noise," Brett hisses, "and I'll put a cap in you myself."

I shut up and in the momentary silence that descends we can hear the puttering of an outboard motor approaching. A small skimmer slides out of the night, lights swinging through the mist hanging above the water's surface, and comes to a stop parallel to the sea wall by a short set of steps. Nobody disembarks from it.

"My clients are waiting, señors," Martinez says. "It is time to decide whether you want to do business or not."

The brothers exchange a glance that suggests they are seriously not happy with this, and the tension in the air crackles. I try surreptitiously to look around me, checking to see if I can catch even the smallest glimpse of the reinforcements that are waiting just around the corner, but there's no sign. I feel my heart beating harder against my ribs as a low-level, drug-infused fear begins to take hold.

"OK," Brett says at last. "Let's do it. But I wanna tell you, Martinez, this better be the one and only surprise of the evening, otherwise your dago ass is gonna be going swimming. You hear me?"

The geek grins that nauseating crescent moon of yellow teeth and nods. "But of course, Señor Dansky. Everything will go smoothly, I assure you." He gestures for us to follow him down the steps and onto the skimmer.

Brett looks at each of us in turn with a glare that says "First sign of trouble, kill 'em all," then heads after Martinez, his brother joining him. We each take our turns to board the vessel, which is about the same size as a Justice Department patrol boat. Despite the arc lights positioned above the cabin, the darkness ensures that I can't get a good look at our two Banana City hosts: one guy is standing beside the wheel, waiting until we're all aboard before cranking the engine and turning the vessel back out to sea, while the other lounges against the side, a rifle slung over his shoulder. Martinez says something in Spanish to him, sharing a joke it seems, then tells us that it will not take more than five minutes to reach the ship. The brothers are staring the rifle-guy out, trying to intimidate him, but it's not working. From what I can see of his face in the moonlight, he just smiles back, rocking with the motion of the boat.

With the flat, black expanse of water all around us, I start to feel alone and trapped. It's easy to see why the dealers chose to meet the Danskys out here, there's nowhere to run to, nowhere to make a stand. You can't even swim for it as very few have fallen into the Black Atlantic and survived. The thick soup of chemicals and pollutants is so strong that if you swallowed a mouthful you'd be in intensive care for days, your stomach pumped dry. I realise that if we don't get back on this boat after the transaction is finished, then none of us are getting out of here alive.

True to Martinez's word, the ship hovers into view in no time at all. The large, sleek yacht is anchored out in the ocean, and I can see shadowy figures moving on its deck. As the boat sidles up against the hull, a rope ladder is thrown down to meet us. The pilot kills the engine and the skimmer bobs on the waves, rifle-guy crossing to portside and beckoning us to climb. The Danskys hesitate.

"Go, señors," Martinez urges.

Cautiously, we ascend. As we clamber over the edge, we find ourselves staring down the barrels of a dozen guns. On the deck, a semi-circle of Banana City gangbangers surrounds us, automatic weapons pointed in our direction. They're armed to the max. The brothers look around hopelessly, as if trying to find a way out, but there's nowhere to go. The greaseballs say nothing, and it strikes me that if they wanted us dead, they wouldn't be taking their time about it. I get the feeling they're waiting for an order, or just keeping us under guard. Either way, it doesn't smell like a double-cross.

"Please excuse my friends," Martinez says behind us, huffing and puffing as he throws himself over the side and onto the ship. "They just like to be extra careful."

"I get nervous in the face of so much killware," Brett says, whipping a pistol from his holster and levelling it at Martinez. "And when I get nervous, I get an itchy trigger finger. You might want to tell 'em to lower their cannons before it becomes a bulletfest."

"Please, Señor Dansky," Martinez says. "Let's not make this unpleasant."

"Give me one good reason why I shouldn't unload into your treacherous drokking face, you piece of shit–"

"Because Enrique has brought an exceptional offer your way," says a voice from behind the Banana City group, and they part to allow a slim, dark woman clad in combat fatigues to walk through to the front. Her ebony hair is pulled back into a severe ponytail, revealing a birdlike, coffee-coloured face. "I trust him implicitly, and so should you."

"Talón," Brett acknowledges.

"Hello again, señor." She nods once. "Now, I believe we are here to do business and not kill each other?" The woman makes a waving gesture and says something in Spanish. The gangbangers slowly drop their guns, though from the murderous glints in their eyes, only reluctantly. "I'm sorry we are not more welcoming, but we make no exceptions. You can trust no one these days."

Brett sheathes his gun and shakes hands with her. "You got that right."

"We should not delay," Talón says, looking uncomfortable. "Evading the forces of law and order is becoming increasingly difficult. I think we should conclude our deal as soon as possible."

"Suits me."

"You have the money?"

Brett taps the briefcase. "Right here. Forty thousand in untraceable paycards, as agreed. And the merchandise?"

"But of course." Talón barks an instruction to a couple of lackeys and they disappear into the hold. Minutes later, they return struggling with a crate between them, dropping it down in front of the brothers. "There are another three like this," she says as the Danskys peer into the crate, pulling out zip guns and random weapon parts. "I trust you are satisfied?"

"All looks good to me," Jonny murmurs.

"Did I not say you would be happy?" Martinez beams, but everybody seems to ignore him.

This is it, Hendry, I'm thinking. Now, now, now. Can't take them all by myself, man…

Brett hands the briefcase to Talón. "You'll help us get this stuff ashore?" he asks.

"I have another two skimmers at your disposal," she replies, then pauses as another of her lieutenants whispers in her ear. He hands her a small package, wrapped in cloth. "Ah, yes." Talón gives Brett a dazzling smile. "We also have this for you. I understand you have a buyer who is interested in such antiquity?" She passes the bundle over to Brett, whose face has gone pale and takes the package gingerly as if he was holding a grenade. "It will cost you a further five thousand–"

Then the whole world turns white.

For a moment, we're frozen, transfixed in the hard light, too stunned to move. Darkness is banished in a heartbeat, as if daybreak has suddenly exploded over the ship. But when I look up, I see a looming shadow moving in the sky, followed a fraction of a second later by the amplified voice coming from it.

"Justice Department! Nobody move!"

The H-wagon swoops in low to hover above the yacht, its engine roaring in our ears, spotlights trapping us in their glare. The sea churns in the downward blast of its jets and sprays filthy water in our faces, and after a moment of utter incomprehension, it serves to break the spell and Talón and her men are moving and shouting, looking for somewhere to hide. They're like roaches, scuttling into every crack and crevice, trying to find safety.

Brett drops the bundle and grabs Martinez with both hands, bellowing into his face. "You set us up! You sold us out, drokker!"

"Señor, I did nothing!"

Jonny puts a gun to Martinez's head and blows his brains out. "We ain't got time for this, bro! We gotta *go*!"

"Talón! Find Talón!"

Lights appear on either side of the yacht, closing in through the mist; patrol boats are approaching. Mauser and Cavell stand at the stern and start firing with their shotguns at the vessels and seconds later, a cannon lets rip from the H-wagon and reduces the pair to bloody confetti. I see the skimmer that brought us here attempt to escape, but a laser arcs out of the sky and destroys it in an orange fireball.

The ship plummets into chaos. The Banana City contingent are trying in vain to hold the Judges off, but they're picked off with ease. The Justice Department boats have now swung alongside the yacht, and helmets are boarding, mercilessly putting down any opposition. Strodem – showing a rare streak of character, or perhaps just wanting to go out in a blaze of glory – leaps at the nearest uniform and the two of them are hurled into the water, disappearing into its inky depths.

Lying flat on the deck, bodies all around me, I see the bundle that Brett dropped and snag it. I stagger to my feet and try to discern where the brothers have gone, smoke now wafting in front of me as the vessel begins to burn. I see Talón and one of her right-hand men untying a skimmer from the ship while keeping the Danskys away at gunpoint.

"You were followed, you idiots!" the woman spits. "You have brought the Judges down on us!"

"It was your drokking middleman that screwed us over," Brett snarls. "Should never have trusted that spic bastard in the first place."

"*Puta!*" Talón's goon swears violently and shoots Brett repeatedly in the chest, knocking the gun-runner back in a blizzard of crimson explosions. He slides against the outside cabin wall, leaving red streaks on the panelling. Jonny yelps in genuine grief, but before he can pull his own weapon there's a blur of movement and Hogg appears out of nowhere, throwing herself at the gunman, thrusting a blade through his neck. He gargles, feebly clutching at the knife, then collapses. Hogg realises for just one moment that there is someone behind her before Talón empties half a clip into the back of her head.

Talón and Jonny stand off against each other, pistols raised. There are tears trickling down Dansky's face.

"My brother... You'll die for that, drokker," he whines.

"Come on then, Mega-City cretin," Talón sneers. "Take your best shot."

Time for me to intervene, I think. I need Dansky alive. "I'm afraid I can't let you do that," I say, levelling my snubnose at the pair of them.

"Trager?" Jonny glances at me quizzically.

"Justice Department," I reply. "You're under arrest."

For a second, they look like they don't believe me, then realisation hits. Talón screams and fires at me. I duck and roll, ears ringing as I hear the wood shattering behind me, then come up blasting, putting two slugs through her head, dead centre. My shooting range tutor would be proud.

Even before she's hit the ground, I have to deal with Jonny. He pumps the trigger frenziedly, bullets flying wild, but I still catch one in the arm, spinning me around, dropping me to my knees, making me lose the snubnose. I yank the Roundlock free from my waistband, but take too long aiming. He kicks it from my hand, then punches me full in the face. I see stars as I lay on my back, looking up at him lining his gun up with my forehead.

"Drokkin' snitch," he says.

My hand finds the boot knife strapped to my leg and I tear it free, ramming it up into his groin. He screeches in pain, and I knock him over, disarming him before he can recover. I tug the blade free and he cups the ragged mess between his legs, whimpering.

"Freeze!"

I turn and see three Judges standing before me, Lawgivers trained. "Drop the weapon!"

"Family man! Family man!" I yell, giving the recognised code word for an undercover officer. I drop the knife with a clatter, holding up my arms above my head. Behind me, I can hear Jonny moaning.

"Stay down," one of the Judges says, slowly moving forward. "Play dead until this is over."

I nod. Play dead? I can do that.

FIVE

High up in the Grand Hall of Justice, Chief Judge Hershey looked out of the window of her office at the panorama of Mega-City One spread out before her. It was sometimes difficult to believe that to all intents and purposes she was in charge of this chaotic sprawl, and that from the lowliest cleaning droid, sweeping the streets of City Bottom, all points of authority ultimately cascaded up to her. It was a dizzying thought that brought home to her just how much responsibility she wielded, and theoretically how impossible her job was.

You couldn't control the Big Meg, no matter how much Justice Department told itself it did; it was merely a holding action, a juggling act. You stamped down on one section of the underworld, ten more sprang up in its place like some mythical, many-headed beast. The city would endure, the way it had always done, and the wheels of society would continue to turn, but in her low moments Hershey sometimes wondered if her position wasn't just a bit futile. She kept the cogs oiled so the whole machine was able to carry on trundling along, but did any decision she make truly change anything?

Of course, times had changed and she wasn't the autocrat that other Chief Judges in the past had been. Mandates had to be passed by the Council of Five, and the heads of various departments all had their say in issuing directives. Ever since she'd assumed the office, she liked to think that she'd been an approachable leader – perhaps a little *too* approachable, she thought, thinking of the hours wasted listening to block committees and dignitaries haranguing her with petty complaints – and certainly her slightly liberal outlook did not go down well with some of the more hardline elements within the ranks.

There was no doubt that some of those close to her were waiting for her to fail. They were just waiting for one of her initiatives that promoted an openness between Justice Department and the citizenry to explode spectacularly back in her face and so prompt a return to the good old-fashioned "back to basics" tactic of pummelling the poor saps into submission. She did sometimes question why she bothered offering the public a platform to voice their opinions, when half the time they clearly couldn't care less. Give them a chance to vote on something and they'd whinge that all the thinking was making their heads hurt. She guessed it came down to not wanting to spend her time shuffling papers and finding things to outlaw; she wanted to see the city develop, and for people to take charge of their *own* lives, rather than her – through the Judicial system – telling them how to do it.

She wondered what Fargo would make of it all, whether he'd accuse her of living a fool's dream. She could imagine he'd certainly be astonished to see a woman of her age as Chief Judge. It wasn't bad, she had to admit. She was quietly proud of being only the second female to hold the position, and she was most definitely the youngest. Ten years ago, she'd been a regular street Judge, with no designs on rapid promotion, and now she was at the top of an incredibly complicated chain of command. The route that had taken her there was an eventful one.

She supposed she'd always been a good organiser and took well to ordering others about, and it was in the vacuum that followed the Second Robot War and Volt's suicide that the opportunity had presented itself. Few others were prepared to contest her, and given the fate of her predecessors, it was perhaps not surprising. It was not a secret that your life expectancy dramatically shortened the moment you donned the robes of office. Goodman was assassinated, Griffin shot as a traitor, McGruder went insane before checking out in the line of fire, Silver was murdered at the hands of Judge Death, and Volt went down with a self-inflicted bullet through the brain. Hershey sometimes wondered if she wasn't safer back on the streets.

Indeed, she'd be lying if she said she didn't miss being back out there on her Lawmaster, enforcing the Law. Standing at the window, watching from a distance as the tiny trucks sped along the multi-lane meg-ways below her like lines of insects following intricate paths, she felt very marginalised from the hub of the city. It was perhaps her biggest sacrifice upon becoming Chief Judge; that she wouldn't get to experience again the rush of adrenalin as she busted a sugar deal or pursued a tap gang. While she was up here worrying about making a difference, at least down on the street you had solid evidence of the fact; a couple of dead perps at your feet spoke volumes.

There was a knock at the door. She hadn't been looking forward to this meeting. It was not that she disliked her visitor's company, far from it, but she could see it turning into a confrontation. He wasn't somebody easily assuaged, and despite her authority she couldn't help but feel intimidated in his presence. She'd served under him many times before, respecting his forthright adherence to the Law, but now the tables were turned in their relationship despite him being a good twenty years older than her, and this made her feel a touch uncomfortable, as if she could always sense his unspoken disapproval. Still, she reasoned, it wasn't as if he hadn't been offered the position in the past. It was clear that he was only content to be at the frontline in the war against crime, receiving and acting upon instructions from HQ.

"Come in," she said.

Dredd opened the door and strode into the office. "You wanted to see me, Chief Judge?"

Hershey clasped her hands behind her back and walked away from the window to stand beside her desk. "Yes, this won't take a moment, Dredd." She looked at him, unblinking, but merely saw her reflection in the mirrored visor of his helmet. "I thought you should know I've just had an irate call from Councillor Matheson Peat, complaining about your handling of the Vanessa Indigo affair."

"I expected he would. He's not usually stuck for words."

"He claimed you unnecessarily put lives at risk. He also says you later harassed him at his apartment."

"I went round there to inform him of developments in the Liz Short body dump case. I thought that he might be interested to know that over a dozen mutilated corpses had been found beneath one of his buildings. Evidently, all he's concerned about is what the papers are going say tomorrow."

Hershey snorted in agreement. "Peat's an idiot, there's no question of that. He's also extremely influential, unfortunately. He could make life difficult for us if he starts publicly badmouthing Justice Department."

"Drokk 'em. What's the worst that happens? You don't get invited to a few functions."

Hershey sighed inwardly. Diplomacy was never Dredd's strong point. He didn't understand the subtle balancing act she had to perform to keep the city ticking over: the captains of industry and media moguls she had to pacify; the foreign ambassadors she had to meet and greet with an eye for overseas trade; dealing with the offworld contingents visiting Earth for the first time. Mega-City One couldn't afford to conduct itself unilaterally these days, despite a history of going it alone. It paid not to burn bridges because you never knew when you'd require allies.

"Even so," she replied, "it might be prudent to play this one sensitively. It's attracted a lot of attention from a number of parties." She paused. "You know I've allowed Indigo and her entourage to return to Euro-Cit?"

"So I heard. You want to tell me why?"

Hershey chose her words carefully. "I've been under pressure from the Euro-Cit foreign affairs representative," she said. "You know what they think of her over there, she's a national treasure. If we didn't to let her go home, they would kick up a stink."

"So what about the charges relating to her bodyguards' weaponry?" Dredd growled. "We're just going to forget about those too?"

"Indigo claims no knowledge of what her minders were carrying. She's a certified neurotic drug addict, with a history of mental illness, so she probably didn't even know what day it was. Her manager, Lubular, says the bodyguards were vat-grown and hired by a cloning agency. He also didn't know anything about the guns."

"He say that under lie detector?"

Hershey shook her head. "It doesn't matter, Dredd. With the Euro-creeps making a fuss and threatening to turn this into a diplomatic incident, it's easier all round if we just let them go."

"Seems to me this sets a dangerous precedent. Just shows what you can get away with if you've got enough money and the right connections."

"That's showbiz," Hershey replied, immediately regretting attempting to joke in Dredd's presence. His stony-faced countenance didn't quiver.

"I thought if you committed a crime in this city, you paid the full price of the Law, no matter who you were."

"It's not always that black and white, Dredd," Hershey said wearily. "I've got to think of the big picture, especially if Mega-City One's relationship with the rest of the world is at stake."

Dredd was silent for a moment. "This complaint of Peat's, it gonna go anywhere?"

"Grud, no. Far as I can see, you acted responsibly and did what was expected of you. I just thought you should know there might be some flak coming your way over the next few days. But the councillor will calm down eventually."

"I'm not so sure."

"Trust me, I'll keep him and his cronies sweet," Hershey assured him, smiling. "Indigo's would-be assassin, did you get any ID off him?"

"Some creep called Norris Bimsley. One previous conviction for shouting in a built-up area, otherwise utterly unremarkable. Uniforms that checked out his apartment in Jack Yeovil found a shrine devoted to her. Guess he must've just flipped when he heard she was coming to town."

"Who'd be a celebrity, eh?" Hershey remarked, raising one eyebrow, aware that even Dredd himself had a dedicated fanbase, hard as that was to believe.

The senior Judge didn't respond, and the brief silence was broken by the buzz of the intercom. Hershey went behind her desk and flicked the switch.

"Yes?"

"Sorry to disturb you, ma'am. Garrison in the med-bay was asking if Dredd could stop by after he'd finished his meeting with you."

"OK, thanks." Hershey turned to Dredd. "Seems you're wanted. This is the Liz Short case, right?"

Dredd nodded. "About time we started getting some leads. Been a dead-end so far."

"Keep me informed of any developments," Hershey said, motioning that he could go. "Oh, and Joe," she added when he was halfway across the room, "appreciate you dropping by."

"No problem," he replied, already out the door.

▪ ▪ ▪

Dredd rode the el' down to the med-labs on the lower levels of the Grand Hall of Justice, thinking over what Hershey had said. It infuriated him that creeps with influence could evade the full weight of the Law simply by pulling in a few favours from their pals in high office, and he was surprised that the Chief Judge was prepared to get entangled in that web of self-motivation and mutual back-scratching. She was certainly a different woman to the young Judge that accompanied him on the Owen Krysler quest. It obviously hadn't taken long before the pressures of the position had started rubbing away at the strict values she'd once held, turning her into much more of a political animal. He supposed he had to see it from her point of view as well; if you didn't want the Big Meg vilified by every nation-state on the globe, you had to make some compromises.

That was probably one of the reasons why he hadn't accepted the promotion – his temperament was not best suited to entertaining the morons that circulated at that kind of level. As far as he was concerned, it didn't matter if you were a two-bit Umpty-bagger or a member of royalty. If you broke the Law, you did time.

The el reached the intended floor and he strode into a white corridor, the large windows set into the walls showing suited technicians working at computers or over corpse-strewn tables. A few droids moved from slab to slab, bone-saws whirring or pushing trolleys containing bodybags.

Here in the med-bays, the Judges performed autopsies, identified the John or Jane Does that regularly turned up after another night in the city, conducted forensic tests on murder weapons or crime scene evidence, and patched up those that had been injured in the course of duty. The area smelled chemically clinical, and Dredd's boots squeaked as he walked across the spotless floor, searching for Garrison. He spotted her sitting in front of a screen, tapping into a keyboard.

Behind her, the blackened bones that had been pulled out of the Elizabeth Short chem-pit lay across several workspaces, tagged and bagged.

"Garrison."

She spun in her chair and smiled when she saw Dredd. "Got a match on that earring," she said triumphantly. "We were right, the titanium *has* been mixed with polymers outside the city. There's a substance called clarrissium present, which originates only from the Pan-African States. The Africans use it for construction purposes because it's extremely heat-resistant."

"So the victim came from Pan-Africa?"

"Almost certainly. No jewellery like this is imported, though we can't vouch for those sent as gifts, of course. I've checked with Immigration and got them to send me a list of all those that have come into Mega-City One from Africa over the last five years." She produced a printout with a stream of names copied across it. "Some of these have since returned, so they can be discounted, as can obviously the men. That leaves two hundred and fifteen women. Narrowing those down to our victim's age, we're left with thirty-two."

Dredd could feel Garrison building to something.

"I cross-referenced those names with the Missing Persons register and got three hits," she continued. "A quick DNA match with Skully here," she patted the skull the earring had come from, sitting beside her desk in its transparent plastic covering, "and we got a name at last: Emmylou Engels."

"You're sure about the match?"

"Yep. She'd been given a medical examination upon entering the city, and Immigration took a blood sample, logging her DNA onto the database. No question, that's her."

"What about the other bodies?" he asked, gesturing to the array of bones.

"Still working on it," she replied. "Computer's churning through data day and night doing citywide DNA searches.

We don't have the point of reference that we did for Engels, so it's kind of a big net we're throwing out."

"When did you ID her?"

"About half an hour ago. Assumed you'd want to be the first to know."

Dredd nodded slowly. "Good work, Garrison." He looked around the room. "Is there a terminal I can use here? I need to access MAC."

"Here, use this one," she said, getting up from her chair. "I've got to go and dissect a brain anyway." She winked and disappeared into another lab.

Dredd sat and logged into Justice Department's central computer, calling up Engels's details. She'd arrived on 14 August 2125 via the Atlantic Tunnel and came looking for work as an actress. Immigration had declared her clean, she had no previous arrest record, and was granted a six-month stay in the city. She'd registered her address as 2242/b George Bush Snr, living with her landlady, one Agnes Petri. The same Mrs Petri had contacted her local Sector House on 17 May 2126, saying that she was worried about her tenant, whom she hadn't heard from in over a month. Despite a note claiming to be from Engels saying that she'd found work in another sector, and a suitcase full of clothes had been taken, Mrs Petri insisted that if Engels had gone anywhere, she wouldn't have disappeared so suddenly. She'd also left a number of possessions and was owing rent.

The investigating Judge – Parris – got in touch with Engels's parents and boyfriend in New Nairobi, but they hadn't heard from her since her disappearance, and she hadn't mentioned anything about a new job the last time they had spoken to her. The Public Surveillance Unit had no record of her movements, and in the end, Parris wrote it off as a Missing Person, adding as a footnote that she'd probably done a moonlight flit with some new beau. As a result, Emmylou had joined the thousands who disappeared in the city every year, with no motive or explanation, and were very rarely seen again.

Now, four months after she was recorded missing, her remains had been discovered.

Dredd trawled through the text, assimilating the information. Reading between the lines, it seemed to him that Parris had done only the most cursory of jobs in investigating her disappearance. From the language used in his reports, he clearly thought he was wasting his time chasing after an adult who'd probably deliberately hidden their tracks and didn't want to be found. Parris was of the opinion that he could detect no criminal activity surrounding her vanishing, and believed the landlady was being overly suspicious simply because she was out of pocket. The trail had gone cold and the last entry was logged at the end of May. Other, more pressing cases had moved to the fore and Engels was forgotten; out of sight and out of mind.

And now she's resurfaced, Dredd thought, looking at the small photo of her onscreen – pretty, plump, auburn-haired – and the investigation was kicked into life once more.

Dredd made a copy of the case file, then left the med-bay. He resolved that his next port of call should be the landlady, Petri, to see if she could remember anything several months on, but first he had to deliver the bad news to the victim's family. This was one of the most unfortunate aspects of the job and Dredd was still not comfortable with it after all these years. Normally, in a situation like this, there would be a liaison Judge to soften the blow and comfort the grieving, but with the parents based over in Pan-Africa he would have to do it via vid-phone. He found their contact numbers amongst the data stored on the disc and steeled himself for the anguish that was inevitably to come.

▪ ▪ ▪

George Bush Snr was in the rough end of Sector 20 and looked like it could do with some major structural repairs. Broken windows had been repaired with tape, and there were a few old laser scars from a years-old block war competing with lurid scrawling to make the building appear an eyesore even from a distance. From what Dredd had learned about Emmylou, talking to her mother and father, she evidently had little money and her acting career had not been exactly going great guns. She'd moved to the Big Meg to try to land bigger roles, but lacked the talent or the drop-dead looks that would've made her a star. According to Emmylou's dad, she'd made noises about returning home, her dream unfulfilled.

The couple had taken the grim news hard, and Dredd tried his best to sound sympathetic while at the same time cajoling information out of them that might be pertinent. They had nothing new to reveal since they'd last heard Emmylou had gone missing, and had been secretly hoping that she'd grabbed herself a plum part in some touring company, even though it was completely out of character for her to go off without a word to anyone. They said they were going to scrape what money they had together and come to MC-1, to bring back her remains. Her actor boyfriend – whom Parris had earmarked early on as a suspect, before checks confirmed that he hadn't left the country for the past year – was equally distraught, but did mention something of interest: in one of the last conversations Emmylou had had with him, she'd said that she'd joined an agency. When pressed, however, he couldn't recall its name and dissolved into more tears.

Dredd rapped on the door of 2242/b, and a wrinkled, rat-faced woman in her sixties answered. She peered up at him, squinting.

"Agnes Petri?"

"That's me. If it's about that goldfish licence, I told the man at City Hall I've already paid–"

"Can I come in, Mrs Petri? It's about one of your old tenants, Emmylou Engels."

She ushered him in, saying, "You after her for rent evasion? She owes me a good three months. I've had to get a new gentleman in and put the rent up so I can recoup some of my losses. People like that I've got no sympathy for–"

"Emmylou is dead," Dredd interrupted, looking around the cluttered apartment. The carpet was threadbare and the ceiling stained with something unrecognisable. Grud knew what people paid to live here, but it was probably too much. Dredd wasn't surprised that only unemployed actors were desperate enough to put up with conditions like this. "Her remains were recently discovered."

Mrs Petri shrank against the wall, her hand fluttering to her throat. "Oh. Oh, how terrible," she stammered. She walked over to a tatty armchair and slumped into it. "Oh my grud, that poor girl…"

"You originally reported her missing, Mrs Petri. When was the last time you saw her?"

"I… can't remember," she said quietly, dabbing her eyes with a tissue. "I went out one evening – it must've been April, I think – and she was in then. She was using the computer. When I came back, she'd gone. There was a note saying she'd got a job on the other side of the city, and half her wardrobe had been packed. I assumed she'd be back in a week or so, because she'd left some of her stuff here. When it got to a month, and still I hadn't heard anything, I got worried."

"There was no sign of a struggle? Nobody had broken in?"

"No, everything was how I left it. I presumed she left of her own accord."

"She was using the computer?" Dredd asked. "Show me."

Mrs Petri got to her feet and led him to a small, old terminal sitting on a table by the window. Dredd checked the files on it, noting the dates they were last revised. The latest was Emmylou's CV, on 6 April 2126. That had to be the date her landlady had last seen her. "Are the block CCTri-D cameras working, Mrs Petri?"

She shook her head. "Juves keep vandalising them. Haven't worked for years."

Terrif, he thought. He scrolled down through the CV, noting her last employers, and decided to print a copy off. "What about Emmylou's things that she left behind?" he enquired.

"I didn't know what to do with them," she said, opening a cupboard and retrieving a box filled with clothes, papers and publicity photographs. "I thought I should forward them to her family, but I never got around to it."

Dredd looked at what was left of Emmylou. On the top was the handwritten note that Emmylou had left; it was brief and vague, with no suggestion of where she'd gone, who she was with, or whether she was coming back. He compared the handwriting with her signature on other documents amongst the paraphernalia – mostly speculative letters, soliciting for work from the major film studios – and it looked convincing enough. A headed missive caught his eye: Mega-City Casting Agency. It was arranging an appointment for her to come in so they could find her work. Dredd mentally logged the address.

He handed the box back to her. "Better keep hold of it for the moment, Mrs Petri. We may need to examine some of the contents more thoroughly. I'll have someone come and collect it from you soon. Thank you for your time." He headed towards the door.

"B-but what *happened* to her, Judge?" she asked, following him to the threshold. "Where did she go? Who would want to kill her?"

"That's what I intend to find out, citizen."

From one end of the spectrum to the other, Dredd thought, as he entered the MCCA building. The carpet was a plush cream pile, and the chairs in the reception area were an artful arrangement of canvas and chrome. The walls were studded with portraits of the agency's top clients – most of which, he had to admit, he had never heard of – and replica movie posters. For one startling moment, he found himself looking at a picture of his own visage, snarling back at him in front of a post-apocalyptic backdrop. The film was titled *Flight of the Eagle*, and the credits said that he'd been played by somebody called Janus Krinkle. The jowls were a little flabby, he thought, but otherwise it wasn't a bad likeness.

"I see you're admiring your alter ego," said a voice. Dredd turned to see a tanned, muscular man in an expensive-looking suit approaching him. "You gotta say, Janus has you down to a tee."

"You're aware that it's illegal to use a Judge's image for monetary gain?"

"These movies have all been approved by Justice Department," he replied, pointing at the little eagle symbol in the corner of the poster. "They're what we like to call our 'promotional pics'. This one retells your mission to nuke East-Meg One."

"They're propaganda, you mean?"

"Yes. A little anti-Sov entertainment goes down well in friendly territories." He stuck out his hand. "I'm Buddy Laskin, one of the partners here at MCCA. What can I do for you, Judge?"

Dredd ignored the proffered hand. "I'm investigating a case involving one of your clients. Emmylou Engels?"

Laskin frowned. "Engels? The name doesn't ring a bell. Come through into my office, I'll check my records." He led Dredd through into an ostentatious room, bedecked in black and gold. Film props adorned a huge desk, and more posters decorated the walls. Laskin rifled through some documents in a filing cabinet, then gave a little exclamation of triumph. "Ah, yes, Emmylou. Joined our ranks some eight months ago. Terrible actress, by all accounts, but she's cheap and punctual, which goes a long way."

"When was the last time you saw her?"

"Well, according to our files, when we last found her some work. That was back in February when she got a gig working for Catalyst. In fact, she hasn't been in touch since then, which is a bit odd, 'cause she came across as very keen. Is she OK?"

"She's been murdered."

"Jovus..." Laskin went pale beneath his tan. "When did this happen?"

"Possibly not that long after you saw her. She went missing in April. What's Catalyst?"

"It's a film studio – Catalyst Productions. They make the propaganda features you saw out there. Big budget, anti-Sov, war movies. We supply them with lots of actors."

"She didn't have any other work after that?"

"Not through us, but then actors work all over. She might've done some vidverts or something through another agency."

"How was she when you saw her? Did she give any indication of being troubled?"

"Not at all. As I said, she was very keen. She was happy to accept any work that came her way."

"And she didn't say anything about going away?"

"No, she made no mention of it."

"How long have you supplied actors to Catalyst?"

"Hell, years. The movies might not be works of art, but they pay fairly well and it's a regular income. That's the most important thing to our clients."

"Any other of your actors disappear?"

Laskin shrugged. "People drop off our roster all the time. They move on, have kids, join another agency, go abroad. It's not our job to keep track of their movements." He fixed Dredd with a stare. "You don't think somebody's targeting our clients, do you?"

"I'm sure Citizen Krinkle can handle himself," Dredd said as he left.

Outside, back at his Lawmaster, Dredd checked Emmylou's CV again. The Catalyst job was the last one listed in her employment record – a subtle number called *Total Annihilation*. If she'd done any work after that, then presumably she would've added it to her résumé when she was updating it. The gigs previous to the Catalyst job were fairly evenly spaced, then there was a gap prior to her disappearance.

The fact that there was no struggle at Petri's apartment suggested that, if Emmylou *was* kidnapped, she may have known her abductors and let them in willingly. There was no mention from her parents of her making many friends in the city, so perhaps she recognised somebody from her acting work. A fellow thespian? A director? Maybe Catalyst, as Engels's last employer, could provide some answers.

Dredd swung his leg over his bike and was about to gun the engine when shots rang out. A bullet clipped his thigh, and he instantly rolled for cover. He yanked free his Lawgiver, then glanced at his leg and saw it was just a flesh wound. He peered over the Lawmaster frame, looking for the source of the gunfire, but a moment later the gunfire came looking for him. A roadster screeched around the corner, a perp riding shotgun and spraying him with the contents of a semi-automatic. Dredd dived out of their path, then came up shooting, putting three rounds through the back window of the car. Without hesitation, he leaped onto the bike and roared in pursuit, crouching down as the creep twisted round and started firing again. Dredd thumbed the bike cannons, and the powerful ammo shredded the roadster's back tyres, making it spin out of control. It hit a central reservation barrier and flipped, crashing down on its roof.

The perp with the semi-automatic crawled out of the passenger door window and got shakily to his feet, still clutching the gun. He saw Dredd bearing down on him and tried to aim, but the Judge fired one Lawgiver shot that caught him directly in the forehead. The back of his skull erupted as he flew backwards onto the ground.

Dredd slid to a halt, just as the driver was clambering out. "Freeze!" he shouted. "You're under arrest!"

The driver looked at him, dazed, then raised his hands, a strange beatific expression passing over his face. Dredd had a fraction of a second to notice before the guy exploded with an ear-splitting blast. The detonation threw him off his bike as the perp vaporised before his eyes, windows shattering behind him and red globules pattering down onto the street. Limping around his upturned Lawmaster, Dredd looked at the spot where the creep had been standing and saw only a sooty epicentre with residue radiating outwards.

Mob blitzer, he thought to himself, waving away the smoke and cordite thick in the air. Evidently, somebody didn't want him following this line of inquiry.

SIX

My shoulder gives me a twinge of pain as I enter Iso-Block 14's infirmary, probably in phantom sympathy to the poor spuggers lying in here with missing limbs, punctured organs and scarred faces. Funny how the baddest, most evil motherdrokkers look like such sorry sacks of shit once they're laid up in bed, regulation PJs on, and heads wrapped in bandages or extremities strapped to a splint. Walking between the beds is like taking a trip into a retired perps' home: a tattooed biker sits upright, coughing violently, a drip running from his arm; next to him, some sickly looking creep with waxy skin is staring at the ceiling, as motionless as a corpse; across the way, an eldster is moaning incessantly, sounding like he won't last the night. If you met any of them in a dark alley, they'd slit your throat as soon as look at you. Now, the only danger they pose is spreading an infection.

That said, the warders don't take any chances, ill inmates or not. There are two guards standing sentry at the entrance, las-rifles slung at the ready, and the med-droids that sweep from one patient to the next administering booster shots or painkillers look as if they could turn nasty if threatened. I instinctively touch my shoulder where Jonny Dansky's bullet shattered the scapula, feeling grateful that it only took a few hours in a speed-heal to knit the bone back together. Something about receiving treatment from a robot gives me the shivers: the cold, metallic fingers grasping your arm as they search for a vein; the stiff, jerky movement of their heads as they look down at you, computing a diagnosis within their circuitry; the realisation that all it takes is one crossed wire and they could be recommending you for experimental vivisection. I, like a lot of people, get queasy around droids. When something checks my pulse, I want to be able to feel a pulse back.

I find Jonny towards the far end of the ward, lying back with his eyes shut. This is the first time I've seen him since he tried to frag me on the ship, and an urge unexpectedly builds inside me to put a gun to his head and give him a permanent kiss goodnight. I haven't taken many bullets in my years with Wally Squad, and when somebody attempts to kill me, I can't help but take it personal. Part of me thinks that pulling the trigger on the drokker would be too quick, and maybe I should try something a little more agonising, like putting his pillow over his head, for example, and watching the bastard squirm as I crush the air out of him. The urge is so strong that my fingers actually brush the butt of the gun jammed in my waistband, but then reason takes over, making me realise that whacking a perp in the middle of an Iso-block med-bay isn't the smartest move, surrounded as I am by several dozen witnesses, including a pair of heavily armed Judge Wardens. Also, I still need information from him. The yearning doesn't go away, but is flattened by the odds of getting away with it. Justice Department takes a dim view of summary executions, especially when the victim is laid up in bed with a severe groin wound and is already looking at life in an iso-cube.

Even if circumstances were different, Jonny wouldn't have the honour of being the first creep I've nailed in cold blood. Occasionally, my undercover status becomes compromised to the point where my own life may be in danger, and a quick bullet to the back of the head can salvage an operation. Sometimes the choice can be hard as it's not unknown for me to grow to like the crims I infiltrate – their ingenuity, their balls-out courage, is sometimes worthy of a grudging respect – and taking out a prospective problem before it grows into a full-blown crisis is a tough decision.

Gangbangers have shared secrets with me like I'm one of their brothers moments before I've slid a blade into their guts, or they've confessed that they think they've got a rat in the house and I've had to act shocked and point the finger of suspicion elsewhere, while at the same time fitting a silencer when their backs are turned. I'm not always proud of the things I've done to protect myself, or the methods I've employed to shake down informants. There are a few pimps and stookie dealers still walking the streets (or rather, limping) nursing broken fingers or cracked kneecaps that have never properly healed.

My light chemical dependency in fact grew out of a need to not dwell on my past. A life built on betrayals is not always easy to live with. My sleep used to be haunted by the faces of those I'd pushed under a zoom train, or battered to death in a dark alley, or dropped a few hundred feet from a hovercar. My desire to keep the truth at a distance, even from myself, meant a not-insubstantial quantity of narcotics was required. The zizz helps me create a barrier between the street player and the lawman inside, struggling to stay in control.

Dansky doesn't open his eyes as I stand over him. Seems hard to imagine that this guy with his head propped on pillows, hands resting on his chest like he's sleeping the sleep of the just, had the drop on me only twelve hours ago. I was a second away from having a slug drilled into my skull by this creep, and the slenderest of margins by which I escaped still gives me heart palpitations. I'm drokking *burning* to drive my fist into his slack-jawed, slumbering face, but it's too public. I opt instead to accidentally-on-purpose bring my elbow swiftly down on his bandaged crotch, while at the same time trying to look as nonchalant as possible as I perch myself on the edge of the bed.

"Motherdrokker!" he screams, folding up, his hands clutching at his wound. "Piece of drokkin' *shit*!"

"Oops. Did that hurt?" I ask, all mock-innocence.

"I'll kill you, you drokkin' asshole," Jonny snarls, reaching for me, then notices the commotion has unsurprisingly brought the attention of the room onto his corner of it. The guards look over, shouldering their rifles, and he slowly relaxes, easing himself back onto the sheets, grimacing as he rides out the waves of pain ebbing from between his legs.

A med-droid trundles across. "What's all the fuss?"

"Sorry, doc," I say. "I think I sat on a sore bit."

"Get this drokkin' bastard out of here," Jonny spits out through gritted teeth, eyes watering. "Spugger wants to kill me."

"Remarkable powers of intuition," I reply, "but that would be against the Law." I reach into my pocket and show the robot my name badge. "Pete Trager, Wally Squad. I'm hoping Citizen Dansky here is going to help me with my current investigation."

The droid peers at my ID, seemingly surprised – if it's possible for a mechanoid to show surprise – that I'm a Judge. A brief flash of self-realisation tells me that I probably look unkempt and dishevelled, and could do with a couple of hours in a sleep machine and a fresh change of clothes. But it merely clicks its eyes up from the badge to my face and nods. "OK. But keep it quiet. I've got sick people here."

"No kidding," I say, motioning to the four hundred pound fattie wheezing and spluttering in the next bed. "Jimmy the Badyear Blimp there murdered three hundred and sixty-five citizens before they caught him." I smile graciously. "Don't worry, doc, I'll try to keep this short." The droid appears satisfied and rattles away, and I turn back to Jonny. "But when it comes to real sickos, you Danskys are in a class of your own."

"Drokk you," he breathes.

"Or should I say Dansky singular, since your beloved brother is at this moment rumbling up the Resyk meg-way to become the ingredients of a grot pot."

Anger flares in his eyes, but he's not dumb. He knows I'm provoking him and he can't do anything but lose in this situation. He looks at me with contempt. "What do you want, Trager? I've got nothin' to say to you."

"Well, on a purely selfish level, I'm just enjoying seeing you suffer." I tap his leg gently and he visibly flinches. "I bet that smarts, don't it? Do they reckon you can still have kids?"

He doesn't reply.

"Ah, well, probably for the best. You rid the world of one Dansky, the last thing you need is more of the shit-eating simps filling up the city. Shame somebody didn't think of doing the same to your daddy thirty years ago."

He takes this on board before saying, "Y'know something, Trager? My only regret is that I hesitated before blowin' your drokkin' head off. You're gonna have to live with the fact you're only breathin' because of that, because of a millisecond of grace. Your ass belongs to me. Your life stood on the edge and it coulda swung either way."

"Does it all the time, pal. You ain't the first," I say dismissively. "But enough with the pleasantries, I wanna know about these and the buyer you had lined up." I pull from my small knapsack the bundle that I'd snagged on Talón's yacht.

Opening it up, there's a clink of metal on metal as I spread the contents across his bed. The strange and troubling array of devices look like they've come straight out of the Spanish Inquisition. There are five pieces in total, some with more obvious applications than others. The thumbscrews are the most self-evident, a set of mini-cuffs forged from black iron. The largest instrument is some kind of skullcap, with a tightening nut at the top and clamps around the neck area. A nasty serrated blade is affixed at throat height, presumably to slice open the victim's jugular if they were to attempt to twist their head away from whatever the torturer was about to do.

Next to that is a complicated, multi-jointed affair with a tight spring at its centre and several needle-sharp barbs jutting out at different angles. So far I've been afraid to touch it, for fear of tripping a catch and having it snap shut on my hand. It reminds me of a portable man-trap. The last two items are all the more bizarre for their immediate lack of purpose: a curved, spoon-like implement that wouldn't seem out of place in someone's kitchen, and a metallic truncheon, not much more than a foot long, with a hook at one end. Despite their innocence at first glance, it isn't difficult to envision an imaginative psycho getting a fair bit of mileage out of the pair of them.

Although the pieces are clearly antiques, they've been expertly looked after by somebody who knew what they were doing. My guess is that Cuidad Barranquilla Justice Department has an entire section of its armoury devoted to shit like this, and probably doesn't have any qualms about using them on suspects.

Jonny's attempt at acting cool fails miserably as his eyes give away his fear almost instantly. He tries to look at the instruments of torture as if it's the first time he's seen them, but recognition is broadcast all over his face.

"How many times have you sold stuff like this, Jonny?"

He says nothing, turning his head away as if to refuse to acknowledge their existence.

"Talk to me, Jonny," I persist. "Who have you been selling them to?"

"Drokk you," he replies, but there's a catch in his throat and his response lacks venom. He sounds afraid. "I-I don't have to talk to you." He looks at me at last. "Why the drokk should I help you, pig?"

I let that one slide. "I ain't gonna lie to you, Jonny. Once you're out of here, you're going to an iso-cube for the rest of your natural life. There's nothing I can do about that–"

"Seeing as you're the spugger who put me in here in the first place!"

Typical perp self-pity. Always somebody else's fault. "But talk to me, give me a name, and I'll see what I can do to make it easier for you. Maybe even decrease your sentence. You could be out in, say, twenty years. You don't wanna die in jail, do you, Jonny?"

The long, hard road of the rest of his life hits him at that moment. I can see him deflating before me, all the piss and vinegar draining out of him as he realises he'll never taste freedom again. He's weighing up the choice that all criminals have to make at some point in their lives: should he rat out a colleague to save himself, or go to his grave a principled idiot? It doesn't usually take the average creep long to make the decision – no honour among thieves, yadda, yadda, yadda – but Jonny seems surprisingly tormented. Perhaps I underestimated just how much he hates us Judges.

"You... you don't understand," he begins, nervously glancing at the black pieces of metal lying only a couple of feet away. "They'll kill me. They're drokkin' dangerous..."

"Who are?" I have to admit his fear's starting to unsettle me. "They're not going to get you while you're in custody, if that's what you're afraid of. You're safe here."

He doesn't look like he believes me. "I ain't no snitch," he says loudly, as if to mostly convince himself.

"Jonny, if your brother was alive and in your place, do you think he'd be making it this hard on himself? He was always the one setting up the deals, wasn't he? He was the one with the foresight. Now, if he was presented with an offer like this, don't you think he'd jump at the chance to grab something for himself from this mess? You're on your own now, Jonny. Can't rely on your brother for backup. You gotta make your own decision."

The mention of Brett makes his eyes leak, and he says his sibling's name in a tiny whisper. I almost feel sorry for him.

"Do the right thing. Give me a name, and then maybe one day you'll be able to raise a glass to his memory as a free man."

He screws his eyes up tight and I think he's going to continue stalling me, but after a moment's silence his head drops forward and he says quietly: "Conrad."

"Conrad? That's the buyer?"

He nods. "That's the only name I know. That's all he calls himself."

Sounds like a cover. "And how do I get in touch with him?"

Jonny runs trembling hands over his face. "The number... it's unlisted. Four-double-two-three-six-eight. I don't know where he's based. We speak to him or one of his men and just arrange a meet. Usually at Tommy's."

"The bar on Bleeker?"

He nods again.

"What does Conrad look like?"

He shrugs. "He's a businessman, he ain't a player. Smart, expensive suits, neat haircut. He's very... sure of himself."

"So why are you so scared of him, Jonny?"

He looks at me, his eyes searching mine. "He's powerful. And we've heard what he's capable of."

I stand up and gather together the torture devices into the bundle and put it back into my knapsack. "You made the right decision, Jonny."

"So you'll talk to them, right?" he says as I start to walk away, gesturing towards the guards standing sentry at the door. "You'll let them know I was willing to help? You'll cut a deal?"

"I'll do my best," I reply, giving him a short wave. Then, as I pass one of the Judge-Wardens, I mutter under my breath "Dansky, in the far bed. He's planning on busting out and taking hostages. Bring him down hard."

I step out into the corridor, smiling, and slightly disappointed that I'm going to miss the fireworks.

Ten minutes later, I'm standing at a public phone, punching in the number. It rings a couple of times before a man's voice answers "Yeah?"

"Speak to Conrad?"

"Who is this?"

"A friend. Is Conrad there?"

"He's busy. Gimme a message an' I'll pass it on."

"Tell him I got his antiques, from south of the border."

The phone goes dead, the sudden silence making me jolt. I replace the receiver, unsure whether I'd said something wrong, though Jonny mentioned nothing about any kind of password. Frustration gnaws at me. This number's my only lead and if I've blown it, then the investigation will grind to a halt. As I'm mulling over the possibility of running a trace on the number, seeing if I can narrow it down to a sector – though I can imagine it being rerouted through several different exchanges, leading me on a phantom search before I finally find myself chasing my own tail – the phone rings. I snatch it up.

"Yeah?"

"Who are you?" A different male voice this time. More cultured. My immediate guess is that this is the enigmatic Conrad.

There's no reason to lie. "My name's Pete Trager." I find it easier if I keep my identities to a minimum as it lessens the chance of me slipping up by getting my assumed monikers mixed up. There's also a veracity to people's voices when they speak their own name, a confidence that's notably missing whenever anybody tries to pass off an alias. "I've worked with our mutual acquaintances, the Dansky brothers."

"So perhaps you can tell me why I'm talking to you and not them?"

"Truth of the matter is, they've been the victims of a small hostile takeover. Our friends in Banana City, they saw my organisation was much more efficient at trafficking certain merchandise, and decided to take their business elsewhere."

"Where did you get this number, Mr Trager?"

"The Danskys passed over all their contacts, and I'm more than happy to carry on doing their business with you. In fact, you'll find my prices are extremely reasonable. They were going to sell what I've got for you for eight thou, but–"

"Please." The smooth voice raises a notch. "I do not wish to discuss consumables over the phone, no matter how secure this line is. Right now, the most pertinent matter is why I should trust you."

"Why should you indeed? After all, I'm just a voice in your ear, right? You need verification, somebody to vouch for me." Uh-oh, I'm gonna have to wing this one. "I'm sure Talón will speak highly of me."

A pause. "You have met Frederica Talón?"

"Sure. You could say we both hit it off. And I'm now her man in Mega-City; all her business goes through me." I cross my fingers and take a leap of faith. "You want me to fix it so she gets in touch with you, lets you know I'm on the level?"

Another beat of silence. I get the impression he wants to avoid contact with his Banana City supplier; the least amount of guilty associates the better. Plus he's probably frightened of fraternising with an honest-to-grud gangbanger. This Conrad seems to be one of those high-flyers who thinks he's above the scum that do his dirty work. "That... that will not be necessary. Senorita Talón's judgement is usually faultless over whom she chooses to deal with."

"Usual place, then?"

"Tommy's at ten. I look forward to meeting you, Mr Trager." He clicks off.

I slam down the receiver in triumph. Oh, Petey-boy, you are *sooooooo* cool!

Tommy's has a certain rep within Justice Department for being a perp-magnet. The joint's namesake was murdered over ten years ago after an extremely competitive game of shuggy, each limb discovered in a different corner pocket, the cue ball placed in his mouth. Despite undergoing several ownership changes and varying managers, it can't seem to shake off attracting all sorts of undesirables. This might be something to do with its location, nestled as it is on Bleeker Street beneath the flyover of a north-west megway, like the building itself is trying to escape detection.

Fat chance. PSU had at least one camera trained on the area almost permanently, sure to catch a few wanted felons passing through. One thing about crims, whether they're smart or dumb, ruthless young Turks or seasoned old lags, they're reliable creatures of habit. No matter what they've done, no matter how many times their mugshot might've been flashed up on every Tri-D set in the sector, they can't seem to stop frequenting the same circles. Dogs returning to their own vomit and all that. I suppose by fostering this sense of community, creating an entirely separate level of society within the city, they reason it makes Judges' attempts to infiltrate it all the more difficult. Poor creeps haven't reckoned just how far the tentacles of law enforcement have already breached their extended family.

I arrive early and case the joint, feeling that organised crime could be reduced significantly just by bulldozing the drokking place. Like its patrons, the bar is squat and ugly, its walls blackened by the exhaust fumes of countless vehicles thundering overhead. The neon sign probably breathed its last back when Cal was in charge and nobody has bothered to give it a refit. The line of hoverbikes racked outside look slightly at odds with the grungy exterior; polished and gleaming, they're the status symbols of the local Harvey Keitel Wideboys.

It seems strange that somebody as evidently high-rolling as this Conrad guy should frequent a dive like this. Surely he would stand out like the proverbial mutant at the school disco? Can't see him cutting much ice with the regulars, unless, of course, they are aware of what he's up to… Jonny knew his rep and it almost scared him to silence.

The moment I enter the joint I can feel hostile eyes upon me. Years on the streets have enabled me to exude the necessary aura of menace and unpredictability that you'd expect from a Mega-City perp, but it doesn't stop my presence arousing the creeps' innate feelings of suspicion. Rather than attempting to avoid their gaze, I ride it out by striding up to the bar and ordering a drink, then turn to survey the room. The place is not that crowded, but the clientele have managed to fill it all the same. The Wideboys, sat around a corner table, live up to their name by being huge, hairy motherdrokkers that look like they could snap you in two with a flick of their wrists. Beside me, a couple of grizzled slabheads burnt out on steroids with arms like sides of beef are resting their enormous torsos against the bar.

Although the room doesn't exactly go silent, I can see glances being constantly thrown in my direction, weighing me up, and I give them the stare back, hoping I look mean enough not to tangle with. The strategy seems to work as the threat of violence drops to a low-lying ebb, and they seem satisfied that I'm not the Law. The barman brings me my beer, looking like he'd be happier wrestling Kleggs. He bangs the bottle down with his huge fist and silently takes my creds, clearly disgruntled that I've mistaken this for some kind of public house where anyone can just breeze in.

I sip at the thick, flat synthi-lager, studying a large, dog-eared photo tacked up next to the bottles on the back shelf of the remains of the original Tommy, spread out over the shuggy table. It must've been taken just before the Judges arrived, as if the killer was rather proud of his arrangement and wanted to capture it for posterity. Some wit has scrawled on it "Now That's What I Call A Break!", and I realise as I catch a glimpse in the mirror behind the bar that the table is still there next to the window, presumably stains and all.

I check my watch. Conrad is late. There's nobody here that even approaches his description and I'm a hundred per cent sure I couldn't have missed him. The thought that the guy might've got cold feet starts to play on my nerves, as I feel a little antsy surrounded by so many crims who would cheerfully rip my head off if they had any inkling of what I was. I buy another beer and nurse it for half an hour while listening distractedly to the meatheads to my left relating unlikely romantic conquests, and watching the entrance in the mirror for any new appearances. I must be looking on edge, 'cause eventually the barman notices that I'm still taking swigs from the same bottle.

"Ain't gonna hatch, if that's what you're savin' it for," he mutters, nodding at it as I roll it between my hands.

"Warm enough already," I reply.

I expect him to take offence, but he concedes the point in surprising good faith. "Ain't that the truth. Fridge got knocked out by those drokking 'bots. Whaddya call 'em, Nacker's lot? Ain't got round to fixin' it."

"You mean Narcos?" I say, wondering with an uneasy gulp just how out of date this stuff I'm drinking is.

"Whatever. Pointy headed spugger. All I know is, he owes me a fridge."

"Long dead, my friend. I think you'll have to write that one off." Some Wideboys come through the door to join the group in the corner, and I automatically look up at their reflection.

"You waitin' on someone?" the barman asks, catching my interest.

I consider my answer, unsure whether to say anything. While I don't want every crook in here knowing my intentions, my options are fast disappearing. I decide to go for it. "Was hopin' to catch a guy called Conrad, meant to drink in here. You heard of him?"

He shakes his head. "What's he look like?"

Good drokkin' question. "Smart, stylish. Snobby type. You heard him speak, you wouldn't mistake him."

"Don't get many like that in here. Ain't exactly the Megapolitan Opera House. If I see him, I can let him know you were lookin' for him. You a friend of his?"

"Just got some business to put his way."

"You got a name, just in case he shows up?"

For some reason, I pause, feeling I'm giving too much away. "Just say that Talón was asking after him." I drain the bottle, more for appearance's sake than the taste. The fear's starting to encroach on me and I need a hit. "Gotta take a whizz."

I go into the bathroom, which is as foul as I'd imagined it would be, and lock myself into a cubicle. I take a wrap of zizz from my pocket, empty a line onto the cistern lid and then snort it up, feeling it burn away the paranoia lurking at the back of my head. I close my eyes and let the drug course its way through my system, my pounding heart pumping it along every vein and artery, igniting my senses and boiling my blood. My jaw clenches and my temples throb as the anxiety is pushed back down into the dark once more, and a chemically infused strength of purpose washes through me.

I open the cubicle door and take a fist straight in the face. While I'm seeing stars I take another two body blows, knocking me to the ground. I feel my gun being wrenched from my belt, and the knapsack containing the torture instruments is ripped off my shoulder. Then I'm yanked to my feet and slammed up against the wall, and I get my first look at the two creeps assaulting me. One of the thugs keeps his arm against my throat, barely allowing me to breathe, while the other pats me down quickly, checking for any other weapons.

“He’s clean.”

“Going on a trip, motherdrokker,” the dirtwad pinning me to the wall says, and he slams my head hard against the tiles. Darkness descends on me like a curtain dropping before my eyes.

SEVEN

"For I will not rest, I will not sleep, until every Sov is wiped from the face of the Earth."

"But, Judge Dredd, half the city is destroyed! Our forces are decimated! We have barely survived the aggressor's assault! How can we possibly return from this?"

"We will rebuild, because it is in our blood to stand strong against those that wish our citizens harm, because it is the Mega-City way. From the founding fathers, from Fargo himself, whose purity and belief in righteous justice flows through these very veins, it has always been our inner strength and uncompromising vision that has seen the city endure. We have stood on the brink of nuclear extinction, but fought against our enemy and threw it back at them tenfold. The whole world knows what happens to those that threaten us, who attempt to mess with the Big Meg. We will stamp on them, and we will stamp on them hard. There is no time for weakness and grief, for we must forge ahead making sure this city will rise again. Now, if you'll excuse me..."

"Dredd, where are you going?"

"I'm sorry, your honour, but I'm needed back on the streets. While this city still stands and crime is being committed, that is my duty: to protect the people and uphold the Law."

Dredd watched himself riding off into the distance on an authentic-looking Lawmaster – although he wasn't sure the bike needed the spoilers at the back – as the screen faded to black and the Catalyst logo emerged in plain white. It had just been a ten-minute short, rough footage cobbled together from recent shoots for a promotional tool, but he had seen enough to know exactly how awful it was going to be.

Dredd knew little about films and he hardly watched the Tri-D (except when an illegal broadcast demanded his attention) but for a supposedly accurate historical epic, he thought the dialogue was laughably over-the-top and the characterisation unrecognisable. He wondered what McGruder would've made of her role in it, as the actress in question had chosen to portray the former Chief Judge as some kind of simpering dunce who went around asking everybody what was going on. As for this Krinkle idiot who was playing him, Dredd had to assume the actor was either writing his own scripts or else he was being paid by the word, because he couldn't recall ever being so verbose. Speeches had never been his forte; he liked to think his actions spoke for themselves.

The lights flickered on and the studio's PR spokesman stood smiling expectantly at him, like he'd just introduced him to one of his children. "What did you think?"

Dredd struggled for a reaction. "You've taken events in an... interesting direction." In truth, he supposed he couldn't fault the sentiment. There was nothing wrong with a little city pride, and he could hardly criticise the representation of Justice Department. In an age when it seemed every cit and his uncle was distributing pro-democracy literature and taking potshots at any Judge they could find, it made a refreshing change to be painted as the good guy for once. Of course, these films were being made with the Grand Hall of Justice's approval, so they were never going to be anything less than complimentary. "You sell these all over the world?"

"To friendly territories, certainly, who share our suspicions of the Eastern Block. Most of our sales go to Texas City, but you'd be surprised how popular they are in Brit-Cit, mainland Euro-Cit and even Hondo. I think events on

Sin City didn't help the Sov reputation to improve, to say the least."

"I guess not," Dredd replied, remembering the time thousands were killed when East-Meg agent Orlok released bacterium on the floating pleasure island. He imagined the televised pictures of the dying, their eyes streaming blood, their faces contorted by swollen growths, would make a horrific impression. After that, who wouldn't enjoy seeing the Sovs getting their butts kicked, time and again? "What's this one going to be called?" he nodded at the now-blank screen.

The PR gimp at least had the good grace to look embarrassed. "*Dredd's Dirty Dozen*. But that's just a working title," he added hastily. "It follows you and your fellow Mega-City Judges in your guerrilla war against the invaders. Y'know, executing collaborators, cutting off Dan Tanna Junction, that sort of thing. We've tried to make it as accurate as possible – you should see the scene where Tanna goes down, it's very impressive."

"I'm sure." Dredd couldn't help but feel distaste for the way a tragic moment in the city's history was being re-enacted for cheap entertainment. He knew this film had a certain role to play, but even so, a lot of good men and women had died in the Apocalypse War repelling the Sovs, and to see their sacrifices captured in such a tawdry fashion was a disservice to their memory. Despite being instrumental in Mega-City's eventual victory, Dredd didn't get any satisfaction from revisiting this specific point in his past, it was too much like picking at a scab, allowing the bad blood that had already been spilled to flow once more.

His overall opinions of Catalyst Productions were mixed; on the one hand, it was without doubt a professional outfit and the various soundstages were all busy in the process of making umpteen different flicks. There was no denying their commitment either, despite the general rottenness of the final product. Serious money was being thrown at these features with a substantial sum of it coming in the form of Justice Department subsidies. The productions utilised advanced special effects and real-life actors (as opposed to the digital versions), which was a cost in itself. Distributing, as it did, its wares all over the world, this was no fly-by-night company.

And yet something about the set-up irked him. Perhaps it was because that very commitment seemed *too* dedicated, going beyond a niche market into something personal and obsessive. He had no evidence of this, of course, it wasn't anything but a niggling feeling, his loony-tune antennae twitching.

Even so, there had to be a particular mindset behind a company to continuously produce something so fastidiously one-track and unrelenting in its depiction of the Sovs as the scum of the earth. It was a psychology of hatred that he found troubling. From what Dredd could see, there was little variation in the pictures. The sets and plots took occasional detours, but the end result was always the same – the East-Meggers got nuked out of existence, and more often than not it was *him* pressing the button. To see his doppelganger up on the screen, as part of this huge, big budget celebration of atomic genocide, made him feel used, as if he was complicit in this institutionalised, corporate xenophobia.

Catalyst's politics had made it friends in high office, however. Prior to his visit he'd read up on the history of the company – what little he could find on MAC, at least – and it had been McGruder, unsurprisingly, who'd seen its potential and helped fund its fledgling productions. Silver had later increased Justice Department's contribution, enabling it to significantly broaden its market share. Both former Chief Judges were hardliners, who probably took no small pleasure in seeing once again that roiling mushroom cloud rise above the remains of East-Meg One. Hershey was a different matter, but he noticed she hadn't removed the financial backing. Ever the diplomat, she was presumably keen to stay onside with the studio's CEO.

And that CEO was the enigma at the heart of his unease; the man behind the movies, Erik Rejin. Records on him were even more skimpy: born in 2066 into a wealthy family who had made their money in kneepads, he later inherited the fortune when his parents and siblings were killed by a Sov missile that was amongst the first payload to hit the city. Eighteen months after that, he sold the kneepad firm to one of the larger conglomerates and used the money to establish Catalyst. A widower with one daughter, Ramona, reports said Rejin hadn't been seen in public for a good twenty years or so. Dredd's attempts to talk to him had so far been benignly stalled and he'd been saddled with this simpering PR drokkwit instead, who'd insisted on giving him a mini-tour of the studio and running through the company spiel. He'd so far neatly sidestepped any questions relating to his boss, and Dredd's patience was wearing thin.

"You keep personnel records of the actors that work on these films?" the lawman asked.

"We have our employees' records on file, yes."

"I need to check the details of one of your actresses that worked for you some six months back."

The gimp looked uncomfortable. "The records are kept in our head office and Mr Rejin is very, *very* sensitive about his privacy. I don't have the authority to take you over there without his say-so–"

"Listen, creep," Dredd rumbled. "I'm all the authority you need. You continue to give me the runaround, I'll book you for obstruction. Tell your Mr Rejin there's no such thing as privacy in this city, and in my experience anyone who insists upon it usually has something to hide." He took a step closer to the PR goon who visibly cowered. "I'm investigating a multiple murder, and I don't have time for the fun and games of rich boy recluses."

The simp nodded quickly and retrieved a tiny phone from his jacket pocket, punching in a number and talking quietly and rapidly into it, turning slightly away from Dredd so the Judge couldn't discern what he was saying. Thirty seconds later, he clicked the mobile closed. "I've been instructed to take you through to Mr DuNoye's office."

"DuNoye?"

"Mr Rejin's legal advisor, and his... well, his second-in-command, you could say," he answered. "He's basically in charge of the day-to-day running of the studio."

He led Dredd through a warren of backstage corridors. They passed metres of cabling, discarded props, and the occasional actor wandering from the movie set still dressed in full costume. Dredd couldn't help but do a double-take as Sov Judges nodded at him in greeting.

"Hey, Janus, heard you scored with that chick last night, you old dog," one of them called out, slapping Dredd on the back.

The PR guy laughed nervously and hurried the lawman along before he could reply. "Sorry about that," he muttered. "Reality tends to get a bit mixed up around here." They climbed some stairs, and the surroundings gradually became less chaotic and more plush, morphing into an office environment. The gimp knocked softly on a door and ushered Dredd in. A silver-haired suit was waiting for them, standing behind a desk. Everything about him looked dry-cleaned: his clothes, demeanour, nothing was out of place.

"Thank you, Marcus. I can deal with Judge Dredd's questions," he said, dismissing his colleague, who withdrew gratefully. "I'm Vandris DuNoye, Mr Rejin's solicitor. You say you're investigating a murder case?"

"I wanted to check one of your employees' records. Emmylou Engels. She was in something called *Total Annihilation*."

He nodded. "I remember Ms Engels. A barely competent actress. Is she a suspect?"

"She's a corpse. She was murdered not long after finishing work for your company."

"My grud..." he whispered, his composure faltering for a moment. "I-I'm sorry to hear that. What did you want to know?"

"Whether her personnel file had any mention of a relationship with another employee, or if she'd talked about any problem she might've had with a colleague. I'm fairly sure she knew her killer."

"I don't think she was here long enough," he murmured, tapping at his keyboard. "She had a minor role, came in for maybe a few weeks' filming, maximum." He looked up from his flatscreen. "No, according to her details, she was paid, went away happy and we didn't call on her again. As I said, she wasn't exactly A-list."

"Any associates that you know of?"

"No, there was no one," he replied, then paused in thought. "Wait... she did say something about a mystery man. Joel somebody, lived a few blocks away from her. I presume she was dating him."

"And that's all, huh?" Dredd glanced down at his lie-detector curled in his fist, hidden from DuNoye's view.

"That's it."

The Judge looked around the office. "Your boss at home?"

"I'm sorry, Mr Rejin is not available to visitors. He's very ill."

"I wasn't requesting your permission, DuNoye," Dredd barked. "I'm getting a little tired of you people stonewalling me–"

"And I can assure you, Judge Dredd, that Mr Rejin is not well enough to answer any of your questions. As his lawyer, I'll make sure that if you insist on disturbing him you will be facing extremely damaging legal consequences."

"Don't spout the Law at me, creep."

"Mr Rejin has some highly influential friends that would make life very difficult for Justice Department if they felt you were harassing an infirm friend of theirs. A number of distinguished Mega-City councillors are all shareholders in Catalyst, including Matheson Peat, whom I believe is already making his opinion of you widely known."

It figured that Peat was part of this rich men's inner cabal. "I couldn't care less what the good councillor thinks of me. Right now, you're hindering my investigation into a multiple-murder case–"

"I've been nothing but helpful to you, Judge Dredd. I've told you all I know. But I will not stand by and allow you to intimidate Mr Rejin. I think I've made my position perfectly clear." He pressed an intercom and said "Marcus, can you escort the Judge back to the studio floor?"

He had to admit this lawyer slimeball was calmness personified and was completely unruffled. "Don't think I've finished with you, DuNoye," Dredd growled, jabbing a gauntleted finger in the other man's face. "If I find out you've been withholding vital information, then even your connections aren't going to save you, understand me?" He stormed out, knocking aside the PR gimp as he came through the door.

DuNoye motioned with his head for Marcus to go after him, then as soon as he was alone, reached for the phone.

Dredd raced along the Steadman expressway, feeling his investigation was taking a route he hadn't anticipated. What had seemed at the beginning like the hallmarks of a nutjob cult killing now seemed to be growing into something more sinister, more sophisticated. The lead that DuNoye had thrown him – Engels's supposed "mystery man" – was a phoney, he was convinced of that. His lie-detector had told him that the lawyer was feeding him a line, and Dredd could only assume that he had been sent on a wild goose chase, to pointlessly hunt down this mythical date of the victim's. He'd briefly interviewed many of the cast and crew before he left Catalyst, and none of them could remember Emmylou talking about this "Joel" character, or that she saw any of her work colleagues out of hours. They all thought she didn't look like somebody with problems, or who was in fear for her life.

He had a call patched through from Control – it was Garrison. "Dredd, we got the next two DNA matches from the Liz Short body dump. Darryk Fellmore, white male, thirty-two. Lived in Zeta-Jones lux-apts. The other is Ricki Haigle, black female, forty-six, resident of John Malkovich. Both single, no dependants."

"Let me guess, both actors."

"How'd you know?"

"Call it thirty years of Judge's intuition. Listen Garrison, I'm not near a terminal. Can you find out their employment history, see what their jobs were in the months leading up to the point when they were reported missing? If you can't do it through MAC, get a helmet round to their last known addresses or contact the next of kin. I'm heading back to the Grand Hall of Justice, you can contact me there."

"Wilco."

Dredd deliberately failed to mention to her what information he was after. He wanted his suspicions to be confirmed independently. If he was right, then he would have to inform the Chief Judge, who no doubt would be less than happy with his suspicions.

He left the expressway, and turned onto Brassard, weaving his Lawmaster through the traffic. A large truck rumbled past him on the outside and pulled into the middle lane to a chorus of angry horns from the other motorists as they had to decrease speed sharply. Dredd looked for a way round, but discovered they were approaching the mouth of the Naomi Watts underpass and he was going to be stuck behind this thing until he could break clear on the other side. The vehicle was drifting lazily from side to side, the driver seemingly unaware of the build-up he was causing, or perhaps being wilfully obstructive. Either way, the creep was contravening half a dozen highway laws. As they swept into the tunnel, Dredd was just about to give his siren a blast and get the idiot to pull over, when – watching the truck take a wide swing to the left – he realised a split second too late what was going to happen.

The truck slid into the inside lane, as if to allow the other traffic to pass, then slammed on its brakes and slewed itself across the entire width of the road, tyres screeching. Those unfortunate enough to be right behind it had no chance, smashing into its chassis with several thunderous bangs, accompanied by the sound of shattering glass and squealing rubber, all amplified within the confines of the tunnel. The vehicles that followed tried to swerve out of the path of the wreckage, but had nowhere to go. They sideswiped the walls of the underpass or buried themselves into the tangle of metal that now completely blocked the thoroughfare.

Dredd twisted his bike in an effort to stop himself ploughing into those in front, but lost control, the Lawmaster skidding away from him. He let go and tucked himself into a roll, his shoulder pads and helmet taking the worst of the damage as the tarmac reached up to greet him like a fist. The impact winded him, but he couldn't feel any broken bones as he staggered to his feet and, to his frustration, found his bike lying immobile beneath the debris.

The air was filled with the stink of oil, gasoline and burnt rubber, and small fires began to spring up in the ruptured engines of the vehicles twisted out of shape by the collision. Some citizens were emerging from their cars, dazed and nursing injuries, others were slumped forward in the front seats unconscious, or were unable to move because of the debris trapping them in. Dredd couldn't even get to the driver of the truck to see what had caused the pile-up, the cab rendered unreachable by the sheer number of wrecks toppled over on one another.

His priority was to call in reinforcements and start cutting the casualties free before the whole tunnel went up.

"Control, this is Dredd. We have a major accident in Watts underpass, med and meat wagons required," he barked into his mike, striding back towards the entrance. "Brassard is now completely blocked. Get helmets down here to redirect the traffic, and we need cutting equipment to free the injured–"

He stopped mid-sentence, momentarily stunned by the audacity of what he was seeing. Nine or ten men in full-face masks and anonymous fatigues were swinging down on ropes lashed to the pedway above the tunnel mouth. They had spit guns and assorted hand weapons – mostly crowbars and axes – strapped to their backs, and they acted quickly and confidently. Once they touched down onto the road surface, they began to move amongst the stationary vehicles, throwing the groaning cits aside.

"Control, this was no accident. We have wreckers working Watts underpass. Repeat, back-up required, wreckers in force in Watts."

"That's a rog. Units will be with you shortly."

Dredd drew his Lawgiver, flattening himself against the wall, thinking that he should've guessed the truck had been used to intentionally block the tunnel. Whilst he'd dealt with plenty of wreckers before – perps that caused carnage by attacking motorists, breaking their way into the vehicles to steal money and valuables – he'd never actually been in the centre of a robbery itself. The creeps had certainly picked the wrong moment to launch an attack, but if they were checking the traffic entering the underpass, they must've seen him going in with it. So why choose now to commence the assault?

Unless…

The perps were splitting up, covering the full expanse of the tunnel. Some of them grabbed rings, wallets and necklaces, smashing car windows and snatching bags from the laps of the barely conscious, but others – while to all intents and purposes appearing to be on crowd control – were scanning the wreckage, looking for something. Or some*one*.

"Move in," one of them ordered. "Keep searching. We've got five minutes, tops."

This wasn't an ordinary hold-up, Dredd was certain of that now. They wanted it to look like a wrecking job, but they were using it as a cover. The robbing of cars was cursory and indiscriminate, as if that was their secondary goal. They'd staged this huge accident for one objective; to eliminate one of those trapped in the tunnel, but not to make it look like the victim had been singled out and was just in the wrong place at the wrong time. Dredd had a good idea who that intended victim was.

Well, he wasn't going to make it easy for them. He emerged from the shadows, Lawgiver raised, and shouted: "I'm giving you creeps one chance to drop your weapons and surrender. Hands in the air, *now*!"

The wrecker Dredd presumed to be the leader pointed the Judge out to the others. *"Nail him!"*

Dredd ducked down behind a car as he was met by a hail of automatic fire. Bullets ricocheted off the bodywork of the wrecks, shattering windows. Those citizens still trapped in their vehicles were ripped apart, jerking in their seats as they were caught in the onslaught, bodies riddled with ammunition. The wreckers were pouring the fire on, squeezing their spit guns dry, paying little attention to who was in the way. Dredd knew he had to finish this quickly before any more innocent lives were lost, and before a stray round ignited the huge tinderbox they were in the middle of.

The barrage halted. Through the wheel arch of the vehicle he was using for cover, Dredd saw feet approaching in his direction. Crouching, he shot two standard execution rounds through the meathead's lower leg. The wrecker collapsed with a yelp, his eyes meeting Dredd's for a second before the lawman put one more through his open mouth, forcing teeth and skull shards to explode back across the tarmac. The Judge crawled rapidly round to the corpse and snatched his spit gun, reasoning he could do with the extra firepower. He stood and sighted two more of the creeps sneaking in from the right and blew them away before they had a chance to aim.

"There!" came a cry, and Dredd rolled over a car bonnet, bullets popping all around him. He felt one ping off his helmet as he came down two-footed on the road and opened fire, both barrels blazing, his Lawgiver in his right hand, the spit gun in the left. A round from the latter satisfyingly took out two of the creeps at the same time, the ammo blowing through the first one's torso to catch his partner as well, slamming them both against the underpass wall.

Dredd moved before the rest could pin him down, slaloming between vehicles, making sure he kept all of his assailants in plain sight; he didn't want any of them getting behind him. By his reckoning, he'd taken down half their number already, and there were five of the drokkers left. Ideally, he would've liked to have fired off some heat-seekers, but he couldn't be sure they wouldn't catch some of the cits still left alive in the tunnel. Armour-piercing was another matter, though. Dredd saw one of the creeps squatting on the other side of an upturned mo-pad and put several AP rounds through the engine block, catching the guy in the neck and chest. He heard sirens in the background, and so did the remaining gunmen.

"Drokkin' jays comin', man!" one of them cried and made a break for it, heading for the tunnel entrance. The lawman sighted his weapon and shot the escapee through the kneecap, sending him sprawling, his screams echoing back along the underpass.

"Heads up, Dreddy," the leader yelled and Dredd had a moment to catch a glimpse of the grenade whistling over in his direction before he was moving again. He leaped onto the roof of a car, twisting away from the rattle of gunfire that followed his movements, and put as much distance as he could before the explosion. Seconds later, the entire structure shuddered as the grenade detonated, blowing vehicles into the air and sending an orange fireball shooting towards the tunnel mouth, incinerating everything in its path. Dredd rolled and found cover, feeling the heat blistering his face as it passed overhead. He had to get out; the fumes and leaking fuel set alight by the blast were going to turn this place into an inferno.

He got to his feet and saw the last three wreckers also charging for the opening. Looking back, most of the vehicles involved in the initial collision were ablaze, and a small chain reaction was going off, spreading to the surrounding remains. Dredd grabbed an injured perp, blackened but still breathing, and tugged him towards the light. Street and Med-Judges were arriving at the scene, leading motorists standing at the tunnel entrance out of the way. As Dredd emerged, he ordered them to get back.

"Move out! The whole tunnel's going to–"

Before he could finish, an eruption inside sent flames spiralling out, the wave of hot air pushed out with it throwing a nearby meat wagon off its wheels and onto its side. Fire licked at the roof and sides of the underpass, the heat forcing the Judges to retreat. A droid fire-fighting crew came forward and attempted to douse the conflagration.

"Some cits still in there," Dredd said, trying not to choke on the black smoke pouring out of the underpass.

"And who's this?" a Judge called Laverne asked, motioning to the semi-conscious perp at Dredd's feet.

"One of those responsible," he answered. "Last three got away. Did you see what happened to them?"

"Nope. Must've escaped the same way they came in." Laverne nodded at the ropes dangling above the tunnel entrance. "If you've got a description, we'll put out an APB."

Dredd shook his head. "Masked. Anyway, they'll have had a change of clothes and are probably headed to another sector by now. We'll just have to hope this creep coughs up some names." He gave the wrecker a gentle kick, getting a soft groan in response.

"Quite a mess," Laverne said, looking up at the smoke and flames. "Guess they didn't figure on holding *you* up as well."

Dredd didn't reply.

"Have you any idea of the seriousness of what you're suggesting?"

"I'm fully aware of the implications, if my suspicions are proved correct, of course. I don't make a habit of casting wild accusations."

Hershey sat forward at her desk, hands clasped together in front of her. "But you're accusing a major film studio – one with links to Justice Department, I might add – of being instrumental in the kidnap and murder of several citizens?"

Dredd nodded. "Something's rotten at the heart of Catalyst, I'm sure of it. Engels disappears a few weeks after working for the company and Haigle vanishes two months after her first gig there. Fellmore appears in three of their productions before his disappearance a year later."

"I've read the report," Hershey said testily, indicating the papers spread out before her. "It might just be coincidence. If someone's murdering actors, then their places of work are all going to be fairly similar."

"It's the single unifying factor between the victims. They've all got different backgrounds, different ages, different sexes, but they all worked for Catalyst at some point in their lives. They also all seem to be single, with no close family ties."

"Meaning?"

"Meaning someone's profiling them, choosing them because nobody's going to notice they're missing for a while. I looked into their Missing Persons files and Haigle hadn't been registered missing until eighteen months after her probable time of death. Nobody knew anything about Fellmore. Both their apartments had been re-let, the presumption being that, as actors, they'd found work in another part of the city, or left the country altogether."

"But you have no evidence," Hershey reiterated. "Nothing concrete. This is all supposition."

"I know that DuNoye creep lied to me, giving me a false lead to further muddy the waters of the investigation. If he's protecting Rejin, I want to know why. Plus there have now been two attempts on my life. Somebody with a lot of money is behind them if they can afford a Mob Blitzer or hire a wrecking crew to take me out."

"But we've got no names to connect them. The drive-by shooter was identified as some lowlife called Jove Parnell, who has already done time for ARVs and who wasn't even gang-affiliated. And that perp you pulled out of Watts knows nothing. Psi-Div probed him and all they got was that he was hired by a voice on the phone to do a wrecking job."

"They're the soldiers. They're not going to be told anything if it means we can use that info to get at the creeps at the top. We're looking at systematic murder here. If we're gonna break the organisation open, we gotta get at the brains behind it."

Hershey sighed. "Erik Rejin is a staunch supporter of this office and he makes many welcome contributions to our funds. If you're wrong about this, Dredd, it could prove very costly."

"I'll stake my reputation on it," Dredd replied flatly.

The Chief Judge sat back in her chair, thinking. Finally, she said: "What are you proposing?"

"We put someone inside Catalyst."

EIGHT

"Wake him up," says a voice even my mind, floating out on the ether, tells me I recognise. My embattled memory tries to put a name to it, but it's frustratingly sluggish. Seconds later, sharp pain lances through the haze of disorientation and consciousness rushes up to drag me out of the blackness. My heavy eyes open slowly and my body takes several moments to realise the situation: I'm being held upright, two pairs of arms supporting my weight. The room is darkened, with no distinguishing features that I can make out, other than the floor feels smooth and cold beneath my feet, like it's bare stone. There is a man standing before me, his features shadowy until he steps into the circle of light I'm in. Must be a spotlight directly above me.

"Is he awake?" the speaker asks, and now I know where I've heard that cultured voice before. His words echo slightly and I get the impression we're in a fairly large, high-ceilinged room, but even as my eyes become accustomed to the darkness I can see nothing beyond my captors.

One of the figures to my side enters my field of vision – it's one of the creeps from Tommy's bathroom – and slaps me hard. I can't help but cry out, my yelp descending into a snivelling cough as I taste the blood filling my mouth. "Looks like it," the meathead replies.

With the return to consciousness, my senses start reporting every injury demanding my attention. My face feels like tenderised munce. Blood's dribbling down my cheek from the cut bisecting the bridge of my nose where creep number two caught me with his ring when he drove his fist into it. I'm guessing it's broken, the cartilage mashed into the walls of my nostrils. I can't breathe out of it and the razor-edged gasps that emerge from my mouth sound like wretched sobs, drawn from the harsh pit of my chest. Each swallow feels like a shuggy ball is being lodged behind my tonsils.

My head lolls forward as bloody drool spills from between my lips and creep number one wrenches me back upright, smacking me forcefully a couple of times against my temples. "C'mon," he mutters. "You ain't dead yet."

The man I know must be Conrad stands there looking for all the world like this is happening on his Tri-D set. He wears a blank expression on his handsome, middle-aged, but curiously unlined face, as if this physical, ugly element of criminal activity is happening to some creature far below on the evolutionary scale; like it's feeding time at the zoo.

My aching, drug bleary mind makes a couple of snap judgements about him: firstly, he is remorseless and incapable of feeling empathy, but at the same time he's not a regular con, but rather someone put in charge of a couple of thugs. Secondly, he's not the arch-perp behind all this, but an errand boy, a gofer acting on his master's bidding. A barely functioning, cogent part of my brain realises that while he could order me dead without a moment's hesitation and wouldn't think twice about it, he's still an employee and answers to his boss. I gotta tip the advantage my way and make myself indispensable, otherwise he'll get his goons to chop me into pieces and flush me down the pan.

"Who are you, Mr Trager?" Conrad asks evenly, flattening down his thousand-cred haircut.

"Just... answered your own... question," I manage to spit out.

He continues as if he hasn't heard me. "You carry no ID, you have nothing to verify that you are indeed who you say you are. True to your word, you have brought the merchandise," he taps the bundle of torture devices that they snatched off me the moment they pounced, "for which I am grateful. But the methods by which you obtained them still vexes me. All attempts by my people to contact the Dansky brothers have been fruitless."

"T-that's 'cause they're… lying at the bottom of the… Black Atlantic," I say, wincing, short of breath. "I told you… there's been a… h-hostile takeover."

"You expect me to believe that you wiped out the Dansky gang single-handed?"

"N-no, I had help. Fuh-Frederica Talón and her men… swapped allegiances."

"And what did you offer them that they found so irresistible?"

A phrase I remember Brett using pops into my head. "K-keys to the kingdom."

Conrad takes a step closer to me, peering into my face. He can't quite conceal his distaste at the dried blood caked to my skin, the bruise swelling up on my forehead, forcing my right eye partially closed, the idiot yawning of my mouth as I gulp for air, my nose a ruined mess. Something about his disgust, the animalistic repulsion of my bloodied state, creeps me out and it occurs to me that maybe the Danskys were right to be scared of this guy. There's clearly an unhinged mind behind that smooth exterior.

Conrad reaches out his fingers to my face and traces the outline of a welt on my cheek with the lightest of touches, moving his hand up past the back of my neck. Then he grabs my hair and yanks hard, tugging my head back, and moves his lips close to my ear, so close that I can hear the wet sound of his tongue as the words curl out, hissed and heavy with menace: "Who – *are* – you?"

"You… think… that I'm… l-lying to you?" I gasp, trying to keep my voice as steady as possible. It's not just the pain that's affecting me now, but a cold, hard dread that's building in my belly. "You don't... t-trust me?"

"I don't like change, Mr Trager. Change is bad. Change brings with it problems, it can upset the status quo. My colleagues, my employer, they don't like to see new faces. They like to keep the system pure and untainted, free from those that seek to enter from the outside."

"I b-brought you the... gruddamn offer of the w-week," I reply, my watery eyes looking up into his, my hair tearing away from my scalp. "I'm your... n-new contact that can g-get you... all the B-Banana City goodies that you want, and you're gonna th-throw that away 'cause you d-don't know my face?"

"The organisation I represent, Mr Trager," Conrad says, pomposity and self-importance oozing from every pore, "takes its secrecy very seriously. We had a beneficial relationship with the Danskys because they were reliable and didn't ask any questions. Now they're gone, and out of nowhere you pop up on the scene. You'll forgive me if I'm not the tiniest bit suspicious."

"S'way it is on the street. Deals come and go, people come and go. The p-point is... whether y-you're prepared to g-grab the opportunity."

Conrad smiles and releases me from his grip, patting my cheek softly. "And now it is time for *you* to go, Mr Trager. You're too much of a security risk, I'm afraid." He glances at the goons holding me. "Take him down to City Bottom and dispose of him."

"Wait, wait," I weakly protest, trying to resist the creeps as they attempt to pull me away. "This... this is a trust issue, right? You don't know me from Aaron A Aardvark, so you're gonna sling me in a garbage grinder?"

"Something like that."

"What's it gotta take, man, to... convince you I'm a square bear? You think I don't have the cojones to join your group? What d'you think happened to the Danskys?"

Conrad pulls an exasperated expression. "Mr Trager, I don't know what has become of the brothers, but I remain unconvinced you were responsible. Now, I have better things to do than stand here arguing with you–"

"Lose me and you lose all your supplies from South-Am. Talón won't deal with anyone else. Take me onboard an' you'll have direct line to torture central. Won't have to bother with middlemen."

"This is bullshit," creep number two snarls.

"Trust has to be earned, I know that," I continue. "I c-cannot be automatically granted your approval... without some show of loyalty."

"Why don't we just whack him here, boss? Only way to get him to shut the drokk up..."

Conrad holds up a hand, looking amused. "Hold on, I want to hear what he's got to say." He gestures for me to go on.

I try to straighten myself, clearing my throat. "You say you don't like those that seek to enter your organisation from the outside. W-what do you do, for example... if you need to replace one of your men? Do you take on the p-person responsible for their removal... The person who has shown themselves to be the s-stronger?"

The question flummoxes him. "I don't... the situation has never arisen–"

"But you're going to need... to replace *him*," I continue, making a sideways nodding motion with my head at creep number two, standing diagonally to my left. "Who would you t-trust to take his place but his most obvious s-successor?"

"But he's not–"

I lash out, my speed and strength catching them unawares. I elbow creep number one in the midriff, loosening his grip, then spin and sweep the legs from beneath creep number two. As he lies prone, I flatten my right hand and deliver a powerful blow to his throat as if it were a blade, directly above his Adam's apple. It destroys his trachea and he gags, unable to swallow or gasp for breath. As his hands go to his neck and he struggles to his knees, his eyes bulging, a horrible spluttering noise emerging from his mouth, I bunch my fist and drive it into his face, demolishing his nose, splintering the bone. He collapses instantly, hitting the floor like a dead weight.

Conrad and creep number one have barely had time to register the attack when I turn back to them, their eyes wide, mouths agape.

"Seems like you have a vacancy," I say.

I'm sitting at a bar on Feltz, nursing my sixth or seventh whiskey, or whatever synthetic derivative that I've been served, and I'm allowing the alcohol to dull my senses and soften the pain. My swollen, bruised face is attracting attention from the other patrons and the barman is giving me distasteful glances every time I order another round, but by now I'm past caring. I want to drink until I can no longer feel the ache in my limbs or the throbbing in my skull or remember the sensation of the perp's windpipe disintegrating at my touch. I think I've fractured some bones in my hand, and I'm having trouble holding the glass without it shaking.

As I suspected, a display of utter ruthlessness was enough to convince Conrad that I was genuine. Although his surviving crony had to be restrained from putting a bullet through my head, Conrad himself didn't seem that upset by the violent passing of his colleague. In fact, he appeared impressed by my casual brutality and lack of mercy, as if wiping out a rival was the way to get ahead in his organisation. Despite managing to wheedle myself into his trust, I thought I had still better watch my step if I didn't want to end up the same way.

Conrad had said he had a job for me, a trial run, that if successful would open all sorts of doors for a man of my talents. I was told to be at Tommy's in three days' time when a guy called Alphonse would pick me up and show me what the job entailed. I was blindfolded and taken on a short, ten-minute journey before being left on a street corner. Clearly, his trust didn't extend far enough to reveal the base they were operating out of. I know that he has just enough faith in me to keep me alive for the time being, but beyond that I was going to be treated with caution.

Despite my conscience telling me that I should be celebrating having penetrated Conrad's mysterious outfit, I merely feel deflated and weary. And maybe a touch scared. My head feels too heavy for my neck to support, and every time I close my eyes I see the faces of the perps I've nixed to maintain the great lie that is my life. A blood-spattered gallery of accusatory glares, existences wiped out... for what? For the greater good? Pawns that could be sacrificed because it got me closer to the Mr Bigs, the creeps who were really pulling the strings. And what did that make me? Someone who saw life as so meaningless that it could be snuffed out at the drop of a hat? Who was I to see madness in this Conrad character, when it seemed I was cut from the same cloth? Perhaps that was what frightened me – there was something about him that was very familiar to me, a kindred spirit. We're bonded by the blood we have no qualms about spilling.

The alcohol is making me maudlin, I realise. I ought to go outside, get some fresh air, shed some of the ghosts clinging to me like cigarette smoke. But maybe one more for the road... I raise my hand slightly, trying to attract the barman's attention, suddenly dimly aware that there's somebody sitting next to me.

"You look how I feel," a sultry female voice says. I turn to look to my right, eyes struggling to focus. An attractive woman – dark hair, bright red lipstick that matches her tight little dress – swims into my vision. She doesn't attempt to hide her shock at my appearance. "Jovus, somebody sure went to work on you."

"You should see the other guy." I smile weakly, even the slightest muscle twitch giving me pain. The barman ambles over and I slide my glass towards him. "Fill her up." I glance at the woman. "You want a drink?"

"Wouldn't be in here if I didn't," she replies. "I'll have the same." When the barman's gone, she asks: "So, you walk into a door?"

"More like two doors walked into me. My fault, really, my head kept getting in their way." She laughs, the first joyful sound I've heard all day. "Let me guess, hard day, right?"

"Hard *year*; one I'm trying to forget," she whispers.

I clink her glass. "Join the club. We can have mutual amnesia." I take a gulp, the fiery liquid burning its way to my stomach. "Whaddya do?"

"Professional heartbreaker."

"I can see that. Does it pay well?"

She smiles. "Not really, but there's plenty of job satisfaction. How about you?"

"Actor." It feels good to be knowingly swapping untruths with someone, both of us aware of the yarns we're spinning, like we're creating new lives just for tonight.

She looks mock impressed. "Wow. Would I have seen you in anything?"

"Well, it tends to be underground stuff, mainly."

"There's some drokking brutal critics out there," she says, nodding to my bruises. She reaches out and lightly touches the swelling above my eye, and it takes enormous willpower not to lay my hand on top of hers and keep it there.

"They don't pull any punches, that's for sure," I reply quietly.

We chat briefly, both circling the truth like dancers. For me, this kind of invention is second nature; another skin to step into, another role to play. She keeps up with me every step of the way, obviously having done this sort of thing before. Despite the lack of honesty between us, there's a warmth to her company that I find beguiling and comforting. I always did have my head turned by a pretty face and an easy smile.

An ache gnaws at the back of my skull and I groan. "Ugh. I've drunk too much."

"Come on," she says, sliding off her bar stool. "Let's go somewhere more private."

The floor seems uneven as I join her, and my legs feel like they're going to buckle any second. Fatigue and inebriation are crashing down on me. She slips an arm around my waist and steadies me. This close to her, I can smell her scent, feel the softness of her body. As she guides me out the door, I ask, slurring slightly: "What's your name?"

"Sam."

"I'm–"

"I know who you are, Pete."

Shock sobers me up fast. I resist her pull, standing stock-still and looking into her eyes. "How do you..."

"I was sent to bring you in," she replies, motioning with her head towards the street. I follow her gaze and see two Judges beside a catch wagon, waiting for us. "Hendry wants to talk to you." She opens her handbag and I steal a glimpse of the Justice Department badge contained within. She smiles reassuringly. "You're not the only one that can put on a performance."

I'm sitting alone at a small table in an interrogation room, several cups of synthi-caf now percolating through my system in a bid to stave off the effects of the alcohol. I find the blank walls, intended to be threatening and dislocating to the suspect, oddly comforting. After too much drug-induced hyper-reality and a brain-deadening comedown, it feels good to be in some nowhere-place, where I can't get over-stimulated. The spartan nature of Justice Department holding tanks evokes the cold, brutal efficiency with which the Law is administered, and is supposed to put the fear of grud into the perp, but for me, it seems like a welcome relief.

The door opens and Hendry walks in, a cane in one hand aiding his limp. He takes one look at my sorry state and shakes his head, lowering himself into the other chair across the table from me. These are the only pieces of furniture in the room.

"I feel worse than I look," I tell him.

"Helmets said you were intoxicated when they brought you in."

"Medicinal. It numbs the pain."

Hendry sighs. "Trager, do you remember our last conversation? I seem to recall giving you a friendly warning about enjoying life on the street too much–"

"Gimme a break, chief. I'd just had the shit kicked out of me. If I'm not entitled to a drink–"

"You gave up your entitlements years ago, when you became a Judge," Hendry snaps. "Exactly what does getting drunk benefit you, other than to lower your defences and leave you compromised? You're an officer of the Law, for drokk's sake, you can't afford not to be alert."

My superior's words cut through me like a las-saw; a napalm-burst ache blossoms behind my eyes. I wince, rubbing my temples. "Sending a pretty face in there was your idea, no doubt?"

"Thought we'd bring you in gently. Good job Harvey was a Judge and not an assassin, you wouldn't have made her job too difficult for her."

"Y'know, your concern is quite touching. You haven't once asked how I came to get all these." I gesture to my bruises.

Hendry pauses for a second, then says softly: "You went ahead with the torture deal? How did it go?"

"Weird with a beard. This creep the Danskys were so afraid of, guy called Conrad, he's a complete fruit-loop. Looks like a regular cit on the surface, but he's a drokkin' nutcase underneath, man."

"Conrad? As in Conn? As in *Beast That Ate the Beast That Ate Mars*?"

"Hey, that was a good drokkin' movie."

Hendry cracks a smile. "Hell of a movie."

"But, yeah, that's all I know him by. Gotta be a cover name. They're drokkin' paranoid about outsiders."

"They didn't trust you?"

"Eventually." I flash back to the creep on his back, my hand chopping down on his throat, the awful gagging of his final breaths. An involuntary shudder travels my spine. "I convinced them I was on the level."

"What do you think he's up to?"

"I got a meet in a few days' time, guess I'll find out then. I think they're trying to test me."

The door opens again and a figure fills the frame. At first, I think it's just a uniform come to deliver a message, but then this gruff, rumbling voice emerges from it and I recognise who it is instantly. I've heard that snarling bark a hundred times on Tri-D, growling at reporters or delivering a warning to terrified viewers about staying out of trouble. "This your wonder boy then, Hendry?"

Grud*damn*. It's Dredd.

He strides in, every bit as intimidating in the flesh as his reputation suggests, a file tucked under his arm. He throws me a look that says he doesn't think much of me at first glance, and I try to give him an unimpressed stare back, but the truth of the matter is that I'm a touch star-struck. The man's a legend, responsible for saving the city half a dozen times over, and he's the benchmark by which every Judge must test themselves. There is so much weight and history flowing through his bloodline that it is difficult not to be nervous in his presence, even if you are a fellow officer. You feel your every word, your every action, is being judged and invariably will come up wanting. There are few that are his equal.

"Dredd," Hendry acknowledges. "This is Trager, one of my best Wally Squad operatives."

I raise my eyebrows at my superior, surprised by my commendation. I had always guessed that I was a little too close to the edge for Hendry's comfort. But I suppose I do get results. "What's all this about, boss?"

"Your infiltration of the torture-buyer's organisation may have links with my ongoing investigation into a number of murders," Dredd interrupts tersely, putting the file down on the table. "You've heard about the Liz Short body dump?"

I nod, thinking back to the piece in the *Mega-Times*. "Yeah, I read about that. Dead were pulled out of a chem-pit, right?"

"The victims that we've managed to identify have all been actors, and have all worked for a film studio called Catalyst at one time or another. They make anti-Sov propaganda movies. I believe that the company is a front for an outfit that is kidnapping, torturing and murdering citizens."

"Whoa." The name Catalyst rings a bell. To be told that it was killing its actors was like hearing that Dave the Orang-utan was actually a gimp in a monkey suit – a big deal to wrap your head around.

"You sold on the instruments of torture from Banana City to your contact, I understand," Dredd continues. "Where did you meet him?"

"I was told the handover usually took place at Tommy's, that bar on Bleeker. Creep never turned up but sent a couple of goons to collect me. They knocked me unconscious and I woke up in this big, dark building. Nothing I could recognise; could've been any kind of warehouse."

"Or a studio?" Hendry puts in.

"Maybe. There was a spotlight right above me. Everything else was in shadow."

"The creeps that grabbed you, would you recognise them again?" Dredd asks.

No drokkin' kidding. You don't forget the face of a man you've killed with your bare hands. "For sure."

Dredd leans in, flips open the file and retrieves several surveillance photographs showing grainy images of three men emerging from a block main entrance with a woman. She's carrying a couple of suitcases. "We pulled these off the PSU camera trained on George Bush Snr. We've narrowed down the day we think one of the victims was kidnapped, and went through the footage. I think this is her being taken away."

I squint at the pics. "They're wearing blur-masks."

"I know. But is the clothing, anything else, familiar?"

I shake my head. "These aren't the goons that went for me."

"What about the buyer?" Dredd persists. "Did you get a good look at him?"

"Sure, when he wasn't having me used as a punchbag." I point at the swelling above my eye. "I got a fractured–"

"Save it for the meds," Dredd replies dismissively. "What did he look like?"

"Grey-haired, suited motherdrokker. Not your average crim, but loonier than a barrelful of muties."

Dredd pulls out another pic. "This him?"

I don't have to hesitate. Conrad's self-important, smooth visage glares back at me. "Hell, yeah, that's him. He got form?"

Dredd shakes his head. "This is his citizen ID. He hasn't got a record. His real name's Vandris DuNoye. He's Catalyst's legal eagle and the right-hand man to the creep behind the company."

"Drokk me," I say, genuinely shocked. "He mentioned something about his employer'."

"Erik Rejin. He's the meathead at the top I want to nail, but the rich creep's surrounded himself with a layer of protection I can't get close to. That's where you come in."

"Get inside the organisation," Hendry says to me. "See what you can find. We gotta blow it wide open from the inside." He pauses, glances at Dredd, then adds: "Rejin's got a daughter, Ramona. Must be in her early twenties. Get close to her. We, uh, know you got a rep with the ladies, so see if you can use that to your advantage. Get what info you can out of her."

"Keep me updated," Dredd adds sternly. "And don't go so deep you can't get out. Remember who you're working for."

I nod slowly. "Nothing I can't handle."

Dredd pulls himself up to full height, a lawbreaker's nightmare. "Don't be too sure. If these creeps are guilty of what I suspect they are, you're gonna have to keep your wits about you. From what I've seen of them, they are dangerous and they are remorseless."

I look down at the photo of DuNoye, his cold, dark eyes betraying nothing. I can still taste blood in my mouth.

PART TWO:
THE ATROCITY EXHIBITION

NINE

"You Trager?"

I glance up at the guy looming over me and it doesn't strain my brain to guess that this is the gimp I've been waiting for. Built like a Manta prowl tank, he's squeezed into a two thousand-cred suit that looks like it's about to burst. His massive arms are barely contained within a jacket stretched to the seams, and his thick-necked bullethead emerges from the shirt collar like pink sausagemeat squeezed out of a tube.

The creep's outfit makes him immediately incongruous amongst the rest of the clientele in Tommy's, and if it wasn't for the shaved head, pinched features and cold, cruel eyes set deep in his waxy skull, then no doubt one of the bad-asses here would question his right to walk amongst them. Also, the drokker's a good six and a half feet tall; he towers over the stumpy little bikers as if they're his pixie followers. Looking like a serial killer on his way to his grandmother's funeral, he exudes an attitude that would keep anyone at a safe distance, allowing him an impressive exclusion zone. Right now, his bowel-loosening stare is fixed on me, his nostrils flaring like he's itching to spill some blood.

Take a deep breath, I tell myself. Don't sound hesitant, don't let him intimidate you. "That's me. You're Alphonse, right?" The name sounds ludicrous, applied to King Krong here. His parents must've been seriously drokking optimistic – you might meet a MCU History lecturer called Alphonse, or it's what you'd christen your robo-servant if you had lots of money and pretensions but little taste, but no way does it suit a bruiser of the magnitude that is standing before me. It's like naming one of Satanus's brood Fluffy or something; just ain't gonna work. Then again, the tag could be bullshit, just another bogus ID.

He nods. "Come on. Got the speedster parked outside."

He turns, not waiting for me to join him, and surges his way through the Friday evening drinkers, the barflies parting almost as one to let him pass. I trail behind in his wake, singularly less threatening, relieved as I step out into the cool night air to be away from the crush, though apprehensive about where tonight's events are going to lead. I won't have much of a chance against this gorilla if things turn nasty, and there won't be time for back-up to mobilise. I just gotta stay on his good side, prove that I will be a worthwhile addition to the organisation.

Alphonse is standing beside his vehicle waiting for me to catch up. It's a sleek, dark, two-man hatchback job and I'm surprised he manages to fit behind the steering wheel. He's eyeing me as I approach, cocking his head to one side as if weighing up in his mind what size coffin I would take, or how much ballast he'd need to sink my body in a rad-pit. What he's actually thinking about surprises even me.

"You got any smarter clothes than that?"

I stop and look down at myself. To blend into the citizenry means a fairly understated wardrobe that isn't going to draw attention to yourself. My outfit consists of lime-green kneepads, Emphatically Yess pantaloons with the third trouserleg tucked stylishly into the waistband, a pair of hightops and a shirt/jacket combo by the Guerre family from Cal-Hab. If you don't want to attract unwelcome comments from passers-by and risk provoking trouble, it pays not to look like a simp.

I shrug at Alphonse. "S'all I got."

He sighs like an exasperated fashion consultant, then climbs into his car, indicating that I should do likewise. "We gotta get you a suit. None of mine are gonna fit a pee-wee like you."

"What's the diff?"

"Difference is," he says, starting the vehicle up and easing it into the flow of traffic, "that it creates an impression. It puts forward an image. Most people make a decision about somebody within the first few seconds of meeting. If you meet someone and they're suited and booted, chances are your impression's gonna be that they're respectable, businesslike, and take pride over their appearance. No reason to fear someone in a shirt and tie."

The casual way he says "fear" gives me goosebumps, as if everybody had a very real reason to fear him and the clothes were just a costume, a distraction, to hide the psycho concealed inside them.

"People look at you," he continues, glancing at me, "an' they're gonna think – no offence – that you're an asshole. No reason why they should give you the time of day."

"Charming."

"Nothing personal. Ninety per cent of the population looks like you and they're assholes as well. If the average Joe on the slab turns up at your door asking questions or needing help, do you let him in? Do you say, 'Hey, whatever you need, use my vid-phone, anything.'? Like drokk you do. You tell him to get lost. You don't owe any drokker anything, right?"

I nod, conceding the point. Most Big Meg citizens barely saw their neighbours, let alone spoke to them. There was too much suspicion, too much nervousness about the consequences of helping – or even getting to know – a stranger. One minute you're helping out some little old lady to cross the road, the next you wake up and find yourself being sold in an alien slave market on a far away rimworld.

The Judges had fostered a society built on dread, in which they constantly reiterated the fact that crime was an ever-present disease and that each second of every day someone was a victim of it. It left cits paralysed, scared to leave their apartments; which, of course, suited Justice Department very well. It was a lot easier to control a city if the population felt besieged by an enemy within. The cits were so busy barricading themselves into their homes that they failed to notice that their supposed protectors were removing their civil rights one by one.

"Now put a man in a suit," Alphonse says, "and watch their reaction change. Automatically, they think you're someone in authority, 'cause you don't look like them. They're deferent, courteous, eager to please – a world away from how they treat others normally, even their own family." He takes one hand off the wheel and briefly adjusts his tie in the rear-view mirror. "Here, watch this."

A Judge suddenly slides up parallel to the car on his Lawmaster and glances in. Sweat prickles in the small of my back, but the helmet simply gives Alphonse the once-over then glares at me for a second before taking an off-ramp.

"Y'see?" Alphonse asks me, waggling his eyebrows. "Model citizen, me."

"Sounds to me like you've made a study of this."

He smiles unpleasantly. "I've seen plenty of meatheads' reactions close-up. I know when I've been taken into their confidence, when they sense there's nothing suspicious about me. You get enough experience at this sort of thing, it's as easy as flicking a switch. You go from Mr Nice Guy to… someone else."

"What, exactly?" I enquire, pushing him slightly.

"You'll see," he says quietly, watching me from the corner of his eye. "Mr DuNoye, he doesn't trust you, you know that, don't you? He's pretty wary of anyone he doesn't know well. Some say he's paranoid, but me, I just think he's careful."

Mr DuNoye, eh? The need for cover names seems to have gone. "You mean Conrad?" I ask innocently.

Alphonse lets out a barking laugh. "Ha! His idea of a sick joke – just one more actor playing a role. Everything I learnt about playing up to people's perceptions I got from him. You've met him, right?"

I instinctively touch my face where the bruises were slowly fading. "Yeah, we've met."

"And you're first impression of him was?"

"He looked like a businessman, like a gruddamn captain of industry. But it didn't take me long to realise that inside he was–"

"Something different," he finishes. "That's how it works, that's how we all work. The image we put forward every day ain't necessarily the same as what we're like in private. Do you know what we'd be like if we were one hundred per cent honest with ourselves? The city would be full of naked, gibbering loons, man."

"So, DuNoye may look like Mr Respectable, but he's buying antique torture equipment from South-Am. He got a taste for the rough stuff?"

Alphonse is silent for a moment, then he says: "Mr DuNoye is a respected lawyer and the public face of Catalyst Productions with many influential friends, including some within Justice Department. He also happens to have a certain... predilection, which he shares with a select client base in a profitable enterprise."

Predilection? Profitable enterprise? Suddenly, the penny drops. "Vi-zines. He's making Vi-zines."

"A rather crude term for what we're actually achieving, but needless to say you can understand Mr DuNoye's reticence to allow outsiders into his private life. You'll see soon enough how our work is so much more than some backstreet criminal organisation, and we shall see if you have the stomach to be a part of it."

I swallow, feeling I could do with a zizz hit. "He said he had an errand for me. A test. So where are we going?"

"Why, Mr Trager," Alphonse replies, that nauseating smile returning to his lips, "we're going to pick up our next star."

We park in the shadow of Dick Miller and take the el up to the one hundred and fourteenth floor, my mentor explaining to me the set-up along the way.

"See, we can't just kidnap people when they turn up to auditions. Their agencies are gonna want to know where they are, and once they start getting suspicious then the talent's going to avoid us like the plague."

"You're talking about Catalyst here?" I ask, acting stupid. I have to be careful and make sure that I don't let it slip that I have more than my fair share of information at my disposal. "I thought it made regular movies..."

"It does. Anti-Sov prejudice sells all over the world. But it's our legitimate front and what you might call our grooming method. Mr DuNoye and Mr Rejin, they monitor the actors and see who they think has potential. Those that they like the look of often get called back."

"Rejin... I've heard of that guy. Never seen in public, right?"

Alphonse doesn't reply straight away. "He's the man at the top," he mutters. "He... tends to keep himself to himself."

"But why don't you just snatch the victims off the street, if they're gonna be murdered anyway?"

"It's all about quality, that's why," he snaps. "Yeah, any two-bit Vi-zine publisher gets its meat by snatching a couple of bums out of an alley, but what do you get? You get shit, is what." He reaches into his inside jacket pocket and pulls out a small, rolled-up periodical, handing it to me. "Stuff like this is pretty much the standard that you can buy off the black market; a shoddy, cheap hack job."

I open it out and catch the title – *Drilling Miss Daisy* – before my eyes are pulled to the explicit cover pic of an eldster getting a frontal lobotomy while clearly fully conscious. The image is grainy and badly composed, the photographer having got so close to the subject that it isn't easy to make out the details. Judging by the lighting too, it had been shot in a gloomy basement with only a bare bulb providing any illumination. I steel myself to flip through the pages and do so quickly and with the minimum of attention, trying hard not to rest my gaze on any one atrocity. The reproduction values are poor, the paper rough. Hard to believe, but a mag like this sells at about fifty creds each on the underground. A sicko and their money are soon parted, that's for gruddamn sure.

"Pretty grim," I say, giving it back to him, relieved to have it out of my sight. I notice ink has rubbed off onto my fingers and I try to wipe them down the back of my trousers, keen to be rid of its taint.

"Yeah," he says distractedly, slipping it back into his pocket as if it were the morning's *Mega-News*. "It's this sort of rubbish that we're trying to avoid. We're going for the high end of the scale – classy pics, quality production and, of course, top-of-the-range screamers."

The el' pings as it reaches our floor and we step out into the block corridor. Alphonse pauses for a moment to check the address. "Three-nine-nine-eight/B, that's what we're looking for," he says to himself. "One Bartram Stump."

"What's to stop this guy having a spouse and six bawling brats?" I ask as we head off in search of the apartment. "I mean, you ain't just gonna be able to walk out with him in front of his whole drokking family."

"Research. The bosses are not only looking for photogenic bods that are gonna look good carved up for the camera, they get us to investigate their personal backgrounds: find out if they've got next of kin or many friends, see if it's gonna be noticed if they disappear. Actors have a habit of going where the work is, so it's not unknown for them to just up and leave one day, 'specially if we leave enough evidence to point the authorities in that direction. We target the ones that are living alone, preferably new to the city, that ain't gonna be missed in a hurry."

"Have any of them ever been investigated?"

"Occasionally a name crops up on the Tri-D as having vanished, but cits go missing all the time. Judges got bigger problems than chasing round after errant actors." He stops. "Wait here." He flattens himself against the corridor wall and slides along to a junction, where up on the corner of the ceiling a CCTri-D camera is operating. He reaches into his pocket and retrieves a small canister, spraying the contents in front of the camera's lens, then he looks back at me and motions for me to follow. When I join him, he murmurs, "Freezed the circuitry. It'll drokk with its time delay. Don't want PSU seeing who Stump's visitors were."

We continue down another corridor until we halt in front of a door. "Here we are," Alphonse says. "Let me do the talking at first, OK? I wanna make sure we don't spook him too early."

I nod. I can feel myself clenching and unclenching my fists, my palms damp with perspiration.

Alphonse knocks briskly. Moments later we hear movement behind the door before it slowly opens, a head peering round the frame cautiously. For a second, the citizen looks bemused, then recognition lights up in his eyes, and he pulls the door wide. All he's wearing is his dressing gown.

"Alphonse! How're you doing?" He reaches out and shakes my partner's hand vigorously. "Long time no see."

"It's been a while, Bart," Alphonse acknowledges, that slick smile spreading across his face. "We were in the neighbourhood, thought we'd drop by."

Stump's attention turns to me and he curiously gives me the once-over. The guy's got matinee idol looks written all over him: tanned complexion, square jaw, thick, dark hair that might or might not be a wig, a smooth forehead showing evidence of several rejuve jobs, pearly white teeth and bright blue eyes. He seems vaguely familiar in a way that suggests I might've seen him in a vidvert recently or staring down from some advertising hoarding; a commercial for toothpaste, maybe, or aftershave. Something in which a gimp grins at himself in the mirror a lot.

Alphonse makes the introductions. "Bart, this is Pete Trager. He's the new casting manager over at the studio. We were discussing a shortlist of names for the next feature, and yours cropped up. I reckon it's been too long since the Stumpster has been wowing the ladies in the aisles."

"Really? A new production?" he says eagerly, turning from me to Alphonse and back again, his naked ambition embarrassingly plain to see.

"No one nails that gruff Mega-City Judge charm the way you do. Ain't that right, Pete?"

I nod, trying to generate enthusiasm. "That's the truth."

"Well," Stump says conspiratorially, modesty evidently a fairly alien concept, "to be honest, I feel playing a Judge slightly beneath me. Not much personality or motivation to work on, you understand. And I always feel a bit unclean conveying fascism so convincingly. But I do so love a challenge." Before I can piledrive my fist into his arrogant face, he adds excitedly: "You better come in and tell me all about it." He ushers us across the threshold and shuts the door behind him.

His apartment gives off more than a whiff of pretty poster-boy fallen on desperate times: the furniture looks ratty, the remains of take-out food is lying on the floor, and the walls are smothered in stills from movies, faded publicity pics and yellowing cuttings. In nearly all of them, Bartram Stump is flashing those dazzling teeth, either at paparazzi as he's snapped with a succession of beautiful women attending some premiere, or in character as he's pouring on the charm to his co-star. The general effect is headache-inducing, as if I'm standing in a hall of mirrors with reflections on every side.

Stump is babbling away to Alphonse. "Grud, when was the last time you required my thespian services? Must've been *Strat-Bat Out of Hell*... That was, what, a couple of years ago? I must say, it would be very interesting working with you guys again. What made you think of me?"

"Let's just say you got the perfect face for our next leading role," Alphonse replies, reaching into his jacket. "Now can you do me a favour?"

"Anything–"

Alphonse levels a gun at the actor. "Shut the drokk up and do what you're told." He beckons me over with a gesture of his head. "Trager, grab him."

Stump is backing away, a look of shock painted on his perfect features as I move forward and put an arm round his throat. He struggles feebly, but doesn't put up much opposition, his eyes are fixed on the pistol in Alphonse's hand.

"What... what's this... all about?" he stutters, an inflexion in his voice suggesting he's hoping that this is a game, or an impromptu role-play session, where his ability to look scared is being tested. If I was a director, I'd say he was doing a pretty drokkin' good job.

"Don't speak unless I tell you to, OK?" Alphonse warns, to which Stump nods in agreement. "OK. Now, Catalyst has a new policy on hiring actors, in which we gotta see you're capable of following orders. Can't have a loose cannon, doing what he likes, can we? Thing about making movies is that everybody has to pull in the same direction. You still wanna be in the movies, don't you, Bart?"

He nods again, fervently. Watching this guy, I realise how easy it's been for the drokkers at the studio to find victims for their sick photo shoots, dangle the promise of fame and fortune, of their name up in lights, and the poor saps are queuing up at the door, happy to be exploited for a fleeting chance at stardom. Whilst they might have known they were selling something of themselves for the lure of the silver screen, few could've expected that they'd end up sacrificing everything for that one big shot at immortality.

"I guarantee, all eyes are gonna be on you. Now, I want you to pack some clothes, 'cause you're gonna be going away for a few days. Anybody likely to come checking up on you?"

"M-my ex-wife. She'll want to get in touch if she hasn't got her monthly payment–"

"OK, then you write her a note. Say something about a job that's come up across town that you couldn't pass up an' you'll get in touch when you're back. Hey, you're the creative, I'm sure you can come up with something."

"Look, what the hell is this all about?" Stump says, trying to inject some authority into his voice. "This is all very unorthodox. You can't just rough me up and drag me somewhere against my will. Is this some kind of method acting procedure, where the actor has to go through the same treatment as the character?"

"Bart." Alphonse cuts through the actor's protestations like a las-knife. "I won't give you another warning. No questions. Just do what you're told."

"Drokk you, and drokk your loathsome pet bulldog here." He struggles to look round at me, and spits, a globule of phlegm pattering against my cheek. "I'm not going to be threatened by a couple of petty thugs." He kicks against me weakly and tries to wrestle free from my grip; with my arm still wrapped around his throat, I pull back hard, cutting off his air supply.

Surrounded by this joker's rampant and misplaced egotism, his puerile handsome blandness looming in from every side like I'm trapped inside his self-obsession, something snaps in my head and I suddenly want to give this deluded drokker a taste of reality. A darkness descends as I increase the pressure until the choking rasp emerging from his mouth ceases altogether and his hands flutter up to my arm in a feeble attempt to wrest it away.

I hear my name being said and the shadows at the edge of my vision begin to disperse as I glance up at Alphonse and see him mouthing at me to stop. I release Stump and he falls to his knees, coughing and spluttering. I edge away from him, a numbness replacing the rage.

Stump makes a gagging noise as he forces oxygen back into his lungs, and gradually words begin to filter through. "Please... don't hurt me... I'll do anything... Don't hurt me..." He doesn't raise his gaze from the carpet, keeping his head bowed as if in supplication.

"No more arguments, OK?" Alphonse says softly.

Stump nods, as meek as a lamb after that, his spirit broken. He silently packs a couple of holdalls, then sits at his desk and composes a short note, which he shows to Alphonse for his approval. My partner gives it the nod, then instructs me to tidy the place up.

"Hey, I ain't clearin' away his shit," I say without thinking, pointing to the dirty dishes piled up in the sink and the takeaway boxes stacked on top of one another next to the actor's armchair.

"You'll do what you're drokkin' told," Alphonse rumbles, the threat so implicit in his voice that even Stump looks up at him, fearful. He checks himself and says more quietly, "This is a disappearance job. You think the Judges are gonna think he went of his own accord if everything's left as it was? This place is gonna stink of a kidnap."

"I'd be surprised if they smell anything over the reek of that sink," I mutter.

"Rubber gloves are over there," Alphonse replies. "Get to work."

Grudgingly, I set to giving the apartment a polish. I know this is all part of the test, pushing me to my limit with menial tasks, but going elbows-deep in someone else's mess particularly yanks my chain. It's times like this that I feel like telling the drokker just who exactly I am and see him crawl through shit for a change, but I control my temper and swallow my pride, letting him feel he's still the boss. For every greasy plate I stack, I visualise the moment when I take the spugger down.

Once the chores are done, we're ready to go. Stump looks shellshocked, like he's retreated into himself, and he dumbly follows Alphonse's lead as he picks up his bags. I try to summon some kind of guilt for nearly killing the guy, but it's surprisingly hard to find, as if my reserves of empathy have run dry.

Alphonse hands me a hood. "Blur mask," he says. "Don't want the street cameras catching our faces with him." He turns to Stump. "OK, let's move out. I'm gonna be right behind you and the gun is gonna be lodged in your spine, so no funny stuff." He gives me a wink. "Don't want to ruin your performance."

I'm standing alone in an empty studio lot – which I'm pretty sure was where I was taken to by the goons from the bathroom at Tommy's – watching over Stump, who's been tied to a battered old chair, and I feel like I'm floating above myself, watching and wondering what in the name of all that's holy I've got myself into.

In the bright, white glare of the spotlights, I can see dark stains on the floor and scrape marks where a number of heavy objects have been dragged. There's a trolley parked next to Stump and upon it are several metallic instruments that sparkle in the light. Amongst them are some of the torture devices I snagged off the Danskys and passed on to DuNoye. The stench of death is everywhere in this place. Grud only knows how many have been slaughtered here.

A groan breaks the silence; Stump has already been beaten unconscious once, when he attempted to resist being strapped down, and now his bloodied form is stirring. I study him and it reminds me of how I was in that position not long ago. As his swollen eyes open and appeal to me for help I turn away.

"Are we ready to start?" a voice from the shadows says, and DuNoye emerges from the darkness with Alphonse tagging along beside him.

"He's coming round," I reply quietly, my throat like sandpaper.

"Excellent." The lawyer looks at me. "And Mr Trager, Alphonse says you acquitted yourself well with Mr Stump's retrieval. You seem to show to a remarkable propensity for violence, which is always gratifying to see in an employee."

I don't answer but try to look flattered by the compliment nonetheless.

"All we await now is our talented photographer," DuNoye says theatrically, turning to the blackness beyond the circle of light. "Ramona, is everything set?"

"Don't wet your pants, Vandris," I hear just before a stunningly beautiful woman in her early twenties joins us out of the gloom. My heart freefalls. Despite the casualness of her clothes, she exudes an authority and confidence that's utterly magnetic. Short, blonde hair frames an exquisite face, with blue eyes magnified by delicate round glasses. Small, kissable lips are offset by a flawless complexion. She has a couple of cameras hanging around her pale neck, the straps dividing her breasts. I try hard not to stare, but I can sense her gaze upon me. "This is the new guy, huh?"

"Indeed," DuNoye answers. "This will be Mr Trager's first session."

"Well, as long as he doesn't screw up the shots," she says, removing a lens cap.

"Oh no," he says. "I think he's going to be quite a natural." DuNoye walks past me, his feet *tip-tapping* on the hard studio floor, and stops beside the trolley. He pauses in thought, glances once at Stump, then picks up what looks like a miniature wrench. Smiling, he holds it out to me and says: "Perhaps you'd like to begin, Mr Trager? Why don't we start with the teeth?"

TEN

The groans seemed to echo from the very walls, as if the building had been passively soaking up the pain, misery and madness it had witnessed over the years. As he passed across the threshold, Dredd reasoned that this structure had probably seen more human degradation and mental agony than most, and wouldn't be surprised to discover that its history still resonated within its corridors, like a psychic illness that had permeated the rockcrete.

The psychiatric Iso-Block in Sector 42 was one of the oldest in the city, and it had housed a good number of the Big Meg's most dangerously insane perps. Its age meant that its technological resources were a long way behind the more recent kook cubes that had sprung up in its lifetime, but the wardens and med-staff here didn't pretend that they were attempting to cure their charges. They were simply locking them away where they couldn't cause any trouble. The prisoners were kept sedated and occasionally recommended for lobotomies if drugs proved insufficient, but as a rule, once a crim entered the Iso-Block it was unlikely they would see daylight again. Futsies that had possibly suffered only a temporary plunge into madness were usually sent to one of the more progressive units where they received counselling. This place was for those who had insanity deeply ingrained into their brains, and who had retreated into some dark centre at the heart of their being from which there was no return.

It was an unnerving environment, there was no question of that, Dredd thought, as he headed into the bowels of the building. The disembodied cries that drifted from beyond the locked doors of the iso-cubes were almost ethereal, and as he passed a pair of wardens struggling with an inmate, he caught the feral look on the perp's face, virtually all trace of humanity gone. The lawman wondered how long a sane man could stay in here before he too lost his mind, succumbing to the sickness that seemed to pervade the air.

Dredd found the records department and entered a small office occupied by a single elderly Judge. It was many years since he'd last seen active duty, and he had taken this administrative post rather than go on the Long Walk. But despite his balding, wrinkled features, his eyes belied a sharp mind still at work.

"Dredd," he said. "Don't often see you round these parts."

"Denton," Dredd acknowledged. "I need to pick your brains."

The old man smiled. "Well, you've come to the right place. Picking apart brains is our specialty."

"What do you know about Erik Rejin?"

"Rejin..." Denton pondered. "The name sounds familiar. He's some kind of bigshot, isn't he?"

Dredd nodded. "He's the reclusive head of a film studio called Catalyst. Hasn't been seen in public for the past two decades. I'm investigating his company for some kind of criminal activity."

"So what brings you here?"

"I've been trying to check up on this creep, but there's some troubling gaps in MAC's data. His early years seem fairly straightforward; his family made a fortune in kneepads, I don't know if you remember them? They were behind the Supafit range."

Denton nodded. "They had the Justice Department contract for a while."

"That's right. There doesn't seem to be anything suspicious in the first half of his life, he lived with his parents and brothers, Troy and Bennett, on the huge family estate. Then came the Apocalypse War and their home takes a direct hit."

"It wiped them out?"

"All of them except Erik. Now, this is where the details go hazy. He vanishes for a substantial period of time, at least a year, I think. MAC has no record of his movements during this interlude. When he reappears – or, at least, when our files make mention of him again – he's inherited the kneepad business, which he goes on to sell off eighteen months later, and then founds the film studio."

"So it's that gap that's interesting you?"

"I can't see how he could've got out of the city, not with the war on, and he couldn't have survived on his own. He might've been injured and it's very likely he was traumatized. The length of time he was missing seems concurrent with possibly a period spent in incarceration. I'm wondering if he was admitted to a Justice Department facility and this would've been the nearest psych-unit."

"But if he was in here, then the records would be on MAC."

"Exactly. That's what's worrying me. It seems too convenient that this bracket of his life has just disappeared into a hole."

"Hold on, I'll enter his name into our inmate database, just in case." Denton tapped at his keyboard and waited while the computer completed its search. "Nothing." The old man stroked his chin. "There are quite a few gaps in our data, Dredd. Wars, Necropolis, Judgement Day, they've all destroyed important records. It's not surprising that a handful of cits fall through the cracks."

"This seems more... intentional to me" Dredd replied. "Targeted. If we'd lost all the details on Rejin, then you could put it down to a glitch in the system. But just to have the details missing for one year strikes me that somebody is covering their tracks."

"You think the data's been erased off MAC?" Denton asked, incredulous. "To do that would mean someone with very high-level clearance had accessed the files. In other words, somebody within Justice Department."

"I'm aware of the seriousness of the implications," Dredd said sternly. "But until I'm proved wrong, that is my suspicion." He glanced at the elderly Judge's terminal. "Can you run an ident match? You can grab a photo of Rejin from before the war off MAC and cross-reference it with your intake from 2104."

Denton did as he was asked, pasting a citizen ID of Rejin on one half of his screen, then instructed his machine to compile any similarities from kook cube detainees that had been processed in that year. Hundreds of faces flickered past as the computer churned through its records: eyes, noses, mouths, all compared and dismissed.

"How old was he when he lost his family?" Denton enquired.

"Late thirties by my reckoning. Thirty-eight, thirty-nine. He was single – didn't marry until a while after his reappearance."

The computer flashed up a message to say it had finished its trawl and all it had was a partial match. The visage it displayed to the right of Rejin's was of a wild-eyed man of roughly the right age, but thinner around the cheeks and with a heavily lined complexion. The screen said his name was Marcellus Blisko.

"Could be him," Denton mused. "Grief and madness can change a man's appearance quite severely." He scrolled through the perp sheet. "Hmm, that's odd. The charges against Blisko, the reasons for him being sentenced here, don't seem to have been entered." He read further, then peered up at Dredd, an uneasy expression passing over his face. "And he was... released."

"When?"

"About eleven months into his stay here. Just says that his release had been approved, but not by whom. That's extraordinary. Next to no one gets freed from here. They're all lifers."

"This was over twenty years ago. Who would've handled the paperwork?"

"At that time, it was probably Judge Warnton. He died a few years back. Heart attack." Denton ran a hand over his hairless pate. "I just don't understand... He was such a stickler for detail. Can't think why there's so little info entered on this Blisko character."

"Unless it's been removed, like the data on MAC?"

The elderly Judge shot a look at Dredd. "Not on my watch. I'm the only one in this Iso-Block that can access these records."

"So we're looking at an outside job," Dredd said. "Some creep hacks into the Justice Department mainframe and removes anything incriminating relating to Rejin."

"Jovus, they'd have to be good to get into our system."

"I think they're getting help from on high, the same way Rejin did twenty years ago. Somebody's covering for him. A friend." Dredd turned and headed for the door. "Thanks for the help, Denton. I'll call in the Tek boys, see if they can run a source program on your terminal and follow the trail back to the hacker."

Meanwhile, Dredd thought, I'm going back to where it all started.

Councillor Matheson Peat sat at his desk in his office in the chambers of commerce, staring at a blank computer screen. He'd been motionless for the past hour, his expressionless face bathed in the green glow of the monitor. He was meant to be composing another of his audience-pleasing speeches – about how Mega-City One needed leaders with vision to drive it forward into the next century, about every citizen facing up to their responsibilities of being part of the most progressive society in the western world, blah, blah, blah – but the words would not come.

Normally, this kind of oratory was his bread and butter, and he'd delivered variations on the theme more times than he could remember. It was a reliable old stand-by, and it went down well with Justice Department. But recently, those phrases that would slip out of his mouth so naturally now seemed hollow and desultory, nothing more than insincere platitudes. He could not summon the enthusiasm to once more praise the city and its custodians without wishing to expose his words for the overcooked mix of hyperbole and lies that they were.

This metropolis was not some sparkling testament to mankind's indomitable spirit any more than the Judges were an even-handed force of truth and righteousness. The reality was that the people were victims, trapped in an industrialised nightmare, bullied into submission by an unelected regime that crushed democracy at every turn. It used every trick up its sleeve to hang on to its precious power, discrediting – even quietly removing, if the rumours were to be believed – those that dared to criticise its authority, and resorted to extreme levels of violence to demonstrate its belief in supremacy through strength. If he stood up now in front of a collection of fellow politicians and judicial representatives and spouted his usual media-friendly soundbites, he felt he would choke on them.

Needless to say, Councillor Matheson Peat's mind was otherwise occupied.

He couldn't concentrate, his thoughts constantly returning to the events of the past couple of weeks. He felt his carefully planned, expertly arranged life was spinning wildly out of control. First the farce at the Fred Quimby opening, then the murder investigation after the unearthing of the body dump beneath the foundations of Liz Short, and now irate phone calls from friends about Dredd snooping around Catalyst and making menacing noises.

It was too much. It was threatening to destabilise everything he had spent his political life working towards, and even now he could sense his intricate network of colleagues and acquaintances coming apart at the seams.

It had been bad enough to allow a star of Vanessa Indigo's standing to be put in a position of danger – the attempted assassination was broadcast all over the city to a dumbstruck Tri-D audience – but questions were also being asked about his working methods following the Short case. His Phoenix Campaign had never had so much negative publicity, and where once his buildings were considered the desirable blocks to be seen in, now it was being alleged that they were constructed on unsafe land. Despite going on a charm offensive after the story broke in the press, he could not shake the feeling that those with influence who had once given him their ear were subtly distancing themselves from him, like he was a pariah. When bad news hit, you soon found out who was prepared to stand by you, and in Peat's case he discovered the answer was not that many.

Even the celebrities, once keen to align themselves with his projects, seemed cool towards him, as if they could sense when someone's spot in the limelight was fading. They were like parasites, he thought angrily, feeding on the attention he had engineered for them, sucking the last drop of exposure they could gain from his connections before abandoning him when the reporters and photographers turned their microphones and cameras elsewhere. He didn't consider any of them close.

In truth, he used their fame to promote his policies as much as they used him to get their faces on the front of the papers, and the relationship was never anything more than pure business. But it riled him to think that they couldn't even be bothered to disguise their loathing of being too near to him, as if he were a social leper, and to come into contact with his ill fortune would spread disease-like amongst their cliques.

The damage seemed irreparable, and he felt trapped in a circle of despair that was alienating Peat from everyone around him. His girlfriend tried to reassure him that it was just a run of bad luck, and that he simply had to ride it out.

"People have bounced back from worse disasters," she had reasoned. "Aren't you always saying Mega-City One will stand tall no matter what is thrown at it? And that the city endures because the spirit of the citizens refuses to be broken? Well, if we can survive wars, invasions, despots and madmen, then you can take a few knocks and still come up smiling."

He wished he could believe her. But as sweet as her naivety was, she couldn't comprehend just how much trouble he felt he was in. He hadn't had a decent night's sleep since the problems had begun, and consequently he drifted through his waking hours like a mournful phantom, a shadow of his normal effervescent self, refusing to be comforted by Sondra, shutting her out of his dark despondency, turning her away from him.

He couldn't blame her for feeling hurt by this, and for wanting to spend as little time as possible in his company. Evenings in their apartment were silent, dour episodes. The frustrations and anxieties inside Peat grew more malignant and bitter the more he brooded on them, and he barely noticed if Sondra was there or not. Peat suspected that Sondra was seeking solace with the apprentice taxidermist down the hall, but he could not bring himself to feel jealous or aggrieved by her infidelities. And this lack of emotion made him start to question his own sanity.

Was he that hollow, to watch deadened as his life fell apart and not attempt to save it? Had he been seduced by the fame game, the need to present an image, to the point where that was all he had left? He wondered if he truly felt passionate about anything, or if it was all just spin to keep him in the public eye, empty words and gestures signifying nothing. He was alone at the centre of his world, and nobody could touch him.

Through his haze of self-pity, Peat suddenly realised that his intercom was buzzing. He sighed and flipped the switch. "Yes?"

"Judge Dredd to see you, Mr Peat," his secretary said sullenly. Keisha too had been affected by his moroseness these past few days, struggling to get him to make decisions on council matters or agree to meetings. She was increasingly having to make excuses for his non-attendance at various functions, and was clearly getting tired of mollycoddling him.

"Send him in," Peat replied, but the lawman was through the door before he'd finished speaking. He stood before the councillor as rigid and uncompromising as a granite statue. Although Peat's stomach tied itself up in knots in the presence of the Judge, he felt anger towards him too, for all the misery he had brought down on him, for almost single-handedly destroying his life and career. He shouldn't be able to get away with it. Peat wasn't some drug-dealing scumbag who offered nothing to society but a cheap hit. He was a well-respected citizen, who'd fought for his city, and he was damned if this jumped-up fascist bullyboy was going to intimidate him.

"Judge Dredd," he said through gritted teeth. "To what do I owe this pleasure?"

"I'd like to ask you some further questions, councillor. I trust you can find the time?"

"I thought I told you the last time we spoke, Dredd, that you had no right to treat me like a common criminal. I have done nothing wrong and for you to keep hounding me like this is really quite unacceptable–"

"As I told you, councillor," Dredd cut in, "you remain a suspect in an ongoing multiple-murder inquiry. Until the case is satisfactorily closed, then I will decide the course of the investigation. Now, we can either talk here or I'll pull you down to the local Sector House for a thorough interrogation."

Peat's face reddened. "Th-this is atrocious! You have no right–"

Dredd had heard enough. He strode up towards the councillor's desk and wrapped his fist in the man's shirt, yanking him over the desktop towards him. The pompous windbag popped sweat immediately, his skin draining of colour as quickly as it had flushed. "And I am drokking tired of hearing your whining, creep. Now if you don't start being a little more cooperative, I'm gonna arrest you for withholding evidence and recommend you for truth drug administration, deep-brain scan, the works. If the only way to get you to talk is to cut you open and physically extract the information, then believe me we'll do it."

Peat whimpered like a kicked dog and Dredd released him, letting him slump back into his chair. He ran a shaking hand over his face, then whispered "What do you want to know?"

"Your association with Erik Rejin."

The councillor stared. "Erik? H-he's a business colleague, that's all. What's he got to do with–"

"I'll ask the questions," Dredd interrupted. "You have an interest in Catalyst Productions, don't you?"

"I'm one of the shareholders, yes. I've helped the company secure funding, a lot of which comes from Justice Department, I might add."

"I'm aware of our contribution to the propaganda market. I'm more interested in how you came to first meet Citizen Rejin."

Peat looked uneasy. "I don't recall..."

"I'm going to keep this simple, councillor," Dredd said evenly and retrieved a small device from one of his belt pouches, placing it down on the desk between them. "That is a lie-detector; what we Judges call a birdie. As the name suggests, it tells me when a suspect is not being entirely honest. Now, you're going to tell me everything about your first meeting with Erik Rejin and every beep I hear from the birdie is a year you're going to be spending in the cubes. Do I make myself clear?"

Peat opened his mouth, then shut it again. Eventually, he nodded, cleared his throat and began to speak.

"Down! Stay down!" Peat ordered as his squad came under heavy fire. The Sovs had them pinned. Their tanks were moving up on Barrymore, crushing any resistance before them, and ground troops were mopping up in their wake. Peat had seen four or five Judges on Lawmasters leading the charge against the invaders vaporised by just one shell, catching them dead centre. Once the smoke cleared, all that was left of Mega-City's finest was a tangle of wreckage at the base of a huge crater. He did not hold out much hope for his Citi-Def unit while they were in the open as they did not have the ammunition to enter into a stand-up fight with Sov artillery. Hit and run, that's all they could do. Guerrilla warfare.

He looked around at his men, crouching low behind the ruins they were using as cover. Not that long ago there'd been twice the number in his squad, which had originally operated out of Charlton Heston Block, and over the course of the past few days, the unit had been gradually whittled down. Run-ins with those drokkers over in neighbouring Mike Moore had caused severe casualties even before the whole city went ballistic, and now, including himself, there were just five left of the Crazy Heston Frontliners.

At first they'd directed all their energies in defending their block, but when they saw the mushroom clouds blossoming on the horizon, they realised that a new enemy was taking the conflict to a whole different level. They might have had their differences with Mike Moore, but upon discovering those commie rats from East-Meg One were looking to take over not just their homes but the entire metropolis, suddenly this fresh target seemed much more worthy. His men hadn't needed convincing – they'd been fighting solidly for forty-eight hours, but their aggression was undiminished and they took to this latest adversary with renewed vigour.

Peat had led his unit proudly into battle with a foe befitting the stature of the Frontliners, but it soon dawned on him just how much he had underestimated the Sov armour. The squad's small arms were barely making a dent in the East-Meg onslaught, and all the time his unit was losing soldiers in every skirmish. They could not afford to take any more casualties.

"What do you think, sir?" his lieutenant, Mattocks, asked, squatting down next to Peat. He absent-mindedly scratched at a las-scar on his cheek.

"We can't stay here," Peat replied, watching the tanks advance through his binox. "Won't be able to get through Sov infantry, and certainly can't hold 'em off. Gonna have to retreat." The commander pointed out a route through the collapsed masonry of nearby buildings. "We'll have to hotfoot it across country, find somewhere we can lie low. Tell the men to get ready to go on my word."

Mattocks nodded and shuffled off on his belly to pass on the order. Peat continued to watch the artillery rumble down the street towards them, black smudges against the boiling sky. They needed a diversionary tactic to keep the Sovs occupied while his squad made a break for it. He spied an overhang, part of a half-demolished structure that lined the route the tanks were taking, and beckoned to Rawlinson who was carrying the RPG.

"Just before the nearest tank is under it, aim for that ledge," Peat instructed. "It's gonna be tight. We're gonna have to wait until they're fairly close before we hit 'em, but we need a smokescreen to cover our escape."

Rawlinson understood. He sighted his weapon on the overhang and waited for the mobile armour to move closer. For interminable seconds, they all crouched motionless, listening to the ever-present thunder of the tank tracks draw nearer. Peat looked at the faces of his men as they anticipated the order to move: some had their eyes screwed shut, others unconsciously fingered their rifles, heads bowed. The noise of the tanks seemed to fill the whole world, the screeching of metal getting louder moment by moment. Then, suddenly, there was a burst of flame, a rush of air, and the RPG on Rawlinson's shoulder bucked in his grip as he fired. There was a fraction of a pause before the explosion split the air, throwing chunks of the building in all directions.

"Go!" Peat yelled, and the unit stood as one, dashing for the escape route. The commander glanced at the advancing tanks and saw with some satisfaction that the rubble had put one of the vehicles out of action, rockcrete piled on top of it. Dust billowed before them, concealing their movements for a few vital seconds. The rattle of gunfire emerged from the clouds of debris and smoke, but the Sovs were aiming wild, evidently unable to see their attackers. Peat patted Rawlinson on the back and told him to get moving since they wouldn't have long before the East-Meg army was on their tail.

The Citi-Def squad moved fast, clambering as quickly as they could through the ruins, but the few minutes' grace they had bought did not get them far before they heard the Sovs shouting to each other and shots began closing in. They had been spotted. A shell arced in the air and detonated to their left, throwing out a lethal rain of shrapnel, and Peat watched helplessly as Mattocks took several hits in the face and chest, his uniform reduced to bloody rags. The lieutenant turned and unleashed a furious burst of fire at their pursuers, impotently trying to channel his rage before falling dead to the ground.

They had to find a hiding place. Peat looked around desperately for somewhere to head to, then he realised that they were running parallel to the perimeter boundary of some sort of estate. Chances were it was big enough for his squad to lose themselves in. He shouted to his men to find a gap in the iron fence. Fortunately, the area had been subjected to intense bombardment, and there were big enough rents along the border of the property for them to squeeze through. They stumbled onto crater-riddled land and fixed their sights on the remains of a large house, which lay at the summit of a shallow hill. Peat glanced back and could see no sign of the Sovs so he felt reasonably confident that they'd given the invaders the slip.

As they drew closer to the mansion, they saw that it must've taken the full brunt of an airburst. The roof had collapsed in places, the walls were blackened, the windows mostly shattered. It looked derelict.

Topley whistled appreciatively. "Must've been some pad, once."

"I think I recognise this place," Peat replied, frowning. "I'm sure I've seen it on the news..."

"Looks like a celebrity shitheap," Marriott said.

"Well, whatever it was, it's our hideout for the time being," Peat murmured, heading towards the front door, dangling off its hinges. "But we'll scope it out, make sure there's no nasty surprises waiting inside." He signalled his unit to follow. "Keep 'em peeled."

They entered slowly, flipping on the torches attached to their rifles to penetrate the gloom. All the power seemed to be out, and the destruction wrought on the inside seemed as extensive as that on the exterior. A grand sweeping staircase led up to the first floor, but it was blocked by a huge shard of the roof that had fallen in. They moved cautiously through the hallway, checking as best they could each room they came across, dust dancing in their beams, the silence enveloping them like a shroud. Whoever had lived here had had plenty of money and taste, the expensive works of art now lying shattered beneath their feet.

"You reckon the residents have fled?" Rawlinson asked.

"Seems likely, if they're not buried under a ton of rubble," Peat answered.

"This place safe, d'you think?" Marriott added, swinging his torch up at the exposed rafters. "One strong breeze and the place could come down like a house of cards."

Peat was wondering the same thing himself. "Can't say for sure. We'll only stay for as long as we have to. Any sign–"

A moan echoed through the structure as if the mansion itself was shifting on its foundations. At first, Peat thought it was the wind, but then it came again, louder, and there was no mistaking the sound's origin as human. His men eyed each other nervously, shouldering their guns, and turned to their commander who put a finger to his lips and motioned for them to spread out. Peat cocked an ear and tried to follow the source of the noise, which seemed to be getting more insistent. He led his team into what had once been the kitchen and stopped, waiting for the groan to come again. When it did, he peered down at his feet.

"Trapdoor," he whispered, gesturing to the opening set in the floor that was partially covered with heavy blocks of rockcrete. "Must lead to a basement. Marriott, Rawlinson, help me clear this debris, then on three, open it. Topley, keep me covered, but don't shoot unless you have to."

The men lifted the rubble clear then stationed themselves around the trapdoor, looking at their superior expectantly. Peat counted down silently, then nodded. Marriott and Rawlinson tore open the door and a crimson blur exploded from the opening, throwing itself at Peat.

They toppled backwards, grappling at Topley's feet, who tried to sight his gun on the attacker but couldn't get a clear fix. It seemed to be a man, but he was coated almost entirely in blood and he was making a keening whine like a wounded animal. Topley reached down and got his arm around the maniac's throat, lifting him off Peat. Close up, he could smell the man's foetid stench and realised that what he thought was a mewl was actually a breathless litany.

"Kill them all... kill them all... kill them all..."

"Drokker's raving," Marriott said, helping Topley as the man struggled in his grasp. "Grud, he stinks too." He glanced at his CO. "You all right, skip?"

Peat got to his feet, rubbing his head where it had cracked against the kitchen floor. "I'll live." He got his hand under the lunatic's jaw, lifting his face into the light so he could get a better look. "Must've been trapped under there for days, poor spugger." He looked closer into the man's eyes, wild with fear and madness, then Peat spat into his hand and wiped away some of the dirt and blood caked to the guy's skin. A gasp escaped his lips. "Jovus drokk!"

Marriott looked at Peat. "Chief? What is it?"

The commander rubbed away more of the grime. "I've seen him before. This place... I thought I recognised it. It-it's the Rejin estate. You know, the billionaires?"

"The kneepad people?" Topley asked.

"Exactly. My grud, this guy must be one of the sons. Erik, is it?" The man moaned louder in response. "They've been all over the press in the past. The Rejins are one of the richest families in the city."

"So where's the rest of them?" Marriott wanted to know.

"Uh, sir?" Rawlinson piped up. He was still standing by the open trapdoor, shining his torch into the darkness below, his face pale. "You might want to take a look at this..."

"He had partially consumed them," Peat said, gazing at his hands folded before him on his desk. "Can you imagine what that did to his mind? Trapped with the bodies of his parents and brothers, crazed with grief and hunger, he'd been forced to cannibalise his own flesh and blood. When we found him, he was covered in them, head to foot, and he was raging, *raging* against the Sovs that had murdered his family."

Dredd stood before the councillor, impassive. "And so you took him to a psych unit under an assumed name.

You were working an angle already, weren't you? You saw an important future ally and you helped protect him."

"I was a businessman before I was a politician, Dredd," Peat replied simply. "Here was the sole heir to one of the largest kneepad manufacturers in the city. I felt I could help both our causes if we kept this as discreet as possible."

"How did you get him out of the kook cubes?"

"The company lawyers, plus some significant leaning on certain elements within Justice Department by myself and my colleagues. We convinced them he could be kept under control."

"But he couldn't, could he? You released a dangerously insane man because it made sense to your career. What did he do? Fund your election campaign?"

Peat stood and crossed to the window, his back to Dredd. He sighed and rested his forehead against the glass. "I... I thought Erik deserved more. He was too important to be left rotting in some padded cell. I believed his energies could be directed into something more... worthwhile." He paused, then added, raising his voice, "For grud's sake, Dredd, this was twenty years ago."

"The Law is the Law. You used Rejin the same way you use everyone else, to climb the greasy pole and to increase your own publicity. And you attempted to cover your tracks by trying to erase the past. How did you hack into MAC's files?"

Peat turned and looked Dredd straight in the eye. "I'm not saying any more."

"Fair enough. We'll talk further down at the Sector House."

"No," Peat replied, reaching into his jacket and removing a small blaster, pointing it at the Judge. "I'm going nowhere with you."

Dredd stared him down, unfazed. "Don't be ridiculous, Peat. You're only making things worse."

"How can they possibly be worse?" he replied, his eyes watering. He sniffed, then shouted "Keisha!" Seconds later, his secretary entered, glanced at the two men, then spied the revolver, her jaw dropping. Before she could speak, the councillor reached over and pulled her to him, his left arm snaking around her throat. He placed the gun barrel against the side of her head. She whimpered and he shushed her quiet.

"Now, I'm walking out of here, Dredd," he declared. "Try to stop me and you'll have blood on your hands too."

ELEVEN

I'm sitting in a small room, adjacent to the studio set, my eyes closed, trying to control my breathing. In the darkness behind my lids, all I can see is blood and a face twisted soundlessly in pain, as if the images are burned onto my retina. No matter how much I shake my head or pound my temples with my fists, nothing can dispel them.

They're imprinted there, indelible, and a part of my mind not paralysed with shock at what I've just taken part in is terrified that they will never fade, like a stain on the inside of my skull. I fear that every time I shut my eyes, I'm going to see the gore-streaked features of Bartram Stump, dying in the most perverse and brutal manner imaginable. And I was the one who was responsible for his horrifying injuries because I had no way of backing out of this horrible mess this group of callous, monstrous perps have dragged me into. It's going to replay in the theatre of my mind like my very own private snuff movie on a permanent loop: star, director and audience all in one, anguish and revulsion keeping the spools turning.

I open my eyes and stare at the ceiling, wanting a hit of anything – zizz, alcohol, even a sugar rush would do – to destroy my nerve endings and render me numb. I want to crack open my head and rip out the darkness festering inside because I know it's only going to grow and grow before it consumes me entirely. What's scaring me even more than the acts I've just performed on another human being is the voice I'm starting to hear asking why I'm being such a hypocrite.

You knew what you were getting into, it's saying. Nobody forced you into anything. Don't act all mortified about what you've witnessed. The truth of the matter is that you took some gruddamn pleasure from it. The first time you met Stump, didn't you want to drive your fist into that handsome, bland face? Haven't you always longed to destroy everything that offends you with its puerility? Look me in the eye and tell me you didn't get a thrill from the power you wielded, released from the moral obligations of being a Judge. You embraced the black, cancerous heart that pulses inside you and allowed it to blossom. It's always been there, don't deny it. It's right there, right at the core of who you are.

I can feel tears trickling down my cheeks and I cover my face with my hands, trying to stem their flow. I don't want to hear what this voice has got to say, it's cutting too close to the bone, but I can't escape it. If I stuffed my ears, buried my head, it wouldn't halt its condemnatory monologue.

You don't want to hear it, it replies, because you don't want to accept the unacceptable. Take a look in the mirror, pal. Come to terms with it.

"No... no..." I murmur, unaware the words are escaping from my mouth.

In answer I hear a different, female, voice. "You all right?"

I lift my head away from my hot, wet face, blinking back the tears. It takes a moment for her features to coalesce into focus, then I see Ramona peering round the door, her camera still dangling from her neck. She doesn't look concerned, merely moderately surprised to see such a reaction. She eyes me curiously as if I'm some sort of freakshow attraction. She glances back behind her briefly, then slips into the room, shutting the door after her.

"No need to ask how it was for you," she says with a little more warmth, a slight smile playing on her lips.

I do my best to straighten my appearance, wiping a hand over my tear-streaked cheeks. "Sorry," I say, clearing my throat. "Not very professional."

She leans against the wall opposite me. "No need to apologise. You wouldn't be the first guy to freak out after a session. Not everybody can do it. Lots of them think they can, but when it comes to it they lose their nerve. It takes guts and a certain strength of will."

"Sounds like you've done plenty of these... sessions."

"A fair few," she says, absent-mindedly removing her glasses and cleaning them with the edge of her T-shirt, affording me a tantalising glimpse of her pale belly. If she notices me looking, she doesn't make mention of the fact. She replaces the spectacles and fixes me with those piercing blue eyes. "Vandris seemed to think you were a natural for this kind of work. I have to say, you looked like you were in control of the situation. The best performers hit a kind of plateau, as if they're sculpting a work of art and are taken over by a... creative reverie. But the comedown can be a bitch, can't it?"

I nod, thinking that sounds like the understatement of the drokkin' century. "Doesn't it ever affect you?"

She shrugs. "I stopped being troubled by my conscience years ago. My father taught me just how transient the human form was, how the flesh was a disguise, hiding our true selves." She taps her camera. "I'm capturing the unveiling of that truth, in all its multi-coloured glory."

I feign understanding, thinking that the daughter sounds as mad as everyone else around here. Gruddamn, though, she *was* beautiful. I feel like a besotted juve, but it's worth hearing her speak just to watch the shapes her mouth makes, the way her tongue flicks against her front teeth, the movement of her slender neck.

I'm suddenly aware that *she's* studying *me*. She's looking me up and down with her photographer's eyes, trying to get the measure of me. "So how did you get involved with Vandris?" she asks.

I actually struggle for a couple of seconds to think of a credible answer. Is she really entrancing me that much that I'm incapable of lying to her? Normally, the cover stories would fly from my lips without hesitation, but for some reason the dishonesty niggles me. I stamp it down quickly. "I was just a street hustler," I reply, which is hardly a lie at all. "Another bum trying to make a living underground. I came into possession of some merchandise, which Mr DuNoye was interested in–"

"The instruments from South-Am," Ramona interrupts. "They're beautiful, aren't they? It makes such a difference, working with a craftsman's tools."

I nod queasily. "They're... unique, I'll say that. Anyway, I wanted... I don't know, to prove that I could be useful to this organisation. Maybe I felt like I needed a place to belong, that I'd been on the streets on my own for too long. Maybe it was my mercenary instincts telling me this was where the money was. Or that I recognised–"

"Kindred spirits," she finishes. "I think it was more than the lure of a quick cred that brought you to us, Mr Trager. You felt the dark pull within your soul, a craving that perhaps you did not fully understand."

I say nothing, and for the first time I can't meet her gaze. I look down at my palms, still speckled with crimson.

"I could see it in you, in your performance out there," she continues. "It's impossible to fake, you either have it or you don't. And you have it very much within you, Mr Trager. It burns, doesn't it, this cold flame that can explode into violence? Directionless, without reason... But here it can be cultured, refined, into a thing of beauty." She steps closer to me and takes my hand in hers. "Let me show you."

Ramona leads me back into the darkened studio, now empty of life. All that remains of what had taken place here is the chair lying forlornly on its side, liquid patches of shadow on the floor around it. The rest of the torturers have disappeared along with their tools of the trade, presumably to dispose of Bartram Stump's corpse in yet another chem-pit somewhere in the city.

I briefly wonder, as I follow her into a backstage corridor littered with props and costumes, just how DuNoye and his men know where to dump the bodies. They seem to have intimate knowledge of every rad hotspot into which they can dissolve the evidence. It smells to me like they're getting help from outside the organisation, and that someone is priming them on the best places to go; someone with a vested interest.

We climb a set of stairs, leaving the filmmaking apparatus in our wake, and emerge into an office area. The lights are off here too, but I can feel the brush of plush carpets beneath my feet. Ramona heads towards a door, then fishes in her trouser pocket for a key.

"This all part of Catalyst too?" I whisper, glancing around me.

She nods. "This is the business section. Vandris's office is just down there," she says, pointing vaguely behind her, "and my father's quarters... are at the far end."

She looks uncomfortable, as if she doesn't want to say anything further, and turns her attention back to the lock, twisting the key and tugging down on the handle. The door swings open and she enters first, slapping on a light that casts an eerie red glow. I follow, pulling the door shut after me.

"Your father lives here? At the studio?" I ask. Once my eyes become accustomed to the lighting, I realise it's a compact but fairly high-tech darkroom: various pieces of photographic equipment and developer chemicals line the shelves.

Most immediately striking is the plethora of pictures – mostly all of them black and white shots – tacked to the walls or hanging from makeshift washing lines. It's a grotesque gallery of suffering as men and women of a wide range of ages are caught in mid-scream, their agonies frozen for the camera. Despite the horrific nature of the photos, and it's impossible for the eye not to be drawn to them, flitting from one atrocity to the next, there's evidently a talent at work that's equally hard to ignore.

Whilst the majority of Vi-zine pics are flat and unimaginative, or grainy to the point of illegibility, these are approaching art, with a style and sense of composition that far outstrips anything I've seen before. I begin to understand now what Alphonse had been talking about when he maintained that Catalyst was going for something more upmarket, and it is clear that the driving force of the talent is Ramona Rejin. She is capturing death and creating something new from it.

"My father's family home was destroyed in the Apocalypse War," she says quietly, setting her camera down on the work surface. "He was the only survivor. After that, he was uncomfortable living alone, so he made his work his life. Catalyst is everything to him; he lives and breathes what we're doing here. And this is where I feel safest," she says gesturing around her. "Alone with my photographs."

"These pictures," I say, continuing to gaze up at the photos, genuinely impressed. "They're like nothing I've ever seen before."

"You like them?"

I pause for a moment, trying to conjure up a word that sums up my simultaneous fascination and repulsion. "They're... unforgettable. I've never seen Vi-zine shots like these before."

She pulls a face. *"Vi-zine."* She spits out the word as if it were poison. "Such a patronising and inaccurate term. It was the Judges that coined that phrase, did you know that? A catch-all expression for something they've sought to eradicate."

"Then what are you doing here?"

She shrugs. "Literally? A Pictorial Study of Human Transformation, if you want to give it a grand title. Does art need to be pigeonholed and labelled? I'm making something new here, something aficienados will not have seen before. You know the kind of rubbish that's out there on the black market."

I nod. "I've seen them."

"Pulp hackjobs like *Dismemberment Today*, *In the Flesh* and *Shreddies* – they say nothing and they offer nothing, other than a cheap voyeuristic thrill. The subjects are often vagrants, the photography is ugly, with no semblance of skill or sincerity, and they're treating their audience with a shameful disdain. However, what my father and I are doing here is creating beauty from the inbuilt flawed nature of human physicality."

"Come again?"

"Us, our bodies, are fundamentally flawed. In our minds, we're misshapen, unable to conform to the aesthetically pleasing archetype that's paraded before us on Tri-D and in the movies. We try to change ourselves, transform ourselves, but rarely to our satisfaction. The image in the mirror is never perfect. In reality, we're prone to infection and disease, constantly fighting against the defects that lead to illness and death." Her eyes glow with a preacher's zeal, sermonising what's clearly her life work. "But take apart this human jigsaw puzzle," she holds her hands to her chest, "expose the interlocking pieces and it takes on an abstract beauty. Through my photographs, I demonstrate that mankind contains an inner light so rarely seen."

The cynic in me wants to ask her to point out the artistic worth in the pic above her head showing some poor sap having the tips of his fingers sheared off, but in truth the passion in her oration is incredibly overwhelming. I feel almost dazzled by the bright flame of her self-belief. If Ramona sees her mission as unveiling our inner light, then it's shining from her right now, sparkling from her eyes and mouth.

"You're tellin' me *you're* misshapen?" I ask. "I've never seen a more perfect example of beauty." I'm laying it on a bit thick, but unusually, I'm not lying.

She looks confused for a second, then smiles to herself, lowering her gaze. In the blink of an eye, her guard is broken and she's gone from zealot to an embarrassed young woman, her cheeks flushing. Her restive fingers look for something to do and she opens the back of her camera, removing a small disk which she then plugs into a terminal.

"I promised to show you something," she says quietly.

She flicks the screen on, opens a desktop folder and scrolls through the digital photos of me participating in the torture-murder of Bartram Stump. After the fourth or fifth picture, I turn my head away, scarcely recognising the man before me, and Ramona glances sideways at me, noticing my discomfort.

"Do you see it?" she asks. "The way you wield the knife, as if it feels natural in your hand? Do you see the violence in you boiling away, looking for an outlet? You can't deny I've captured your true–"

"I'm no killer," I try to assert.

"No? Some kill because they have no choice, or do so by accident, and others do it because it's in their blood and every life they take reaffirms their identity. They kill because they can only know themselves in those final, precious moments. I would say that you're a natural born killer Mr Trager, and that you've at last found your calling."

There's still some small scrap of conscience inside me that wants to refute her theory, but maybe she's right. Maybe it's always been inside me, this ease with which I can take life, and I use the Law as an excuse to give vent to it. I could've easily gone the other way and become one more nutso mass murderer. Instead, I kill for the city; a sanctioned executioner.

"I'm capable of violence, I admit," I mutter unconvincingly, "but it's not who I *am*. It doesn't *define* me." I gesture to the photos. "Your-your audience... Who are they? What do *they* get from it?" There's a hint of desperation to the words. I feel like I'm falling apart before her, or at least, the character I've thrown up around myself is crumbling. The light blazing from her is melting it.

"We have an established client base which is growing all the time as word of mouth spreads," she replies, fixing me once again with her unwavering stare, stepping nearer. "The distribution network of Catalyst's propaganda films ensures that my pictures are shipped all over the world. All sorts of people are interested in my work. Perhaps they like to feel so close to death because it makes them closer to a higher being or something. Maybe they're drawn to taboo. The bottom line is that nobody else is doing what I'm doing. I'm breaking through boundaries."

She reaches out past me, her arm brushing my shoulder, and removes a pic from the wall of a semi-flayed face, which looks in close-up like the spread wings of a butterfly. She studies it, smiling. "Transformation, you see? We're all capable of taking on new forms." She glances up at me. "Even you, Mr Trager."

The room suddenly feels suffocating, surrounded by so much horror, and the red light is beginning to make my head ache. My hand fumbles for the door handle. "I'd better be going."

She waits until I've turned away before she speaks. "Thank you for what you said."

I pause. "Hmm?"

"The compliment. It was very sweet. You weren't just being polite?"

"No," I reply, with a short shake of my head. I still haven't actually turned back to face her for fear that she will see how much I'm trembling. My heart's pounding like crazy.

A hand alights on my arm and gently pulls me round so I'm gazing into her brilliant blue eyes once more. "My father has always taught me never to trust anyone," she says softly. "He says that everyone is steeped in lies and the truth was buried deep within. But I see in you no need for lies because the truth is so close to the surface – we've both witnessed it emerging tonight. You have demonstrated that you have nothing to hide from me."

"Ramona, I–"

"Would you like to kiss me?"

"Listen, your father…"

"He brought me up on his own when my mother died, sheltered me, instructed me as to how the world works. He taught me everything. But I'm making this decision for myself." She puts a finger to my lips briefly. "Now, answer my question."

My throat has dried up, so all I can do is nod. She smiles prettily, removes her glasses and places them on the worktop, then pulls me forward and we embrace, my hand cupping the back of her neck, my mouth locked to hers. Her skin feels wonderfully soft and smooth as my fingers trail beneath her T-shirt, caressing the small of her back and her waist. I close my eyes to shut out the frozen screams of the dead hanging above us.

I awake with a start, disorientation flooding through me until I see the curve of Ramona's back as she slumbers beside me, her shoulders imperceptibly rising and falling. We'd talked into the early hours, lying in each other's arms on the floor of the darkroom, until we drifted off into sleep.

I sit up gingerly and struggle into my clothes, careful not to disturb her. My joints protest at having been trapped in an awkward position for too long. Gently stroking her hair, I gaze down at her. In sleep, she looks just as beautiful, her lips slightly parted as she breathes lightly, the soft exhalation the only sound in the room.

I've never met anyone quite like her, the magnetic power she exudes is so powerful. It's her self-belief that's so compelling, her total conviction behind her "art" and the truths she's uncovering about the human condition.

In a city in which dumbness and moronic gullibility are the pervading traits of the population, to come across anyone as fiercely intelligent as Ramona – no matter how *disturbed* – is a moment to be celebrated and cherished. Coupled with her extraordinary beauty, the desire she evokes in me makes me ache with a need to take her away, far away, from the corrupting influence of her father's homicidal insanity. I don't know whether she can be cured of her funereal fixation, or indeed that she *wants* to be. But however this mess is resolved, I want to keep her safe from harm. With this in mind, betraying her is going to feel like slow torture from which there's no escape.

I stand and snatch a torch from the work surface, also grabbing a small camera, then cross over to the door, easing it open slowly and checking behind me that Ramona hasn't stirred. I peek out into the corridor and, discovering it empty, slip out of the room and into the shadows. My watch says its 3:30 am and I'm hoping that Catalyst goons don't habitually patrol this area. I hug the walls, my ears attuned to the silence, listening out for any sign of life, the soft carpet absorbing my footfalls. It's almost oppressively quiet, my breathing sounding unnaturally loud.

Passing an office door, I flash the torch on and catch DuNoye's name stencilled on the glass, the room beyond in darkness. I swallow nervously and try the handle but it's locked. Crouching, I slip my hand into my shoe and retrieve my Justice Department lock override, inserting it into the mechanism. Seconds later, the door clunks open. Another quick look around me to check that I'm alone then I disappear inside.

The beam of the torch highlights an expensive office with posters for studio movies on every wall. Moving across to DuNoye's desk, I pick up a couple of folders left strewn upon it and give the contents a quick look: it's mostly a list of shipments for Catalyst products, detailing quantity and destination.

Jovus, they're going everywhere. Ramona said that the Vi-zines were shipped out through the company's distribution network. If that was true then they were being sold all over the world.

The Vi-zine racket, by its very nature, is a small-scale, covert operation that deals with a highly selective client base, and I've never seen an outfit with such huge resources behind it. Catalyst must be flooding half the major cities in the world with their brand of high-quality snuff rags: Texas City, Hondo, Brit-Cit, Emerald Isle, Pan-African States... Serious numbers were being pushed out to all of them, right under their respective authorities' noses. As the propaganda flicks were coming with Justice Department approval, Customs must be rubber-stamping them automatically. The lists didn't specify customers but I have a feeling they would be held on DuNoye's computer. I'm loath to touch it, however, in case it's alarmed. This is one for the Tek-Judges to hack into once the uniforms were called in. I take a couple of quick snaps of the shipping documents as evidence. It was disturbing just how many sickos must be out there, lapping this material up.

Exiting the office, I pad further down the corridor, discovering meeting rooms or supply cupboards containing shelves groaning with glossy torture mags. *Click, click*, goes the shutter on my camera. I poke my head round the door of an empty edit suite, the bank of monitors gleaming in the torchlight.

The corridor ends in a large, ornate door, which I can only assume leads to Erik Rejin's quarters. I place my ear to the wood but hear nothing on the other side. I weigh up the choice: if I'm discovered breaking into Rejin's rooms, then it's game over. No amount of fast-talking is going to convince them I don't have a suspicious agenda. But this is the gruddamn dragon's lair, the point where all roads have led to. Dredd and Hendry instructed me to explode Catalyst from the top down, and finding proof that the big cheese is fully aware of what his company is up to will be enough to close the whole operation down for good. There's no argument. I unlock the door and tentatively twist the handle, wincing at the smallest creak.

Playing my torch over the surroundings, it's clear that this is some kind of viewing room. An impressive wall-mounted screen dominates the area with chairs and a sofa positioned in front of it. On the far side, there's another, smaller door, and crossing over to it quickly I can hear the rhythmic sound of snoring coming through the divide. It must be Rejin's bedroom. To be in such close proximity, and knowing that it's probably not going to take much to wake him, galvanises me into action.

Ramona had made a fleeting mention of her father watching movies here and presumably Rejin would approve anything that the studio produced, so I check the Tri-D system standing before the screen, sorting through the labelled discs lying next to it. I try to find something incriminating, but they all seem to be typical Catalyst films, with names like *Eagle Down*, *East-Meg Apocalypse*, *Perils of the Black Atlantic* (rough cut) and *Sov Strike Squad*.

I dig deeper, moving the discs aside to get a look at the others that appear less new. Some of them have no titles and I can only guess at their contents, but one catches my interest – *Anna*. I retrieve it, turning it over in my hands, casting a glance at the connecting door which separated him from the slumbering CEO behind it. My curiosity won't be denied so I insert it into the Tri-D, making doubly sure that the speakers are disconnected, then turn the machine on, light and shadow dancing on the ceiling. I listen for any disturbance in the snoring pattern coming through the wall, but there's no change, and I turn my attention to the three-dimensional images projected in front of me.

It's not a professional movie; it's been shot with a hand-held camera, jittery and unfocused. The subject is a young woman, maybe in her thirties and I immediately recognise similarities with Ramona, but the woman onscreen is too old to be her. Also, the woman's clothes and those of the occasional bystander that crosses into view date this film to be a good ten to fifteen years old. I suddenly realise that this is Ramona's mother – Erik's wife.

The opening shots are of her performing onstage, evidently an actress of some note. With the sound off, it's impossible to gauge her performance, but judging by the applause and bouquets presented to her, she's clearly popular and talented. I fast-forward through cuts to parties and holidays, sometimes catching a glimpse of a five year-old Ramona running into shot, or being held in her mother's arms, but the focus of attention is always on the woman, Anna. There's no sign of Erik, and I guess he must be operating the camera, the adoring onlooker.

I continue to flash past more images of her, but as time goes on she appears troubled by the camera rather than welcoming its presence. At one point she seems to be shouting, pushing the intruding lens away. Then a jump-cut and the material changes entirely: Anna is tied to a chair, her mouth gagged, her eyes terrified and pleading, and as the camera moves closer to her a knife emerges from under the frame, presumably grasped in the cameraman's hand.

I watch Ramona's mother's protracted murder for several minutes before I look away, my eyes blurry with tears. My gaze rests on the threshold to Rejin's bedroom and I take an involuntary step towards it, shaking with anger and an insatiable desire to go in there and throttle the sick old drokker in his sleep. My trembling fingers reach out to turn off the Tri-D, but before I can do so the main lights flicker on. I whirl round to find DuNoye standing in the main doorway, a couple of creeps behind him.

"Enjoying Mr Rejin's home videos, I see," he says, smiling menacingly, and he takes a moment to stare up at the events displayed on the screen, the violence reflected in his face. "Not quite happy families, is it?"

I start to instinctively back away. "Look, DuNoye, t-this isn't what you think..."

He waves my protestations away. "There's no need to explain. I know everything... Judge Trager."

TWELVE

"I want spy-in-the-sky cameras trained on him every step of the way," Dredd barked into his radio mic, swinging astride his Lawmaster. "All units to relay his movements, but not to apprehend unless expressly instructed. Fugitive has a hostage at gunpoint – we can't move in until we can secure her safety."

"Roger that," Control replied. "PSU cameras report vehicle matching your description is heading north on Massey, approaching Kevin Spacey Interchange."

"Keep me informed," he muttered, gunning his engine and speeding off in pursuit.

It was ridiculous, there was nowhere for Matheson Peat to go. Surely he would be aware that Justice Department was not just going to let him waltz out of the city, with or without his secretary as a prisoner? They had the surveillance technology to trace his route across the city, and with the Black Atlantic on one side and the Cursed Earth on the other, he couldn't make his own way beyond its walls.

The spaceports and harbour guard were put on alert and were told not to allow the councillor passage but to stall him as much as possible. Justice Department had a roster of excuses it could use to stop potential hijackers commandeering a craft to escape in: mechanical failure, weather problems, unnecessarily convoluted red tape. By the time the perp had experienced enough of these, they were ready to just about give up.

It was a risky proposition, when a citizen was being held against their will and could end up being whacked by a frustrated gunman, but Dredd felt the alert would work with Peat – the man was not a murderer. He was a coward and a weak-willed idiot who had covered for others to help advance his own career, and who had used his position of power to aid and abet a series of horrific slayings.

It gave Dredd no small sense of satisfaction to think that when he apprehended the councillor, the creep would be staring at the inside of an iso-cube for a very long time, but even so, the man was not violent or cruel or capable of taking life. Peat was panicking, that was all. His secrets had been discovered, and fleeing was the only response he had left, even if it was just making the situation worse for himself and simply delayed the inevitable.

It had been frustrating for Dredd to watch as Peat had backed away, out of his offices and onto the slab, his gun jammed under his secretary's jaw, a look of fevered desperation on his face. He had known the game was up, but was going play it out right to the bitter end. Sweaty, wide-eyed, his cheeks stained with tears, he appeared every inch a man on the brink, and it was difficult to tell who seemed more scared, the captor or hostage. In such a state, Dredd knew that the councillor's finger could squeeze the trigger at the slightest provocation and so he had to relent, reluctantly permitting him to make his way out onto the street. With the barrel jabbing into her chin, the lawman sensed too that if he tried to bring the perp down with a leg-shot or even go for a straight standard execution between the eyes, all it would take would be a nervous twitch and the secretary would be minus a head.

Dredd carefully shadowed Peat's movements, all the time telling him to give it up now before events got even more out of hand. He couldn't tell if the councillor was listening to him – the words certainly had little effect – and in truth he wished his negotiation skills were a tad more polished, allowing him to project a note of empathy with the criminal. However, even the most judicious of his colleagues would admit that he was not known for his sympathetic side so Dredd tended to leave that aspect of the job to those who were trained for it. All he wanted to do was get the cit out of the way so he could take a shot at the meathead.

Nobody messed with the councillor as he made his way down to ground level. The office staff had stared as their employer had passed them, stumbling backwards, one of their colleagues held close to him, her head tipped back by the gun barrel wedged under her jaw. Some of them had risen from their seats, their mouths dropping open in shock and disbelief at what they were seeing. They'd looked enquiringly at the Judge, but he'd just made a calming motion with his hand, his attention focussed on Peat, and they could do nothing but silently watch as the three figures disappeared down a set of stairs and onto the street.

Outside, Peat had ploughed his way through the crowd, citizens parting in waves when they saw the blaster, and once at the kerbside had managed to force a vehicle to stop. He'd swung the gun in the driver's direction, yelling at him to get out, smashing the barrel against the side window. The man didn't argue and tumbled out onto the tarmac, arms held high in surrender, as the councillor threw his hostage into the passenger seat then jumped behind the wheel. The speedster had torn off, tyres squealing, the other traffic swerving wildly to avoid it as it careened across the lanes and powered onto a meg-way. Dredd had called in a full description of the vehicle and approximate location, knowing that the cameras would do the rest. Peat couldn't escape. He was running in tighter and tighter circles, and eventually he would come to a stop.

"Suspect still heading north, now on Gulacy," Control crackled in his ear. "He's left the main thoroughfare and it looks like he's heading into a residential district. Might have a particular place in mind."

"What sector is that?" Dredd asked, thinking the name sounded familiar.

"Thirteen."

"I'll be on his position in five," Dredd said. He had an inkling about where Matheson Peat was heading.

Keisha had stopped crying. She was curled up on the passenger seat, staring straight ahead, an expression of grim stoicism on her face. Peat glanced across at her as he drove, his left hand gripping the wheel, his right still pointing the gun in her direction; she looked mighty pissed. He'd always been slightly intimidated by her when they'd worked together – he found her no-nonsense efficiency and frankness disconcerting – and he'd often suspected she took him for a self-serving fool. Maybe she'd been proved right.

"Keisha," he started, "I'm sorry I've dragged you into this. You've got to understand... I had no choice."

She didn't answer at first, continuing to gaze blankly out of the windscreen. When she finally spoke, her voice was strained. "Are you going to hurt me?"

"No... Not if everybody does what they're told." In truth, he hadn't planned for that eventuality. He wasn't cut out for the life of crime, he decided, that was becoming abundantly clear. He wasn't nearly ruthless enough. "I don't want any... unpleasantness."

"What is this about?" she demanded, at last meeting his gaze, her temper rising as she sensed she wasn't in any immediate danger. "I knew something was wrong, but I never thought you were in trouble with the Judges. Is it some financial thing?"

"No," he snapped, then added softly: "No. I just made a mistake, many years ago. I thought what I was doing was for the best, but... these things have a habit of coming back to haunt you."

"And you think this is going to help?" She snorted derisively, her glare withering. "You're an idiot, Matheson.

Where do you think you're going to go? The Judges will get you, no matter where you try to hide."

Her words stung him, but he attempted to maintain his composure, anxious to prove that he had the power here. He was the one that was meant to be calling the shots. "They won't stop me, not while I've got you. They'll have to do what I say."

"Jovus, what drokking city are you living in, man?" Keisha was shouting now. "You're going to end up arrested or dead, that's all."

"Keep your voice down," he warned.

His secretary ignored him. "You've got to give yourself up. Stop the car and maybe we both won't be going to Resyk."

"I said shut your damn mouth. I won't tell you again."

"Stop the car!" she yelled and lunged forward, grabbing hold of the wheel, wrenching it to the right. The speedster swerved across the road, oncoming traffic having to screech out of the way. Peat fought to wrest control back from her, but he only had one hand available. Desperately, he swung the gun and slammed the barrel into her face. Blood spattered the dashboard and windows as her nose shattered and she let go instantly, slumping back into her seat. He steered the vehicle back into the correct lane, casting a glance at his hostage who was holding her face and trying to stem the flow.

"Keisha... I'm sorry, but I'm not stopping, not now. I'm not going to the cubes." He was impressed by the newly defined, steely resolution in his voice. Maybe his future lay in crime after all. He'd certainly descended into violence quickly enough, even going as far as to pistol-whip a woman. Perhaps this potential had lain dormant within him all along, and he was at last discovering his true calling. Whatever the case, it seemed he was set on a path from which there was no return. "The Judges are going to fly us out of the city, and once my safety is assured I'll let you go. Just stay calm and you'll have no reason to fear."

She studied him, her bloodied hand masking the lower half of her face, her eyes burning hot with fury and contempt. "They're not going to let you step on an aircraft. They'll have every spaceport in the area under observation, there'll be snipers to take you out the moment you try to board–"

"We're not going to the spaceport," he interrupted. "We're going to be picked up in more... neutral territory."

Even her anger couldn't disguise her curiosity. "Then where?" she asked, her brow furrowing.

In answer, he swung the car off the main slab and headed towards an unpaved, fenced-off area, roped with Justice Department "Crime Scene" markers. The gate set in the fence was locked shut, but Peat made no attempt to decrease his speed.

"Hold on," he said.

"Peat, what the hell are you doing?" Keisha screamed, but any reply was lost as the vehicle smashed through the gate, wire ripping shreds from the bodywork, the air filled with the cacophony of rending metal. Once they were through, the councillor struggled to keep control of the car, the wheels sliding on the soft earth beneath, the tyres torn from the collision. He stamped on the brake and it began to skid, threatening to tip over onto its side any second. In response, he steered into the swerve and directed the vehicle towards a mound of soil, bracing himself for the crunch. It hit the bank and shuddered to a stop, the two of them banging forward then back in their seats.

For a moment, there was silence, the only sound the quiet ticking of the engine as it cooled. Then Peat recovered his senses. He wrenched the door open, staggering slightly as he climbed out, then walked round to the other side and dragged a dazed Keisha from the car.

"W-where are we?" she asked, looking round at the excavated land and construction machinery in puzzlement.

The councillor couldn't resist a little theatricality. "Welcome to Elizabeth Short," he said with a grandiose flourish, motioning to the half-built block towering above them.

Dredd arrived at the site minutes later, following the trail of destruction. Swinging himself off his bike, he drew his Lawgiver and cautiously checked the battered car, its bodywork dented and scratched, the doors left hanging open. He noted the scuffed footprints in the mud heading away from the vehicle towards the block itself, and started to follow. The diggers and trucks stood silent within the shadow of Liz Short as they had done since the bodies were discovered. The only sound was the wind whipping over the tent the Judges had established to examine the remains, the tarpaulin ruffling and flapping in the breeze.

"Control, can confirm fugitive Peat and his hostage have abandoned vehicle at Liz Short construction site," he murmured. "I suspect they are in the building itself. Continuing pursuit."

"That's a roj. Units are rolling to surround the area. Will have Short cordoned off within the next ten minutes."

Dredd made his way into the rubble-strewn entrance hall, wondering where the councillor was likely to be hiding. He couldn't get very far because there was simply nowhere to go; the upper floors had not been built yet, plus the el' would not be working. Peat would have been forced to drag his hostage up the stairs. Dredd guessed that it wouldn't take Peat long to tire of the chase. He must know by now that he was cornered.

The Judge had begun to move up to the first floor when he heard the woman scream. He gauged it had to be several levels above him and began to run, taking the steps three at a time. With the block little more than a shell, the corridors he passed through often opened into empty air, exposed beams jutting out, semi-finished floors revealing the cabling beneath. On more than one occasion, he had to catch himself as the set of stairs he attempted to climb had no supporting wall and to his right was a drop of a couple of hundred feet. The cityscape stretched around him, the growing wind whistling off the scaffolding and swirling rockcrete dust. Dredd tried to ignore the realisation of just how easy it would be to lose his footing and plunge to the ground below, and continued his ascent.

Another scream, much closer, and Dredd doubled his speed, concentrating on throwing himself up the steps. At last he caught sight of Peat and his secretary standing on one of the rafters that poked out of the building, his gun held to her temple. The rafter was little more than five feet across, and there was nothing beyond them but the vertiginous descent to the streets.

"Didn't take you long to find me," Peat said as Dredd appeared before him.

"You were never going to escape us," the lawman replied. "Plus I had an idea where you might be heading." He motioned to his surroundings with his Lawgiver. "It always comes round full circle eventually. What did you hope to achieve?"

"Don't presume too early, Dredd. You try to arrest me, I'll blow her drokking brains out."

"You're not a murderer, Peat. You haven't got it in you."

"You think so? Are you prepared to take the risk?"

Dredd could see that the secretary had taken a beating; her nostrils were caked in blood and a livid bruise had swollen across her face. She looked understandably terrified, her eyes constantly darting either side of her to the dizzying drop. Maybe he shouldn't underestimate the councillor, he thought, as he was evidently quite capable of meting out acts of violence when pushed.

"You're going to get yourselves both killed if you stay out here," Dredd said, a conciliatory note to his voice.

"That's where you're wrong," Peat answered. "You're gonna order us up a hover-cab, just a small one, enough for the two of us and the robot driver. It's going to pick us up from here and fly us out of the city. Any attempts to stop me, she dies. Once my safety is guaranteed, I'll let her go."

"Only got your word for that."

"Then that's all you'll have to go on."

"I'm not in the habit of negotiating with creeps, Peat."

"Too bad, 'cause I don't see you have much choice. Not unless you want Keisha here to go splat."

"You kill your hostage, then what are you going to do? Hand yourself in? Jump?"

"Maybe. But imagine what the papers'll say about how Judge Dredd stood by and allowed an innocent cit to die. The very people you're sworn to protect. Won't do your public profile much good." The councillor jabbed the gun harder against her head. "Now get that gruddamn cab here."

Dredd radioed in the demand, then listened to the response. "It'll be here in a couple of minutes," he said.

"It better, or I'm gonna start getting impatient."

The Judge took a small step forward. "Seems to me, councillor, that it was always *you* that was worried about the press. You were always the one courting the media. They're going to have a field day with you after this."

"Yeah. Shame I won't be around to see it."

"You had quite the career, didn't you? Quite a celebrity. And you've thrown it all away protecting a madman. Was it really worth it?"

Peat didn't reply immediately. "You take your chances when you see them. I wasn't the only one covering for Erik. He's got plenty of friends in high places."

"Fixing to get him released from the kook cubes, wiping his files, and I'm guessing more than one of your Phoenix Campaign Blocks is built upon a body-dump. You were guiding Rejin's operation to the best rad-pits, then constructing over the evidence, weren't you? Half your rich pals are living on top of mass graveyards while you lapped up the fame and exposure."

"Where's this cab?" the councillor demanded angrily.

"And what about you, Peat?" Dredd continued, taking another step along the rafter. "You ever get your kicks from a little torture-murder too?" The secretary looked at the lawman questioningly and Dredd played on it. "Didn't you know your boss had a sick little sideline, citizen? That he's partly responsible for the disappearance of an unknown number of men and women, all of whom had been tortured to death? Kept that council business to himself, did he?"

Control crackled in the Judge's ear. "Vehicle will be with you in thirty seconds. Stand by."

"Matheson, what the drokk are you involved in?" Keisha whispered.

"Tell her," Dredd said evenly. "Tell her what your friends get up to."

"Drokk you!" Peat roared and swung the gun from his secretary to bear down on Dredd.

At that moment, an H-platform piloted by a couple of Judges rose vertically and slammed into the rafter with a sharp clang. It was enough to knock the councillor off balance, and the lawman snatched hold of the hostage and pushed her onto the safety of the platform.

Peat lost his footing and stumbled, then slipped off the beam, his gun spiralling downwards, one arm snaking around the cold metal as he fell. He dangled precariously, yelping in panic, as Dredd inched along, holding out a gloved hand for Peat to pull himself up with.

"Quickly!" the Judge shouted at his colleagues as they lowered and positioned the H-platform below the councillor, then pulled him roughly aboard. Dredd swiftly followed, leaping onto it from the rafter.

He snapped cuffs on Peat, then spun him round and lifted him up by the lapels. "Now," Dredd snarled in his face, "you and me are gonna have a chat about your best pal Erik Rejin."

Peat's numbed, sandblasted expression cracked to give way to a tiny smile. "Y-you might want to t-think about *your* l-little friend too..."

"What are you talking about?"

"Your u-undercover friend. The one you've g-got inside Catalyst. I imagine he's in very s-serious trouble right about now..."

"How did you–"

Peat giggled. "That's classified."

"Drokk!" Dredd turned to the pilot. "Get us down now! I've got to get to Catalyst studios!"

THIRTEEN

I'm dreaming I'm flying over the city. I'm drifting on the breeze like a batglider, clipping the rooftops, twisting through the rockcrete canyons, my feather-light body reflected in a million windows, flashing silver in the sunshine. It looks so peaceful from up here, this heaving metropolis that I call my home, the meg-ways snaking through the sectors like fast-flowing rivers, condos rising like immense cliffs. It stretches for as far as the eye can see in every direction, the landscape a mass of buildings and pedways knitted together; a nest of humanity.

But as I float here, buffeted by currents of hot air, diving and climbing, enjoying the freedom and beauty of my surroundings, I realise the reason that it's so peaceful is that there's no trace of life beneath me. I'm all alone, without a skysurfer or a dog-vulture to keep me company, soaring over a deserted city. The thought of my isolation casts a shadow across my mind, souring the pleasure of my flight, and there is a crinkling at the corner of my brain that tells me something isn't right.

I decide to investigate closer, tumbling down into the gloom of the towering citi-blocks, searching for a sign of occupancy. After the cool, crisp taste of the air up above the furthest spires of the metropolis, down here it smells rank, like the liquefying underbelly of roadkill. The lower I go, the worse the stink gets, a putrid, cloying odour that seems at odds with the sparkling curves of the architecture. Nothing moves down here: no citizens walk the streets, the freeways are empty of traffic, shops, factories and offices are abandoned. The silence is oppressive, the background hubbub of a busy conurbation noticeable by its absence. Even the air is still, as if thick with disease. It coats the back of my throat and makes me gag.

I feel uneasy passing through these empty avenues, wondering what has happened to everyone, what has happened to my home. The darkness seems to be encroaching as I drift ever downwards, as if the buildings are closing in and blocking out the light, stopping me escaping. I decide I don't want to be here anymore. I want to be free, wheeling across the blue sky, leaving this decaying industrial wasteland far, far below me. I want to ascend back up to the heavens, but I can't. It keeps dragging me down, the atmosphere growing heavier, more stifling, to the point where I think I'm going to suffocate.

Then I spy something below me, gleaming pale white amidst the grey surroundings, and moving closer I can see it is a skeletal arm sticking up through the rockcrete from the centre of a square, bony fingers left grasping at nothing but air. I understand at last what has become of the inhabitants. This is a city of the dead, an enormous mausoleum under which the population rests and rots, returning to the earth. Paved over their remains, the metropolis endures, a tombstone for four hundred million people, it both conceals and commemorates the deaths that it clutches to its black heart.

My feet finally touch City Bottom, the darkness looming around me, and I can hear a faint noise cutting through the silence. It seems to be coming from beneath me, so I get to my knees, my ear pressed to cold stone, trying to discern the source of the sound. I close my eyes in concentration and realise that I'm listening to the wails of the dead rising up from their burial ground, weeping and moaning and screaming, trapped perpetually within the shadow of this great sprawling cemetery. It gets louder, as if the dead masses are travelling up from their deep abode to meet me, to claim me. I try to get to my feet, but the skeletal hand suddenly grabs my hair and grips me, vice-like. I panic, struggling to be free, but I cannot pull away from its grasp. The screams rise in pitch and the ground begins to split open, light rushing up, burning my sight, my name repeated over and over again...

"Trager." The word is punctuated by a slap across the face, and I'm pulled into consciousness like a newborn, kicking and mewling. Even though I'm awake, the vestiges of my dream still cling to me for the screams continue to ring in my ears. I open my eyes, trying to gauge where they are coming from, then I see they belong to Ramona. She's being held back by the companion of that meathead whose throat I destroyed and she's looking at me, her cheeks wet with tears, and she's struggling to reach out to me but the creep won't let her come near. Something about her face tells me I probably don't want to look in a mirror right about now. There's pity there, and a horror at what has been wrought on me.

The instigator of the mess that has been made of me is the one who called my name, and he's standing over me, his suit spattered with blood, his hands dripping. Vandris DuNoye. He seems slightly out of breath, but his smooth face and expensive haircut are unruffled. I can't quite decode his expression; it falls somewhere between hatred and the pleasure he'll get from exacting his retribution.

My memories of what happened prior to being strapped to this chair in the middle of an abandoned Catalyst soundstage start to filter through. I remember being caught in Rejin's screening room, of making a feeble attempt to talk my way out of the situation and not even believing myself, let alone convincing this lawyer spugger. I remember thinking that once they had me there was going to be little to stop my inevitable execution, and I fought back desperately, trying to recall my Academy training. I landed several satisfactory punches, and put one guy on the floor with a suspected broken rib, but I was shocked at how rusty I'd become, at how slow my responses were, at how long it took me to recover from every blow landed. Too much chemical indulgence had blunted my edge.

So here I am, the man in the chair, shortly to be the recipient of the pain that not long ago I had administered with a frighteningly eager hand. I've got a fair idea what they're going to do to me. The camera's set up on a tripod – I doubt they'll get Ramona to take the photos this time, so my moment in the spotlight is going lack a certain finesse – and the trolley's standing beside me, a smorgasbord of torture weapons laid upon it. Amongst them are several of the Banana City devices obtained from Talón an eternity ago, and in a nice slice of grim irony, my way in seems also to be my undoing. I take deep breaths. I don't want them to see just how scared I am.

"Back to the land of the living, Mr Trager?" DuNoye asks me softly.

"Vandris, please, I'm begging you, don't do this," Ramona cries, still trying to pull free from her captor.

"Ramona," the lawyer snaps, turning his head in her direction. "I've asked you to be quiet. Your father is on his way down. He will deal with you."

She locks stares with me and I can see a conflict raging inside her. On the one hand, I've betrayed her and she drokking hates me for it: hates me for making a fool of her, for lying to her, for using her to get further inside the operation. That side of her would quite happily see me gutted and dismembered, the occasion captured in a series of graphic glossies. But there's a genuine stirring within her that means she can't stand by and watch me murdered. She broke free of her father's shadow for once to be with me, and that intimacy meant an enormous amount to her. For her, it was possibly one of the bravest things she had ever done. I'd got under her skin, and had been closer to her than anyone since the death of her mother.

DuNoye fixes his attention back to me. "It seems I was right to mistrust you, Mr Trager. I had my doubts right from the start, but... let's just say that your enthusiasm impressed me. Rarely do you meet someone with such a natural propensity for casual brutality. Of course, now that I know you work for Justice Department, it seems obvious."

There seems little point in continuing the charade. I cough, finding my voice. "How did you know?" My words sound slurred, unsteady, as if they have trouble leaving my lips.

"We have a little bird close to the Grand Hall of Justice," he says, taking no small delight in imparting the information. "He has access to all sorts of sensitive material." When he sees me bow my head, DuNoye adds, "No one likes to discover that their organisation has been infiltrated, do they, Mr Trager? You've compromised our operation, you've put us all at risk, including Mr Rejiin's daughter. You're a danger to us and you have to be eliminated."

"Give it up now, DuNoye," I breathe, fatigue starting to take its toll. Every muscle and bone seems to be aching simultaneously. "Your sick little studio is finished. You think that by whacking me you're gonna stop them coming to take you out? Wheels are already in motion, pal. They don't hear from me, they're gonna blitz this place."

The lawyer laughs. "Oh, don't worry about us, Mr Trager. We've already made our emergency plans to get out of the city. We still have a few friends of influence that can ease our passage, and some substantial donations here and there will keep Justice Department off our backs. Still, it's nice to know that you care so much about Ramona that you're happy to see her carted off to the cubes."

I can barely summon up the courage to look at her. She's stopped struggling and is just studying me, like a laboratory specimen; some new species of human being that is worthy of investigation. I want to tell her that not everything I said was part of a performance, that my actions were motivated as much by a genuine attraction and desire as it was by the demands of my role as a Mega-City Judge.

I don't want to see Ramona hurt. She's been brought up by an insane father, bombarded by his mad, monstrous philosophy, and no doubt knows nothing about the truth behind her mother's death. He's made her in his own image, corrupting her view of other people to the point where her talent only emerges as she strives to reveal the secrets beneath the skin. She needs counselling, maybe a spell in a psych-unit. Encubement could only prove to damage her further. I resolve that if by some miracle I come out of this alive I will recommend she gets help. But she, along with the rest of these creeps, needs to be stopped right now.

DuNoye's watching me, sensing my discomfort. "Not pretty, is it, coming face to face with someone you've been deceitful to?"

"That's rich," I hurl back, determined not to have his gloating features be the last thing I see before I die. "She's been lied to all her life. Born into this drokking charnel house, she's known nothing but her father's warped vision. What story did you spin for when her mother disappeared?"

"Trager, what are you–" Ramona blurts out, her words tremulous.

"Ramona!" DuNoye barks again, silencing her. He glares at me, fiery eyes looking straight into mine. "I'm growing tired of the sound of your voice, Mr Trager. I'm thinking it might be best all round if we cut that devious tongue from your head."

He reaches for the trolley beside me and plucks up what looks like a pair of tinsnips. He studies them for a second, as if he were a surgeon selecting the right equipment, then moves closer to me.

"Alphonse, if you would be so kind to capture the moment?" DuNoye asks as my erstwhile partner mans the camera. "Don't want to go for the money shot too soon," the lawyer says to me quietly, grabbing my hair and pulling my head back, "but a little blood will make a nice opening splash image." He motions to another goon standing nearby. "Get his mouth open."

The meathead grasps my jaw and wrenches it apart, despite my best efforts to avoid his clutches. I'm squirming in the chair, trying to make it as difficult for them as possible, but they're both holding on tight. I attempt to retract my tongue until it's virtually choking me. DuNoye edges in closer with the implement and I feel the cold steel against my lips, taste the merest hint of oil upon them. I summon my strength and twist my head a few centimetres, enough for the snips to graze my cheek and chin. Pain lances through me, but it's enough to grant me a few seconds respite as the lawyer stops briefly, looking exasperated at his minion.

"Hold him the drokk still," he says tersely.

"Vandris, I don't want this," Ramona howls. "Not this way, please–"

"Ramona, I won't tell you again–"

"No, I agree, DuNoye," a new voice says, immediately silencing the room. "Not this way."

I'm released at once, my mouth clamping shut automatically. DuNoye drops the snips back onto the trolley and turns to meet the newcomer, who moves further into the light. "I'm sorry, Mr Rejin, I thought you wanted the traitor dispatched," the lawyer says, deferent.

"And so he will. But by *my* hand. His soul belongs to *me*."

Finally, I can see the figure: Erik Rejin, the moviemaker, the elusive creep at the heart of Catalyst. If I was expecting the Devil, a wizened creature whose physical appearance matched the evil deeds that he had presided over, then I was disappointed.

This was very much a man, and all the more terrifying that insanity could reside in someone who is normality personified. He's surprisingly sprightly for his years hidden from public view, his movements not betraying his age – he had to be somewhere in his late sixties – and there's not a trace of the ravages of madness across his face. On the contrary, he has bland, almost nondescript, features: pale blue eyes behind tiny glasses, a tidy sandy-blond haircut going to grey, a small pursed mouth. His skin is unnaturally white, as if he hasn't seen sunlight for most of his adult life.

The more I look at him, however, the more I think that this person possibly doesn't belong to the same species as the rest of us, that he has in fact distanced himself from the human race. There's not a trace of emotion behind those watery eyes, no cracks appearing in that blank mask of a face. He's a cipher; a hollowed-out character who's found that the only way to feel is to see others reduced to the same basics as him. He's the nearest thing I've seen to a living, breathing robot, and when he speaks, his voice has the monotone timbre of someone who died inside long ago.

"What did you want here, lawman?"

I don't know how to answer. He's regarding me strangely, like he's looking through me, and the effect is unnerving.

"You want her, is that it?" Rejin grabs Ramona's arm without even turning and pulls her close. "You want this offspring of mine for yourself?"

"Father, please, I-I didn't know," she sobs, looking petrified of her own parent.

Rejin's head swivels mechanically towards his daughter. "You have betrayed me, child, welcoming this snake into our home. Everything I taught you about the untrustworthy nature of man, you have disregarded." He walks her forward and picks up a las-saw off the trolley. "Haven't I told you that truth lies within? That only once you go beyond the flesh can you slough off the reptile skin and reveal the light of purity? Look, I shall show you that even this being, this *man* of *law*," he spits the words at me, "contains the simple beauty of truth." He goes to raise the saw above my chest.

"No," she replies, shaking her head. "I don't want to see..."

"Then you are a fool!" he rasps and lashes out at her with the handle of the saw, smacking it against her temple. She collapses to her knees, holding the side of her head, weeping.

"Rejin!" I roar, finding my voice at last. "This has to *stop*!"

"You are not in a position to give me any kind of order, deceiver. You have infected my daughter with your lies, you have spread their taint around my domain. And damned though you may be, I shall show that redemption can be extracted from even the most foulest of creatures."

He whips the saw across my chest and the short laser beam crackles as it slices through my shirt and parts the meat beneath. I scream, straining against the ropes binding me to the chair, smoke rising from the slash-mark, the stench of burning flesh reaching my nose. He strikes again, higher, catching my bare neck and shoulder, and white-hot agony paralyses my left arm. There's little blood, as the laser cauterises each wound even as it appears, but the skin around each blow blackens and crisps.

"I want this lawman's transformation on record," Rejin demands. Alphonse hurriedly starts snapping, zooming in on my face contorted in pain. "Can you imagine what this will sell for?" the madman continues. "What the connoisseurs will say when they get to see this Mega-City Judge broken apart by my very hand? It will elevate my work up to a whole new level!" He swipes the saw downwards and slices me across the face. I feel my hair burning, then I black out.

I come to possibly only seconds later. Ramona is clutching at her father, staying his hand, repeatedly asking him to stop.

"Vandris, take her up to my room," Rejin says.

"Sir, we should really be thinking about leaving," the lawyer replies. "We don't know how much the Judges know about us, but they could have the building under surveillance–"

"Not until I have finished with our friend here," Rejin says, gesturing to me. "There is still too much work to be done." He suddenly grabs me under the chin and lifts my head up, levelling the tip of the saw just above my right eye. "I want my revenge on this offender..."

At that moment, an explosion rips through the outer part of the studio. Rejin releases me, steps back and looks around. DuNoye just has time to say, "What the hell?" before there's another burst of automatic fire and the far wall of the soundstage collapses in a cloud of dense smoke. There's a rumble of a powerful engine and Dredd comes surging through the rent in the wall on his Lawmaster, screeching towards us.

FOURTEEN

Smoke. Confusion. The perps scattered as if a grenade had been lobbed into the centre of the room.

"You are all under arrest!" Dredd hollered as he sped towards the group. "Drop your weapons now or face the consequences!"

"Sir! This way!" DuNoye shouted to Rejin, dragging Ramona with one hand in the direction of a back exit. The CEO followed rapidly, bodyguards shielding him and returning fire.

Dredd ducked low and powered into the melee, bike cannons blazing, cutting a swathe through those creeps that had remained to take him on, bodies jerking as they were riddled with high-power slugs. A meathead let loose with a zip gun and Dredd rolled off the Lawmaster to seek shelter, leaping behind a stack of crates. While the bike slammed into a wall with a jarring crunch, he unslung his Lawgiver and came up shooting, putting three standard execution rounds through the crim's skull with barely a fraction of a second's aim.

The survivors saw that this was a good time to flee and backed off, pouring on the automatic fire to cover their escape. The Judge timed the gaps in the barrage and picked his targets, taking out a further two with pinpoint accuracy before those that were left disappeared from view. When he broke cover and headed across to Trager, the soundstage was deserted, the floor littered with rubble and half a dozen bodies. As the lawman reached him, the undercover officer was slouching in the chair as far as his bonds would allow.

Dredd crouched down beside him, lifting his head up to check his wounds. There was a livid gash across his face from his hairline to his jaw, the skin puckered around it like a burn. He could hear the man breathing lightly, and his eyes flickered open, taking a few moments to adjust to Dredd's presence.

"Hold on, Trager," the senior Judge said. "Back-up is on its way." He quickly untied the straps and lifted him to his feet, noticing the scorched marks on his chest and belly. "Can you stand?"

Trager nodded. He swallowed several times and tried to push himself away, attempting to steady himself without Dredd's aid. "I... I can make it," he breathed. "How did you know I needed help?"

"Matheson Peat. He must've alerted 'em that they had a Judge in their midst. As a politician he had access to sensitive Justice Department records, so he could've discovered files relating to your infiltration."

"The councillor? He's involved in this?"

"Up to his damn eyeballs. Been covering for Rejin and the whole Catalyst operation, him and his circle of rich pals." Dredd nodded to the camera set-up. "Vi-zines?"

"And then some."

"Guessed as much." The senior Judge looked Trager up and down. "You were lucky we found out your cover had been blown when we did. It's unfortunate that you had to be put in this position. We'll have to review our security procedures."

"All part of the job," he murmured, wincing as he ran his fingers over his facial scar.

"Wait here for the med-wagon," Dredd said, noting his discomfort and already starting to head off in the direction that the perps had taken. "It won't be long."

"No," Trager replied, his voice growing stronger. "I'm coming with you."

"You're in no fit state to pursue them, Trager. You'll put both yourself and me at risk."

"I'm seeing this through to the end. Give me a gun."

"This is no time for heroics."

The Wally Squad Judge looked behind him, then uneasily walked over to one of the bodies, stooped and retrieved a couple of blasters, his face grimacing in pain. He turned back to Dredd. "I'm coming with you whether you like it or not. Don't worry about me, I'm fine."

"You're not and you know it," Dredd growled. "I don't have time to argue, but I will say this: you collapse when you're meant to be watching my back, you'll have me to answer to, understand?"

"You're all heart, Dredd," Trager said, striding past him.

The two of them reached the door that led into the backstage area. Dredd signalled for Trager to cover him as he edged his way through and appraised the corridor beyond. It was empty. He nodded and the undercover Judge followed him, a gun in each hand, head moving from side to side as he checked both left and right.

"There an escape route this way?" Dredd asked.

Trager shrugged. "No idea. This leads out to the admin offices, though DuNoye did say they had their passage out of city sorted."

"Terrif," the senior Judge rumbled. "Well, we've got units in the area, and an APB's out on them. Won't take long for them to be picked up if they get past us."

"Dredd, I gotta say something." Trager turned to him. "The daughter, Ramona, you gotta go easy on her. She's emotionally unbalanced. Rejin murdered her mother and brought her up, instilling some fruitcake philosophy into her. He's brainwashed her into thinking this whole operation is like a psycho art exercise; cutting open cits to reveal their true nature. He's off the looney-toon scale."

"No kidding. Rejin was trapped with the bodies of his family during the Apocalypse War and went full-blown nutso. Ended up eating half of them."

"Jovus drokk..."

"But the daughter's just as responsible," Dredd continued. "She'll take her chances with the rest of them."

"She didn't kill anyone," Trager replied, his voice hardening. "I'm not excusing her actions, but she just took the pics."

"She's an accessory to multiple murder, no matter what her mental state is. You were warned at the beginning not to get too close, and I can see it's already affecting your judgement. Don't make this personal. You were sent in on a job and it's now time to take these freaks down. If you haven't got the guts for that, then sit it out. But if you have, don't let feelings get in the way."

"I told you I wanted in on this," Trager said, starting to move along the corridor. "Come on, let's get it done."

Dredd watched the undercover officer make his way, wobbling slightly, through the backstage area and followed, wondering just how much of a liability he was going to be. Despite putting on an impressive front, the man was clearly in a great deal of pain, and he was allowing his effectiveness to be blunted by some personal mission of his own. Did he really think he could save this daughter of Rejin's? In Dredd's experience, such an enterprise was normally doomed to failure. When a Judge started getting too close to the perps – whether it became an obsessive vendetta to bring them down or a relationship was growing between the two parties – then the Law itself became compromised. Justice should be delivered with absolute objective authority, otherwise they might as well just hand over the city to mob rule right now.

Dredd resolved he'd have to keep an eye on Trager as well as the creeps they were hunting. Both could equally cause trouble.

The Wally Squad Judge had reached a corner, and was peering round it furtively. He looked back at Dredd and motioned him over. "Thought I saw the glint of a gun barrel," he whispered when the lawman reached him. "Smells like the ideal place for a trap."

Dredd took a peek and silently agreed. The corridor ahead was littered with discarded props and several large boxes had been stacked against the walls to create a narrow channel that someone would have to squeeze through. They could conceal any number of triggermen waiting for them.

"What do you reckon?" Trager asked.

"Let's tease them out," Dredd replied, reaching down into a nearby crate and pulling out a replica stumm gas grenade. He turned it over, grudgingly impressed by its realism. Catalyst had certainly known what it was doing. "As you haven't got a respirator, we'll have to see if they can be fooled by an imitation."

The lawman crouched and threw the grenade down the length of the floor, watching as it skittered between the boxes. The result was instantaneous; two meatheads leaped from their cover, panicked by the device. They moved to kick it away, emerging into plain sight and Dredd gunned them down where they stood.

He got to his feet and crossed to the far corridor wall, Lawgiver clutched in both hands at waist height, alert for any more resistance. He edged further up towards where the bodies lay, smoke still rising from their wounds. It was ominously quiet. He glanced back to see if Trager was following; the undercover officer was sliding along the opposite wall and met Dredd's gaze. At first, his expression advised caution, then his eyes widened and a split second later Dredd was turning, aware that someone was behind him.

"Dredd!" Trager's shout came a fraction too late.

A perp had jumped onto one of the boxes and pointed a sawn-off shotgun in the lawman's direction, letting off a deafening blast. Dredd threw himself sideways, feeling the high-calibre ammo shred the back of his uniform and pepper his skin with buckshot. He rolled, twisted and fired in one movement, pumping the trigger of his Lawgiver, but the pain igniting his back threw his aim off as he drilled a series of holes in the wall before catching the creep in the leg, shattering his kneecap. He squealed and dropped to the ground behind a stack of boxes, but Dredd sensed he wasn't out of the game just yet.

Trager scuttled alongside him, ducking low, and laid a hand on the senior Judge's shoulder. "Bad?" he asked.

"Had worse," Dredd answered, looking back and seeing a fine spray of his blood on the wall. "More pressing, spugwit ain't finished with us. I think I just winged him."

"OK, stay here. I'll deal with him."

"You're worse off than I am."

"Yeah, but I'm younger than you, old man. I carry it better."

"Shame your instincts weren't sharper. You might've spotted the punk earlier before he nearly plugged me." Dredd winced, his back felt as if it were on fire. He still had feeling below his waist and his legs were doing what he told them, which was a good sign, but he wondered how close the shot had come to his spine. That was all it took; one lucky creep with a half-decent chance and he could be put out of action permanently, spending the rest of his days teaching cadets interrogation techniques from a wheelchair. It wasn't how he had planned to spin out his twilight years. "But be careful," he added. "Creep's gonna be reloaded and waiting for you."

Trager nodded and started to inch through the channel, blasters slippery in each sweaty palm. His breathing seemed to reverberate between the walls in the eerily silent corridor. He came to the edge of the boxes and stopped for a second; the gunman was more than likely on a hair-trigger and the moment he put his head round the corner, the guy was going to blow it off. Trager knew he had to cause enough confusion to get a clear shot at him.

He looked back at Dredd, who had pulled himself to his feet, and signalled to the ceiling of the corridor and made a rebound motion. Dredd nodded, raised his Lawgiver, selected the correct bullet, aimed and fired.

The dum-dum ricocheted off the right angle where the wall met the ceiling and arrowed down behind the boxes, the creep yelling in surprise. Trager took his chance and leaped sideways, pumping both triggers before the man had a chance to recover, ammo hitting him in the chest and neck. The Wally Squad Judge curled and rolled as he crashed into the floor, coming up two-footed, feeling the wounds on his torso scream as they were torn open.

He stumbled, unconsciousness bearing down on him, the agony sending stars pinwheeling before his eyes, and leant heavily against the wall, covering the creep's death throes. The guy was feebly kicking his legs against the floor and holding his hands up against his throat to stem the flow of blood spewing forth, his shotgun lying forgotten beside him. Trager booted the gun away and crouched next to the dying man, waving a blaster barrel in his face.

"Your drokking boss," Trager breathed, swallowing down the nausea that clawed at him. "Where is he?"

The meathead gurgled. The Judge reached forward and grabbed his hand, pulling it away from his neck, the severed artery spritzing a crimson arc into the air.

"Tell me and maybe I'll get a med-wagon here in time to save you."

A glint of hope sparked in his rapidly dulling eyes. He opened his mouth to speak, a raw sound emerging from between his lips. "Th-they're b-burning it all," he gurgled, coughing up strings of bloody matter. "Whole d-drokking studio's gonna go up..."

"Where are they?" Trager demanded. "Where's Ramona?"

The creep was barely conscious enough to answer. He pointed further down the corridor, his head flopping back weakly as if the bones within him were softening.

"Where are they, you drokking piece of shit?" he snarled, but there was no reply. In a fit of anger Trager blew a hole in the guy's skull and let him drop to the floor. He got to his feet, breathing out slowly and trying to control his temper, aware that Dredd had emerged behind him and was hovering at his shoulder.

"What happened?" the lawman asked.

"Drokker wouldn't tell me anything, then tried to make a fight of it. Had to waste him."

Dredd looked at the ground and noted the shotgun lying several feet away. "That right?"

"Creeps never learn," Trager muttered dismissively, then started to continue along the corridor. "Come on, we're losing time."

Dredd looked once again at the gore-spattered remains of the gunman, then at the limping form of Trager disappearing around another corner, and followed without a word.

On Dredd's order, Judges had sealed off all exits around Catalyst studios, plus DuNoye's description had been circulated to every unit in the area. They were instructed to apprehend him on sight in the unlikely event that he should escape their barrier. Helmets were also told to be on the lookout for an eldster and his daughter attempting to flee – Erik and Ramona Rejin were wanted in connection with numerous fatalities.

A squad had already entered the building and were mopping up the destruction that Dredd had left in his wake following the firefight. Med-Judges carried out body bags to waiting meat wagons and Tek-Division were also starting to analyse the evidence, taking away the camera equipment and torture implements for study.

From the periphery, Judge Devenson watched the activity with interest, curious and quietly amazed at what was being discovered within the building. He remembered he'd once worked crowd control when some of the actors in a Catalyst feature had made public appearances and he'd been impressed by the company's attention to detail.

To learn that the outfit was a front for all sorts of nefarious deeds was a shock. He was certain repercussions were going to be felt in the Grand Hall of Justice itself. Catalyst had been approved by Justice Department as a producer of propoganda flicks, and questions were going to be raised about how it could have operated so secretly and automonously within the Judges' protection. By all accounts the man in charge of the studio was madder than a sackful of spanners, but surely somebody must have pulled some strings at a very senior level to keep all this under their hat.

The media too, couldn't believe their luck. Tri-D crews were clamouring behind the Judges' line, trying to get a statement from the helmets on duty, but so far they had been told zip. It was the kind of story that reporters loved; a famous recluse is discovered to be harbouring a terrible secret, there was a substantial bodycount, and enough dirt to throw at the authorities for them to editorialise about.

The stories they were filing at the moment were filled with spurious suppositions and accusations in the absence of any hard facts. The realisation that Dredd was still in the building hunting down the lead perp led many to speculate that the lawman was using the opportunity to cover up Justice Department's involvement in the company by destroying vital records. Some rumours had Dredd actually aiding Rejin to escape so as to not publicly embarrass the Chief Judge. Devenson watched this circus with a certain degree of distaste, feeling they could do with cracking down on the freedom of the press even further.

He turned his head to survey the crime scene, making sure that nobody was attempting to cross the lines, and caught sight of a vehicle parked fairly close to the Catalyst offices. It was an expensive model, and not the sort you expected to see stationed on the slab. A couple of cits were seated inside it, seemingly waiting for something, explicitly ignoring the commotion. Eventually, the driver clambered out and wandered over to a gate set in the wall a few hundred metres away. Devenson recognised it as one of the many bolted entrances to the Undercity. The driver loitered nearby, trying to look innocuous, cocking an ear as if expecting a message to come from the other side.

"You!" Devenson shouted, striding over to the car. The creep jumped and turned, guilt written all over him. He eyed his colleague in the vehicle nervously. "What are you doing here?"

"N-nothing," the guy replied. "Just taking the air, Judge..."

"Don't mess with me, pal," Devenson snarled, pushing him against the wall. "Let's hear the truth." He signalled to the meathead sitting in the passenger seat. "You too, creep, out of the vehicle."

"We're not doing anything wrong, sir," the first gimp said.

"I'll be the judge of that," Devenson muttered as his partner slid from the car. "Come on," he called out. "Over here, now."

There was something about the way this second creep was taking his time that sent alarm bells ringing in Devenson's brain. He looked like he was building up to something, angling for the right moment. Out of the corner of his eye, he saw the driver fractionally moving his head; a slight nod indicating something to the other guy.

Devenson threw his suspect to the ground where he was out of the way and unholstered his Lawgiver, all in one movement. "Hands in the air!" he ordered, pointing his gun at the oncoming creep. "Don't move!"

The guy was either stupid or had a death wish. He must have plainly seen the game was up and yet he still went for it. His right hand delved inside his jacket and pulled out a semi-automatic, just in time to be blown backwards by three shots from Devenson, all catching him in the chest area. He spasmed onto the car bonnet, a bullet passing straight through him and shattering the windscreen. He lay there unmoving like a hood ornament.

The Judge yanked the driver up by the scruff of his neck and growled in his face. "Start talking, creep, or you'll go the same way as your friend. What are you doing here?"

Trager and Dredd had reached the carpeted Catalyst admin area and smoke was drifting in the air, getting thicker the further they went. The orange flicker of flames crawled up the walls, devouring promo posters and files, melting furniture and computer terminals.

"They... They're destroying the evidence," Trager gasped between swallows of thin oxygen, his arm held across his nose and mouth.

Dredd didn't reply and barked instead into his radio mic. "Control, we need a fire-fighting team in here, priority one. Suspects have set fire to offices."

"That's a roj. Any sign of the perps?"

"Negative."

"A street helmet has just picked up a creep hanging around outside, close to an entrance to the Undercity. We're shaking him down now but we think he was going to be the fugitives' means of escape."

"Who does he work for?"

"That's what we're trying to establish, but it seems likely one of Rejin's business associates arranged it. In the meantime, the logical conclusion is that the suspects are using the Undercity to flee the building."

"The Undercity? How the drokk are they accessing the Undercity?"

"We don't know yet. But be aware that that's where they are likely to be heading."

"OK. Dredd out."

"What's happening?" Trager asked, coughing as the smoke began to billow before them in black clouds. A glass panel nearby shattered from the heat.

"Creeps are going underground somehow," Dredd replied, sliding down his respirator which gave his voice an even more menacing, mechanical timbre. "If you want to turn back, go ahead," he added. "No point getting this far and choking to death."

"I'll be all right." The Wally Squad Judge wiped his sooty brow and strode ahead, looking to Dredd like he was increasingly desperate to prove himself.

They ran down the corridor, half crouched, trying to stay low enough to escape the worst of the smoke, passing offices now fully ablaze. Trager recognised Ramona's darkroom and stopped momentarily to watch her works of art turn to ashes. The screaming faces that festooned the walls blackened and crisped, curling up and disappearing before his eyes.

"You know where they could've gone from here?" Dredd demanded.

"Rejin's living quarters are at the end of the hall. That seems the likeliest."

The two of them reached the double doors and shoulder-barged their way through, recoiling instantly at the heat that exploded in their faces as flames crawled all over the viewing room. The big screen at the far end had warped and split apart, the Tri-D set below it a molten mess of plastic and chrome.

"His bedroom!" Trager yelled, pointing to the connecting door.

They barrelled through, just having enough time to mentally note that the fire had not yet spread to this antechamber before the realisation of their surroundings hit home. The grand four-poster bed, the exotic furnishings, the expensive furniture they expected were all there, but what made them pause was what lined the shelves of every wall. Sitting there like a private art collection were hundreds of jars filled with human body parts.

For a second the two Judges were speechless as they gazed up at the sight before them. Hearts and tongues and scalps floated in liquid like pickled specimens. Some specimens were difficult to identify: pink jellyfish wafting lazily in a yellowish brine, brown stumps like wet, chewed cigars. Others stared back, dead eyes impassive.

"Son of a bitch..." Trager murmured.

"Missing Persons are gonna be busy," Dredd said.

"How did the insane drokker get away with all this for so long?"

"You'd be surprised at what we've got away with," a voice behind them said, and both Judges turned as one in time to see Alphonse swinging a massive fist and connecting with Dredd's jaw, sending him flying backwards.

Trager fired and put two bullets through Alphonse's chest, but the creep barely flinched. He walked forward and wrenched the weapons from the undercover officer's hands, then smacked him onto the ground. It felt like a block of concrete landing on his head and Trager struggled to remain conscious. Meathead must be pumped on something; blood was flowing freely from his wounds and he didn't even notice.

Alphonse picked Trager up clean off the ground. "Drokkin' rat," he growled. "We drokkin' trusted you an' you ruined everything." He casually threw Trager away from him, slamming him against a wall, the specimen jars wobbling off their shelves and raining down in a blizzard of moist flesh. Trager felt glass cutting his hands as he rolled out of their way, his own injuries screaming in protest.

There was the sound of several rapid bangs as Dredd shot Alphonse half a dozen more times with his Lawgiver, one even catching him on the side of the head, but they didn't seem to slow him down at all. The perp launched himself at the lawman and the two of them flew onto the bed, Alphonse's mammoth paws fixed around Dredd's windpipe.

The Judge couldn't throw him off, his weight pinning him down, so he tried to improvise by flicking the ammo selector on his gun with one hand to armour piercing, ramming the barrel into the creep's side and pulling the trigger. Alphonse's midriff blossomed with a crimson halo as a substantial chunk of his torso was vaporised. The pressure eased off Dredd's neck for a moment, but incredibly the guy wasn't going to be stopped.

Dredd felt somebody yanking his boot knife from its sheath before Trager appeared behind the goon, pulled his head back and drew the blade savagely across his throat. Alphonse released Dredd and stood, his jugular spraying in all directions. He turned to face Trager and took a couple of steps forward, but the severity of his wounds finally caught up with him. An expression of puzzlement passed across his features before he started to stumble, then careened into the walls. One hand went to his neck in a futile attempt to stem the flow while another pounded the paintwork, a rough gasp emerging from his mouth. As he sank to his knees, he feebly punched the wall nearest to the bed and a portion of it disengaged, swinging open like a door. He shuffled towards the threshold, then collapsed and was at last still.

Trager took a peek beyond the secret doorway and saw stone steps descending into darkness. "Gruddamn."

Dredd joined him, his uniform ripped and drenched in red stains, livid welts on his neck. "Let's just get this finished."

Fear began to grip DuNoye, an emotion that he was unused to. Overseeing the running of Catalyst Productions, he'd always been confident of his abilities to sweet-talk the authorities, and draw on the company's resources and network of allies. But maybe it was overconfidence that had destabilised the operation. They had underestimated the Judges as well, thinking they could get away with their little operation right under Justice Department's nose. DuNoye suspected the Judges had stumbled on it by luck rather than skill, but that hardly mattered anymore. They were undone. Once the Liz Short bodies were discovered, they should've ordered a retreat there and then, escaping out of the city – even off-planet – before the heat came down on them. But DuNoye's arrogance had led him to believe he could deal with Dredd himself, trying to throw him off the investigation. That was a gross error, and all their work building up the outfit came tumbling down as a consequence.

Now, as they attempted to scramble to some kind of refuge, they found that that too was rapidly vanishing. Attempts to contact that idiot Peat had proved useless and he was no doubt at this moment in custody. The help that should have been present to aid them in their escape was nowhere to be seen, and their exit from the Undercity seemed to have been blocked. The gate was supposed to have been altered so it could be opened from the inside, but it wasn't budging, which left them trapped in this netherworld. They'd known from the beginning that it would be a risky route to take, and now they couldn't get out, and they couldn't go back to the studio either. They'd literally burnt their bridges. All DuNoye could do was keep trying to contact one of Rejin's associates in the hope that they could get to them before the Judges.

The old man was standing with his daughter, looking out at the blasted cityscape of New York. It was difficult to judge how Erik was feeling, or indeed what he was planning to do. He was completely emotionless, his face a blank mask. Ramona had tried to apologise to him for getting too close to the undercover Judge, but he hadn't answered and simply gazed at her as if seeing her for the first time. DuNoye felt uneasy, unsure how this was going to resolve itself.

But it wasn't his only worry. He could feel eyes upon him, shapes moving in the darkness, a whispered grunting echoing between the concrete canyons. DuNoye was aware of the dangers that lurked in the Undercity, and the longer they lingered here the more they became a vulnerable target for attack. He tried his vidphone again, nervousness starting to claw at him, his fingers visibly shaking as he punched in numbers for someone to get them out of this hole. He wished they'd kept back a couple of triggers for situations like this, but the drokking Judges had wasted half his men.

A rising whistle sliced through the air and the lawyer yelped in surprise as a crudely fashioned spear arced out of the gloom and knocked the phone from his grasp. He looked around for the weapon's owner, but heard only the sound of running feet.

"Sir," he said, his voice breaking with panic. "We've got to go."

Rejin turned and studied him. They were standing on steps leading away from the ruins of a twenty-first century bank, its palatial columns long since crumbled to rubble. "Go where? We are nowhere. We are abandoned amongst the dead, reduced to history like everything else."

"But if we stay around here..." DuNoye began, watching the shadows as pallid faces leered from them. They were everywhere. He backed away, head turning from side to side. "We've got to get out of here."

"Father, please, they'll kill us," Ramona pleaded.

"They are the ghosts of our pasts, come for revenge. We cannot deny them their vengeance."

DuNoye started to run, all thoughts of loyalty forgotten. His footsteps clattered in the oppressive silence as he descended towards the street, but he didn't get far. Another spear fired out of the darkness and sank into his thigh, sending him tumbling. He yelled in pain and fright, trying to crawl to shelter, but the underground dwellers now emerged, their misshapen forms like something from a nightmare. They wore only rags to cover their pale, scabrous skin, carried flint axes and daggers, and they gibbered to each other in a guttural, impenetrable language.

DuNoye tried desperately to escape them, but they descended upon him with ease, the forerunners swinging their weapons above their heads with a whooping noise and burying the blades into his back. The impact laid him out flat, and they grabbed his arms, pulling him into the shadows, DuNoye struggling weakly. The hunger got too much for one so he hacked off a hand, bringing the severed wrist to his mouth and tore at the flesh.

When another beheaded him, Ramona screamed.

The two Judges entered into the slate-grey environs of the Undercity when they heard a shout rebounding off the ruins. Trager recognised it instantly.

"Ramona!"

The Wally Squad officer tore off at speed, following the scream's dying echoes, Dredd trying to catch up with him. They ran up a main street, spotting a group of troggies descending on a pair of figures ahead. Dredd fired his Lawgiver in the air several times and the subhuman creatures scattered instantly, shielding their eyes from the muzzle flash. He put a bullet through a couple of them to make sure they'd keep their distance.

Trager was the first to reach the pair. Rejin was pulling his daughter close to him, slowly retreating. The undercover Judge halted a few feet away from them, breathing heavily.

"Step away from him, Ramona," he ordered.

"She is not yours to command," the old man said.

"It's over, Rejin. Your little business is finished." He turned back to the daughter. "Please, Ramona, come with me. I can help you."

She looked at him, wary and scared. "I trusted you... and you lied to me. Everything you told me was a lie. You used me."

"I know," Trager replied, feeling his guts churn with self-loathing. "And I'm sorry. But this had to be stopped. Your father, DuNoye, they all had to be stopped. You can see that, can't you?"

"We don't have time for this," Dredd growled. "Troggies are gonna be back for more, and grud knows what else."

He levelled his Lawgiver at the couple. "You creeps are under arrest. Hands in the air, now."

"Dredd, please," Trager said. "Can I just speak to her for a sec-"

"Trager, the operation is over. Your role is done. Now these two are lookin' at serious cube time."

Rejin suddenly crouched and grabbed a flint dagger from a nearby troggie corpse, jamming it against his daughter's neck. "We created such beauty, and you infected it all with your lies," he said to Trager. He studied her ashen face. "You even corrupted my flesh, to the point where I don't recognise this creature as being mine."

"F-Father," Ramona whispered, "I never wanted to hurt you..."

"Ramona, you don't owe him anything!" Trager yelled, fury boiling out of him. "Everything you've been brought up to believe in, everything you've been told, is a sham!"

"Don't listen to the deceiver," Rejin murmured.

"What did he tell you about what happened to your mother? That she left when you were a child? Was that it? That bastard murdered her! Strapped her down and filmed himself killing her!"

"No..." Ramona said quietly.

"I saw the film myself, Ramona. Anna was just another of his victims."

"You don't understand..." She started to weep.

"How can you carry on defending him?"

"Because she knows the truth," Rejin retorted. "Because you only saw what you wanted to believe."

Trager felt himself pause. "What?"

"Once she was old enough I had to teach my daughter how purity lies within the human body. That could only be done if she were to discover it by her own hand."

A terrifying realisation slammed through Trager like a ten tonne truck, stunning him to silence. The movie flashed back in his head and he remembered how he never saw the hands that wielded the blade or the camera, only the fear on the woman's face. Was it horror as she watched her own child approach her?

"Ramona," the Wally Squad Judge pleaded. "Tell me that isn't true..."

She looked at him directly, tears flowing freely, but there was a steely hardness behind her gaze. "What do you know about truth?"

"She is her father's daughter," Rejin said. "And you will never have her."

"This has gone far enough," Dredd barked, shooting a warning glance at Trager before turning his attention back to the old man. "Drop the weapon and step away from the girl, meathead."

"You think I will allow you to corrupt her further?"

"Drop it!" Dredd demanded again.

"Better that she is free, away from your touch," Rejin continued. Ramona closed her eyes as if in resignation. "Better she remain unsullied." And he plunged the dagger into her throat.

Trager didn't hear the gunshots as Dredd put half a dozen bullets through the old man's chest. His ears were filled with a roaring sound as he collapsed to his knees, cradling Ramona's head and keeping a hand pressed to her wound. He was shouting for a med-wagon, but his words seemed distant and muted like he was underwater. He was dimly aware of Dredd standing over him, saying something, but all he could do was gently rock the young woman in his arms and sob into her hair, feeling the slow beat of her heart beneath him and her shallow breath brush his skin.

When the med-droids finally arrived, it took them several minutes to extricate her from his grasp, but by then it was too late.

EPILOGUE: FADE TO BLACK

There was a brilliant blue sky hanging over the Mega-City One skyline when Dredd pulled up outside Resyk. Striding inside the monolithic building, it never ceased to amaze him how quiet it was within; all he could hear were his boots echoing off the solemn corridors and gentle organ music lilting in the background. He knew that massive machines were at work beneath the surface, taking apart the corpses that were fed into its maw and reducing them to their usable components, but you wouldn't know they existed from the tasteful reception area. Here, grieving relatives could be consoled and were led to believe that their loved ones were going to a better place.

But once you entered the cavernous inner sanctum, the factory-like workings of the recycling plant became very clear. A huge conveyor belt dominated the space, upon which hundreds of cadavers travelled to the bonesaws waiting for them, and it was on a walkway above it that Dredd found Trager listening to the final words of the priest droid. There were no other mourners, and the robot was evidently on a default setting, giving a pre-recorded sermon and inserting Ramona Rejin's name where necessary. He supposed there would be nobody to give a personal touch to her passing because nobody ever knew her. Having been brought up in seclusion by her demented father, would anybody in the city actually know she was gone? Like Catalyst's victims, she became one of the metropolis's many disappeared.

Dredd hovered behind Trager until the droid had said its piece and trundled off to the next group of bereaved, then joined him at the safety rail looking out over the belt. The Wally Squad Judge didn't turn to face him, his hard, stern face simply watched the naked bodies tumbling past. Only his eyes betrayed his emotions.

"Dredd," Trager finally acknowledged.

"Trager."

"She's down there somewhere," he said, his voice cracking slightly. "I thought I might catch one last glimpse of her before she… before she went." He swallowed. "But there's so many down there, I've lost her. Lost her completely." He gripped the rail, his knuckles whitening.

"How are you feeling? Physically, I mean?" Dredd asked.

Trager glanced at the lawman for the first time and a light smile grazed his lips. "I'll be OK. A spell with the speed-heal sorted me out. I won't lose this," he gestured to the scar down the right side of his face, bisecting his cheek, "but I don't mind. It means every time I look in a mirror I won't be able to forget."

"Trager, you did what you could. You did what was asked of you as a Mega-City Judge. You can't afford to take it so personally."

The younger man shook his head, gazing below him. "It's easier for you, Dredd. You've had your feelings… severed. I just can't turn mine off like that. Every treachery, every lie I tell, is like a knife twisting in my guts. I disgust myself sometimes, the way I sell these people out."

"But justice has been served, that's the important thing. Creeps broke the law and paid the price."

"We all pay the price," Trager said quietly.

They stood in silence for a moment, a muted sobbing coming from the far side of the walkway. Eventually, Dredd asked, "You want to know what the inquiry found?"

"Go ahead."

"First off, they commended your actions throughout the operation, which brought down a major criminal organisation. And the ripples are continuing to spread as we follow up leads from both Catalyst's records and Peat's contacts. There was a big ring of premier-league businessmen involved in the distribution of the Vi-zines, and who helped cover for Rejin in return for substantial kickbacks. So far, seven companies have had their accounts frozen pending investigation."

Trager raised his eyebrows, impressed.

"The inquiry also felt your life was put unnecessarily at risk by Peat leaking Justice Department files, following which the Grand Hall is undergoing a review of security measures. Tek Division ran a source on the MAC infiltration and we've arrested a hacker that was working for the councillor. It looks like, thanks to you, politicians are going to be cut out of the info-loop even further."

It was the first time Trager had heard Dredd sounding genuinely grateful.

"However, my report mentioned certain times where I felt you overstepped the boundaries of being a Judge, and where life was taken at a personal level. Some of these charges were serious enough to warrant a trip to Titan... but given the circumstances, the inquiry edged towards leniency, and the final ruling was that you should be stripped of your badge. Also, that you leave the city."

The undercover officer nodded slowly. "What did Hendry say?"

"He walked out halfway through. Said we were throwing away a damn fine Judge."

Trager smiled. "And what do you think?"

"I think you threw it away yourself."

Trager was silent for a moment. "Maybe. But I won't miss it. I've seen enough death, enough broken lives." He looked the lawman in the eye. "You know how many people you've killed, Dredd?"

"No."

"No, neither do I." He pushed himself off from the rail and started to walk back towards the entrance. "I'll see you around, Joe." Then, he was gone.

Dredd stood for a moment, watching the dead pass beneath him. The case still troubled him. The degree of Rejin's insanity and the scale with which Catalyst had got away with mass murder, right under the nose of Justice Department itself, made him uneasy. He couldn't help feeling that McGruder or Silver – who had been strong supporters of the propaganda material in their day – must've realised the extent of his madness, and turned a blind eye, content that his raving anti-Sov films were being distributed all over the world. How much else could they have condoned, in the spirit of a "special relationship"? It was impossible to tell now, just more secrets that had been taken to the grave.

He wandered down the walkway, wincing as his back injury flared up. Getting old, Dredd thought, as he headed out into the light.

ABOUT THE AUTHOR

Matthew Smith was employed as a desk editor for Pan Macmillan book publishers for three years before joining 2000 AD as assistant editor in July 2000 to work on a comic he had read religiously since 1985. He has been editor of the Galaxy's Greatest since December 2001. He lives in Oxford.

THE BIG MEG GLOSSARY

Black Atlantic Tunnel: A tunnel located below the Black Atlantic that connects Mega-City One to Brit-Cit.

Citi-Def: The City Defence Force (a civilian militia): a voluntary civilian army organised on a block basis that saw action against the Sov-Bloc invaders of the Apocalypse War in 2104.

City Bottom: The pre-Atomic rockrete foundations of Mega-City One, littered with the architectural, human and sub-hume refuse of the city. Also known as The Pits, this area is not recognized as one of the three city levels, and is often the last stop for Slummies who do not wish to live within society.

Council of Five (The): The central ruling council of Judges, consisting of the heads of the main divisions of the Justice Department, that acts as the Chief Judge's advisory body.

Cuidad Barranquilla: Located in the former Buenos Aires, 'Banana City' is considered to be one of the poorest and most corrupt cities in the World.

Dave the OrangUtan: Widely regarded as Mega-City One's finest mayor, Dave won a landslide mayoral race after gaining fame by appearing on the Tri-D show Tipsters Tonite. Sadly, Dave's term of office only lasted a couple of years as he and his owner, Billy Smairt, were murdered by Billy's best mate, barman Mo Molinsky.

Heatseeker Round: Also known as a Hotshot, this specialised ammo is made by capping a guided warhead onto a standard execution round, and rarely misses its target.

Hondo City: Also known as Hondo-Cit; the Japanese counterpart of Mega-City One.

Iso-Cube: The standard imprisonment for criminals; a huge block full of very small, plasteen, isolation cubes.

Long Walk (The): A tough journey a retired Judge decides to make to bring Law into the Cursed Earth or the Undercity. Once gone, few Judges are ever heard from again.

Luna-City: Also known as Luna-1, Luna-City is a colony on the moon established and maintained by the American Mega-Cities.

MAC (Macro-Analysis Computer): Referred to as the 'brain' of Mega-City One, MAC can even predict crimes before they happen, as well as being the information centre for all citizens and Judge activity.

Otto Sump: This extremely unattractive citizen won sixty million credits on the Tri-D show *Sob Story*, and started a chain of beauty parlours with his winnings. When the beauty treatments started turning people ugly, the look caught on and created a subculture of 'Uglies'. As Sump's new products were deemed unhealthy, a hefty 'Ugly Tax' was established. Despite this, demand for Sump's anti-beauty products have still persisted.

Pedway: A pedestrian-only pathway found all across Mega-City One at all levels. Motorised pedways are known as slidewalks and eeziglides.

Power Tower: A controlled volcano, the Power Tower obtains red hot lava from beneath the Earth's crust to provide most of Mega-City One's energy supply.

Robot Wars (The): In 2099, a renegade construction droid called Call-Me-Kenneth waged war against the Judges, killing thousands of cits and Judges. Dredd was able to bring the rebel droid down with the help of other loyal robots and Weather Control.

Sector House: A miniature version of the Grand Hall of Justice, of which there are hundreds located around the city. Sector Houses carry out all routine judging activities for their area.

Statue of Judgement: A massive rockcrete statue of a Judge erected for the second time in 2117, found in Sector 44. Unbeknownst to the public, the Public Surveillance Unit is housed within the statue's head.

Tri-D: The shortened term for three-dimensional holovision; thousands of both legal and pirate channels are available in Mega-City One.

Troggies: The blind descendants of a group of people who remained underground, the troggies have adapted to their dark environment, and have also in the past, made violent and dangerous forays into the city above them.

Umpty Candy: Formerly the most popular confectionary in the city, it was eventually banned due to its extremely addictive nature. Later, the Mega-City Jong family procured the recipe from its creator, Uncle Ump, before killing him, then proceeded to establish the Umpty black market, selling the substance as a fine powder.

Undercity: Formerly New York City and Washington DC, this area was covered with a huge slab of concrete upon which Mega-City One was built. The Undercity is populated by a small number of mutants called 'troggies', who have adapted to live in the cold and dark.

Wally Squad: A group of undercover Judges who infiltrate criminal organisations. Wally Squad Judges are not well thought of by other Judges, as they are prone to become perps themselves.

Wreckers: Also known as street pirates, these armed gangs raid moving vehicles and rob them.

The
Connell Guide
to
Margaret Atwood's

The Handmaid's Tale

by David Isaacs

Contents

Introduction

"The Handmaid's Tale," Margaret Atwood wrote in The Guardian in 2012, summing up its extraordinarily long life,

> has not been out of print since it was first published, back in 1985. It has sold millions of copies worldwide and has appeared in a bewildering number of translations and editions. It has become a sort of tag for those writing about shifts towards policies aimed at controlling women, and especially women's bodies and reproductive functions: "Like something out of *The Handmaid's Tale*" and "Here comes *The Handmaid's Tale*" have become familiar phrases.
>
> It has been expelled from high school... People – not only women – have sent me photographs of their bodies with phrases from *The Handmaid's Tale* tattooed on them... The book has had several dramatic incarnations, a film (with screenplay by Harold Pinter and direction by Volker Schlöndorff) and an opera (by Poul Ruders) among them. Revellers dress up as Handmaids on Halloween and also for protest marches – these two uses of its costumes mirroring its doubleness. Is it entertainment or dire political prophecy? Can it be both? I did not anticipate any of this when I was writing the book.

It seems that every few months an article appears

somewhere about the novel's continued relevance. In March 2015, for example, an article appeared in *Bustle,* which argued that it's "more important now than ever". In April 2016, the *Evening Standard* said that it was "just as vital today" and would "stay with you for the rest of your life". In August 2016, another article appeared in the *Guardian,* labelling it "a book to give you hope". Atwood herself, speaking in April 2016, when the cast was announced for its forthcoming HBO adaptation, claimed: "It's more relevant now than when it was written."

So what is it about *The Handmaid's Tale* that makes it so enduring? What makes it so vital? And what relevance does it have, more than 30 years after it was published?

A summary of the plot

I Night

An unnamed female narrator remembers being held prisoner in what was once a school gymnasium with a number of other girls, kept in check by women called "Aunts", armed with cattle prods.

II Shopping

She describes her present situation: an empty room in which she's held prisoner by a military dictatorship, Gilead, founded on theocratic principles. The house she's in belongs to a man called "the Commander". She's let out only to go shopping, with a "double" called "Ofglen", a woman just like her. They wear floor-length red dresses, white headscarves with "wings" that mean they can"t see anything except what's directly in front of them, nor can they be seen. As she leaves the house, she passes a "Guardian", a sort of caretaker, who winks at her: a forbidden gesture. They come across another woman dressed like them, heavily pregnant, and many others dressed the same way cooing over her. On their way home they pass the city wall, where they see the bodies of three men hanging from hooks; they've been executed for carrying out abortions.

III Night

In bed that night, the narrator, Offred, remembers happy times with her mother and her best friend, Moira, neither of whom she's seen for many years.

IV Waiting room

Offred is surprised to find the Commander standing outside her room one day. When he sees her, he nods hesitantly, and disappears. It's illegal for him to be there; what is he trying to say?

Lying on her bed, she remembers how, on first arrival, she had tried to find out more about the woman who was in the room before her, but is refused any information.

She recalls a visit to the doctor the day before: a check-up, to see if she's pregnant. During the procedure, the doctor offered to impregnate her. Offred is a "Handmaid", we learn: a member of a slave class of women whose sole purpose is to bear children for her Commander and his wife, who can't. If she fails beyond a certain time, it's implied, she will be killed.

Offred is prepared by the household's maids ("Marthas") for a "Ceremony" that will take place later that night.

V Nap

Waiting for the Ceremony, Offred lies on her bed and remembers being with Moira at the "Rachel and Leah Centre" – the re-education centre she described at the start of the novel. They were not permitted to talk there, but managed snatched conversations when they sat in adjacent toilet cubicles. She then returns to a traumatic memory: she's running away with her husband, Luke, and her daughter; they are being chased. Luke is shot at, and her daughter taken away. She hasn't seen them since.

VI Household

The members of the household assemble in the living room: Offred, the Marthas, the Commander, the Commander's Wife and Nick, the Guardian.

The Commander unlocks a box, takes out a Bible, reads from it and they pray in silence. As they pray, Offred remembers Moira's attempted escape from the Rachel and Leah Centre, and the punishment that left her feet looking like lungs.

Then the Ceremony, in the Commander's bedroom: the Commander's Wife lies at the head of a four poster bed; Offred lies nested in her lap. On top of her, the Commander is all but raping Offred.

During the night, Offred creeps around the house. In the living room, she sees Nick. It's forbidden for both of them to be up at this time; it's forbidden for them to be alone together. But Nick has a message: the Commander wants to see her, alone, in his office the following day. Again, this is strictly forbidden.

VII Night

Offred lies in bed wondering what happened to Luke: is he alive or dead, imprisoned or free?

VIII Birth day

During breakfast one morning, Offred hears a siren. It is a Birthmobile: a van sent to drive all the local Handmaids to the house where one of them is in labour. They watch Janine, now Ofwarren, giving birth. It's another grotesque ceremony: the Handmaids sit on the floor, chanting, while this Commander's Wife sits on a stool above Janine, legs wrapped around her, as if it's she who's giving birth.

Offred, "tired" of telling this story, retreats again to her memories and starts to tell another one: the story of Moira's successful escape from the Rachel and Leah Centre. (She kidnapped an Aunt, changed into her clothes, walked straight past the security guards, and hasn"t been heard of since.)

That night, Offred meets the Commander in secret. She's terrified about what will happen, but all he wants is to play Scrabble. When she leaves he asks her to kiss him.

IX Night

In her room, Offred reflects on the strange episode and, climbing into her cupboard, erupts in a fit of hysterical laughter.

X Soul scrolls

Offred and the Commander's relationship intensifies. He starts giving her presents: contraband items, such as magazines from "the time before"; moisturiser for her dry skin.

Out shopping one day, Ofglen says something punishable by death: she questions the existence of God. Offred is thrilled. Ofglen reveals that she is a dissident, part of an underground resistance network called Mayday.

We learn how Gilead came into being. A group of ultra-conservative American activists stormed

Congress, killed everyone, blamed it on Islamic terrorists, and founded their own state. Women lost their jobs, their money. Fundamentalist Christian women became Commanders' Wives; fertile women became Handmaids; working class women became "Econowives"; all other women (and gay men) were sent to the "Colonies," to clear up nuclear waste.

Offred learns what happened to her predecessor: she also had an affair with the Commander, which was discovered. Knowing that she would be arrested, tortured, and killed as a result, she hanged herself in Offred's room.

XI Night

A Romeo and Juliet moment with Nick outside her window; they don't speak, but exchange meaningful glances. The sexual tension is building.

XII Jezebel's

The Commander's Wife is frustrated that Offred isn't pregnant and suggests, heretically, that it might be the Commander who's infertile, not her. She suggests Offred sleep with Nick in secret. In return, she will show Offred a photo of her daughter. She makes good on her word.

The local women attend a "Prayvagazna" – a mass devotional event, in this case to celebrate a number of arranged marriages. There, Offred sees

Janine looking thin and pale; Ofglen tells her that the baby she gave birth to was disabled – an "Unbaby" – and Janine has been reassigned. Ofglen knows that Offred has been seeing the Commander privately; she asks her to do some digging.

When they next meet, the Commander produces an old burlesque costume made of feathers and sequins. He makes her wear it and smuggles her into a debauched, elite club: a brothel. There, Offred finds Moira dressed as a Playboy Bunny. They retreat to the toilet to talk. Moira tells her about the aftermath of the escape – her attempt to get across the border to Canada on the "Underground Femaleroad" – and that Offred's mother was sent to the Colonies as an Unwoman.

The Commander takes Offred to a room where he tries to sleep with her; she can't do it.

XIII Night

At the Commander's Wife's behest, Offred and Nick sleep together.

XIV Salvaging

Offred and Nick begin a passionate affair; she loses all interest in trying to escape or aid Mayday.

The women are called to the steps of the old university (Harvard) for an event called a "salvaging". Three women are hanged, their crimes never revealed. Then a man is brought out. They're told he's a convicted rapist. What follows is a "Particicution": an execution in which all the Handmaids can participate. They're allowed to do anything they like to him. Ofglen beats him violently until he loses consciousness. Furious, Offred turns on her. He's not a rapist, Ofglen replies, he's "one of ours", a political dissident, a member of Mayday. She knocked him out so that he doesn't have to experience what happens afterwards.

Later that day, Offred waits for Ofglen to go shopping. When Ofglen arrives, it's someone else. Ofglen, she discovers, hanged herself after the Salvaging. She saw the secret police, the "Eyes", coming for her, and escaped.

When she gets home, the Commander's Wife greets her at the door. She has found out about her and the Commander. Offred goes to her room, her fate uncertain.

XV Night

Nick arrives at Offred's door, with him two Eyes. They will take her, torture her, execute her. But Nick tells her that he works for Mayday; they've come to rescue her. They escort her off the premises.

Is *The Handmaid's Tale* a feminist novel?

It's possible to work out what *The Handmaid's Tale* is about before you even get to the first chapter (and without reading the blurb or seeing the cover): there are enough clues woven into what publishers call the "front matter"* for a reader (a particularly clever reader, admittedly) to get a fairly clear picture of the book.

First, look at the copyright page.** Ordinarily, you wouldn't think to, but you'd miss two significant dedications: "For Mary Webster and Perry Miller", it says at the top. This might not seem unusual: writers are always dedicating books to loved ones. But if you happened to know a bit about early American history, then it might. Mary Webster was a Puritan settler who was hanged as a witch in the 1680s, and Perry Miller was an American intellectual historian who specialised in the early settlers, taught at Harvard and died in 1963.

When asked about the dedication, Atwood said Webster was an ancestor.

> She was accused of witchcraft. She was hauled off to Boston – this was just before the Salem witch

* The title page, author's bio, list of other works by the same author, etc.

** The page on which all the legal information about the current edition is printed.

trials* – put on trial and exonerated. She went back to her hometown. The townspeople were not pleased with the verdict, they lynched her anyway... they strung her up more or less just like a flag and let her dangle around and when they came to cut down the body in the morning, she was still alive... She lived another fourteen years, the man doing the accusation, however, died.

It's not the most revealing of answers. Twenty years after publishing *The Handmaid's Tale,* Atwood published a poem about Webster called "Half-Hanged Mary" (1995), which might help us flesh out her significance.

Written from Webster's point of view, the poem describes the night of the hanging. "I was hanged," Webster says,

for living alone
for having blue eyes and a sunburned skin
tattered skirts, few buttons,
a weedy farm in my own name,
and a surefire cure for warts;

Oh yes, and breasts,

* A case of mass hysteria in Boston, 1692-1693: the people of Salem were so certain that the devil was in their midst that they hanged 20 innocent people as witches. The whole town turned brutally against anyone who showed the slightest sign of abnormality. It's often thought that their undiscriminating cruelty was the result of the extreme repressiveness of the Puritan way of life, which prohibited even dancing.

and a sweet pear hidden in my body.
Whenever there's talk of demons
these come in handy.

In this account the townspeople turned against Webster because of her independence ("living alone"), the appearance of her body ("blue eyes", "sunburned skin"), the shabbiness of her clothes ("tattered skirts, few buttons"), her ownership of property ("a weedy farm in my own name"), her enterprise ("a surefire cure for warts") and, most importantly, her sex (the "breasts" and "sweet pear hidden in my body"*). She was demonised, attacked, tortured and nearly murdered by her community for the sin of being an independent woman who didn't conform to the repressive expectations of appearance and behaviour that were placed on women in 17th century New England.

But what makes her remarkable, for Atwood, is her survival; the poem is, above all, a survival narrative. In her book, *Scarlet Letters*, the academic Lee Briscoe Thompson credits this "bizarre incident in her family history" with giving Atwood "a predisposition to see women as survivors, a consistent characteristic of her protagonists".

From this first dedication, then, you might infer that *The Handmaid's Tale* is a novel about a victim of some kind of misogynistic municipal repression, whose significance is that she survives. And you'd be right: the narrator, Offred, is a prisoner in a military

* The uterus is pear-shaped.

dictatorship whose existence is ruled by her "sweet pear" – that is, her ability to bear children. And, as we"ll see, it's her survival that interests Atwood more than her oppression.

You might also infer that the novel will fit into the tradition of feminism which sees women as victims, historically oppressed, seeks liberation and demands equality. And you would be largely right.

It's certainly true that in Gilead women are a kind of slave class – worse, even: "I am a national resource," says Offred (75). For Gilead, the Handmaids are "containers, it's only the insides of [their] bodies that are important" (107); they are "two-legged wombs" (146). And they get the blame when things go wrong: "There's no such thing as a sterile man any more, not officially... that's the law" (70-71).

Femininity means, for Gilead, to borrow terms from the 19th century feminist Marion Reid, "self-renunciation" and "self-extinction". "Any symptom of independent thought," Reid wrote in *A Plea for*

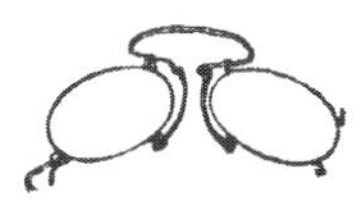

HISTORICAL NOTES ON *THE HANDMAID'S TALE*

The perspective abruptly switches. It's the year 2195 and we're at an academic conference devoted to Gilead studies. A man called Professor Pieixoto tells us that he pieced together the text we've just read from fragments. His society seems to be a happy one: his senior colleagues are women. They seem to be free. But he makes a few too many misogynistic jokes. ■

Women (1843), of women's education in the 19th century, "is quickly repressed"; "the majority of girls are subdued into mere automatons", trained for a "mechanical performance of duty... their own minds all the while lying barren and unfruitful". And so it is in Gilead: "They used to have dolls," Offred says at one point, "for little girls, that would talk if you pulled a string at the back; I thought I was sounding like that, voice of a monotone, voice of a doll" (26).

The novel fits snugly into the discourses of feminism. One of the most common tropes in feminist writing is the image of imprisonment. Offred is, of course, literally imprisoned in the Commander's house. Before she got there, she and others were penned into the re-education centre by a "chain-link fence", like cattle, and only allowed out for "walks, twice daily", like dogs (22). More than just a prisoner, she was treated like a caged animal.

But Atwood engages with the trope on a less literal level, too. Consider this quote, for example, from one of the early and seminal feminist texts, Mary Wollstonecraft's *A Vindication of the Rights of Woman* (1792):

> Taught from their infancy that beauty is a woman's sceptre, the mind shapes itself to the body and roaming round its gilt cage, only seeks to adore its prison. (That is: women are imprisoned by the standards of beauty expected of them.)

The quote makes me think of the Commander's Wife, Serena Joy, whom Offred often hears "pacing back and forth" in her sitting room, as an animal does in its cage (19). The sitting-room, with its twee design, its fetish for objects, its frilly conformity, is Serena Joy's "gilt cage", a room constructed from feminine kitsch. It's a kind of prison for her, one built from the norms of femininity.* As such, Atwood associates her throughout the novel with those instruments of femininity intended to enhance "a woman's sceptre": beauty products. "Her lips were thin," Offred says, "with the small vertical lines around them you used to see in advertisements for lip cosmetics". (24) Later:

> *What a stupid name. It's like something you'd put on your hair... to straighten it. Serena Joy, it would say on the bottle, with a woman's head in cut-paper silhouette on a pink oval background with scalloped gold edges. (55)*

It's not for nothing that the Aunts – the "crack female control agency" (320) who function, in some

* The image of a woman trapped in the sitting room suggests another common trope in feminist discourse. The Irish philosopher William Thompson describes women as the "movable property" of their husbands; "of all [his] fixtures the most abject is his breeding machine, the wife". A man's wife, in other words, is part of the furniture. Thus, in *The Handmaid's Tale*, when the Commander enters the sitting room for the Ceremony, where the women of the household have assembled, "He looks us over as if taking inventory. One kneeling woman in red, one seated woman in blue, two in green..." as if they're items of furniture (171).

ways, as prison guards – are named, we discover in the Historical notes at the end, after beauty products from the "the immediate pre-Gilead period" (321).

Serena Joy may be unlikeable – monstrous, even – but hers is a portrait of feminine conformity as extreme loneliness. When she begins to cry silently during the Ceremony, "trying not to make a noise... trying to preserve her dignity", her husband "opens his eyes, notices, frowns, ceases to notice" (101). She may "seek to adore" her "gilt cage", but that doesn"t mean she's happy in it.

All of which suggests that *The Handmaid's Tale* is, yes, a feminist novel. It may be surprising, then, that so many people have questioned whether Margaret Atwood is a feminist, among them Karen Yossman, who asked in *The New Statesman*: "Is Margaret Atwood a feminist? That's what I'm trying to work out... *Obviously,* you might roll your eyes, *Have you read The Handmaid's Tale*?" But even if you *have* read *The Handmaid's Tale,* as Yossman suggests, you might be unsure.

There are two self-defining "feminists" in the novel: Offred's mother, and her close friend, Moira, both of whom exist mainly in Offred's memories. Offred's mother is a fierce, headstrong feminist, an attendant of "abortion riots" and "porn riots" (189). Moira – masculine, nonconformist – is an enraged, radical activist: she writes university essays about date rape and later works for a feminist printing press, putting out books about "birth control and rape and things like that" (187). They are both likeable characters, fun to be around, with admirable energy and compelling arguments.

But Atwood's presentation of them is critical. They are second-wave feminists – feminists who, after the early 20th century battles for civil and political equality had been more or less won, sought equality in the home and in culture, fighting for sexual and family rights.* "The personal is the political" became a popular slogan in the 1970s. Offred's mother and Moira have taken that slogan to such an extreme that they have allowed men no role in their lives.

Offred's father, whom she never met, was "a nice guy and all", her mother tells her, "with beautiful blue eyes", but "there's something missing in them, even the nice ones" (131). "A man is just a woman's strategy for making other women," she offers as an explanation for having kept him and Offred apart (130). "Just do the job, then you can bugger off" (131).

Moira, who admires Offred's mother, has taken the rejection of men further: she presents her lesbianism as a political choice. Offred remembers criticising her for it:

> *I said there was more than one way of living with your head in the sand and that if Moira thought she could create Utopia by shutting herself up in a women-only enclave she was sadly mistaken. Men*

* Key second-wave feminists, inspired by Simone de Beauvoir, include Betty Friedan and Germaine Greer.

were not just going to go away, I said. You couldn't just ignore them. (181)

As we'll see, the accusation of Utopianism is a severe one.

In her review for the *New York Times Review of Books*, the novelist Mary McCarthy saw in the novel an indictment of "“excessive” feminism... the kind of doctrinaire feminism likely to produce a backlash... exemplified in the narrator's absurd mother". McCarthy's language may seem a little harsh, but Atwood's writing warrants the criticism. When Offred's mother first appears, it is in a memory of a ritual burning of pornographic magazines to which she dragged a very young Offred. During the event, the women are "chanting... ecstatic" (48). It's a mindless, frenzied ritual, troublingly recalled later in the novel in the descriptions of Gilead's own ritual burning of provocative women's clothing: at this event, women are "throwing their arms up thankfully into the air" (242). Again: it's mindless, frenzied, and reminiscent of the Nazis' infamous book-burnings. Which begs the question: if this is a feminist novel, why on earth would Atwood implicitly compare committed feminists to Nazis?

Atwood isn't criticising the politics of these characters so much as their attitudes. Offred's mother, Moira, the architects of Gilead, Nazis, are all troubling to Atwood because they are fundamentalists, and if the novel is a criticism of any one thing, it's fundamentalism. As the academic

A scene from the 1990 film adaptation of The Handmaid's Tale, *based on a screenplay by Harold Pinter, starring Natasha Richardson (centre) as Offred.*

Priscilla Morin-Ollier put it, they share the same "moral absolutist vision". There is no room within their systems for anyone who doesn't wholly agree with them. The logical end point of the fundamentalism of Moira and Offred's mother, it is implied, is not so different to the logical end point of Gilead's. "Mother," thinks Offred at one point, "Wherever you are. Can you hear me? You wanted a women's culture. Well, now there is one" (137).

So is Margaret Atwood a feminist? It depends, she might answer, what you mean by "feminism". In a lecture called, "Is *The Handmaid's Tale* a feminist dystopia?", she attempted to define it. "Going back into history," she said,

> once upon a time, if you disagreed with the ancient Greek opinion that women were simply perambulating wombs you would have been a feminist. If you disagreed with the early Christian fathers' point of view that women had no souls, you would have been a feminist. If you disagreed later on in the nineteenth century with the view that women ought not to be educated because it would cause their brains to enlarge at the expense of the rest of them – the more important rest of them – then you were a feminist... If you entered the twentieth century and took the position that women had the right to their own property, which was certainly denied to them under nineteenth century English law, you would have been a feminist... my point is that feminism is a general tendency rather than a set ideology.

If what you mean by "a feminist novel", then, is propaganda for a political cause, then you'll be disappointed. If, however, what you mean is a novel that questions orthodoxy, thinks for itself, and seeks to be on the right side of history, that's probably what *The Handmaid's Tale* is.

Why does Puritanism feature in the novel?

So what about the second person to whom Atwood dedicates her novel, Perry Miller, the Puritan historian? When asked about him, Atwood revealed that he had taught her at Harvard:

> It's through him that I knew what I did about seventeenth century Puritan America, a theocratic*, oppressive regime not to be confused with the happy democratic fathers of America that some people are sometimes taught about in school.

You might imagine, from this, that *The Handmaid's Tale* will be set during the Puritan era. You'd be wrong about that, but not wholly wrong. Gilead is Puritan America 2.0; Atwood is inventing a grim American future by reaching into its past. She imagines what would happen if the Puritans returned, and what they would be capable of doing with all the technology now available to them.

The academic Gina Wisker has documented some of the ways in which the Handmaids' lives resemble those of Puritan women ("Handmaids of the Lord," in the words of the noted Puritan minister

* A society run along religious lines; the Puritans were "a people amongst whom religion and law were almost identical", as Nathaniel Hawthorn put it in *The Scarlet Letter* (1850).

and persecutor, Cotton Mather (1663-1728)). For a start, they were renamed in ways that overtly denoted their repression, names likes "Silence, Fear, Patience, Prudence, Mendwell, Comfort, Hopestill and Be Fruitfull". Further:

> The upbringing of New England women, like the retraining of the Handmaids, included a rejection of mirrors, combs and any clothes that were more than functional. Each has reading restricted to teachings of the Bible.

Likewise, the Handmaids take names that define their repression ("Offred", or "of Fred": belonging to Fred). Beauty products are banned: "There's no longer any hand lotion or face cream," Offred says, "not for us. Such things are considered vanities" (107). (They've been spared their gilt cage, at least.) And reading and writing are forbidden, apart from the Bible teachings that are read *to* them.

Imagining a Puritan inheritance in contemporary America was not difficult. *The Handmaid's Tale* is a response to a political movement that was nascent in America in the 1970s and 1980s, which saw itself as "a return to traditional values" and which many saw as a reaction to second-wave feminism: The New Right. This was a groundswell of fiery campaigners who would say, for example:

> God's word says that the man is to be the head of the home, and frankly as a woman I delight in

> that. I would hate to have to make the decisions for the home that he has to make. And I'm very thankful that I can lean on my husband and submit to him. (Mrs Bob Jones)

Or:

> The woman who is truly spirit-filled will want to be totally submissive to her husband... This is a truly liberated woman. Submission is God's design for women. (Beverely LaHaye)

For the New Right, as Morin-Ollier puts it, "the greatest lie of the century is the claim that women are unfairly treated and in a position of inferiority in the United States"; the New Right believes that "feminists were to blame for all the nation's ills".

This is the ideology of Puritan America and it's the ideology of Gilead, most powerfully dramatised in *The Handmaid's Tale* in Janine's re-education at the Rachel and Leah centre. Traumatised after being gang-raped at the age of 14, she is forced to admit that it was her fault. "*Her* fault, *her* fault, *her* fault," the other girls chant at her. "I led them on," Janine cries, "I deserved the pain" (82). By the end of the novel, she has suffered a nervous breakdown.

Serena Joy – who is a parody of real "televangelsts" like LaHaye, Phyllis Schlafly and Tammy Faye Bakker – embodies New Right ideology in the novel. In what is known as "the time before", she hosted a Christian fundamentalist TV show. "Her speeches," Offred remembers, "were about the sanctity of the home, about how women should stay at home" (55). The sanctity of the home: in *The Handmaid's Tale*, the home is shown to be, in Edward Howell's words, "a charade of sexual coercion, enslavement, and political expediency". The ideology is bankrupt.

It is, of course, significant that Serena Joy consciously aligns herself with Puritanism; she has hung two paintings of miserable, circumscribed Puritan women in her sitting room, with "the intention of passing them off as ancestors" (89). They are portraits of immense repression: "their backs and mouths stiff, their breasts constricted, their faces pinched, their caps starched, their skin greyish-white, guarding the room with their narrowed eyes" (90). Atwood's language is powerfully evocative here: "stiff... constricted... pinched... starched". The horrors of Gilead don't represent a violent break from the American tradition, she wants to suggest, but a conscious continuation of some of its worst currents.

This brings us to the next page of the book: a page of epigraphs. Like the dedications, they are rich in implication. The first comes from the Bible – Genesis, 30:1-3:

> *And when Rachel saw that she bare Jacob no children, Rachel envied her sister; and said unto Jacob, Give me children, or else I die.*

And Jacob's anger was kindled against Rachel; and he said, Am I in God's stead, who have withheld from thee the fruit of the womb?

And she said, Behold my maid Bilhah, go in unto her; and she shall bear upon my knees, that I may also have children by her.

This is the novel's plot in miniature. Serena Joy is Rachel, the Commander is Jacob, Offred is Bilah – an arrangement repeated in households around the country. The ceremony in which the male ruling class attempt to impregnate the slave class of fertile women (and before which they read aloud this passage) is a grotesque parody of this story: just as Bilah "bears upon [Rachel's] knees", so the Handmaids literally bear upon the Commanders Wives' knees during the intercourse.

But more than simply foreshadowing the novel's plot, this quote functions to root the grimmest aspects of Atwood's fictional totalitarian regime in the text at the heart of Western Judeo-Christian tradition.

The institutionalised misogyny of Gilead invokes the Bible as a way of legitimising its violence: "she probably longs to slap my face," Offred thinks of the Commander's Wife. "They can hit us, there's Scriptural precedent" (26). Like many theocratic societies, Gilead's scriptural emphasis is more about control than faith. Accordingly, there is little concern for accuracy. One of the phrases the

Handmaids are made to recite as part of their re-education is: "From each according to her ability; to each according to his needs." "It was from the Bible," Offred says. "St. Paul again, in Acts" (127). But we know better: it's not from the Bible, it's Karl Marx. Or rather, it's a bastardisation of a phrase that Karl Marx once used, often wrongly attributed to him: "From each according to *his* ability; to each according to his needs." It's an appeal for socialism, about as far away from Gilead, politically, as you can get.

Atwood shows, throughout the novel, how the word of God is misused by the state, a state which seeks to justify everything it wants by pretending it has been decreed by God, and is thus inarguable. The state seeks to stamp out any scriptural ambiguity and stamp its own authoritative and final interpretation on the text. The reference to Marx is sly; another phrase he made famous is: "religion is the opiate of the masses".

But there's no denying that Gilead's misogyny really is rooted in the Bible – the book around which many societies, like America, have, historically, sought to fashion their identities. The fact is that women don't come out of the *Bible* very well at all; think of Eve, directly responsible for the fall of mankind. Margaret Walters has written about how Saint Paul, in the 16th and 17th centuries, the Puritan era

was regularly invoked against any woman who

> spoke out, or asked awkward questions about the Church's attitude to women: "Let your women keep silence in churches, for it is not permitted to them to speak", he instructed the Corinthians. And again, in the epistle to Timothy, "If they will learn anything let them ask their husbands at home: for it is shame for women to speak in church".

Timothy forms the backbone of the religious ceremonies in *The Handmaid's Tale*; the Commander who holds the Prayvaganza is quoting Timothy 2:11-12, for example, when he says: "Let the woman learn in silence with all subjection... I suffer not a woman to teach, nor to usurp authority over the man, but to be in silence" (233). Saint Paul is regularly invoked in the novel, too, as when Aunt Lydia decrees: "Hair must be long or covered... Saint Paul said it's either that or a close shave." Again, she is referring to real scripture, Corinthians 11:6: "For if the woman be not covered let her also be shorn: but if it be a shame for a woman to be shorn or shaven, let her be covered" (72).

With this quote, then, Atwood is signalling, as Howells puts it, that "her tale is an act of resistance to masculinist fiction conventions, including that archetypal patriarchal text, the Old Testament".

FIVE FACTS ABOUT *THE HANDMAID'S TALE*

1.
Men like the novel less than women. Basing her statistics on all the reviews the novel garnered, Lee Briscoe Thompson found that whereas 93% of American women liked the novel, only 59% of American men did. Similarly, 76% of American women found it plausible, whereas only 50% of American men did. More strikingly, 93% of British women found it plausible, and only 43% of British men did.

2.
Not content with merely being a novelist, poet, journalist, memoirist, essayist, screen-writer, literary critic and historian, Margaret Atwood is also an inventor. In 2006 she invented the LongPen – an electronic pen that allows her to sign copies of her books from the other side of the world.

3.
The playwright Harold Pinter's original screenplay for the film of the book was rejected for being "too feminist": it was thought that it would actually harm the reputations of the actors.

4.

Atwood toyed with a number of different epigraphs for the novel. One she very nearly used was the following quote from a UN report: "Women represent fifty percent of the adult world population, one third of the official labour force, perform nearly two-thirds of all working hours, receive only one-tenth of world income and own less than one percent of world property."

5.

In 2015, Atwood wrote a novel, *Scribbler Moon,* for the Future Library Project, that no one is allowed to read until the year 2114.

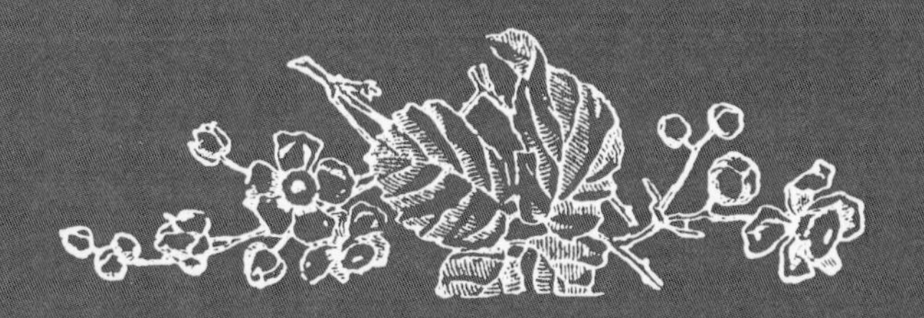

What kind of novel is *The Handmaid's Tale*?

So we're edging towards a fuller picture of the novel. You've worked out that it's going to be about a persecuted woman in a Puritan society which uses iron-law religious morality for political oppression, and is going to seek to transcend a misogyny rooted in Judeo-Christian tradition. What you don't know, yet, is what *kind* of novel it's going to be – what genre. The next epigraph helps with that.

This one's from a text by the 18th century satirist Jonathan Swift (1667-1745), called "A Modest Proposal" (1729):

> *But as to myself, having been wearied out for many years with offering vain, idle, visionary thoughts, and at length utterly despairing of success, I fortunately fell upon this proposal.*

"A Modest Proposal" is a satirical tract – its target being the use of rational argument to solve difficult human problems – that proposes a solution to the chronic poverty in Ireland in the early 18th century: that the Irish eat their children. There is hardly a fault in the logic yet the reader knows instinctively that the argument is absurd. It's an example of what philosophers call a *reductio ad absurdum* (literally: a reduction to absurdity), in which a philosophical approach is followed to its quite obviously absurd logical conclusion in order to reveal the flaws in the premise. In this case, it aims to show the lack of empathy and compassion in political approaches to tackling poverty. The "vain, idle visionary thoughts" he is "wearied out" with making refers to the sensible contributions Swift has already made: suggestions like raising taxes for the rich. The joke is that simple solutions to problems often get ignored because they don't fit into prevailing discourses.

So what does this tell you about the novel you're about to read? If you were particularly sharp, you might be able to extrapolate from it that it's going to be a dystopian novel. Dystopian novels tend to be satirical *reductios ad absurdum* of the societies in which they're written (in some ways, you could call "A Modest Proposal" dystopian). Like *The Hunger Games,* or *1984,* they're set typically in a near future in which worrying trends in the socio-political organisation of the author's society have been followed to their logical conclusions – which tend to be violent, repressive, pessimistic – and are thus shown to be cause for concern.

Atwood has said that her model for *The Handmaid's Tale* was George Orwell's classic novel *1984,* so it's worth thinking briefly about that novel's dystopia, Oceania. Oceania is a place of total surveillance: security cameras watch you day and night, wherever you are. They even have ways of detecting independent thought – "thoughtcrime" – which the state has sought to replace with a uniform "orthodoxy". Emotional attachments and loving relationships have been purged: emotional energy goes into worshipping the spectral, omnipresent figurehead, Big Brother, and flinging hate at public enemy number one, Emmanuel Goldstein.

Oceania achieves its total control in two main ways. First, by repressing sexual impulses: "sexual privation induced hysteria," the narrator explains,

> *which was desirable because it could be transformed into war-fever and leader-worship... There was a direct, intimate connection between chastity and political orthodoxy. For how could the fear, the hatred and the lunatic credulity which the Party needed in its members be kept at the right pitch, except by bottling down some powerful instinct and using it as a driving force?*

Second, by seizing control of words. The elite of Oceania are working on a new language, Newspeak, whose purpose is to make individual communication all but impossible. By reducing language to just a few words, it means to eradicate "vagueness" and "useless shades of meaning". "You don't grasp the beauty of the destruction of words," one of its inventors tells the novel's protagonist, Winston Smith.

> *Don't you see that the whole aim of Newspeak is to narrow the range of thought? In the end we shall make thoughtcrime literally impossible, because there will be no words in which to express it... In fact, there will* be *no thought, as we understand it now.*

Orthodoxy means not thinking – not needing to think. Orthodoxy is unconscious.

Individuality is erased: life is uniform, a matter of going through the motions. Anyone who breaks routine, however slightly, is punished. "You had to live – did live, from habit that became instinct – in the assumption that every sound you made was overheard and... every move scrutinised." "Nothing was your own," says the narrator, "except the few cubic centimetres inside your skull."

It should be obvious how much *The Handmaid's Tale* owes to *1984*; Gilead's mechanisms of repression are much the same as Oceania's. It has a kind of total surveillance, though its instruments are more implied than seen: "I don't see the floodlights," Offred says, "I just know they're there." Similarly, there is a secret police force – the Eyes – whose presence is implied, by means of black cars with darkened windows. It's an "exhaustive surveillance", in the words of Foucault, "which makes all things visible by becoming itself invisible".

Close personal relationships are forbidden; as Lee Briscoe Thompson has it, only one relationship is sanctioned in Gilead, "that between an individual and the collectivity of the State". Gilead has made "unnecessary communication or exchange of information" punishable, "using isolation and uncertainty to effect docility". It has used its strict colour-coded uniforms to dissolve individual identities; it's impossible to have friends in Gilead because there's no way of seeing anyone as an individual. The regime has, in Gina Wisker's words, "reduced people to their functions: control, reproduction, service, and those who regulate those functions". Language is controlled by the state. When the Handmaids greet each other, for example, they follow a Biblical script. "Blessed be the fruit," is how Ofglen greets Offred, "the accepted greeting among us": "'May the Lord open,' I answer, the accepted response"* (29).

Daily life has been ritualised, "to grind out of peoples' lives," as Thompson puts it, "the nonconformities and the opportunities for even small choices (and therefore freedom of action or thought, and the retention of individual identity)."

The sexual impulse has of course been repressed, and sex controlled almost entirely by the state. You might even detect Gilead in embryo in *1984* when the party's representative, O"Brien, explains its plans for the future: "Procreation will be an annual formality like the renewal of a ration card. We shall abolish the orgasm..."

And, as in *1984*, in *The Handmaid's Tale*, the state wants its citizens to internalise its ideology. "The Republic of Gilead," says Aunt Lydia, "knows no bounds. Gilead is within you" (33). "I have failed once again," says Offred, when her period starts, "to fulfil the expectations of others, which have become my own."

* Note that it isn't the *official* or *enforced* response, but the *accepted* response: it doesn't need to have been enforced. The climate of fear has worked.

Another striking similarity is that, like Swift, both Atwood and Orwell have carved dystopian societies not out of problems they see in the real world so much as out of proposed solutions to those problems. Orwell was a socialist and Oceania is a socialist state, whose initial purpose was to overcome what Orwell thought were the problems of capitalism. Likewise, Gilead is an attempt to solve what, for Atwood, are very real problems.

In *The Handmaid's Tale*, "the time before" is not a happy time for women. Misogynistic violence was rife, date rape and violent pornography the norm. Women were scared to go out alone. Offred describes the "rules that were never spelled out but that every woman knew: rules like, 'don't open your door to a stranger", or 'don't stop at the side of the road to help a motorist pretending to be in trouble." (34) There were terrible sexual pressures on women: "the meat market," the Commander calls it, recalling how women "starved themselves" or "pumped their breasts full of silicone, had their noses cut off. Think of the human misery" (231).

We've seen how both feminists and the architects of Gilead responded similarly to the proliferation of pornography – well, you can see why. When Offred goes to the magazine burning, a woman hands her a magazine, open on a page with "a pretty woman on it, with no clothes on, hanging from the ceiling by a chain wound around her hands" (47). As part of the re-education, the Aunts show the Handmaids similar material: "women tied up or chained or with dog collars around their necks, women hanging from trees, or upsidedown, naked..." (128).

Gilead's injustices are justified as solutions to these very real problems. "We've given [women] more than we've taken away," the Commander says (231). "There is more than one kind of freedom," Aunt Lydia says, insightfully. "Freedom to and freedom from. In the days of anarchy, it was freedom to. Now you are being given freedom from."

What both Orwell and Atwood might have a problem with is actually *utopianism*. As Atwood understands them, utopias and dystopias have much in common. For a start, they are both planned societies, highly organised and rigorously structured. Thus they necessarily involve punishment for anyone who chooses not to go along with the plans. "Everyone has to be made to fit the pattern in one way or the other," said Atwood in her lecture on the novel. "Is *The Handmaid's Tale* a feminist dystopia?... Both utopians and dystopians have the habit of cutting off the hands and feet and even heads of those who don't fit the scheme." "Better," the Commander tells Offred, "never means better for everyone... It always means worse, for some" (222). Indeed, Atwood said, "whether it is a utopia or dystopia depends on the point of view of the narrator."* "[A]ll dystopia," she went on, "begins in

* Dave Eggers's novel *The Circle* (2013) is a good example of a novel that plays on this tension: you're never quite sure whether the protagonist sees the world she lives in as a utopia or a dystopia. Accordingly, you're never quite sure which it is.

utopia... Most dystopias are attempts at planned societies that somehow go off the tracks. The longing for perfection has an unpleasant habit of producing tyranny."

And Gilead certainly views itself as a utopia, envisaging, in Gina Wisker's words, a "future state in which women are not expected to carry out a debilitating variety of roles".

> *For the generations that come after, Aunt Lydia said, it will be so much better. The women will live in harmony together, all in one family; you will be like daughters to them... Women united for a common end! Helping one another in their daily chores as they walk the path of life together, each performing her appointed task. Why expect one woman to carry out all the functions necessary to the serene running of a household? It isn't reasonable or humane. (171)*

She has a point.

The Handmaid's Tale is a *reductio ad absurdum,* then, portraying a culture in which some of the obvious solutions to violence against women have been overlooked in favour of a grand solution which, though patently absurd, doesn't involve the inconvenience of shattering the patriarchal structures of the world it comes from. Like "A Modest Proposal", it's a satire about people who would rather suggest extreme cruelty (let the Irish eat their children) than go to the trouble of shifting their world view.

So what is the solution? Atwood doesn't offer one – she is a diagnostician, not a healer – but she suggested in her lecture on the novel that rather than aiming for perfection, or utopianism, we should make the best of what we have. She ended with a quote from the Wallace Stevens poem, "The Poems of Our Climate": "The imperfect is our paradise."

What is the novel telling us about power?

The final epigraph, a Sufi proverb, is more mysterious than the others: "*In the desert there is no sign that says, Thou shalt not eat stones.*" The only explanation Atwood has offered is this comment she gave when asked what it meant, during her post-lecture Q&A session: "We aren't forbidden to do things unless we have a tendency as human beings to do them."

I think she is saying something about power. Power is Atwood's great theme: the workings of power, the consequences of power, the desire of power, the fear of it. Power, for Atwood, is everywhere. As she wrote in "Notes on *Power Politics*" (*Power Politics* being an early collection of poetry): "Power is our environment. We live surrounded by it: it pervades everything we are and do, invisible and soundless, like air..." For Atwood, as the critic Pilar Somecarrera has put it, "our identity is always determined by a net of relations of power".

What *is* power? Throughout her career, Atwood has defined politics (the study and practice of power) as "everything that involves who gets to do what to whom". "A lot of power," she says, "is ascription. People have power because we think they have power, and that's all politics is."

Somecarrera has shown how Atwood's conception of power resembles that of the 20th century cultural critic Michel Foucault, who preferred to think of power as a verb than a noun. As he puts it in *Power/Knowledge*,

> Power in the substantive sense, "le pouvoir", doesn't exist. The idea that there is either located at – or emanating from – a given point something which is a "power" seems to be based on a misguided analysis... In reality power means relations, a more-or-less organised, hierarchical, co-ordinated cluster of relations.

Power, in other words, is in our interactions with other people; it's what you expect of people, it's what people expect of you.

As power is "diffused throughout social relations", says Somacarerra, it is not real in Atwood's world, "not really there: people give it to each other". This is why there is no great villain in *The Handmaid's Tale*: there doesn't need to be. Men and women are "political prisoners... trapped as victor/victims in their own reflections of the world and of each other".

The Handmaid's Tale powerfully demonstrates how power emanates from and infuses our relationships. Almost every social interaction is a power game that replicates the power games of wider society. Look, for example, at Offred's arrival at the Commander's house, when Serena greets her:

> *She didn't step aside to let me in, she just stood there in the doorway, blocking the entrance. She wanted me to feel that I could not come into the house unless she said so. There is push and shove, these days, over such toeholds. (23)*

Or there's the moment when she passes a pubescent Guardian at a roadblock who looks sex-starved. She seductively wiggles her hips at him: "It's like thumbing your nose from behind a fence or teasing a dog with a bone... I enjoy the power: power of a dog bone, passive but there...." (32). Everything you do, for Atwood, expresses your positioning within power structures.

But there *is* a way out. And this is where the Sufi proverb comes in. Power, I think Atwood is using it to say, is an attempt to repress human instinct, to remove humanity from the political subject, to dehumanise. There is no sign in the desert saying don't eat stones because humans don't want to, so there doesn't need to be; power only needs to be exercised over those things that make us human beings. Power wants to erase the unfortunate reality of being human, what the writer Philip Roth would call "the human stain".

In order for power relations to function, individuals must, at least momentarily, dehumanise one another. Offred remembers the painful realisation that she and Luke would have to kill their cat when they fled for the Canadian border:

> *I'll take care of it, Luke said. And because he said* it *instead of* her, *I knew he meant* kill. *That is what you have to do before you kill, I thought. You have to create an it, where none was before. (202)*

This revelation resonates at the end of the novel when the Handmaids are forced to participate in the group execution of a political dissident. The state makes the murder possible by labelling him (falsely, it's implied) a "rapist". The word dehumanises him and thus the women are able to tear him to pieces; as Offred says, "He has become an it" (292).

But in the strange affair between Offred and the Commander, we begin to see how power structures break down when people enter into human relationships with one another – that is, when an it becomes a she. Through their barely sexual, certainly unromantic relationship, the Commander becomes "more than a shadow" for Offred. "And I for him. To him I'm no longer merely a usable body... To him, I am not merely empty" (172). At the end of the novel, when Offred is rescued by Mayday, the Commander believes that she is being taken away by the secret police, to her almost certain death. And he looks on – he, the architect of this totalitarian atrocity – aghast at what's happening to her: "He looks worried and helpless" (306). When, earlier in the novel, he tries to explain the utopian dimension of Gilead to her, he finishes by asking, "What did we overlook?" "Love," she says, simply (231). This is not exactly love catching up with him, but something approaching it. She's no longer a caged animal, part of the furniture: she's become a human being.

How is the story told?

The first thing you notice when you actually read the novel is that it is written in the first person. And when a novel is written in the first person, one question you need to ask is: who is the narrator talking to? One answer might be that she's talking to herself. For Atwood, identity is a kind of compulsive, revisionary storytelling; "every human being," she says.

> is always telling or retelling the story of his or her life. In that case the storyteller is you and the listener is also you. There's a lot of rewriting that goes on throughout your life.

But Offred herself rejects Atwood's hypothesis: "You don't tell a story only to yourself. There's always someone else" (49).

And as we discover in the Historical Notes, the text we read is not an interior monologue – it doesn't come from inside Offred's mind at the time of action – nor is it a diary, nor anything written down: it is a transcription of 30 cassette tapes discovered by an academic, Professor Pieixoto, who has arranged them into what he imagines to be chronological order. Offred spoke the whole story aloud, then, and recorded it. So there must have been some intended listener, beyond herself. But who? I hope an answer will emerge through an analysis of how she tells her story, and then – crucially – *why*.

Offred takes care, throughout her narrative, to alert the reader (or listener) to its constructedness. "This is a reconstruction," she says. "All of it is a reconstruction" (144). As such, she acknowledges, it can only fail to represent the complex reality of her lived experience:

> *It's impossible to say a thing exactly the way it was, because what you say can never be exact, you always have to leave something out, there are too many parts, sides, crosscurrents, nuances, too many gestures, which could mean this or that, too many shapes which can never be fully described, too many flavours, in the air or on the tongue, half-colours, too many.*

Offred's narrative consistently fails to tell it like it is. But she goes further than that, often deliberately telling it like it isn't. When the Commander first asks her to kiss him, for example, she imagines embracing him then stabbing him: "I think about the blood coming out of him, hot as soup, sexual, over my hands." It's a vivid, dramatic moment, punctured entirely by the following sentence: "In fact I don't think about anything of the kind. I put it in only afterwards" (150). Or, later: "If there were a fire in the fireplace, its light would be twinkling on the polished surfaces, glimmering warmly on flesh. I add the firelight in" (193). The conditional becomes the actual.

Offred is letting us know that her story is at least partially invented, and that this is thus only one possible version of it. To intensify that, she sometimes presents *more* than one possible version, as when she thinks about what might have happened to Luke after their failed escape. She says, "I believe Luke is lying face down in a thicket," having been shot and killed; "I also believe," she says, "that Luke is sitting up... on the edge of something, a bed or chair", in prison. "I also believe," on the following page, "that they didn't catch him... that he made it, reached the bank", escaped (115). "The things I believe can't all be true," she acknowledges. "But I believe in all of them" (116).

When she pictures Luke in his prison, Offred draws our attention to the process of rewriting. "He hasn't shaved for a year," she says, "though they cut his hair short... for lice they say." Then: "I'll have to revise that: if they cut the hair for lice, they'd cut the beard too" (114). By saying, "I'll have to revise that", rather than simply revising it, she is implying that the text is meant to change beyond its present state.

The version we read is provisional, unfinished: not the first draft, nor the final form the text will rest in. In fact, it's not only Offred who hasn't finished. Pieixoto's ordering of the text is, he explains, "based on some guesswork and [is] to be regarded as approximate, pending further research" (314).

Why has Atwood presented it like this? Partly it's because she wants us to feel, as she does, a distrust of closed narrative forms. Gilead uses closed narrative forms for political control. It lays a simple, positive narrative over the infinite complexity of its grim reality and trusts that that version will be regarded as truth.

Think, for example, of the public execution at the end: three women are hanged and one man ripped to pieces by the Handmaids. And what's the event called? It's not an execution, it's not a punishment: it's a "salvaging". The story told by that word – that the dead people have been saved from sin, rescued – overwrites what might be considered the 'real" story: that they are murdered, like Mary Webster nearly was, because they don't fit into the system.

This is why the Handmaids are forbidden to read or write: reading and writing means control of language, and control of language means control of narrative. And the state wants a monopoly on narrative. When, during the procreation ceremony, the Commander takes the Bible out of its locked box, Offred laments that he "has something we don't have, he has the word" (99). And this is why, when he invites her to play Scrabble with him, she feels strangely empowered: "The feeling is voluptuous," she says. "This is freedom" (149).

It's also why Offred has such a mania for appreciating the surprising resonances and multiple meanings of words; a mania manifest mainly in the preponderance, in her postulating, of polysemy and paranamasia. Or, in English, her puns. They're everywhere, puns. Some of them are bawdy – as when she describes the young Guardians she has deliberately aroused as "two men, who stand at attention, stiffly" (32). Sometimes they're telling puns, as when she says, of the Handmaids' dresses, "some people call them *habits*, a good word for them. Habits are hard to break" (34).

This mania always manifests itself at the most intense moments in her story: "I sit in the chair and think about the word *chair,*" she says on the morning of the Birthing. "It can also mean the leader of a meeting. It can also mean a mode of execution. It is the first syllable in *charity*. It is the French word for flesh" (120). Or, when she is describing the coup that led to the founding of Gilead, and remembers being fired from her job:

> Job. *It's a funny word. It's a job for a man. Do a jobbie, they'd say to children, when they were being toilet-trained. Or of dogs: he did a job on the carpet...* The Book of Job. (182)

If Offred can hold on to the fact that words have multiple meanings and surprising resonances, and that they're not always connected to one another – "None of these facts has any connection with the others," she says about the variations of "chair" (120) – then not only can she, in the words of Marta Dvorak, "critique the institutional linguistic practices serving to promote ideology", but she can actually resist some of that control. If she can see the many possible stories that exist inside single words, single worlds, then she doesn't have to accept the state's version of reality, of her. She can be multiple. "These are the litanies I use to compose myself," she says (120).

Why do flowers feature so much in *The Handmaid's Tale?*

But the punning is only one side of Offred's stylistic coin. On the other side is the poetry. Much of the poetic writing in *The Handmaid's Tale* is about flowers. Like puns, flowers are everywhere. They're part of the story Gilead wants to tell about women. They speak of a kind of compliant femininity: pretty, silent, in the background, and solely for the purposes of procreation. Thus the only non-essential item in Offred's room is a picture of flowers: "Flowers are still allowed" (17). And Serena Joy is surrounded by them. When not roaming her gilt cage, she can be found, sedentary, in her botanic one: "sometimes

[she] has a chair brought out, and just sits in it, in her garden. From a distance it looks like peace" (22). Looks like peace, but isn't: in the words of the French feminist Hélène Cixous, "women's lovely mouths [are] gagged with pollen".

One day, Offred finds Serena Joy in her garden,

> *snipping off the seed pods with a pair of shears... She was aiming, positioning the blades of the shears, then cutting with a convulsive jerk of the hands. Was it... some blitzkrieg, some kamikaze, committed on the swelling genitalia of the flowers? (161)*

It is an image in miniature of what Gilead does to its citizens: desexes them. Tellingly, Serena Joy here is "Saint Serena, on her knees, doing penance".

But for Offred the garden tells a different story. "Here and there are worms," she says when she first describes it, "evidence of the fertility of the soil, caught by the sun, half dead; flexible and pink, like lips" (27). Uninterested in the docile, passive prettiness of flowers she hones in on these vaginal worms, complexly symbolic of life ("fertility"), sex ("pink, like lips") and death ("half dead").

For Offred, then, the garden becomes symbolic – what Gilead wants to write out of the picture. Thus flowers adorn her relationship with Nick, the kind of romantic, mutually-desiring relationship that Gilead wants to stamp out. "The tulips along the border," she writes after her first subversive encounter with him, "are redder than ever, opening,

Margaret Atwood (b. 1939)

no longer winecups but chalices; thrusting themselves up, to what end?" The deepening red of the tulips, their "opening" and "thrusting" project Offred's erotic charge back at her.

Later, when her desire is becoming unbearable, she passes Nick and the air "stinks of flowers, of pulpy growth, of pollen thrown into the wind in handfuls, like oyster spawn into the sea" (190). The stink, the pulp, the explosion of pollen in the wind, the semen-like oyster spawn... Offred's repressed feelings are seeping into her imagery. Later, suggestive "stains on the mattress" are "like dried flower petals" (61); after all, as she reminds us, flowers are "the genital organs of plants" (91).

Offred wants to reclaim the association of women with nature, which Gilead has attempted to disinfect; she wants to tell a darker, earthier, more real story: she wants to bring the filth back to flowers. When she sees Serena Joy snipping off the seed pods, she immediately makes the scene her own, describing the changing seasons.

> *Well. Then we had the irises, rising beautiful and cool on their tall stalks, like blown glass, like pastel water momentarily frozen in a splash, light blue, light mauve... (161)*

These are images, now, not of regimentation and control, but of free-floating flux, flowers caught, momentarily, in their twisting. The garden becomes a source of political hope.

There is something subversive about this garden of Serena's, a sense of buried things bursting upwards, wordlessly, into the light, as if to point, to say: "Whatever is silenced will clamour to be heard, though silently..." (161).

It's an image of the triumph of individual sexuality over totalitarian oppression. The strict binaries of Gilead's system, their false certainties and oppressive narratives, their narrative impositions, have yielded in Offred's imagination to this imagery of flux and mutability. Things shift, suggest, glimmer, change form like words do when punned on.

> *The summer dress rustles against the flesh of my thighs, the grass grows underfoot, at the edges of my eyes there are movements, in the branches, feathers, flittings, grace notes, tree into bird, metamorphosis run wild. Goddesses are possible now and the air suffuses with desire.* (161-162)

She can even *feel* the change in the world ("the grass grows underfoot"), the futurity of desire. No longer is the garden associated with Christian, male oppression; it's an image now of pagan, female, freedom. *Goddesses* are possible now.

I want to pause for a moment, as Offred does, on those irises "momentarily frozen" in time, and consider the significance of freezing time in this novel.

Offred has a strange relationship with time. There are a disorienting number of time periods repres-ented in the novel, and it's often hard to know which one she's describing at any given point. Sometimes she seems to exist in more than one time in the same sentence. This one, for example: "We wait, the clock in the hall ticks, Serena lights another cigarette, I get into the car" (94). This is when the household has assembled in the sitting room and they're waiting for the Commander. The car, though, is in Offred's past; as she waits, and the clock ticks, she starts reliving her escape attempt with Luke and their daughter. In this sentence there are two present tenses.

This is regularly the case for Offred, who spends

a lot of time in her memories. Sometimes it's unintentional – "attacks of the past," she calls them (62). It can be the smallest sense memory that draws her back in time, often to her daughter, as when she's lying in the bath:

> *she's there with me, suddenly, without warning, it must be the smell of the soap. I... breathe her in, baby powder and child's washed flesh and shampoo, with an undertone, the faint scent of urine. (73)*

At these moments, as the critic Jagna Oltarzewska has argued, Offred appears to be suffering from post-traumatic stress disorder. Traumatic events, Oltarzewska writes, have a kind of timelessness: they are at once outside time and continuously present, forever relived. "The trauma is thus an event that has no beginning, no ending, no before, no during and no after"; it has "a timelessness, and a ubiquity that puts it outside the range of associatively linked experiences, outside the range of comprehension, of recounting, and of mastery". Experience

> separates out into a sluggish, monotonous present and what is referred to as the "time before", between them lies a "marker", a moment *out* of time which is unbridgeable, indescribable and involves an irreparable sense of loss.

Offred's "marker", her moment out of time, is of course the disaster of her attempted escape: her daughter taken from her, her husband lost, both their fates unknown.

Often, though, her double presence is intentional: she has learned to spend time in her memories. Thus, when we first see her walking around town, she says,

> *I'm remembering my feet on these sidewalks, in the time before, and what I used to wear on them. Sometimes it was shoes for running, with cushioned soles and breathing holes, and stars of fluorescent fabric that reflected light in the darkness. (34)*

Notice the level of detail she goes into, and the sensual enjoyment she finds in it: the sing-song rhyme, indulgent alliteration and ebullient rhythm of "cushioned soles and breathing holes, and stars of fluorescent fabric". Her memories tend to be more richly sensual than her present experience; she picks up on small details and lets their fullness wash over her, savouring even the most banal objects. Sense – scent, usually – is a kind of door on to her past. When she smells nail polish on a tourist, for example:

> *I remember the smell of nail polish, the way it wrinkled if you put the second coat on too soon, the tiny brushing of sheer pantyhose against the skin, the way the toes felt, pushed towards the opening in the shoe by the whole weight of the body... I can feel her shoes, on my own feet. The smell of nail polish*

has made me hunger. (39)

Her past seems to have more reality to her than her present, which often has a hellish, dreamlike sluggishness to it. It's like a room she can enter at will, always there, to escape her prison.

It's a [illegible]ns of resistance. As Marta Dvorak [illegible] way of resisting "Gilead's control [of] [illegible] d history". Gilead, she says, has tried [illegible] of "utopian stasis and timelessness". [illegible]ead's present is oppressively static, gloopy. "There's time to spare," Offred says. "This is one of the things I wasn't prepared for – the amount of unfilled time, the long parentheses of nothing. Time as white sound" (79). "It seems to have stopped at summer," she says elsewhere (209). Then, watching a dandelion disintegrating in the wind: "All that time, blowing away in the summer breeze" (224). "There was no night and day; only a flickering" (149).

For Dvorak, Offred is a "time traveller who breaks out of her temporal and spatial closure. Memory allows her to "step sideways out of [her] own time"* to turn stasis into movement". Her ability to live in her memories, in other words, is another way of escaping Gilead's control of her narratives: she is creating her own mental space, a private, imaginative

* This is what Offred says when she is lying in bed at night: "The night is mine, my own time, to do with as I will, as long as I am quiet. As long as I don't move... I lie... and step sideways out of my own time. Out of time. Though this is time and nor am I out of it." (47)

world in which Gilead can't reach her.

Those irises, then, represent her ability to snatch time, to snatch moments of beauty, joy, and to hold them so that they stretch on forever (flowers, after all, decay and die). As with her response to Gilead's control of language, Offred wants to resist closure, and she does that, paradoxically, in her poetic embrace of the fleeting and momentary. As she says of Luke in the early days of their relationship: "He was so momentary... And yet there seemed no end to him" (61). It even becomes a way of dealing with her trauma: remembering "pull[ing] her [daughter] to the ground and roll[ing] on top of her to cover her, shield her", just before she was taken, Offred remembers a leaf close to her eyes, "red, turned early". She says: "I can see every bright vein. It's the most beautiful thing I've ever seen" (85).

There's another counter-world Offred sometimes steps into: the world of her own body. Offred is defined and determined by, and valued because of, her body. And, like everything else, Gilead wants to write its own narrative on to it. In her essay, "Margaret Atwood's Female Bodies", Madeline Duries explores how, in Atwood's novels, "wider power structures are written onto female flesh"; Offred's body is a "battlefield" between her and Gilead. As a result, it becomes alien to her, not her own. "My nakedness is strange to me already," she says when she takes a bath (72).

But it's all she has. And, as such, she often settles into it, mindfully, as into a landscape. To begin with, it's an alien landscape, defined by the state's expectations of her (fertility), and looking like the set of a science fiction movie. "I'm a cloud congealed around a central object," she says,

> *the shape of a pear, which is hard and more real than I am and glows red within its translucent wrapping. Inside it is a space, huge as the sky at night and dark and curved like that, though black-red rather than black. Pinpoints of light swell, sparkle, burst and shrivel within it, countless as stars. Every month there is a moon, gigantic, round, heavy, an omen. It transits, pauses, continues on and passes out of sight, and I see despair coming towards me like famine. To feel that empty again, again. I listen to my heart, wave upon wave, salty and red, continuing on and on, marking time. (84)*

It doesn't sounds like a happy place to go. Elsewhere, she describes how "I sink down into my body as into a swamp, fenland, where only I know the footing. Treacherous ground, my own territory" (83). For Gina Wisker, "Offred's own body is not a place of safety – she feels that it is a swamp threatening to overwhelm her". But what Wisker ignores is the fact that, in Offred's fenland, only she knows "the footing". It might be a place defined by her function within this patriarchy; it might be "treacherous ground"; but it's still her own place, her "own territory". No one else can go there.

Duries, along with many other critics, has noted

the debt Atwood owes to Hélène Cixous in this kind of body-writing. In her seminal essay, "The Laugh of the Medusa" (1975), Cixous puts forward her idea of écriture *féminine* (feminine writing), urging female writers to find inspiration in their own bodies: "By writing her self, woman will turn to the body which has been more than confiscated from her, which has been turned into the uncanny stranger on display."

She "calls on women", as Duries has it, "to reject male, rule-bound language in favour of a language connecting body with text". She wants women to weave imaginative worlds from their bodily experience, creating a "unique empire", over which they are "sovereign". Is this not what Offred is doing? She is rewriting and reclaiming her body from the state. Significantly, for Offred, it takes falling in love, and entering a fulfilling sexual relationship, to fully reclaim her body: "I'm alive in my skin," she says after consummating her desire. "Write yourself. Your body must be heard," Cixous commands. And Offred does.

The way Offred tells her story – with its postmodern distrust of narrative forms, its overflow of wordplay, its flower poetry, its strange timelessness, and its landscape writing of the body – is an attempt to wrest some control from the oppressive, patriarchal state in which she lives: control over language, over narrative, over body, over imagination, over identity. It's an act of resistance.

It's not an *entirely* successful act: her story is

presented to us, remember, by two men (Professors Pieixoto and Wade) who surround their account of the reconstruction of her text, and their retitling of it, with misogynistic jokes before dismissing her story as "crumbs" of History (323). As Howell puts it, Pieixoto abuses her "as Gilead abused her, removing her authority over her life story and renaming it in a gesture which parallels Gilead's patriarchal oppression of women".

But nor is it entirely unsuccessful: far from the rule-bound, regimented "masculine" story that Pieixoto and Wade want history to be, her story – herstory – is ambiguous, uncertain, and open-ended. It is, in Dvorak's words, a "rebellion against utopian closure and uniformity", which deliberately cultivate[s] uncertainty, blurring, ambiguity, flux – all threats to perfect regularity and normality".

So why does Offred tell us about her life?

Most critics argue that Offred tells her story in order to survive. Atwood has always been interested in survivors – those victims like Mary Webster who pull through against the odds. One of her first books, a work of literary criticism called *Survival* (1972), explores the subject. In it, she outlines four different ways of dealing with one's victimhood:

> Position One: To deny the fact that you are a victim... Position Two: To acknowledge the fact that you are a victim, but to explain this as an act of Fate, the Will of God, the dictates of Biology (in the case of women, for instance), the necessity decreed by History, or Economics, or the Unconscious, or any other large general powerful idea... Position Three: To acknowledge the fact that you are a victim but to refuse to accept the assumption that the role is inevitable... Position Four: To be a creative non-victim.

It's this last position that interests her. The "creative non-victim" uses her victimhood as a source of inspiration and, in doing so, transcends it. Storytelling – writing – becomes an act of survival.

The problem with this reading is that Offred is telling her story *after* the event, from implied safety. She has already survived before she starts speaking. So, again: why tell her story?

One answer might lie in the care she takes to reimagine the world she's escaped from. She weaves together sensuous details she can't possibly remember to create an immediacy, a living-through, of experience. She tells us, for example, that "through the almost-closed door I could hear the light clink of the hard peas falling into the metal bowl" (20). Does she really remember this detail? Probably not; it's probably like the crackling fire she adds in to the text, included to create atmosphere. But, in its vividness, it makes readers feel more present in her world than they otherwise would, and thus care more.

Often she goes into a great deal of detail when describing things she can't possibly know. When she pictures Luke in his imaginary prison cell, for example, she says:

> *the hair is ragged, the back of his neck is nicked, that's hardly the worst, he looks ten years older, twenty, he's bent like an old man, his eyes are pouched, small purple veins have burst in his cheeks, there's a scar, no a wound, it isn't yet healed, the colour of tulips near the stem end, down the left side of his face where the flesh split recently. (114)*

She's taking care to make this imagined scene as realistic as possible* (see that revision: "there's a scar, no a wound"), but it's pure invention.

Or, there's the bit when she imagines a meeting between Aunt Lydia and Janine at the Rachel and Leah centre, a meeting she wasn't present at and only heard about third-hand. It begins in the conditional tense: "Blessed be the fruit, Janine, Aunt Lydia would have said" (139). But the level of detail she goes into moves far beyond the probable, the possible, and ends up in the realm of pure invention, even of the poetic. Janine's voice, for

* And reusing material in order to do so: earlier, she notes that the tulips in the garden look like wounds: 'red, a darker crimson towards the stem as if they have been cut and are beginning to heal there". (22) Here, Luke's wound is, "the colour of tulips near the stem end".

example, is "transparent" and a "voice of raw egg white" (139). The conditional tense disappears ("Janine looked down at the floor") and Offred's imagination takes over: "Aunt Lydia allowed herself one of her pauses. She fiddled with her pen" (140).

There's something odd about that phrase, "allowed herself one of her pauses". Why not just say, "Aunt Lydia paused"? It's because Offred wants to suggest what might be going on in Aunt Lydia's mind. She doesn't just pause, the phrase implies, but she *deliberately* pauses ("allows herself") in order to create a certain dramatic effect, one she has used before ("one of her pauses"). This is an example of *free indirect discourse,* a novelistic device in which a third person narrator (here, Offred) lets the voice and vocabulary, the language, of a character (here, Aunt Lydia) bloom into the narration in order to give an impression of interiority. Other examples in this passage: "It was true that the toilets sometimes overflowed. Unknown persons stuffed wads of toilet paper down them to make them do this very thing"; "several pieces of disintegrating fecal matter" (140). Unknown persons; fecal matter: this is not Offred's language. It's the prim and euphemistic language of officialdom and propriety. It's Aunt Lydia's.

Offred is using the tricks of the novel trade (a build-up of sensuous and evocative detail to create immediacy; free indirect discourse to create interiority) to tell her story. She is, essentially, a novelist. And so, in order to understand why she might be telling the story, we need to think about why Margaret Atwood tells *her* stories: what, for Atwood, is the function of the novel?

"I believe that fiction writing," she wrote in her essay, "An End to Audience" (1980), "is the guardian of the moral and ethical sense of the community... Fiction is one of the few forms left through which we may examine our society... through which we can see ourselves." She goes on:

> The writer is both an eye-witness and an I-witness, the one to whom personal experience happens, and the one who makes experience personal for others. The writer *bears witness*. Bearing witness is not the same as self-expression.

The writer, for Atwood, uses her personal experience to bear witness to suffering, and to communicate that suffering to others. So Offred is not just telling her story to survive: she is bearing witness, to herself and to others, in the hope that her reader will gain a degree of self-perception to effect self-correction, both individual and communal.

But this story takes place in a fictional universe, and all the suffering it describes is fictional; she is bearing witness to nothing. How does that square with the idea of fiction as "the guardian of the moral and ethical sense of the community"? Why be a guardian to a non-existent community?

Well, Gilead is not so non-existent. The past – *our* past – continuously peeps through the gauzy veneer of its present. It does so from the very first sentence: "We slept in what had once been the gymnasium" (13). Obsolete codes and marks from the time before abound, like the symbols on the gymnasium floor, the "stripes and circles" of the old basketball court; "the hoops for the basketball nets were still in place, though the nets are gone" (13). Even the "music" from dances that were once held there "lingered, a palimpsest of unheard sound, style upon style..." (13).

Palimpsest is the most important word in these early pages. A palimpsest is literally a sheet of paper on which one or more new texts have been written on top of an older one, which is visible under the surface (this is from the time when paper was scarce and it was often necessary to reuse the same sheet). History is a palimpsest for Atwood – *reality* is a palimpsest. The present is the newest text, but older versions are always visible beneath if you look hard enough.

When Gilead hangs its criminals, it strings up their bodies on the city wall and covers their faces in white hoods, to try to erase their individuality. "The heads are zeros," Offred says, blank pages on which new texts can be written. But, for Atwood, there's no such thing as a blank page: "if you look and look" at the hoods, "you can see the outlines of the features under the white cloth" (42).

There are marks and traces of a vanished past everywhere, from the "little mark, like a dimple, in each of [Rita's] ears, where the punctures for earrings have grown over" (58) to the initials carved into the top of Offred's desk at the Rachel and Leah centre (once Harvard University, where Atwood studied):

> M. loves G., *1972. This carving, done with a pencil dug many times into the worn varnish of the desk, has the pathos of all vanished civilizations. It's like a handprint on stone. Whoever made that was once alive. (123)*

Whoever made it not only *was* alive, but *is* alive: "M." stands for "Margaret" and "G." for "Graeme", Atwood's partner Graeme Gibson. This is the old text that peeps through Gilead's present: the real world that Margaret and Graeme and you and I inhabit.

And, in many ways, Gilead is just another rearrangement of the text of our reality. As Winston Smith thinks in *1984*, with piercing insight into the function of dystopian fiction: "The best books... are those that tell you what you know." It's a fictional world, yes, but all of its elements are factual. As Atwood has said, "I did not use any details in this book that have not already occurred somewhere in history". Every grotesque element of her dystopia comes either from our past or our present.

Part of the inspiration for the novel came from trips Atwood took in the 1970s and 1980s to Iran and Afghanistan; in her article for the *New York Times* in 2001, she recalls how putting on the chador during her visit there in 1978 influenced the outfits worn by women in *The Handmaid's Tale*. Some of the academic papers that Professor Crescent Moon mentions during the conference at the end of the novel suggest other analogues: "The Warsaw Tactic: Policies of Urban Core Encirclement in the Gileadean Civil Wars" suggests that Gilead learnt much from Nazi Germany (312). "Romania," Pieixoto then tells us, "had anticipated Gilead in the eighties by banning all forms of birth control, imposing compulsory pregnancy tests on the female population, and linking promotion and wage increases to fertility" (317). Gilead's "simultaneous polygamy", he says, was "practised both in early Old Testament times and in the former State of Utah in the nineteenth century" (317).

The white hoods over the corpses come from Canadian history, as do the red uniforms from "the uniforms of German prisoners of war in Canadian P.O.W. camps of the Second World War era". In the Philippines they really do call political executions "salvagings". The resonances multiply. As Pieixoto says, "there was little that was truly original or indigenous to Gilead: its genius was synthesis" (317).

It's our community, then, that *The Handmaid's Tale* wants to be the moral guardian of. By transmuting it into fiction, Atwood wants us to reconsider the world we live in, to see it with new eyes, and re-evaluate the things that we have long since ceased to notice. She wants us to see, as Hawthorne's narrator puts it in his great novel of early Puritan life, *The Scarlet Letter* (1850), "the awfulness that is always imparted to familiar objects by an unaccustomed light". She is warning against complacency, incuriousness.

And *The Handmaid's Tale* powerfully dramatises the danger of complacency and incuriousness. In their memories of "the time before", Offred and Luke ignore or laugh at details that, in retrospect, are troubling. When, lazily flicking through television channels, they come across Serena Joy's programme and find it ridiculous: "We thought it was funny." But Offred concedes, with a hint of hindsight: "really she was a little frightening. She was earnest" (56). Or, when their daughter is nearly kidnapped by a religious fundamentalist in a supermarket: "she's just crazy, Luke said. I thought it was an isolated incident, at the time" (73). But nothing is an isolated incident.

We "lived as usual", Offred says, in perhaps the most important passage in the book.

> *Everyone does, most of the time. Whatever is going on is as usual. Even this is as usual, now.*
>
> *We lived, as usual, by ignoring. Ignoring isn't the same as ignorance, you have to work at it. (66)*

The usual is just whatever's happening in the present. "Ordinary," said Aunt Lydia, "is what you are used to. This may not seem ordinary to you now, but after a time it will. It will become ordinary" (43). Atwood wants us to feel that what we consider normal is, in the words of the novelist J.G. Ballard, "a stage set that could be dismantled at any moment". If we take our freedoms for granted, and ignore the oppression and fascism that always seeps in at the edges of society, we might find ourselves living in a new normal.

Early in the novel, Offred passes some Japanese tourists in the street. The tourists look like people from our world. The women wear make up, high heels. To them, the Handmaids look strange. But to Offred it is they who look strange. She describes

> *the high-heeled shoes with their straps attached to the feet like delicate instruments of torture. The women teeter on their spiked feet as if on stilts, but off balance... They wear lipstick, red, outlining the damp cavities of their mouths, like scrawls on a washroom wall... (38)*

And so they start to look strange to us, too ("their spiked feet as if on stilts"; "the damp cavities of their mouths"). Suddenly, we think: why *do* we make women smear paint over their lips; why *do* we make them walk on stilts? We see the gilt cage.

When the journalist Nancy Gage asked Atwood if *The Handmaids Tale* is meant as a warning, she answered:

> Let me put it this way: If you see somebody walking toward a large hole in the ground and you want them to fall into it, you don't say anything. I don't know whether you saw Time magazine a few weeks ago. It had on the cover "Politics,

> Religion and Money". And it was about the potential presidential nomination bid that the evangelical right is making in 1988. If I were an inhabitant of this country, I would be worried about the low voting rate. That means that 25, 26, 27 percent is controlling the rest."

What do we make of Offred?

Critics have been divided. As Lee Briscoe Thompson has written, "reviewers have reacted variously to Offred, but almost always with considerable energy", either praising her courage or denouncing "her wimpishness", celebrating her understatement or deploring "her monotone". There has been a "palpable feminist desire to set Offred up as a political symbol: of woman victimized, of woman resistive, of woman triumphant". But she can also be regarded as self-interested. Her "capitulations" to Gilead are "many":

> abuses of Janine, identification with Fred's household, rapidly decreasing taste for freedom, defense of Fred and intermittent fondness for him, complicity in Salvagings, dependence on Moira to be the rebel spirit for them both, failure to help Mayday, and the final agonized realisation

> that to stay alive and out of physical pain she would betray "anyone..."

Plenty of critics, writes Thompson, have "berated her for her passivity and her infuriating inclination to forgive her oppressors".

Some critics believe that Offred, and women like her, are, in their subservience, in some ways *responsible* for Gilead. Patricia Kamal writes in "A Woman's Dystopia":

> By choosing as the central character a woman who, with or without autonomy, does not identify with victims and cares only about a man's love, Atwood warns how a Dystopia for women could succeed.

Others just find her too boring to care about. Alan Cheuse, for example, thinks Atwood "gave us far too little action and far too much of the *longeurs* suffered by the interned Offred".

But no one ever said she was supposed to be heroic. "I think she is an ordinary sort of person," Atwood has said, "caught up in extraordinary circumstances. She proposes no solutions beyond escape... She's somebody who wants just to live her life."

There's a line from Milton that recurs a couple of times in the novel, from his sonnet, "When I consider How My Light is Spent" (1673): "They also serve who only stand and wait." One reading of this line is: those who stand around and do nothing and wait for things to improve are as responsible for tyranny as those carrying it out. It could be seen as a condemnation of Offred's inaction. But is it true that she only stands and waits? We've seen that the very act of telling her story is an act of resistance. "I don't have to tell it," she says. "I don't have to tell anything, to myself or to anyone else. I could just sit here, peacefully. I could withdraw. It's possible to go so far in, so far down and back, they could never get you out" (237).

And, unlike Winston Smith who, at the end of *1984*, has allowed his own identity to be totally subsumed into that of the Party, she retains her identity from beginning to end; she hasn't gone so far down and back that they could never get you out. She is, at all times, herself: "*I am, I am*. I am, still" (243). It's because of that that she has a story to tell and thus that her story can act as inspiration to her readers.

Whatever you think of Offred, the one thing you can't accuse her of when you close the book is dishonesty. She makes no attempt to tell a better story than the one we're reading, to paint herself in a better light. "I wish this story were different," she says just before its end.

> *I wish it were more civilized. I wish it showed me in a better light, if not happier, then at least more active, less hesitant, less distracted by trivia. I wish it had more shape. I wish it were about love, or*

about sudden realizations important to one's life, or even about sunsets, birds, rainstorms, or snow.

...I'm sorry there is so much pain in this story. I'm sorry it's in fragments, like a body caught in crossfire or pulled apart by force. But there is nothing I can do to change it.

I've tried to put some of the good things in as well. Flowers, for instance, because where would we be without them?

Nevertheless, it hurts me to tell it over, over again. Once was enough: wasn't once enough for me at the time? But I keep on going with this sad and hungry and sordid, this limping and mutilated story, because after all I want you to hear it, as I will hear yours too if I ever get the chance, if I meet you or if you escape, in the future or in Heaven or in prison or underground, some other place. What they have in common is that they're not here. By telling you anything at all I'm at least believing in you, I believe you're there, I believe you into being. Because I'm telling you this story I will your existence. I tell, there you are.

So I will go on. So I will myself to go on. (279)

And, here, perhaps is the answer to question of who she's talking to. "I believe you into being," she says. She means *you*.

FURTHER READING

Primary

by Margaret Atwood

Bodily Harm (1981)
The Handmaid's Tale (1985)
Cat's Eyes (1989)
Alias Grace (1996)
The Blind Assassin (2000)
Oryx and Crake (2003)

by other authors

Cixous, Hélène 'The Laugh of the Medusa' (1976)
Hawthorne, Nathaniel *The Scarlet Letter* (1850)
Huxley, Aldous *Brave New World* (1932)
Ishiguro, Kazuo *Never Let Me Go* (2010)
Orwell, George, *1984* (1949)
Piercy, Marge *Woman on the Edge of Time* (1976)5)

Secondary

Cooke, Nathalie *Margaret Atwood: A Biography* (1998)
Dvorak, Martha *Lire Margaret Atwood*: The Handmaid's Tale (1999)
Howells, Coral Ann *Cambridge Companion to Margaret Atwood* (2006)
Howells, Coral Ann *Margaret Atwood* (2006)
Ingersoll, Earl *Margaret Atwood: Conversations* (1990)
Thompson, Lee Briscoe *Scarlet Letters: Margaret Atwood's* The Handmaid's Tale (1997)
Wisker, Gina *Margaret Atwood An Introduction to Critical Views of Her Fiction* (2011)
Wynne-Davies, Marion *Margaret Atwood* (2010)
Slettedahl Macpherson, Heidi *Cambridge Introduction* (2011)

Notes

First published in 2017 by
Connell Guides
Spye Arch House
Spye Park
Lacock
Wiltshire
SN15 2PR

10 9 8 7 6 5 4 3 2 1

Picture credits:

p.21 © Cinetudes/REX/Shutterstock
p.51 © Guidicini/REX/Shutterstock

A CIP catalogue record for this book is available from the British Library.
ISBN 978-1-911187-68-4

Design © Nathan Burton

Assistant Editors:
Brian Scrivener and Paul Woodward

Printed in Great Britain

www.connellguides.com